Behold, A Pale Horse

~ a novel ~

Robin Kellum Teachey

American Literary Press, Inc.
Five Star Special Edition
Baltimore, Maryland

Behold, A Pale Horse

Library of Congress
Cataloging in Publication Data
ISBN 1-56167-396-X

Library of Congress Card Catalog Number:
97-077975

Published by

American Literary Press, Inc.
Five Star Special Edition
8019 Belair Road, Suite 10
Baltimore, Maryland 21236

Manufactured in the United States of America

For my mother
"Miss Essie"
who was always there
for me
and always thought I could!

—Prologue—

THERE IS A LOW LYING COUNTY in the eastern part of
Carolina that is a mite different from any other spot on earth—
and yet those words have been spoken since time began about
one's birthplace, and will go on being spoken until time is ended.
Here the people cling to one another in time of trouble, separate
and go their bigoted ways in time of prosperity, ridicule one
another, belittle those who fall from grace, gossip whenever
two or more are gathered together, worship in their own peculiar
fashion, and have their own particular kind of preacher; and if
perchance he is called and doesn't suit them, they do not hesitate
to throw him out and call another, and if he bucks up and won't
let himself be thrown out, they move down the road a piece and
build themselves another church, leaving him in the old one to
preach to thin air, for they will have their way in the end.
Moreover, they are born to this place, grow up here, marry and
raise their big families, die and are buried here, for they would
no more sell their land or move than they would cut off their
arms. Anyone outside their county is considered a Yankee or a
foreigner. Even their language has its own queer tone, and its
sons return from foreign wars talking the same, and pick up
their same hoes and follow the plow again as if the in-between
years had never been. There they tend their tobacco and corn
and peanuts and cotton and raise their hogs and chickens and
cows. They look no different, but they are a people unlike any
other on earth.

Part I

—Chapter 1—

HER FRIENDS THOUGHT HER A SILLY CREATURE, vain and self-centered too, because she loved to watch her own reflection in the clear swamp water going and coming from school. The only mirror they had at home was an old one that had eroded on the back until you weren't sure whether your face was clean or the mirror spotty, even when you peered closely.

I'm going to pick honeysuckles when school is out, she told herself, and put them here beside my bed. Then my room will smell like the clean woods and I can make believe I'm walking in it even when the lamp is turned out.

She carefully arranged her spit curl right in the middle of her forehead, braided the rest of her long curly hair into one far braid, and tied a faded blue ribbon about an inch from the end of it. Echoes of the quarrel she had heard between Pa and Ma last night still rang in her ears and made the tight band circle her heart again.

"Ain't listening to no more tom foolishness 'bout it. We done put up with too much schoolin' for her already. Girls don't need it. Soon as it's out, she can marry Ben's boy, and that'll be that!" Pa had been real mad sounding.

"Can't we wait on pushing her into that? She hates the sight of him. And it'll be for all her life. Maybe somebody you'll like better will show up."

"Show up!" he'd shouted. "Where in the hell is he going to pop up from? I want her to marry somebody whose land joins mine. Can't you get that through your thick skull? And I want her to do it while Ben and his boy is still in the notion. What difference does it make whether she likes him or not. If she loved him, a year or two of marriage would cure that, wouldn't it?"

And the argument had been so loud that she had put her hands over her ears and slipped out on the side piazza so that the cool night air would dry off the hot beads of perspiration that were pouring from her forehead.

Damn old Ben Simpson and Ben Jr. too, for that matter. In particular damn Ben Jr. Him with his sissy-ways and his fast balding head and his long sharp nose. I'd rather be dead than married to that beast. He's pinched every girl's bottom in Miss Justice's school. She leaned over the side of the porch railing and gagged.

"If you're going to walk with me, you'd better get away from that mirror and get a move on," Kate called.

"And here's your dinner bucket, too," Ma added.

The bucket was all warm and smelled of hot biscuits that she knew would be filled with grape preserves and fried pork. And what could fill an empty spot better than biscuits with preserves or meat come dinner time?

How can they be so different and still be cut from the same cloth, Ma thought as she watched them walking down the dew dampened dusty road toward the cut off piece. Kate, so dependable, so smart and quick at housework, maybe plainer to look at but so much smarter; and Ella, so lovely to look at and yet so rattle brained. When she turned to go in and get the water bucket, something in her heart whispered, yes, but you love that rattle brained one the best, don't you? And she didn't bother to deny the little voice accusing her.

Two of the Morton girls waited at the cut off for them so that they could walk together through the woods. It was a full mile as the crow flies from the cut off to the school, and though there was no real danger, they felt safer in numbers. An occasional snake in the late fall or early spring slid across their path, but they walked around him. Or a big possum with its youngins hangin' to its uplifted hairless tail strolled nonchalantly across the path and looked at them out of its small black beady eyes as if it had all day to cross. These were not the dangers. Those stupid Parker boys occasionally stepped out suddenly from the thick underbrush and nearly startled them to death. The oldest one, Tom, would leer at them then laugh his head off. More than likely they had been to their traps and were carrying an otter or 'coon home. Several times he had grabbed hold of Ella's sash and untied it as she walked gingerly past him, and rather than try to make conversation with him or retrieve the sash, she would go on to school without one.

Once when she had fallen behind the others about midway, where the path crossed the swamp water, and was re-braiding her hair and admiring her own reflection, he had stepped out quickly and grinned from ear to ear at her. She stepped back quickly and almost fell from the foot log that lay over the stream. Were the girls so far ahead that it wouldn't do any good to call? Her mind was muddled and she couldn't think what was best to do. He kept looking at her and grinning.

"Wanta, wanta, you wanta see my traps?" he stammered, but he held out his hand forcefully to take hold of her arm.

"I'll be late for school. Please move off the log now, Tom."

"You'll be late, you'll be late,' he repeated in his stupidity and he grinned again as drops of saliva ran down the corner of his bearded face.

The girls had missed her and started back. They rounded the corner and called, "Better come on, Ella. You're going to make us all late."

Tom kept on grinning, but he stepped backwards off the log and let her pass.

"You'll be late," he whispered as she passed him dubiously, and then he added, "ha, ha, ha."

—Chapter 2—

MA HAD A BIG TATER PUDDING on the back of the stove cooling when they got home. And there were some black-eyed peas left over from last night's supper that she had warmed over with a hog jowl. The aromas were delectable and made one's mouth water, and they hurried and changed their clothes so that they could get right at the business of cutting that pudding.

"Better hurry up with the changing, youngins," Ma hollered from the porch that separated the house from the kitchen. "Pa thinks maybe the sow has had her pigs. She ain't been up to waterin' today. He wants one of you to go and look for her and the other to help me finish with the washing."

Go and look for the sow! Through the lovely green spring woods with the wild azaleas blooming and yellow jasmine bursting out all over the stumps and roots, and the swamp water high and swift, and all the birds singing and making nests. I must be the one to go, Ella thought frantically. I can think there. And be by myself, don't care if everyone does think I'm vain and self centered because I want to be alone. Anyway, who's ever alone in the woods. It's a three ring circus, all acts going at once, if only you have eyes for it.

"Please let me look for the sow today, Kate? You can next time, if you just please will this once."

Kate's sailor dress was stuck halfway over her head and she muttered, "Help me out, you nilly willy. Some looking you'd do for the sow. You'd most likely sit on a log and look at yourself in the run till night."

"Please, Kate. Just this once, let me be the one."

"Oh, I don't know," she flippantly declared. "I might and I

might not! I haven't even decided yet whether or not I'm going to tell Pa about that last note Leonard stuck in the holler for you last week."

"How'd you know that? I haven't told a living soul."

"You didn't have to tell a living soul, dearie. I simply read it after you went to sleep sniffling."

She reached deep into her chemise, pulled out a scrap of paper, and waved it through the air like a matador waving the red flag in front of the bull, just teasing, just taunting a little more, begging the bull to come on, hoping he will, hoping he'll charge so that he can have the right to kill the innocent.

Ella was stunned. She wanted to say, "I'll tell Mama." But not even Mama would approve of their communications and their means of delivering the notes.

"Please, Katie. Give it to me, please. It's mine anyway and you don't have any right to read it or keep it. Please."

Kate smiled sarcastically and gently waved the note back and forth, back and forth, still teasing and enjoying the tortured look on Ella's face.

"Nooooooooooooooo. I don't think I will give it back. I just think I'll keep it as a kind of insurance in case you're tempted to go tattling to Mama about me again. And in case I need you to do my homework, or any other little thing that just comes along. But if you're very nice, I will let you be the one to go look for the sow. I'd rather help with the wash any old day. You'd better be practicing up on your washing, too. Won't be long, you know, afore you'll be in charge of such things."

🙰 🙰 🙰

WILD DAISIES WERE BLOOMING all over the meadow, so close together that it was impossible to walk without stepping on them. Ella munched on a big square of potato pudding which had been cooked like a pone of bread, and half sang with her mouth full. She stepped high, like a colt just let out to pasture after having been long shut in the stable, lifting one foot higher than the other, swinging her arms freely, sash tail flying behind in the breeze like the colt's tail. Occasionally, she'd stop and look around and holler, "Pigg. Pigggg," and wait to see if the daisies moved or the grass rustled.

But she seemed to be the only living creature in miles. There was a thin stretch of tall virgin pines that lay at the end of the meadow fields and just beyond lay the big swamp that drained the Pocasin. It was soft and spongy and its mire was filled with crayfish. Lily pads floated on its deep red water, and giant cypresses stood in the middle of the run, their roots exposed and bleached out. Here the coons came to wash their food, the bear to eat his corn, the squirrel to hide his nuts, and those horrid Parker boys to set their traps. Everyone knew they spent more time in the swamps than anywhere else. "I do hope she isn't in the swamp. I couldn't bear it to run into Tom and Tim alone and this far from the house. Maybe I shouldn't have been so eager to dash out and look for old Bessie. Me and my big mouth! I could kick myself."

She stood on the edge of the pine thicket and looked around again. Here the meadow ended sharply and the ground was blanketed with thick pines needles. It was here that she had come often with Pa and the mule and wagon and got loads of pine straw. They used it in the pig pens, hen's nests, and cow stables. In the fall they heaped their potatoes in piles, covered them with pine straw, and then banked them in round mounds of dirt so that they could keep them all winter. The pines were so thick here that all other forms of vegetation had been choked out, and it was lovely to walk in or see. Again and again she turned her voice with the wind and called, "Pigg. Pigggggg," and waited and waited, but no stirring came from any direction. She was beginning to get in a state of great perturbation, not knowing whether to go through the pine thicket and into the swamp or whether to turn back and say she simply couldn't find the sow. Then Kate would dramatically state at the supper table that she had wanted to go, that she could have found the sow, but Ella had insisted on going, and she would then hint that perhaps she had only picked flowers and dillied. Why did everyone think she was brainless just because her face was pretty. Unbeknownst to Ella, her face had an eternal look of innocence. That thought of ridicule and persecution by Kate drove her through the pine woods and into the swamp. She slipped off her old shoes, tied the strings together, and slung them over her shoulder. Deeper and deeper she walked until she could see the run of the swamp. She wanted to call for the sow again, but here her voice would carry and she was afraid someone might hear her, someone of whom she was afraid. The long ancient moss swayed with the gentle spring wind. The mud was soft and cozy between her toes and spring cold; for the sunlight never hit the ground in this densely wooded area. Leaning against one of the old trees and watching the deadly swiftness of the current, she did not hear the footsteps approaching from behind and when a strong, work worn hand placed itself on her soft shoulder, she opened her mouth to scream but no sound issued from her lips. Did she dare turn around? She could already see the foam on Tim Parker's thick lips. Cold chills began to tighten the flesh on her legs when the owner of the hand spoke.

"I could tell your hog calling a mile away, honey, and I hurried through my chores so I could come afore you went back home."

"Oh, Leonard! You scared the plumb daylights outa me. I thot you were Tim. I didn't hear you comin'."

She turned around and leaned against him for a moment.

"Why, you're really scared ain't you? I shouldn't a'done it, honey, but I thot you'd a knowed it was me."

"Let me get my breath and I'll be alright." She continued to rest against him for a few moments. It was the first time their contact had been this intimate and it was electrifying for both of them. He had held her hand a few times at pea shellings, and kissed her briefly on the cheek at corn huskings, but he had only dreamed how wonderful it would be to have her young and lovely body pressed close to his. He knew the buckle on his bib overalls must be hurting her flesh as it was his, but the pain was exquisite and he did not want to mention it for fear she would move. She was tinier in his arms than he had dreamed she would be, much smaller and much softer. Why had it never crossed his dumb mind, he berated himself, to dream how soft she would be. His own Ma was as hard as any man and he had just assumed that all women were the same. It was like falling into your pile of cotton before the wagon came along and picked it up in sheets. His hands slid down her shoulders and then her waist and below, and all was still softness.

His head fell on her neck and he whispered, "My God, Ella. You're so soft to hold. So sweet. So pretty. You don't know how I dream about holding you like this. You just don't know."

"I dream, too. But don't you pay any mind to what I write you? You just ignore my questions in your notes. Leonard, Pa ain't foolin'. He's a fixin' to marry me off to Ben. I'm afraid it's going to be this summer. You know I hate him and his old long ugly nose. If he kissed me with that long cold thing on my face, I'd die. Why won't you leave here and take me with you. Please. We could get on the train when it stops for water and we'd be in Wilmington by morning and we could get married. You could work. I could do something."

"You know why, Ella. There's Pa. And the land. All that land will be mine as soon as he dies and then I can marry you. He can't last much longer."

"Oh, damn that land. And he won't die for forty years. He'll outlive you. He's mean enough to try to do it just for spite, too. I don't care about the land. I don't care about him, or my family either when it comes to choosing between them and you. Don't you believe what the preaching man said last Sunday. You gotta leave your Ma and Pa and cleave to your wife. Weren't you listening?"

"No, I was looking at you, like I do at all the meetings. You know I never hear a word they say. The only reason I go is so I can look at you all day."

"You shouldn't say that, Leonard. God hears everything."

"Let him hear. Let him hear me say you're pretty, too. I don't give a damn who hears it."

"You're trying to be wicked now, Leonard. I'm not going to listen to you talk like that any more. Anyway, I have to look for the sow and it's almost dark. I had forgotten her."

"I know where she's at. In the meadow side of that old burnt out stump hole. With little ones, too. Your Pa borrowed our Hampshire boar but there was some red one's in the bunch. There's been a nigger in the woodpile somewhere with that old sow."

"I'm, not listening to you now, Leonard." And she clamped both tiny hands hard over her ears.

He reached up and pulled her hands off of her ears and said, "Now you're listening. I say you don't have to marry Ben, no matter what your Pa says. You ain't a slave. These is modern times. You just stand up and tell him, and let that be that. I'm going to marry you, hear that?"

He reached out as if he would embrace her again, but she darted like a cotton tail rabbit out of his reach and picked up her dress tail with both hands and ran swiftly. Even as hot tears were falling from her eyes and falling into the slime below her feet, he called after her, "I'll see you at the camp meeting Sunday. Hear that, now?"

She did not stop running even when she reached the pine thicket, but ran breathlessly through it and into the meadow field. Sure enough, right in the old burned out stump hole lay the sow, and six little pigs, four black with white bands around them, and two orange-red ones were lined up on her belly, grunting and sucking and wiggling their tails in satisfaction. Their tongues were red and they were pulling on her tits with a primitive fierceness even though they were only a few hours old. Pa would be aggravated about the red ones because he had thought he had bred to a full-blooded Hampshire boar. And now it was evident that their own Jersey boar had gone to her before Pa had noticed that he was in heat. It was a community practice to take one's sow with a rope around her back leg, and walk over to a neighbor's house who had a boar like you wanted to use. Inbreeding of their stock was unheard of, but they didn't mind in the slightest if their children married their double first cousin.

The one kerosene lamp gave a soft comfortable glow on the eating table. This was the only time of day that Ella thought the kitchen looked pretty. It was too dim to see the long sooty cobwebs that hung in the unceiled loft above the table, and yet light enough to see how white the boards were that the walls were ceiled with. Ma had scrubbed them with lye soap until the natural color had disappeared and they were bleached as a bone.

The remains of the 'tater pie and some warmed over black-eyed peas made their meal. Only their elders were allowed to drink coffee and it was a distasteful drink with coarse grounds settling in the bottom of their cups. Ma only ground the beans in the morning and made a big pot full before daylight, and this sufficed for their three meals. By the time it had been warmed over three times, it would curdle the palate, but Pa drank it with relish. Invariably, he would declare dramatically that when he was a youngin', coffee was a luxury that their parents only indulged in on Sunday mornings, and that Missouri should be grateful that he provided so nicely for her and the children. And if Missouri had complaints on how he provided, she did not voice them.

"Well, I'll be damned. I can't get over that cussed sow having red pigs. How in the hell that happened, I'll never know. That old hog of Percy's hopped right on her two or three times, and I just knowed that was that."

Their Ma looked as if she wanted to tell him to be careful what he said in front of the girls, but she knew if she corrected him, she would wind up with a lecture directed to her on how soft the girls were raised and on how she had failed to produce a boy he needed so desperately to plow his fields and slop the hogs, and inherit his land. The land . . . that was everything. It came before anyone else or anything. He was sober on Saturday night, which was a rarity in their community, and he had never beat Missouri other than with words, but he was obsessed with obtaining more land and hanging onto what he already had.

"Perhaps your other sow won't disappoint you," Missouri spoke softly.

"She damned sure better not. She'll wind up in the pork barrel if she does, and I won't be long putting her there either. How'd you happen to come across her, Ella?"

She had a mouth full of peas and the question came unexpectedly. Blood shot to the roof her head, flooded her cheeks and lips, and moisture came to the corner of her eyes.

"Well. I do believe you're nigh choked to death, honey. You want me to pat you on the back?" Behind this solicitous gesture from Ma was a deeper insight than Pa possessed.

When she could speak, she stuttered it out. "I looked everywhere. In the meadow. In the swamp, too. I was scared cause it was getting dark. It was when I was coming back that I heard her grunting and went over to where she was. She was vexed at me, too, for finding her, I think. She grunted like she would bite if I got any closer."

"Probably would, too. I'll carry a lightwood knot with me when I go after her in the morning and if she tries anything on me, I'll knock hell out of her. That'll teach her not to bite the hand that feeds her. I'll need you too, 'Souri, to bring the pigs in a sack. Why in the hell they go that far from the house to have them, I'll never know."

"May I be excused now and get my lessons?" Ella asked.

"You may not. You can stay and help you Ma do the dishes. That's what you can. Need the practice, anyhow."

"I won't need her tonight, Jacob. They're not pots and pans tonight, just these plates and Kate and I'll do them."

"Contradict me when I try to make them work! Let her do nothing but keep her head in a book. You think that book learning's going to help her tend babies and scrub floors and cook?"

No one answered and as soon as he saw he was the only one who cared to argue the point, he waved one arm, cup and all, and said, "Well, go on. Study. Who's stopping you?"

It was safe here in the privacy of her own dark room. She wished she need never light the lamp. Here in the black of night, no one could read her face, hear her soft words, learn the secrets of her own young trembling heart. There is safety in the dark, she thought. It's almost as if I can feel Leonard here with me. She hugged herself and cold shivers crept up her legs. His strong hands had left their imprint on her neck and shoulders and she wished that the imprint would never leave. You must have the courage to leave home, Leonard. There is going to be no second chance. You must see that love can be enough and that your Pa is only using you as he would a hired hand. Anyone can shock his fodder, plow his soybeans, bust his corn middles, plant his sweet potatoes, slop his hogs, and tend his piney woods cows, but there is no one else in the world who can ever love you like I do. I could go on loving you the rest of our lives, Leonard. Please understand that Pa isn't fooling about me marrying Ben Jr. Then old man Ben would see him the field next to ours, thirty cleared acres, and Pa would do anything for that. Anything at all!

"Are you going to stand here and moan all night in the dark, or are you going to light the lamp and study some like you claimed you just had to get to doing," Kate asked sarcastically as she brushed past her and struck the match and lit the lamp. Not many families in the community had two lamps and they were very proud of the second one. Of course, the Ben Simpsons, not only had a kerosene one for every room in their two story house, but also a gas chandelier for their parlor that lit the room up like daylight. But then, no one expected to have things like they did. He not only owned the biggest farm, he owned the community store and sold everything from dry goods to fish meal. Most of the community ran credit with him until late fall when they sold their cotton, and being in his indebtedness, they felt obliged to be nice to his most unlikable family.

"Well. What were you doing? Are you deaf or not?" Kate persisted.

"I'm sorry, Kate. I was trying to arrange my thoughts a little before doing my work."

"Only an addlepated person would have to arrange their thoughts. Anyone else would keep theirs in order. By the way, I coulda sworn you turned beet blood red at the table when Pa asked how you found the sow. Couldn't a been that you just accidentally ran into Leonard and he helped you through the bushes and brambles till you found her, could it?"

"You and your wicked mind! I'm not answering you when you talk like that."

"The time might come when you'd be glad to talk to me when you get in that prissy Simpson family. I can just see you trying to talk with those high hats. They'll look down on you like dirt. Me, I can't understand it, but I heard Pa tell Ma that old man Ben was interested in improving their family line as they are weak and run down from marrying kin, that he would like to see Ben Jr. married to a young strong girl like you, one who can give him strong grandchildren. They say his wife is not taking to the idea at all. At all! And his sisters! They'd as soon as speak to dirt as to us. I can imagine how nice living with them would be. But I could take anything if Ben Jr. was interested in me. And that automobile. Imagine. I hear tell it will go twenty miles an hour. You'd be the talk of the neighborhood. Honestly, Ella. What can you see in Leonard when someone like Ben Jr. is really interested in marrying you?"

"I can tell you this, Kate, if he ever tries to kiss me, I'll do my best to knock his head off. He tried to hold my hand at the last meeting and his hands were wet. I coulda died. And the way he looked at me, it made me feel all dirty. I began to wonder if I'd put on enough clothes so that he couldn't see through them. I wish you had him, because I don't intend to be caught dead married to that damp louse." And she flounced on the bed with a thud and a heavy sigh and opened her book to page 232, review questions for Friday. When was the first air mail route established between New York and Washington? When was the first communications radio broadcast at Pittsburgh, Pennsylvania?

When was the League of Nations established? What are the common rumors concerning an income tax on $300 or over?

And for a while, the threat of the distasteful marriage was pushed into the background, and the joy of learning filled her mind and heart. After the lamp had been turned out and the odor of burned wick and kerosene filled the small room, she lay awake staring out the small window. The moon was a ball of red fire, more like a late September moon than an early May one, and a small flattened out dark cloud floated over the bottom of it slowly. It looks like the waves of the ocean kissing the moon, she thought. Is it so far away that no one can reach it. Did God really put it there? Does he know that I love Leonard with all my heart?

For Leonard was a simple young man. Of the earth, he was, and cared nothing for the ways of the city. He had none of the complexities of personality that Ella had and could never begin to understand her. She was lovely, yet unaware of it in a true sense of naivete. She was simplehearted, but not so simple in learning as most of the other girls her age. She had none of the impertinence of Kate, yet little of the humbleness of her mother. She did not long to be like either, only to be left alone to be like herself and to love Leonard. Why is the moon so far away tonight, and why will it be gone in the morning? Why does that little star sit right near the end of it like it has nothing to do but sit there? Star light, star bright, first star I've seen tonight, I wish there were no Ben Simpson and that Leonard was old enough to be his own man and marry me. Ben Jr. with his choleric looking nose, filled her with incalculable misunderstandings and apprehensions, and the vision of him that came in the night was really worse than his true appearance. No one could truthfully say that it was his own fault that he was spoiled. His father had been over forty when he had married, and that this marriage had produced a boy nine months to the day of the marriage had filled him with a pride that twenty years had not dampened a bit. From the very first, when the baby had cried, the baby was held. When the baby wanted anything, he got it. As a young boy, when he saw anything in pictures he desired, they had ordered it even if it had to come all the way from San Francisco or St. Louis. He had been the only boy to own a bicycle, a pony, and was now the only person within ten miles who owned a car. Even Ben Sr. did not own one and did not want to own one. The train still carried him where he wanted to go, and for local trips, he could still hitch his horse to his buggy. And now Ben Jr. wanted Ella for a wife, and by God, he intended to get her for him, even if it was going to cost him thirty of his best acres of cleared land. Two girls had followed close behind Ben Jr., but whatever they needed and wanted was taken care of by their more conservative mother. Mrs. Simpson had no illusions about who handled the boy. He had never asked her for anything and it was obvious to everyone that he considered her a nonessential member of the household. He tolerated everyone, but he loved his father in spite of the fact that he knew he held the reins over him.

Moreover, he too looked out at the night skyline, the tall thick pines borderlined the fields, the sky filled with twinkling stars, the air dotted with fireflies, and he filled his mind with dreams of the girl with the long yellow hair and knew that she would be his.

—Chapter 3—

IT WAS THE FIRST WEEK IN JUNE, and the event was an annual one that the entire community lived for from year to year. Sister Carrie Whalis and her troupe came with their tent and they sang and preached for two days and nights. The preaching was loud enough to drive any devil out of the ground and woodlands and the singing was mournful and tear rending enough to melt the hardest heart. The community had a small country church, but the land it stood on had been donated by Mr. Ben Sr. and most of the money to build it with had been given by Mr. Ben, and Mr. Ben's daughter played the only organ in miles every other Sunday, and Mr. Ben's wife led the singing and Mr. Ben's boy led the closing prayer and Mr. Ben put the most money in the plate. His daughters wore the most expensive hats and shoes and dresses and took up the front row every meeting. No one would have dared go up and sit in their pew. You'd sooner take a neighbor's horse than get on their bench. So even though the little church was filled most Sundays, the people of the land did not have a feeling of belonging to it. The music was a little above their raising and they did not get the spiritual uplift from it that they did when Sister Carrie's boys played their banjos and sang, "Lord, I'm going to lay at Jesus' feet. Ain't that sweet. I'm going to lay at his feet. And he will heal me there. Oh, yes. He'll heal me there."

And from the back of the tent or the front or the middle, or even from the front pew would come a loud "Amen, brother. Amen, I say." And more amens would follow. All of this cavorting was below Mr. Ben and his family, but he had to come anyway just to make sure nothing happened in the community that he didn't know all about. Of course, his wife and daughters had never come with him, but he attended anyway and had carried Ben Jr. with him since the boy was three. Even then, the young boy had been a cut-up and could sing and recite long before other children his age.

The local gentry arrived by mule and wagon or mule and cart, according to what they had at home. A wagon was a come up over a cart and not too many people owned the four wheeled contraptions, where as a cart was much cheaper to own. But there was no snobbery among the one mule families and the two mule ones. If a body needed a wagon for the day he simply carried his cart and traded, and a thank you and a much obliged were all the barter that ever traded hands. The women packed the carts full of bed quilts, their best of course, and enough cooked vittles to last two days. When bedtime came, they simply spread the quilts out on the ground under the carts and put the children to bed. Later in the night the women would join them, but the men rarely slept. After the preaching ended in fire and brimstone, they gathered around a fire and refought the big war, tramped the fields of France again, smelled the wicked odor of the poison gas, the cramped quarters of the troop ships, the cold of the Alabama nights at training camps, the damned mosquitoes in the Carolinas, and when every other subject had been exhausted, they lit in on politics. It was a strictly Democratic community, in a Democratic county, in a Democratic state, and a Republican running was a mere formality. Abraham Lincoln had not received a single vote in their country and the Republicans who had followed him had not done much better. Anyone who even suggested a very small Republican view point was considered ripe for the state hospital. And it was a rare person indeed who voiced his opinion contrary to the majority. And the only problem now seemed to be how to get those damned varmints out of office and get another good land loving Democrat back in his rightful place.

Ella had looked forward to the big meeting for months. Here would be a chance to see and be with Leonard. No one paid much attention to what the young folks did as long as they were in the tent and the tent could get very dim by smoky lantern light. Here Leonard could hold her hand beneath the folds of her dress and it made the blood pour in her cheeks and her head feel giddy and light. Ma had told her last time that she had noticed her during the meeting and felt sure that the Lord was speaking to her, and why hadn't she answered His call and confessed her sins?

Their wagon was loaded down with preparations for the two day trip. Sister Carrie always held the meetings on the river bank because it was like Jesus at Galilee. And she, too, wanted to let down her nets and haul in souls for Jesus.

There were boxes of fried chicken, baked sweet potatoes, cold boiled ham, corn bread and biscuits, homemade pickles, and several cakes. No one could out do Ma when it came to good vittles. Ella and Kate sat in the back and let their legs hang out and swing along with the jolting movements of the wagon. Even Kate was in a patronizing mood, and not many things put her in a really good mood.

The river lay just as Ella had remembered it. Wide and deep and rare blue, bordered by pines and gums and oaks, all filled with long swamp moss. Here a body could lie down and die from the sheer loveliness of the land.

They arrived fairly early and it gave them a chance to get a good place to tie up their wagon. Pa inevitably picked the spot closest to the water. It was here that he would have loved to have built his home, but this land was not for sale and never would be. It had been in the Barns family for over two hundred years and no one would have had the audacity to approach them with an offer to buy a part of it.

She and Kate slipped their shoes off and hurried down to the river's edge where they began wading around. The sand was as white here as it was on the ocean's edge, for the river led directly into the sea only a few miles downstream. The water was salty and the ocean's fish came in here to spawn and spend the summer. The mullet already were swollen with roe. Crabs darted hurriedly to a safer spot, leaving little muddy pools and swirls where they had been. Hundreds of the young crokers swam near the shore and moved in schools. The girls found it delightful to watch them. And the river's cooling breeze was a thing often dreamed of while hoeing down corn middles and cutting down Jerusalem weeds, or turning potato vines in the June sunshine. They held their skirts and various petticoats high to keep them dry and occasionally shot a furtive glance up to see if Ma was disapproving, but she was already engaged in a conversation with Dr. Kellum's wife, and they knew that would be lengthy and exciting. Everyone knew all about how bad Dr. Kellum's patients had suffered in childbirth, how brave or how cowardly they had been, how prematurely the baby had arrived, or how dark he was colored, almost as if Indian blood had outed. And Mrs. Kellum delighted in telling all she knew.

They were soon joined by Eva Belle Morton, Ella's dearest friend. Dearest, perhaps, because she lived close to Leonard, was not interested in him as a boyfriend, knew and understood how interested Ella was, and acted as a mediator between them. If her best laid plans were thwarted by Kate, they were promoted by Eva Belle, a short dumpy happy creature. She squealed with delight when her feet first touched the cold water, but she soon was wading around with them and chattering much like the squirrels in the trees overhead.

"Leonard's goin' to be late. Said tell you it'd probably be night before they get here. They're still laying by corn. And he said to tell you he wanted to be your eating partner tonight. Be sure and tell you that, he said. I do declare, Ella. Are you making any headway at all with him?"

"I don't know what you mean, headway." Ella wished that she wouldn't talk about Leonard in front of Kate, who relayed everything to Mama with added attractions.

"Like the dickens you don't. I mean has he asked you something special? Now that school is out and you ain't going on to boarding school, what else is there for you? I mean what else? You don't want to be one of those women who just goes around and stays with the sick and old for the rest of your life, you don't now, do you?" she said all in one breathless breath.

"I wouldn't mind waiting on sick people. In fact, I'd like to go to nursing school in Rocky Mount, but you have to finish high school first, and Pa isn't going to let me go on. I'd have to board in town and I guess it's true that we can't afford that. You know how long it's taken me to get through grade school, what with the weather so bad in the wintertime and me having pneumonia twice. I do wish Ma had a sister or somebody who lived near the school. I could just die. That's how bad I want to go on. All Pa thinks of is me getting married, I believe."

This trend of the conversation excited Kate, for though she was one year younger than her sister, she tried to act older than Ella and Eva, and her air of superiority helped her to succeed.

"If I were Ella, I wouldn't be so bull headed about marrying Ben Jr. I just melt away when he goes by in his car. If he asked me to ride in it with him, I just know I'd faint. And he's so clean. How 'bout how white his shirts are all the time? I'll tell you, I'd rather have a school teacher for a husband than an old dirt farmer. You won't never catch me married to one. You can just mark my words on that and mark them well." She emphasized her words with a vicious kick at the water.

"Well, you can have him. And I wish you did. I had just as soon get in the bed with a red belly moccasin."

"I'm going to tell Mama you've been talking ugly again, Ella. You know it ain't nice to talk about getting in the bed with a boy."

Of all the things Kate loved best, she loved to tattle to Mama. She should have been named "I'm going to tell Mama."

"Well, if you're going to tell your Ma everything we say, you can go on right now and stay with her, cause you're sure not going to stay with us and tell everything we say this time like you did last time. If I were Ella, I'd have stomped the life outa you before now. And you'd better believe it, too." Eva glared at her and waited for the answer that Kate couldn't think of for once.

They saw his cloud of dust long before they heard his twelve cylinder engine and knew that Mr. Ben and his boy were high tailing it to the meeting. If there was anything Mr. Ben didn't want to happen, it was to be left out of any conversation at a gathering. And conversations slowed to a halt when the 1921 Lincoln jerked to a stop, and Ben Jr. hopped right over the front door and went around and opened the door for his father. He never failed in a chance to add butter to his already well-buttered bread. Young boys began to gather around the car and to admire the rear tail lights and the chromed running boards. They hoped a shower or rain would come up so they could see Ben Jr. put the top up and down. As much as they admired it, they knew a ride in it was beyond their expectations. Moreover, their parents would have flailed them when they got back home if they had asked for a ride in it. He deposited his Pa with the elders and meandered down to the river's bank to watch the girls with their dresses held up to their knees wading and splashing.

Eva Belle was the gayest and loudest of the three and nothing bothered her etiquette wise. "Don't look right this minute, but you know who is watching," she half whispered to Ella.

"I don't care if you know who falls in the river and drowns."

"Shame on you, Ella. I'm going to tell Ma how ugly you talk about him. It ain't even Christian besides, and in particular at the meeting."

"Oh. Go drown yourself, Kate," Eva spat out. It was what Ella would have liked to have told her sister but lacked the courage.

Kate would have stomped out and reported to Ma, but she didn't intend to leave as long as there was a chance that Ben Jr. might speak to her. And he cared to speak to her about as much as he did to the back end of a mule.

Their continued giggling and whispering irritated him and made the blood climb to his prematurely balding head, but he tried to suppress his sharp temper and spoke evenly if not pleasantly.

"Aren't you ladies afraid a crab will bite your toes?"

Ella whispered, "It's not the crabs in the water that I'm afraid of. It's that rich crab on the bank . . ."

After that nothing could control the convulsions of laughter that issued from Eva Belle.

Kate walked closer to the shore.

"I think they're downright silly today, don't you?"

"Well, I wouldn't know. There's a difference between true laughter and silliness. I don't know why they're laughing, so I wouldn't know which is the case."

His maturity awed Kate and she walked out of the water and dropped her skirts and sat down on the sand.

"I do so greatly admire your car," she continued the one sided conversation.

Ella wished to kill her when she heard her say this because she knew it was the only lead he needed.

"I'm glad. I drove all the way to New Bern yesterday and had the motor tuned up. They have the only garage in a hundred miles that can do the job. I'd be delighted to give all of you girls a spin out to the main road and back if you'd like."

"We'd be ever so grateful. Oh, we'd be thrilled, wouldn't we Ella?"

And from the look that Kate flashed on her, she knew she'd better say she'd be thrilled or she would regret it for days afterwards in the privacy of their room where Kate's piercing tongue whiplashed her.

For this and other reasons not understood by her own self, Ella asserted their willingness to go for the ride. Perhaps it was in hopes that they would meet Leonard coming in and perhaps she could wave from her high seat in the car to him in his low cart and perhaps he would feel a pang of jealousy so hard that this very night he would declare that she meant more to him than anything in the world and that he would marry her now, in spite of losing his birthright to the rich lowland, that he would be willing to clerk in a store if necessary for a few dollars a week if only she were his.

Naturally, it worked around so that Kate and Eva sat on the

red leather back seats and she had to sit beside him on the front. He reached under the seat and pulled a lever and the front seat moved backwards a few inches.

"This will give you more room, I believe."

He assumed that they appreciated the fact that only this kind of car had an adjustable front seat, but they did not know it and did not especially care. The motor purred, he spun around in his eternal cloud of dust, and they were off. Ella was so startled that she grabbed hold of the door with one hand and the windshield with the other.

"I'm not frightening you girls, am I?" He did not give a damn about the occupants of the back seat, but he did not dare address Ella alone. He could feel her antagonism for him and wanted to break down that barrier if possible.

"We love it," Eva hollered. "How fast will it go?"

Ella turned and looked behind. Eva's hair was blowing in the wind like a red pony's tail and she really was enjoying the ride. So was Kate. Why then did her stomach feel like a tiny ball moving around? Surely it was safe. Quite a few people were using them nowadays. Why, in the cities the sidewalks were lined with them. She had seen pictures of it and surely the pictures were real. Nonetheless, she tried to sit as close to the door as possible.

He rounded the corner with an ominous screech and she fell over on him with a lurch. Squeals of laughter came from the back seat as she tried to sit back straight. He slowed to a stop and began to rapidly apologize.

"I'm so used to driving by myself going and coming from school that I didn't realize how sharp I've been turning. I hope you're not too upset."

"We're fine back here," came from the back seat.

"I don't think I care for riding in an automobile. Maybe we'd better go back now before Mama begins to get worried."

It was the best excuse Ella could think of at the moment.

Kate was furious. She punctuated her lines with daggers as she stated, "Mama is not worried at all. If you're such a fraidy cat, get back here with Eva and I'll sit up front. I can sit there without falling all over Ben Jr., I know."

She made as if to change seats, but Ben Jr. quickly said, "That won't be necessary. I'll drive slower the rest of the way and there really is some beautiful scenery a few miles farther down the road. The trees there look just like the coastline of Florida. You'd enjoy it. I'm sure."

And as usual, Ella was worn down by persuasions she did not believe in but did not have the fortitude to stand up against.

True enough, the scenery was beautiful. It was a crooked dirt road that ran parallel with the sound for miles and led to the ocean. It was necessary to take the ferry to cross over from the sound to the beach, but they did not go all of the way. Old gnarled cedars lined the road, their tops broken out by the strong ocean winds and all looking as if a giant mowing machine had just run across the tops of them. Behind the cedars stood scraggly pines. They, too, were beaten to death by the whip of wind. Clumps of pea grass were scattered around the base of the rarer juniper trees. The land which did not look as if one thing could possibly survive on it gave life to hundreds of sturdy plants and trees. They were not quite ten miles from home, yet the landscape was as entirely different as if they had moved to another state.

The sun was beginning to settle low over the trees when they reached the river road again and sure enough, Leonard's mule and cart was just ahead of them at the turn off. Confronted with reality, Ella wished she didn't have to look at him as Ben Jr. sat on the horn, started the mule, and impatiently waited for him to pull off the road and let them pass. They passed close enough to touch the wagon but it was not a look of jealousy on Leonard's face she saw. It was a hang dog look she hated in him, the look of defeat, the look of passive loving.

"Oh. Damn you, Leonard," she whimpered to herself. "Please fight for me. I could be worth fighting for."

As they purred past the cart and covered its occupants with dust, Ben Jr. observed, "Old man Johnson's boy has made a strapping young fellow, hasn't he? First time I've seen him in a year or two."

Ella prayed silently that now wouldn't be the moment that Kate chose to come out with her remarks about Leonard, and for the moment her reprieve was granted. Eva was enjoying her afternoon to the maximum. Nothing, not even Kate, was spoiling the ride for her and she leaned over the folded down top of the car and hollered, "Put the mule in high gear and come on, slow poke!"

Small is sometimes little, and little can be tiny, and tiny can become a speck, but Ella felt as minute as a grain of sand as she sunk down low in the seat.

"I wish I was home hoeing cotton. Damn these meetings. Damn Sister Shalis and her confounded preaching. I wish I was home," she mumbled half under her breath.

But under the roar of the big engine her words were lost.

The families had congregated and lit fires near their own wagons and carts, and the aroma of fresh coffee beans boiling over the open fires filled the air. They all carried old faded tablecloths that were used to spread the supper on the ground. They would doctor their red bugs all next week, but they would enjoy the outdoors tonight. Ella and Kate took the plates of cold chicken and warmed over baked sweet potatoes and coffee and went back to the river bank to eat. Ma and Pa would be joined by the other adults to swap vittles, and the young folks were not interested in hearing the old folks talk tonight.

"Can I eat supper with you, Ella?" rang in her ears as soon as they were seated and she looked sideways and saw his big legs standing right beside her, almost standing on the tail of her dress. Just looking at a part of him made her heart hurt in her breast and the bite of food in her throat grow larger until it was impossible to swallow. Leonard was her life . . . he had to be . . . she intended to make him be whether he had the courage or not. She might be weak with Kate and Pa, but she did not intend to be with Leonard. From this moment on she intended to do anything to get him. Time was running out, just like the sand at her feet running madly into the channel and on into the ocean, and she could not help herself anymore than the sand could help.

And then Ben Jr. appeared in the shadows beside Leonard. No one in the world would ever have expected it, but Kate blurted right out, "Can I eat supper with you tonight, Ben?"

There was a serious silence.

For the first time in her life, Ella saw fright on Kate's face. She didn't know whether she was afraid that he would accept or afraid that he would refuse. If he failed in a lot of things, he did not fail to be a gentleman in public situations and he quickly put her at ease.

"That will be very nice. If you've finished your meal, we'll get a good seat early, if you like, Kate."

Kate had not finished. She had barely started, but she declared she had eaten all she could hold, and she excused herself in a manner unlike herself and took his arm and left. Only a few steps away, he stopped and turned and said, "May I have the honor of eating breakfast with you, Ella, or has Leonard asked for that, too?"

She wanted to say yes. Leonard had asked for everything for the rest of her life, but she could not bring herself to look at him and tell him another lie. He was really trying to be very nice and she was a little sorry she could not like him at all. And perhaps before breakfast, all would be settled between her and Leonard and she could tell him then.

"That would be very nice, Ben Jr."

For the first time that day, the choleric look left his face and laughter liens appeared around his eyes. Even the hard line at the corner of his mouth disappeared and he smiled.

"I'll be looking forward to it, then. Tomorrow morning."

And he turned again and he and Kate went to find their seats.

"Why didn't you say that I had asked you already."

"Why did not YOU say that you had already asked me? I waited for you to say that."

"I just didn't think that you'd tell him yes. I guess that's why."

"Oh. Darn it all. Forget the supper. And the breakfast. Can't you see where this is leading? Don't you care that Pa is breathing down my neck to marry Ben. He wants that land and he can't get it any other way. He wants me safely married to a good man, too. And he thinks he's killing two birds with one stone. He don't mean to be mean about it, I don't think so anyway. And I do know we can't afford for me to go on to school. If anyone goes to boarding school, it ought to be Kate. She's so much smarter than I am in books. And Ben is really serious. If I even be nice to him, my goose is going to be cooked. And if I'm not nice too him, old man Ben might cut off Pa's credit and we just couldn't make it without it. He might cut off your credit, too. How do you think you'd manage to get your fertilizer come spring. But if me and you were married there would be nothing anyone could say. It'd be too late to cry over split milk. Are you listening, Leonard?"

He was busily drawing pictures in the sand with a twig. But from the agonized look on his face, she knew that he was listening. Moreover, he was thinking about what she was saying.

"I can't take you home with me, Ella. Pa wouldn't let me bring another mouth to feed there. Not now. Even if I could marry you and I couldn't unless we run away to South Carolina. That would take money to go by train for the two of us. And I don't know nothing about any other work but farming. I don't know if I could even get a job. I want to marry you more than anything, but not now. I just don't see how right now. You believe me, don't you?"

"No. I certainly don't. If you wanted to you would. If you loved me you wouldn't think of taking a chance on losing me. I couldn't bear it if someone was pressuring you to marry some other girl and I thought there was a chance you might. You don't care a darn about me!"

Big salty tears fell on her plate, splattered on the peeled potato, ran down the side of it and under the chicken bones. And still they fell.

"Please, Ella. Please, don't."

He tried to touch her hand, but she jerked it away and held it under the folds of her dress.

"Please," he begged her piteously. I can't stand it for you to cry like this."

"You don't care. You've never cared. You just let me make a fool out of myself all this time believing that you loved me. I hope Ben Jr. does ask me now."

"Say you don't mean that. You can't."

"I can and I do." And from the look of pain on her face, he did not doubt that for the moment she did mean it.

Fire and brimstone spewed from Sister Whalis's mouth that night. The men puffed their pipes and blow the smoke out as if they did not hear, but the womenfolk moaned and rocked back and forth and felt the wrath of God in all of her words . . . and her words were voluminous. If a fool's voice was known by the multitude of his words, Sister was a fool indeed.

She raised her eyes to the star filled night and cried out, "And when he opened the fourth seal, I heard the voice of the fourth beast say, 'Come and see.' And I looked. And behold, a pale horse; and his name that say on him was Death, and hell followed with him. And power was given them over the fourth part of the earth, to kill with the sword and with hunger and with death, and with the beast of the earth . . . and they cried and said, 'How long?' O Lord, holy and true, dost thou not judge and avenge our Lord on them that dwell on earth? . . . Oh vanity. Vanity. All is vanity. Do your young ones here tonight believe they are innocent? Wicked. I tell you in the blessed name of Jesus that they are sinful. Conceived in sin. Carried in sin. Born in sin. Dwell in sin. Surrounded night and day by sin. I tell it to you by his precious grace. None can be saved 'cept through his Grace. Who will come . . . Who will come tonight and say he belongs to Jesus. Don't sit there and warm those seats all night. It's hot in hell. Cool in heaven though. Clouds everywhere and soft flowing breezes. How in His precious name can you delay? I'm going to close my eyes and I want every eye here closed tonight and I want just those hands raised that are lost in sin. No one will see but Jesus. No one will look. And then I'm going to pray for the lost ones, whether they come here tonight or not. Nobody knows the burden on their heart but God. O sweet Jesus. Every eye closed now. Every head bowed. Not one eye open. There goes a hand. And another and another. Praise Jesus. I'm going to pray for you. And you. And you. Bless your heart. No one knows but me and Jesus. I'm going to pray for you. And another. Praise God. I'm not going to close this meeting tonight with this many people lost in sin. No sirree. My heart wouldn't let me rest another night of my life. We're just going to raise our heads and stand and sing, 'Amazing Grace,' and then I'm going to preach just a little longer, and I want you to search your hearts. You may never see another sunrise. Never see another day. Oh, God! Think of the rich man who filled his barns and said, 'Now me and my family is a going to take it easy for the winter,' and God looked down and said, 'You poor ignorant thing. You're just a big farming fool. This night I'm going to claim your soul.' AND HE DID! How can your heart be so cold to God's word. This night, he said . . ."

And they sang another hymn, and another, and the Sister preached between hymns, and they moaned and prayed and closed their eyes again and again, while Sister Whalis wet her palate from the tin dipper that sat in the ten quart water bucket beside her portable pulpit. A moonlit lacquered world surrounded them and all of their daily cares of fields and livestock were as far away as if they had been transported to another world.

It was well past midnight when they spread their quilts beneath the wagons and crawled between them. The ground was lumpy and hard beneath but their souls were filled with enough fire to ease their physical woes for the night. The air was moist and smelled of yellow jasmine and wild azaleas and the green bay trees. And all around was the aroma and sounds of the salty blue river. Its very being made all others seem insignificant, for it was the widest river in the world for its length; it was so wide that one couldn't see across it in several places, and it was deeper than anyone had ever dived. Its blueness was unpredictable. It ranged from a bright blue green to a huckleberry blue, depending upon its depth and on the weather.

Ella was not sleepy in the slightest, even though Ma and Pa and Kate had been asleep for some time. The center camp fire had died out and the only movement now was an occasional shifting of feet by the mules and horses, and an occasional mullet breaking the water and splashing as he reentered the river. These were the sounds she loved and she wished they could go on living here the rest of her life. How cool the water would feel to her feet. And why not? Tomorrow all of this would be gone and they would be back on their own dry acres, and besides, everyone was asleep and no one would know she had left the quilt bed. Kate shifted sides ominously as she tried to crawl past her, but she settled down and did not open her eyes. Her bare feet made no sound on the pine needles and the naked white sand as she lifted her white muslin gown high above her knees and ran between the wagons and down to the river's edge. The water was afire with moonlight and its ripples looked like the ocean's waves. She had never seen the ocean, even though they lived only ten miles from it, but she had seen pictures, and pictures were the gospel to her. The debility of her situation with Leonard engulfed her for a moment and she hugged her own bosom. She was standing ankle deep in the cool water when she heard a footstep break a pine cone behind her and she turned so quickly that the hem of her gown fell into the water and she almost lost her balance trying to get out of the river.

"I've been awaitin' for you."

"Leonard! Do you have to come up behind me all the time. You nigh scared me to death. I didn't tell you I was coming here."

"I know that. But I knew you'd come."

"You think you're pretty wise to me, don't you?"

"Nope," and there was an inflection of sadness in his voice. "I know I'm not wise about you or about anything for that matter. I wish I did know more answers. But how will I ever be able to leave the farm and do anything in the world with no schooling. I might could get a job pushing a broom in the depot. That's about all I could do."

"Please don't. I know you're smart. It can't be helped about going to school for you or me for that matter. Things are just the way they are. We're born in them, that's all. Sometimes though, it seems as if a body thought the stakes was high enough, a body would be willing to buck circumstances, even if he didn't win in the end. Even if there was just one chance in a million that he might win."

Until this very moment, she had not known what form her plan would take. But she knew that she had to have a plan and to execute it by herself if she were to save Leonard and herself from the snapping jaws of land lovers and the ruts of circumstance. And the plan was older than the tides that brought in amoeba and deposited them upon the twisted oak trunks and left them and returned again to do the same age after age after eon. The plan was simply man plus woman. Boy loves girl. No other plan could work. And she could only hope that this one would.

She turned around to face him, full gown swinging loose and free and blowing all around his cotton trousers and between his parted legs, her high youthful bosom pressing hard against his chest, her tender unpainted lips eagerly seeking his, arousing in him instincts that can lie dormant in a boy for just so long and then must spring to life fiercely, instincts that he had suspected and half feared but never obeyed, and which were not being kept under control by her pulling his shaggy head down to her own. His lips tasted kisses of brine and the tears aroused a fierce pain in his chest that ran over and circled his heart, ran down to his navel area, divided like a streak of forked lightning darting from cloud to cloud on a hot July afternoon, and ran down his groin and on into his thighs. She continued to brush her lips lightly across his own, and purposefully press her breasts tighter against him. He felt the sobs rise in her and heard her breathless moan between kisses. This new feeling was stronger than the wind that came cutting across the wide river, stronger than the bare cypress roots that stood naked in the water, stronger than the promise the skies gave that the sun would rise early in the east. This was a thing called "nowness and hereness." Later it would be reduced to the vulgar when it was exposed to the raw threads of daylight, but now it was only the sweet, the undeniable, the immediate.

Later it was damp lying on the bed of pine needles well away from the camp, and their bodies bathed in perspiration, which was quickly evaporating and making them even more chilly. It had been different than Ella had dreamed and hoped it would be. Surely it would be like his kisses, only sweeter, but it had been painful and embarrassing to both of them. If there had been any other way possible, she would have backed out at the last possible moment, but there was no other way, and she had closed her eyes tightly and prayed that it would soon be over and that she would be pregnant and then the only road left open to Leonard would be marriage. Sure fire . . . it was a perfect plan.

Moreover, Leonard had known that he was hurting her and could not help himself. He had seen these things happen in hog pastures and cow stalls and had heard older boys talking behind the country store, but these things did not help him at this moment. He had never expected things to get so far out of control that he couldn't stop it if he desired and here he was now, hurting the one person he loved more than anything, kissing her wet cheeks and eyelashes, whispering words he did not recognize as his own. He had dreamed many times of how wonderful it would be to love Ella, but the dreams had not been like this. He had dreamed of a big bed of good feathers swallowing them in its belly, leaving no place for them to be except side by side, and the window shutter left open for the stars to peep in if they wanted them to. But here the whole moon gazed on them and he felt the awareness of too much nakedness. He too, had not been ready for the moment that had passed, taking them beyond the point of no turning back.

Boyhood had passed tonight, but not without regrets. That a boy becomes a man suddenly is always filled with pain and sadness. The days of marbles and windmills in ditches are lost in the land of yesterdays and the tomorrows will be filled with the cares of everyday living from that moment until he dies.

Ella was busy trying to arrange her slips and night dress and he turned his back to her. When he turned again and looked she had scooped a hole in the sand beneath the thick pine start and buried her bloomers.

He reached out to touch her in a pathetic gesture.

"I'm real sorry, Ella."

"Well, I'm not!"

And he was to think about her answer for all the years to come, and to wonder . . .

—Chapter 4—

THE WEDDING was more elaborate and more expensive than Ella had imagined it could be. Mama had sold all of her laying hens and had bought yards and yards of white creamy satin and had sat up late every night for weeks making every stitch by hand for Ella's wedding gown. The dress had a high round neck and fit tight under her bosom, billowing freely from that point downward. It was not only stylish, it was appropriate for the bride's condition.

Pa had stopped work and cleaned up the churchyard, slinging down the young bushes sprouting up right near the church door, and burning off the last years dried sage. Inside, the church was decorated with red and white dahlias, lovingly given by their neighbors, all of whom would be there.

And the tears that gathered in the corners of the bride's eyes were considered normal for a young and fluttery bride of sixteen. And the bridegroom was dressed in clothes that his father had tailored especially for the occasion. Only the best was good enough for Ben Sr.'s son. The wedding of his only son would be attended by every farmer for miles around. Some would come to see the bride, some to see the bride's mother weep, some to see what the groom's mother and two sisters would be wearing, some to see how his mother reacted to the marriage, and some came to see just anything that could be seen. The intricate stitching on the wedding gown was admired by every woman present, and the groom was kidded by every male present. His choleric appearance was heightened by his harassment and he mentally counted sheep until the whole thing would be over.

The wedding recessional was a little squeaky on the old

organ, but very few present knew whether it was on key or off key. And all in good time, the bride and groom climbed into his Lincoln convertible, waved good-bye to everyone, and were off to their honeymoon, destination unknown to everyone except the groom.

If anyone two months before had told Ella that she would be riding beside Ben Jr. as his lawful wife and promised life companion, she would have laughed in sheer disbelief. The complexity of the events leading to the marriage even now left her totally bewildered. And the events paraded before her eyes even as the gray telephone poles with their green glass fixtures slipped past their automobile. Stand still, car! Stand still, her heart begged. You are carrying me too fast and too far in the wrong direction and with the wrong person. This is my life and it is all headed down the wrong road. If I close my eyes and open them, all of this will be a dream and I'll wake beside Kate and the moonlight will be flooding into my room just as it has all the nights of my life. And I'll be glad it was just a dream and turn over and go back to sleep with a relieved sigh. But it was not a dream that his long fingered hand reached over and tried to take her hand in his. He accidentally touched her leg and a tremble of fear and revulsion shook her from her new stockinged feet to her newly bobbed hair. At least, she had stood Mama down on that. If she could not marry Leonard, Ben Jr. would never have the pleasure of caressing her long golden hair. And she had taken the scissors and sheared herself so badly that Mama had to relent and let her have it bobbed.

Ben was certain that she did not respond warmly to him, and had talked it over with his father who had instructed him in the art of marriage and love making as if he needed instruction. Any bride worth her salt was never responsive before the wedding. This was a virtue to look for in a bride. Ben Jr. wasn't sure of his father's wisdom, but he was so elated over Ella's acceptance of his proposal that he put his doubts in the back of his mind and hoped that time would make her warm and loving.

The chain of events leading to the marriage was set off the

night of the revival on the river bank. Ella had given herself freely in a pine bed of love and pain to Leonard, and after that, she had thought it would be up to Leonard to make things right. There was never the slightest doubt in her mind that if she had conceived, Leonard would rush to her side, propose marriage, and all would be well for the rest of her life. In her childlike innocence, this seemed the only thing possible for him to do.

Three weeks later she awoke and felt her stomach get up and walk. There was the slimy feeling of bile rising in her throat and she jumped from the bed, rushed to the chamber pot, and vomited until it seemed as if her bowels would surely be the next thing to come up. Missouri heard her retching all the way from the kitchen and came running, wiping her flour covered hands on the front of her apron as she came.

"In the name of the Lord, do tell me what you ate last night. Or most likely too much sun. That's what I been telling Jacob, but he doesn't listen to a thing I say. A girl just can't stand too much sun."

And she rang out a wet cloth and put Ella back to bed with the cloth on her head. She soon had Kate standing beside the bed wetting lily leaves in a pan of cold water and putting them on her head. Only a stomach fever could make a person vomit like that, she declared. No more hoeing until the heat subsided! Absolutely!

In an hour, she felt as well as she ever had and was up at work. And though her illness mystified her mother, it did not mystify Ella, for she suspected the truth. The next morning, however, her illness gave a repeat performance. And again, they put damp lily leaves to her head and made her lie in bed during the morning. Missouri wrung her work worn hands together and declared it must be an attack of malaria coming on. But where was the hot fever that came with malaria, or "malery" as the local people called it?

The vomiting went on for a week before a seed of suspicion planted itself in Jacob's mind and he hitched the cart to the mule and set out after old Dr. Kellum. He might not be a medical school graduate, but he could cure most of the ailments of woman and child and all the ailments of hog and mulehood. He might not be the choice of the town, but he was certainly the saviour of the country folks.

"Hitch me up the buggy," he hollered at the top of his bassoon voice at his little wife, and she hurried at a trot to take down the bridle and hitch the horse.

"Don't sound like nothing serious," the Doc boomed to Jacob. "Most likely been eating green peanuts and got her belly out of sorts. A little good ash tea will cure that. Then again, her appendix could be acting up. Vomit a lot with them these days. Hope not, though. That'll mean ten days in the hospital. Cost money to have them appendix out and them doctors won't take no ham or taters for pay, either. It's cold salty cash they're after and they don't give a damn if they take out your liver to boot, if they can get more money out of you. Most likely it's not that, though. Don't get your dander up. I'll pass you on the way."

He took the reins from his wife's hands and climbed into the buggy.

"I most likely will make some more calls before I get home. If'n it's dark, don't forget to tend the hogs and get in the cow. I ain't wanting to traipse the pasture over at night looking for that bellowing creature. And have the gate open when you see me coming. I don't want to wait and sit out here while you meander out to open it."

If she minded him talking to her thus, she showed no sign. Her face was as impassive as a piece of granite and she neither told him good-bye nor heard him say it to her. They shared the same table, house, and bed, but their companionship was a thing that had never been. When he hollered, "Bessie," she dropped whatever she might be doing and came. It was better than an argument. He was so loud that he couldn't hear her side of any story, even if she tried to tell hers. And the more calls he made, the better she liked it. She was content with her sewing and her flowers. Why, she could turn a cockle burr into a rose bush with a little water, her neighbors declared. And she also enjoyed the prestige of being the only doctor's wife. She knew almost as much as he did about doctoring and often went with him to deliver babies. Her presence helped to ease the local women's embarrassment at having a man present at such time. The nearest hospital was sixty miles away and that made it impossible to have the baby anywhere except at home.

Missouri wanted to stay in the room when the doctor talked to her daughter, but he wouldn't hear of it.

"Patient's privacy," he boomed and laughed. "Me and Ellie got things to talk about. Mamas ain't so bright as they like to think. Out!" And there was no one around, not even old Mr. Ben, who dared to defy the doctor's orders.

"Now, young miss. What's this tomfoolishness 'bout you being possum sick every morning?" He ignored the fact that she had the thermometer in her mouth and he had told her to keep her mouth closed. She shook her head slightly that she couldn't talk, but he ignored that and rattled on.

"Ain't no point in nothing as young and healthy and pretty as you ever being sick. Now let's take a look at that stomach and feel that appendix."

The thermometer fell out of Ella's mouth and she pulled the quilt tight around her neck. "I want to talk to Mama."

"I don't think so! You need to talk to me most likely," and he took the quilt by the ragged edge and snatched it back with a dramatic sweep and left her lying there huddled in her gown. "Now up with it, young lady, or I'll lift it the same way."

Much as she hated to, she raised it inch by inch until he said she could stop, and he mashed her stomach in the side, middle, naval area, shaking his head negatively all the time.

"Now, young miss. I want the truth about this thing. Which one of these neighborhood young bucks has stabbed you recently?" He tossed the quilt back on her with an air of indifference and dropped down in the chair beside the bed. Until the look of terror came into her eyes and tears began to fall down the corners, he had been playing it by ear, but he knew now he had hit the nail on the head.

He pounded his balled fist into his other palm repeatedly as he listened to her revelation.

"I haven't been able to get out a second. As soon as I can tell Leonard, we'll be married, but Ma has watched me like a hawk every minute of this week. And I can't send a note by Kate. She won't take them for me anymore. And I wanted to be sure before I told him. You don't think my baby will be marked for my sins, do you?"

"If there's one thing I'm sure of, it's that such things are hogwash. It may be marked. Anybody's may be marked, but sin has damn little to do with it. It's breeding. Same as with the hogs and the horses. Pick a good stud, breed him to a good mare, and you'll get a good colt. Pick a runty stud, a runty mare, and you'll get a puny colt. Pick a fine stud, a poor mare, and you have a fifty-fifty chance of getting either. Same works for humans, too. Pick a fine mate, that's what I tell people, and they look at me like I'm mad. They believe it with their damn hogs, and they want to tell me about love when it comes to picking a wife. Hell with love. Love will come later. Pick a good mate first. Now, what do you want me to tell your Ma and Pa? That's the most pressing problem right now."

"Oh. Would you tell them something else is wrong with me until I can talk with Leonard, I mean, I mean . . ." and she realized that she had spoken his name for the second time to the doctor.

"Of course, I can and will tell what I please. But you get word to him right off and get hitched. These things don't wait for no marriage license. You understand? Right away, now. If you don't do something soon, I'll be obligated to be honest with your family. Understand?"

And he satisfied them with the details of a bowel complaint, they paid him with a piece of smoked side meat, and he stood on the porch and talked politics and smoked his pipe for an hour or two afterwards.

"Well, I never. Infected bowels. What new ailments will they come up with next?" Dr. Kellum said that he had just read about it in his new medical journal and it was exactly what she had. "No ash tea this time, either, just sassafras. You love it too, so it won't be like taking medicine."

And Missouri had been quite satisfied with his explanation.

Two days later Ella was considered well enough to go back to work and she took her woven straw basket filled with shucked yellow corn on her arm and set off for the hog pen. The male hog was kept penned a good ways from the house because it was indecent for the women folk to know and see the breeding of hogs. And feeding him gave Ella the opportunity she had been wanting all week. She flung the corn over the lightwood fence, dropped the basket right beside it, and took off at a fast run through the meadow and on through the pine thicket. Down through the branch thicket she ran, slowing down on the foot log, crossing the mire where the crayfish squirmed this time of year, on up the steep hill to the clearing. Even though the sun was near setting, Leonard was still plowing the big mule team, rope tied round his neck to free both hands to guide the big turning plow, as around and around he plowed. She stood in the bushes and waited until he came to the end near the woods. So intent was he on keeping the plow point in the right furrow that he did not look up when she called his name the first time. She called more urgently.

"Whoaaaaaa." The lead mule wanted to jerk forward, but the slack mule stopped dead in her tracks at the first syllable to whoa. "Whoa, damn you."

"I've got to talk to you a moment."

"Ella! What on earth are you doing over here?"

"Come over here where your Pa can't see me, Leonard."

He took the rope from his tanned back and wound it around the aged handle of the plow and stepped across the furrow and into the edge of the woods.

"I've been missing seeing you at church," she hedged with pitiful words, not knowing how to start an embarrassing conversation.

"I've been ashamed to go, Ella. I didn't want to look at you.

I been knowing you hated me."

"I've not been ashamed to go. I was hoping to see you there. I been 'fraid maybe you were sick. I been sick, you know."

"No. No, I didn't. What ailed you?"

"Oh, Leonard! Darn it. Don't you know? What we was hoping would happen did happen and now everything will be right for me and you. There's going to be a baby. Mine and yourn. And Dr. Kellum said the sooner the wedding, the better off we'd be. There's nothing Pa can say agin' it now, or anybody for that matter."

The color drained from his face as quickly as a starved leopard plant in a bed of sand gulping up its first water in months. He rubbed his cheeks and chin with his grimy hand and pinched his lip with his forefinger and middle finger. Ella took these mannerisms to mean that he was in deep study, but in truth they were expressions of bewilderment. He was a young boy, bucking his manhood, part child-part man, afraid to be a grown man for fear he would be a tyrant like his Pa or would not be able to shoulder all the responsibilities of a family alone, still terribly afraid of his bellowing fire-belching-cursing-seven-days-a-week father. He loved this lovely golden creature with her beautiful golden curls here in front on him with her hands folded in front of her, her stance was confident, her face eager to hear him say the only words that she thought he could say under the circumstances.

"It'd be nice, just you and me. I can cook anything Ma can. And care for the baby too. And when you come in nights from your job, I'll be there with your supper steaming, all of it just waiting for you to come."

To marry her would mean leave this land. It was not the richest land in the county, but it was the richest in their community and that was what counted. It was dark new ground, cleared by their own hands, and it would grow corn taller than a man's head without adding fertilizer. They had to part the stalks of cotton to walk down the row so spreading did they grow in the row middles. All these virgin pines that bordered their land would be his for the waiting. He had only to out last his Pa who couldn't live forever, not at his age or at the pace he kept. Why were things crowding him so quickly? To leave it now would be to lose his birthright forever, his younger brother would then inherit it all. To stay was to lose Ella, and the knife in his guts turned round and round as he writhed in the agony of decision.

"Why can't you see it, Ellie? I didn't want that to happen down there at the river. The devil possessed me, I reckon, but the Lord knows I didn't want it to happen. And I'm real sorry. But I can't leave my land. It'll be mine one of these days. It could be ours. All ninety acres ours. Can't you go off and have the baby and give it away? The Salvation Army takes in girls like that. And keeps the babies. And in a year or two, maybe three, I could take care of us. Maybe if Pa is still living, he'll mark off some of the land and let it be ours."

"Damn your Pa! And his land! That bull ox is not going to die. He's going to outlive you and your brother, and laugh about it, too. You'll never live to see the day this damn land is yourn! He don't intend to die and ever leave it. Understand, you fool!" Hysteria had gripped her voice and she was shouting at the top of it.

"Please, Ella. Pa might hear you."

"Hear! Hear! Let him hear. I hope he does. And if he doesn't, I'll go over and tell him so he can hear. I'll stand on the top of the hayloft and shout so that everybody in the neighborhood can hear! You can't mean you'd be willing for a me to go off and have our baby alone and give it to a bunch of black-frocked loonies who would give it to the first family who wanted it!"

"Ella. People nowadays adopt babies and love them like they'd born them. There ain't no shame to adopting a baby. And you'd forget it in time and we could start over as soon as we are able."

"Oh, damn it, Leonard. Can't you see? This little baby is not going to wait for your Pa to die, or mark off land, or for you to decide you want me enough to leave here with me. He's not going to wait for anything. He's growing every living minute of his life. And if you don't marry me, let me tell you, I intend to stay right here in this community and have him, and raise him, and let you see how fine our baby turns out to be. I ain't going off nowhere, understand? And I don't intend to stop pestering you till the time you tell me you don't care for me anymore. Long as you say you love me, I'm going to keep worrying you till you say you'll marry me."

Never had the sun seemed so big and red and round, and half of it had slipped already behind the dark green pines and the flat topped cypresses. The clouds that only moments ago had been feather white, now took on a dark shade of pink and pale blue. They moved quickly across the night as if a cloud might work itself up into a storm. One of the darkest clouds was shaped like a horse with no head or tail. Death rode a pale horse, Sister Whaley had said. But what about a horse with no head or tail.

He could not look at her and speak, so he looked far out beyond the skylight and softly told her. "I guess I don't really love you like you said, Ella. If I did I'd know right off what to do. And you ain't had a chance to know if you love anybody else either. Maybe we'd better let it go like that for a while."

What had gone wrong with her perfectly planned scheme? All of the stories she had read had ended with the man rescuing the woman from such a bad situation. But only she could rescue herself from this one.

"You're as sorry and no count as Ma and Pa said you were, Leonard." She spoke between clenched lips so he could not see her lips trembling. "You're sorry and you're no good, and you think you've ruined my life, but by God, I'll show you. You're right. You don't love me. A body can't love another and not care what shame and pain falls on them. Go on to your damn fields and your hateful land. One of these fine days I'll send your fine son through these fields to take a look at his father. I want him to be sure and know what a coward looks like."

Sobs choked her and she turned so swiftly, she almost fell headlong across a root, but she regained her balance, and ran swiftly through the branch, over the footing, and deep into the meadow before she stopped and lay down in the broom sage and wept. Convulsions shook her small frame all over. This was a complex situation for her and she was not good at complexities. She punctuated her sobs by hammering the ground with her fists, and was not the least upset by the darkness that had come suddenly as it often does in the late summer.

When the tears had run dry, she began to think again and it ran through her mind that if one plan doesn't work, one may always try another one. Who said that? Why Miss Justice, of course. She had said it often in school. Maybe she didn't have this situation or even one similar to it in mind when she said it, but it was the only advice Ella could think of at the moment and it seemed to be her salvation. She had got into this thing by her own scheming and now she must do her best to remedy it.

¤ ¤ ¤

SHE WORE HER WHITE BATISTE DRESS with its pale blue sash to church the following Sunday, and with her rose red complexion and eyes as blue as the wild blue berries, she caused the young and old heads alike to turn when she came out of the church. Kate wore an identical dress and it only made her more pathetically plain at she stood close to Ella. Now was the time for socializing, which was the main reason most people went to church in the first place. Men went off in groups of three and four and exchanged their farm news; women clustered around whoever had the newest baby and knew, of course, just whom it favored and how much it weighed by looking at it. Then the baby's mother related how often it had the colic and at what times, and that started a chain reaction among the other ladies who had all had the same experience, only worse, of course. Over by the rusty wire picnic table that ran the length of the church yard, the young folks congregated and under the watchful eyes of their parents. They, too, laughed and talked and teased.

Ben Jr. had been standing with a group of older men, but

when he saw Ella join the young people, he excused himself quickly and joined them also. This was the one day he was not going to give her the change to use the excuse that someone else had already asked her to ride home with him. He had attributed her recent coolness to the fact that he had scared her in his automobile and he had made up his mind that if her ever got her in it again, he would drive more carefully. The conversation was mostly of how hard they had worked and how most longed to return to school, but it soon changed to a teasing one.

Eva Belle was up to her same antics and said with sheer delight, "Same dresses, same beaux, I always heard say."

"I don't think you heard any such thing, Eva Belle Morton! You made it up like you always do and added the 'I always heard say.'"

"I did no such thing, you hateful baboon."

He looked anything but a hateful baboon. She was addressing one of the community boys, Leslie Humphries, and he was more like a colt just ready for stud. There had been some German in his ancestry and it dominated his features—thick blond hair, wide face, and deep-set blue eyes which combined artfully and made him by far the most handsome boy hereabouts. His father had a small farm around the loop road and it supported his father and mother and nine brothers and sisters. With the exception of Ben Jr. he was the only boy in the area who had been to high school and this was made possible only by helping Dr. Kellum and saving the money to buy a second hand bicycle. He rode the bike down the railroad track seven miles each way daily to the country high school. After his graduation, he hoped to enter college and work his way through. Nothing in this community called him to stay. Just as far away and just as high up a he could go was his aim, and he did not intend to be steered off it by a skirt, in particular such a flighty skirt as Eva Belle. She knew more things to say to him, but the nearness of him left her senseless and speechless, and whenever she did manage to utter anything, it sounded as if it had come from the lips of an idiot. She was the only local girl who lost anytime in mooning over him. The rest accepted his ambitions and knew he would make his way to the big city, and never look back when he made it.

Times when Eva Belle had spent the night with Ella and Kate, they had laughed and talked all night, and in their fanciful imaginations, Ella was married to Leonard, Eva Belle to Leslie, and Kate to Ben Jr. They even named their children and mentally picked out furniture for their future homes. It was wild, but it was fun, the fun of the young whose hearts can be broken today, and whose fences can be mended by tomorrow's sunrise. Ere the rooster crows for dawn, the words of youth can be healed. Even as their bones knit more quickly, so do their dreams die and are reborn time and time again.

"How 'bout you and Eva Belle and Leslie and myself riding down and looking at the new courthouse they're building? It's going to be all brick, Pa says." And for once his face retained its normal color.

Leslie was the first to answer. "Thanks, Ben. But we left this morning with some hogs out and we've got to hunt for them as soon as we get back. Thanks mightily, though, Ben."

"Well, I'd love to go whether some folks would or not," and Eva looked Leslie squarely in the eye as her words dripped with icicles.

"I'd enjoy it myself." The group was so surprised to hear these words from Ella that all chatter came to an abrupt halt. Even Ben Jr. was stunned. He had hoped to hear those words, but in his heart, he hadn't really expected that she would say yes.

"I'll go with you, Eva Belle. If Leslie wants to run hogs, let him run them by himself, I say." Neil was not as handsome as his older brother, but he was certainly more fun to be with, and was not afraid of community entanglements.

Ella had expected it to be a perfectly miserable afternoon. Pa and Ma had been delighted when she asked their permission to go riding with Ben Jr. and for this at least she was glad. The hurt she would inflict on them later would be bad enough and she was happy to make them happy even for a moment now. But the afternoon had been fun. Her hat had blown out of the car once and they were a third of a mile down the road before the car rolled to a halt. Ben Jr. backed it slowly around. No cutting corners and braking hard today, he kept telling himself mentally. Do right, for once. They stopped in town and Ben Jr. went into the lobby of a hotel and bought them all a root beer. It was the first Ella and Eva had ever tasted any and just the word "beer" added to it made it seem a little naughty and forbidden. Something in the drink seemed familiar to Ella, but she did not want to seem ignorant, not with Ben Jr. so intelligent and a school teacher besides.

But Eva Belle certainly had no qualms about stating what she thought it tasted like.

"Why this is plain old sassafras tea. Just ice had been added. Ain't that right, Ben?"

He laughed hard before he could answer. He was glad Eva was along today to fill in the gaps. Wherever Eva was, laughter was there, too. And they needed laughs today.

"Yes. It is made from sassafras flavor. It's not supposed to be called plain old stuff, however."

"I knew it," she declared with an air of authority as if she could not have possibly been mistaken.

Kate would have loved to have been riding with Ben Jr., but she did not let it show on her face. At least this way, she was close to him and that was better than nothing. Eva Belle would have preferred to have been with Leslie, but she was not one to let one bad apple spoil the cider. Even though she was perplexed as to why Ella had accepted Ben Jr.'s invitation so quickly, she did not tax her flighty mind long over the situation.

The new courthouse was a building the county had long needed, having outgrown the old one years previously. The local gentry had gone to the old one to vote and to try and be tried for seventy-five years, and its long dark hall now sagged in the middle with the weight of years and rotting sills. Ben Jr. explained the history of the old one to them as if they were his seventh graders in Stone's Bay Elementary. In guiding them around the construction, Ben Jr.'s arms and shoulders occasionally brushed against Ella, and he was glad that his trousers had loose legs so that she could not feel the flesh on his thighs quivering. However, this bodily contact filled her with revulsion which she was desperately trying to conquer. It was one of the things she must do, and what had to be, simply had to be.

That's was Sister Whalis always said and who was she to doubt Sister Whalis and the Lord. Her one step into sin in no way made her feel that God was not still her Keeper and she intended to go on calling on Him whenever she needed Him.

The winding dirt road was the width of one car, and it was lucky that they didn't meet but two other cars, for each time they had to take the ditch and wait until the other automobile had edged past them.

The road led through colored town, and here the small planked gray houses sat close together and close beside the road. Some had no porches. Some had dirt floors. All were filled with laughing children and boisterous parents. It wouldn't be long before cotton picking time and Ben Jr.'s father would be down here hiring them by the cart load to pick his fields of waist high cotton. Ben Jr. knew who lived in every single house, and there were children standing all along the roadside staring at the bright red car as it went by, and waving at Mr. Ben Jr. This too was a first for both of the girls as their parents did not hire outside labor, and they had no association with the colored folks other than seeing them getting paid off at Mr. Ben's store occasionally.

Did he dare to ask her if she would like to go to night preaching with him? She had said yes one time today. Did he dare risk her saying no now? Ella looked over at him and thought, "Why, he isn't a middle aged man at all. He's not much more than a boy. Just because most of his hair is on the back of his head and he teaches school, those things don't make him old. He's probably just as scared of me as I am of him. And there isn't time for a long lengthy courtship. Dr. Kellum had said the sooner the better, young lady. She visualized just how his walrus mustache quivered when he told her those words and she hugged herself as if she were having a chill.

"Would you like for me to stop and put the top up, Ella?"

"No. I don't think so. I'm not really cold. Maybe it's because the sun has got behind the trees. I think Mama will be getting worried though about us by now. She's not too sure these automobiles are safe."

"That's how Pa feels too. He still thinks that darn buggy is the best way to get there. Anywhere the buggy won't take him, the train will, is what he tells me when I offer to carry him places. Not for me though. It won't be long before everyone round here will be buying one. Roads will be better then too, Praise God."

"I don't think Pa will ever buy one. He's too interested in saving money and buying land. That's all that counts with him." A note of bitterness flavored her words and Kate was quick to defend their father.

"Shame on you, Ella. You know that's not true. Pa cares mightily about all of us."

"I'm sure he does." He was not at all sure whether he did or not, but the day had been too nice to be spoiled now by a petty quarrel between the sisters, and he thought to put a stop to it before it got off the ground.

"Would you girls care to go to the night preaching with me. I usually drive Mama and the girls out on Sunday night, but I could run them over first and pick you all up in plenty of time." He wanted to say that if one missed part of Preacher Cornaby's sermon, they hadn't missed much, but this wasn't the time to express such a radical viewpoint.

Again, it was Ella who spoke first. "I think that be real nice. I've never been in an automobile at night. I don't know what Pa'd say though. Maybe we oughta ask him first."

"I'd be obliged to ask him."

And naturally Jacob was willing for Ella to go with Ben Jr. to the night preaching. It was a step in the direction he had been draggin' her for the past year or two.

If Ben had been a pusillanimous character before, he was an over confident one now. The fact that Ella encouraged him made him grow taller, act manlier, and draw away from his formidable father. Their courtship progressed so rapidly that his mother did not even have time to line up all of her objections and his sisters were caught unaware of the seriousness of the situation. Within three weeks it was announced that they would be married immediately following the morning church service and everyone was invited to stay for the wedding.

"I do declare. You amaze me, Ella," her mother said. "Here you don't even have your four quilts made. Every bride should have four quilts at least. And you with not a one. We'll just have to make them 'afore cold weather is all there is to it. I don't want Mrs. Simpson saying my daughter came unprepared."

The autumn laden community buzzed with the news.

"If anyone had told me I'd live to see the day that Ella Horne said yes to Ben Jr., I'da called him a liar right there on the ground he stood on. Hasn't she said anything at all to you, Kate?" Eva Belle was more perplexed than most because she alone knew how deeply Ella loved Leonard.

"Not a blooming word. But I don't think love has got much to do with it."

"You can't mean there is a more urgent reason. Not about your own sister."

"I ain't saying. Cause I don't know. But I do know she don't look at him like she used to look at Leonard. That was a pure cow and calf look they did. I just don't understand it. Less she's a trying to spite me. And I can't think she'd throw her life away to spite me. Do you?"

Eva would have liked to have said that she was easy to spite because of her spiteful ways, but this was not the time or place.

"No. There's note a spiteful bone in her body and you know it. Some thing's bothering her, though. Where is she now?"

"How should I know. Most of the time, her and Ma are shut up together talking and I'm not allowed in, naturally. Woman talk, they say. And what time she's not doing that, she and Ben

Jr. are off somewhere in his hateful, plagued devilish red car. I wish I'd never said I'd ride in it. Ella didn't want to that first time and we made her. It's all our fault. We cooked this goose on the wrong wide, Eva Belle."

"Oh, hush. You're too young to know anything but puppy love. Anyway, he'll soon be your brother-in-law and you'll feel different. Tell Ella I stopped by and I wish her happiness in case I don't see her 'afore the wedding. Hear?"

Only a few of the leaves in the swamp had started to change their colors. Autumn in Eastern North Carolina is a precious time to its people. The cotton is laid by and only time can tend it now. The sows have their pigs and weaned them and are pregnant again and happily rooting all over the pastures. The mules have plowed their last furrow of the year and their bridles hang limp on a rusty nail on the stable door. No more work till wood hauling time. The white potatoes are dug. The onions are hung up on nails in the barn, dried and seasoned. So is the red pepper and the sage. Soon the sweet potatoes will be ready to dig. Just in time to eat with the fresh hog meat. The corn has made its ear, but isn't quite ready to pull from its stalk. Acre after acre of the fields lie brown and rattly. Waiting. Waiting. The water runs slow in the swamp for the rains have been few this summer. Even the mud beds are dried out and cracked. Crayfish find it hard to find a mud hope deep enough to hide in and their popping noises can be heard all around the branches. The red bird tree stands watching it all. The time for praying is over. Now is the time for thanks. A few stray pine needles have begun to fall on top of last year's needles, now inches thick and brown-black.

Ella sat on the foot log and dangled her bare feet above the red water. Perhaps a water moccasin floated in it. Perhaps a snapping logger head turtle lay nearby. But these were not things that disturbed her. These were normal, everyday accepted parts of her life. It was the tomorrow and the days afterward that held the unknown for her. Could she fool Ben Jr. on their wedding night? Only Mama knew the real reason for the marriage and she would never tell. She hadn't meant to tell her, but the enormity of the problem had engulfed her and broken her determination to go it alone. Together they had talked and schemed and perhaps it would all work out. She hoped so. At least, if he cast her aside, her baby would not be branded a bastard. O tiny baby. Poor innocent thing. Her heart wept and tears fell and splashed on the branch water flowing under the log. I'm a doing it all for you. I do hope it's for the best.

The water and the tears flowed to the creek, and from there to the ocean, but no one was the wiser.

And now here in the car beside him, dust and miles flying by, she was still dubious that it could work. But, at least, she had to try and, after all, there had been no other way.

—Chapter 5—

SHE ROLLED OVER AND RAISED HERSELF on one elbow, her short golden hair tousled in knots, her flannel gown unbuttoned to the waist, and stared at her sleeping husband. She had done likewise every morning for the past two months: awaking each day surprised to find herself in bed beside a man and even more surprised to find herself not too miserable about it. Looking at him did not make her flesh tremble, or her heart begin its frantic pumping, or cause constrictions in her throat, but neither did it fill her with revulsion such as she had known for him before their marriage. She now knew how sensitive he was about his balding head and his sharp nose and pitied him, and it is hard to pity a person and hate him simultaneously. Even now the look on his face made her want to bend and kiss his forehead.

She slipped quietly out of bed, so as not to awaken him, and dressed in the cold room. At first he had arisen before her and made a fire in the fireplace for her to dress by, but she liked to have his breakfast on the table before she called him and he had not protested too long or too loudly. Other mornings he slipped quietly out first and dressed and took his rifle and went squirrel hunting a short piece from the house. They were only a couple of miles down river from where Sister Whalis held her camp meetings, but the scenery was quite different. The river was wider and deeper, the moss was thicker and longer, the river oaks larger, their naked roots standing higher out of the water. Also, the water had a higher salt content. Some called the river a backwash of the ocean, but the Indians had called it a river, and the white people who came continued calling it that. It was surrounded by a hundred thousand acres of snake infested swamp that the Indians had called a pocasin which meant "swamp on a hill."

It was one of those oddities in nature that no one could explain. It lay below sea level even though it ran a hundred miles inland. A man could not wish for a more ideal hunting ground for it abounded in deer and black bear. But, Ben Jr. did not care for hunting the big game. He was content to walk quietly on the damp leaves, his little spotted squirrel dog running ahead, and kill an occasional chattering squirrel. No one could say that Ella had been too young to cook. She could cook a squirrel stew with rice, black pepper, and flour pastry that made a man's mouth water just thinking about it. He knew that he had disappointed his father in not continuing on the farm and keeping the general store, but he was glad that at least Pa approved of his wife and, maybe in time, he would understand the pleasure that came from teaching the small children.

"I can't read, and look at me!" That was Pa's standard argument, and for the life of him he couldn't go him one better than that.

Before, he had been at loose ends when the last paper was marked and the three room structure stood quiet after a very loud day, but now he hurried home because he knew Ella would be there. And she was such a gay charming child and a woman combined. At home he had heard three women bicker all of his life. Over hats. Over the church music. Over the Christmas program. Over dresses. Over who sat here and who sat there. Over this is mine and that is hers. Over anything! But there was no nickering or nagging from Ella. She was pleasant every moment, and he was trying desperately to control his own hot temper. Even when he blew a valve over little things, she left him alone until he cooled down and did not add fat to the fire. Dear and glorious, he thought. That's what these days are.

Autumn ran into early winter and all the days were short and golden. To look at the woods, one would not know the season, for the pines and holly and junipers were still green.

Only the oak and the sweet gums were barren and they were covered with swinging moss. It's not a barren time at all. Last year I thought this season was bleak and bare, but it's a ripe golden time. Even the holly has more berries than usual.

Walking home one afternoon he recalled the night of their wedding and just thinking of it made blood run to the top of his head. They had driven all the way to Wilmington and had taken a room at the old Cape Fear Hotel. It was the first time that Ella had ever been on an elevator and she had reached out and held tightly to his arm. It was the first time in their relationship that she had touched him first and he knew then that it would be difficult to control himself once the door to their bedroom was closed behind them. He knew just how he would like to love her, but what he didn't know was "should he try it?" This was not one of the women he had taken to a hotel room for a few hours since he was seventeen, one of the local women whose doubtful virtue could be had for a dollar. This was a young girl, now his wife, and the only one he had loved with his heart. He had heard of young brides who panicked on their wedding night and packed their baggage and went home to mama. It would take time and patience and he was trembling so when the door closed behind them that he fumbled trying to light a cigar.

"Let me do that for you. Pa buys them when we sell out cotton in the fall."

He was surprised at her serenity, but she had resigned herself to being his wife. She had told the swamp and the moon and the trees and the wind good-bye to Leonard and good-bye it had to be. Whatever was required of her now to get a name for her baby, that was what she would do. And he had soon drawn the blinds, blocked the door, and taken her to bed. She had made it as difficult for him as possible, just as Ma had told her, and in the dim light that filtered under the blinds from the street below, he thought her the loveliest woman he had ever looked upon. Later in the bathroom, she squeezed a few polk berries on her gown and came out with trembling lips.

"I'm scared, Ben. I'm a bleeding to death. Look here."

Had he been a rooster he would have hopped on the highest fence post and crowed a long shrill note. He had possessed her and, though he had not doubted her virginity, he was bathed in pride at the proof. And now she was asking for his help! The memory of that night would warm him as long as he lived. And he hastened his steps toward their house.

As for Ella, she had truly resigned herself to marriage. Being married to a man with modern ideas did not tie a woman down like being married to Pa with all his notions of what was proper and what wasn't fitting for a lady. The only two places Pa approved of Ma going was to the hen house and to her church meetings. But not so with Ben. He wanted to take her everywhere, to his committee meetings and in particular to show her places and things she had never seen before. Her fright of his automobile had completely disappeared and some of his recklessness had returned. They were soon a regular sight on the dusty river road, her hair flying in all directions at once. Any idle chickens in the road either made haste out of their way or were splattered into a conglomeration of guts and feathers and dirt. And the baby was behaving itself most proper by not moving yet. She did not plan to mention her condition until it moved or Ben noticed it first. She could not decide which was most dangerous. To wait or to tell. If she didn't tell, time would beat her to it. Would that be wise? Just how much did Ben know of babies and their timetable? She did not know what literature had been available to him when he had gone off to school. Some folks said there were whole books written about having babies and love and marriage, but she had never seen one herself; therefore, she wasn't too sure about the matter.

He liked to see the white gray smoke coming out of the chimney when his car rounded the curve each afternoon. He knew then supper was cooking and thought of how good the whole house would smell. But today, there was no smoke from the rooftop. Nor was there any sign of Ella on the front porch. Hastening his footsteps, he found her inside packing his best suit and some of his shirts in their largest suitcase.

"In the name of God, what are you doing, Ellie?"

"I been awaiting for you, Ben. School's been out nigh on an hour."

"I just decided to stay till I was through grading papers. What are you doing putting my clothes in a suitcase?"

"Dr. Kellum sent Tom on his Pa's horse to tell you the news about your Pa. We've got to go there as soon as we can. He's had a stroke and is asking for you."

"A stroke! My God. Aren't they fatal?"

"I don't know. Tom brought a note. I put it down somewhere. I've been so addled trying to think what to pack, I've mislaid it. Let me see now."

"To hell with the note. Sling something in the bag and let's get off."

"Hadn't you better tell someone you might not be able to be at school tomorrow?"

"We can do that on the way out. Pack you best dress. We don't know what we'll find when we get there and we won't have time to come back most likely. I know Mama is running around like a hen with her head off. Gertrude and Faye Ellen are about as much good in an emergency as a raccoon. They always make Mama worse than she'd be by herself. Do get ready and don't keep standing there with your mouth hanging open."

It was the first time he had talked to her rudely, but he was beset with mental images of what was taking place at home and none of them were good.

While packing her best dress she was filled with premonitions. This little wood, unceiled house was their own and she had it as clean as a new reed whistle, and some foreboding told her she was telling it good-bye. But there is no reason for this feeling, she kept telling herself as she folded her dress and petticoats and snapped the locks of the case.

Even if Mr. Ben dies, there will be no reason why we can't return here. Ben will have to finish out the year teaching. I couldn't bear it if we had to move in with his mother and his horrible sisters. They had not spent the night with his family since their marriage, but during the Sunday visits there Ella had plenty of time to feel the coldness in the air. The only warm person in the household was Mr. Ben, and his booming voice embraced her as tightly to his bosom as it did Ben Jr. No one would dare say a slighting word to her as long as the old man lived. It was his household and his women would behave like he wanted them to as long as they lived under his roof. They had no doubt about it and needn't have had, for he was lord and master of his domain. The only weakness in his character was his boy and he was satisfied that all would be well for him now that he was safely married to a good girl.

He had let him sow his wild oats all over the county, bought him everything a young man could desire, educated him, let him go his own way even though he had been set on the boy running the big farm and the general store. Eventually he was sure the lad would see the folly of making forty dollars a month when all of this would be his someday. No one could be that dumb.

Surely his overseer could keep on looking after things and Mrs. Simpson and the girls could run the house the same as ever, Ella thought silently as the car sped down the dirt road, the pines and the oaks and the moss all pitch black beside the road. An occasional rabbit ran in front of the car. Sometimes a possum sat beside the road, trying the decide whether it would be safe to cross now with all these bald tailed babies clinging to her tail. Every time they hit a bump, the metal suitcase bounced up and down in the back seat, adding to the feeling of fear that both were feeling right now for different reasons.

All of the lamps in the house were lit and Dr. Kellum's buggy was still tied up to the elm tree in the front yard. The wind was swinging the porch swing to and fro and the chains squeaked and groaned when moved as if swung by some invisible hand.

The November air in this place was a different kind of night air from that of any place else in the world. The day preceding it may have been warm with filtered golden sunlight, warm enough for a man to turn under his corn stalks barefooted, but the night air was so cold that it took two quilts to keep the chill off a body.

Ella was chilled to the bone and the sight of the yellow lamp light made her shiver and hug herself, then sign with relief. Warmth had to be inside. Ben Jr. jumped out on the running board of the car and bounded into the house a full ten steps in front of her, suitcase forgotten. Time turned backward to when Pa had broken his leg when the team ran away and dragged him all over the new ground, and he had sat beside the bed and cried big boy tears falling on Pa's patched up leg, hands grubby and trembling, voice pleading with Pa to please be well again. Or the time the moccasin had bitten him in the cotton field and he had taken his belt, corded his own leg, cut it with his big black handled Barlow pocketknife, and sucked the poison out. Mama had nearly fainted when he came in all bloodied and belted up. What a man Pa had been at his age. He was a boy again running through the front hall and dashing into the sitting parlor.

Faye Ellen and Gertrude were seated on the settee, Faye Ellen dabbing her eyes with an inch wide lace trimmed hand embroidered handkerchief, but Gertrude was sitting bolt upright, dry eyes. She launched into Ben immediately as if she had been preserving herself for this task.

"Is this the soonest you could get here? Pa's been at death's door since morning. You're the only one he's asked for, naturally."

"Where is he? Where's Ma?"

"Where do you think Pa would be? He had them carry him to his room, of course."

He took the steps three at a time and, as he turned the landing, he saw Ella come timidly in the front door and pause at the door to the parlor. For a brief moment he wanted to go back down and fortify her in being with his sisters, but the moment passed as quickly as it had come and he dashed on down the portrait lined hall to his Pa's room. Brushing aside his ma, who stood just inside the door, he strode quickly to the bed side and knew instantly that he was gazing upon the face of death. And rightly so, for his Pa's face was drawn down at the corner of his mouth and one eye looked wildly out the corner and the flesh on his cheek twitched intermittently. Old Dr. Kellum was wringing out a cold cloth in a white china wash basin and preparing to exchange it for the one on the forehead.

"Glad you made it, boy. 'Bout given you out. You had a long drive though."

His moustache went up and down as he talked and his quid of chewing tobacco looked as if he had got a walnut stuck in the side of his mouth and couldn't figure out how to get it out again.

"What happened. In the name of God, what happened to him?"

Dr. Kellum motioned for him to be quieter and to come over to the corner of the room. There his raspy voice tried to whisper, "Stroke. Worse kind. Lost his voice. Vocal cords paralyzed. He can hear you plain as anything though. Knows everything. Just can't talk. You can talk to him, but don't expect much response and don't mention his sickness to him. Get you Ma out if you can. I can't. Haven't been able to do a thing with her all day."

He went back to the bed which was covered with home made quilts of many patterns and colors and each fancifully quilted in tiny artful stitches. A great deal of juicy gossip had passed over these quilts before each had been completed. He picked up his Pa's knotty veined hand and held it. The old man roused and looked as if he wanted desperately to tell something. He made a sign with his fingers as if he were writing.

"I'm here now, Pa," was the only thing Ben Jr. could think to say.

The old man's eye that was still alert was begging to be understood. He continued motioning as if he were writing.

"Do you want to write something to me, Pa?"

Tears flowed instantly to the old fellow's eyes and ran down his age wrinkled face. At last some one had understood what he wanted all day and did not simply think he was crazy. Did they think him an imbecile or dead already that he could not see them weeping and talking in whispers. Thank God that his boy had come in time and had the good sense to know what he needed and wanted.

Ben put a nickel tablet in front of him and took a pencil from behind his own ear. He had put it there when he left the school house this very afternoon and miraculously it had not fallen off in all the haste and running around. Was that only this afternoon when everything had been right with the world? The old hand shook but he wrote quite legibly. "Get that fool doctor out of here. Get this damn wet rag off my head . . ." He rested and wrote again. "Tell you Ma to leave, too . . ."

"Please," Ben Jr. told Dr. Kellum, "Pa wants you to leave for a few minutes. Take Ma downstairs too and get some hot tea in her if you can. Go on with him, Mama."

She was a tiny vivacious woman, a woman whose only claim to this son was that she had borne him. Her husband had never let her discipline him, teach him, mother him. "Girls are yours," he'd told her. "Ben Jr. is mine." Twenty years younger than her husband she did not have the courage to go against any of his wishes, even if it had done any good to try. The doctor led her downstairs to the parlor where he quickly sent Faye Ellen to the kitchen for a pot of hot tea.

"They're all gone now, Pa."

He was not the little boy any longer. The figure on the bed was the little boy now. He would never be the little boy again until the wings of death flapped and beat him down like they were doing to Pa now.

The old man tried to smile, but he only succeeded in making his mouth pull down at one corner and Ben Jr. was glad that he could not know how hideous it made him look.

All day he had wanted to be propped up on the pillows, but that damn quack doctor had insisted that he lie flat on his back. How could a body write lying flat as a board. He'd always said that Dr. Kellum could only deliver babies and colts, and for everything else he gave coffee grounds and molasses to cure any

ill. Ben read the paper again and knew that it could not do any
harm now to prop him higher. The only way the old man could
utter thanks was to try to smile and Ben Jr. turned aside as he
tried it again. Again and again a knife turned and twisted its
sharp blade in his stomach . . . who says a sympathetic pain is
not real? The question ran through his mind, and the pain was
for the old man, not himself. Or is there a madness in us all that
makes us glad we are not the one death has marked? he thought.
Or is that merely a human feeling of survival? This man was all
parent encompassed for him. All family. All everything before
Ella had become a part of his life.

The old man wrote again. "I'll not get over this. All I have
is yours. Mr. Summerville has the will. I want you to promise
me you'll come here to live and take care of your ma and sisters.
I'm not leaving them anything. But I want you to come here and
tend our land and run the store."

Ben read and he could not hold back his tears any longer.
They fell and splattered off the cheap rough paper.

"I'll take care of them, Pa. You know that."

His answer angered the old man and he tried to rise. He
shook his head angrily and wrote again. "No . . . no. Promise
you'll come here and live and tend the land and the store. I want
you here. This is yours. This is where you belong."

As much as the younger man would have liked to explain to
him that his work with the children at the school was rewarding,
he knew that it was not the right time. Pa would never understand
anything that did not pay off well in plain dollars and cents.
Surely it could do no harm to agree with a dying man. This was
not the time to argue with him. Perhaps he would get over this
and be like himself again after all. Rather than run the risk of
agitating him, he sighed and swore. "I'll come and take care of
it, Pa, if you want me to. But you'll be up soon riding everywhere
on Big Red."

All of the lights burned all night in the big house and
neighbors came and stood on the porch or in the hallway or
talked under the cold dripping trees. They might not have

approved of him, but he was the cornerstone of their community. He had given the land for the church, bought the organ, he ran the store—the only store—he bought their eggs and smoked hams and shoulders, allowed them credit if the mood was upon him just right. And they were upset that the dark rider had struck at one of their community. Besides, it gave them a chance to discuss their brand new President.

The black adder has a sharp long tongue and he can thrust it out and in with a terrifying swiftness. He is despised more than he is feared, but he is feared aplenty and Warren Harding was an adder to them. He had not received a single vote in their county and it was beyond their comprehension that a majority of the nation had wanted this damned Republican with his soft smooth voice. They had heard him speak on the store radio and his voice purred as if honey were dripping from the comb. Sitting around the pot bellied coal stove and listening to him promise to return the country to normalcy after the war years, did not sway them in the least. Republicans and black snakes were one and the same to them.

They had flocked in record numbers to the poll holding places, but their votes had been cast in vain and that damned pug nosed Vice President could not be depended upon. No man that looked that much like a bull dog could be much of a Vice President. The only bright spot in the administration seemed to be that Charles Hughes had been appointed Secretary of State. If a man had a leaning to a Republican in this county he did not have the courage to lean very far and he did not make his opinion audible.

While the lamps burned on and the night grew colder they discussed the national and international affairs, the local hog news, and the community gossip, occasionally glancing up at old man Ben's window to see if the lamp was turned out. As long as the light flowed through that upstairs window they knew that he lived. Without him they did not know whether the community would live or not.

In spite of the fire that burned steadily in the fireplace, Ella kept shivering and hugging herself and of all times the baby started a faint stirring in her womb and made her stomach want to stand up and walk. She knew that she must control the urge to vomit here tonight. Gertrude and Faye Ellen were like a couple of old hawks watching a young mocking bird out trying his wings alone for the first time, and she knew that anything suspicious she did would not go unnoticed. She wished desperately that Ben Jr. would come downstairs and ask that she go up and stay with him. She was not afraid to be with the old man, even if he were dying. He had been her salvation in this house and her insides quivered at the thought of what it would be like here without him to back her. But Ben did not come downstairs and when his mother went up, he would not let her back into the room. The old man had written that he wanted all of them out, including the damned doctor and he intended to do like the old man wanted for this one time at least.

It was around quarter to four when Jacob Horne looked up and said, "The old fellow's gone." They all looked up quickly, all conversations ceased instantly, and saw that the light had been extinguished and the window raised. A tip of white curtain swung out the window with the wind and fluttered a time or two, unaware that it flapped gaily in the presence of death. From inside the house moans could be heard, but there was nothing the people could do tonight. They would meet again in the morning and dig his grave, but for now there was nothing left to do but go home.

The following night, crowds sat up with the widow and the body, but Ben Jr. did not concede to the old custom and soon followed Ella up to his room. The whitest sheets and the softest feather bed that she had ever seen were on the iron frame bed. The feather bed was made of duck breast feathers and all she had ever been used to were geese and turkey feathers mixed with some from the hen house. She felt wonderfully clean and was glad that Ben had decided against sitting up all night. She had become accustomed in the past few months to his long frame curling up around her as soon as she went to bed. Time makes liars out of us, she thought as she watched him undress, carelessly throwing his trousers on the floor and flinging his white shirt across the foot of the bed. It made a liar out of me. I wanted to go on hating him, using him, but here I am enjoying being with him, actually looking forward to his coming to bed with me. The sight of him undressing aroused her more than she dared admit even to herself yet. Later, with the light extinguished and the cool air whipping in the window, lying warm and snug and safe under two quilts and a big counterpane, he pulled the back of her gown up and pulled her up close to his own body.

"Not tonight," she whispered. "Not with him lying dead downstairs."

"Why not? Pa'd be the first to approve. He never turned down a piece of tail in his life and he wouldn't want me to miss a piece either."

"Please, Ben. You don't sound respectful at all."

"Sex is always respectable. People aren't sometimes, but sex is."

"You and your books, Ben. You shock people too much. You shouldn't use the word sex so often. People will think you're not normal or something."

"Not normal, huh?" And he rubbed the inside of her soft downy thigh until the flesh quivered and jumped under his touch and he heard her breath coming in gasps and knew that he had won his point.

She always planned on playing hard to get with him. She would resist for just a little while next time. Maybe he thought her too easy a mark. Mama had said play hard to get all of your life with a husband and he would keep coming back to the same bed, but be too easy to possess and he'll soon look for someone harder to make. She thought it sounded like sensible advice, but she did not have the willpower to carry it out. But next time she was going to try it. Maybe tomorrow or the day after, but tonight it was easier to say yes and enjoy his gentle kisses that started in the heart of her breast and worked their way up her neck, around and under her arms, and soon found her lips. Yes. It would be better to resist tomorrow!

Afterwards she turned to face him and told him that she was pregnant and he accepted it as she had hoped that he would—as the inevitable.

"It's about time," he exploded and patted her bottom.

"I was beginning to wonder if I was any damned good. Are you sure?"

"Yes. I spoke to Dr. Kellum today and he gave me a bottle of root tonic to take. He said I needed it to keep my blood built up to prepare me for all I'll lose later on. You aren't mad, are you?"

"Mad? Why should I be made? Don't babies usually come with marriage?"

And he gently rubbed her bottom again and sighed and went to sleep, knowing that tomorrow would be difficult with the funeral and his mother and sisters, but all was right between him and Ella and that was what really mattered.

—Chapter 6—

IT SEEMED AS IF SPRING would never come again. The winter rains had been prolific and the roads that had been dusty beds all summer had now become miry ruts on the warmer days and frozen ones on the colder days. The roads had been so impassable that Ben had not taken the car out of the car shed within the past two months. He used the horse and cart to go over the farm and to bring supplies to the store from the depot.

Christmas had come and gone. So had January and most of February. Ella was heavy with the child now and much nearer to her time than Ben or his mother realized, but not nearer to it than Gertrude and Faye Ellen suspected with their suspicious minds.

Now that the sun had decided to shine again for a few days straight, the roads were filled with farmers with their mules and carts, hauling pine straw to put in their hog pens and chicken houses and hen's nests. They hauled almost everything in these carts with their big wheels. Sometimes it was burned charcoal they picked up under the water trestle. They scattered this around in their hog lots and the hogs chewed the coke. Sometimes it was stove wood for kitchen ranges, or lengths of fire wood for the fireplaces, or slabs that could be hewed into roof shingles, which were a vital part of building in the country. They hauled their sows from the pasture to another man's farm for service in the carts; they carried their shelled corn to the grist mill to be made into meal in them. They hauled stable manure in the spring in them and broadcasted it all over their fields and pastures and garden tracts; then on Sundays they transported their families to church in them. Someone would sweep the cart out with a broom and on Sundays they spread a quilt on the bottom of it and the women and children sat in the floor and the men and boys sat on a board laid across the body of it. While the man held the reins, a young boy would switch the mule.

It was an inauspicious moment for Ben Jr. when he had promised to stay at home and care for the land and the store and his family. He had not seen a moment's peace since they had moved their few personal belongings upstairs to his childhood bedroom. They had taken over all of the upstairs and turned Pa's room into a sitting room. Perhaps, if they had turned it into a kitchen and could have cooked separately, things might have gone more smoothly, but with four women in one kitchen and each one wanting to cook something different, things seldom went peacefully. Long before nightfall, Ella had been reduced to tears every day, but one thing her husband could say in her behalf, she seldom had words to tell in her own defense. She seldom told him anything that happened, in fact. Her silence was made more noticeable by the fact the Gertrude and Faye Ellen told him volumes every time they could corner him long enough.

. . . Ella didn't do her share of the dishes . . . Ella didn't peal the potatoes to please Mama. Some of the eyes were still left in them . . . Ella didn't know how to make soap from the pork rinds like they did . . . Ella talked back to Mama about when the baby was due and Mama cried . . . Ella wasn't making enough warm things for the coming baby . . . Ella visited her own mother too often . . . Ella sang too loudly at church last Sunday . . . Ella didn't follow the music when they sang.

It all reminded him of a pussy cat parade in which each cat tried to out meow the other cats. These endless tirades against Ella tempted him to tell them all to go to hell or threaten to take her and move. He felt if only his sisters would marry, he could live with mother and Ella fairly peaceably. But how could they get husbands when they felt they were better than everybody else? he wondered. And he was beginning to wonder if he could go on affording them. They frequently took the train into town and bought fifteen dollar shoes and then screeched like scorched magpies if Ella bought two yards of cotton at fifteen cents a yard. Each time that he had tried to talk to them about spending too much, Mama had burst into tears and dabbed her eyes with a very white, lace trimmed, home edged handkerchief and sobbed. "When your father was alive, we never wanted for anything. He bought anything we wanted and he was proud of us to do it, too. Now we have nothing and you begrudge us of every stitch we buy. We'll be in rags and you won't care."

"Well in the meantime, while you're in rags that is, of course, how about wearing some of those thirty dollar dresses hanging in your closet that I got the bill for yesterday. Thirty dollars for one dress! The country is not even back on its feet and you spending like wildfire. We'll all go busted. Us, the country, and you're not moving me with those damn tears either. No wonder Gertrude and Faye Ellen don't use good sense. They model themselves after you."

And he stomped out of the house and went back to the store. In the three months he had been running it, he had found that he had a kindred bond with these local folks that he did not know was possible to feel for them. He enjoyed hearing their tales of poverty, their nigh starvation stories, their livestock ailments, and he was beginning to know for the first time the man who lived inside him. It had been wonderful when all his time had been spent in books, but they had opened a door for him to understand these people. These are my people, he began to feel strongly and it made him damn mad that Mama and his sisters did not share or understand his feelings. With Ella, there was no need for words. She had always been one of them and always would be, regardless of how rich or poor they became.

That night as they prepared supper, Mama sobbed to Ella in her artificial way, "I don't know what will ever become of that boy. I don't know who puts him up to his mess, but he never used to be mean to me before he was married. I'll tell you that much. He used to be such a good boy. I just don't know him anymore. What will ever become of me and the girls? I just don't know."

"You have so much, Mrs. Simpson, that you can't see beyond it. You have more'n anybody I've ever known. Don't all these things make you happy?"

Ella had never seen a table cloth spread except on Sundays, and one was spread every meal here. It seemed a rare and lovely thing and she could not conceive of them being dissatisfied with their lot in life.

"A fine lot you know about it," Mrs. Simpson stormed. "A fine lot you know. You've turned my boy against me. That's what."

Ella wanted to say that he had never been her boy. Not really, that there was nothing, absolutely nothing, to turn against her, that he had never felt a strong bond of love for her or his sisters, that he lived here only because of his promise to the one member of the family he had loved. But in all her youngness, she still had the wisdom to be silent and to let the harsh words lie unspoken.

Aside from that, the baby was laying low in her stomach tonight and had not moved all day. She did not know whether that was a good sign or a bad one. It seemed as if her air was all cut off and a knife stabbed her back every time she tried to take a deep breath. She longed to struggle upstairs and fall on the bed, but she knew that it would never do not to try and help cook supper if she were able to hold her head up. The cured smoked ham frying in rich red gravy made her stomach turn and twist and a bubble rose in her throat that she could not swallow down, but she stumbled on around the table and set every fork and spook and knife and napkin in its right place. Gertrude was supposed to be cooking the rice and she had stopped in front of the wash basin and mirror and was fluffing her hair while the rice bubbled over and ran down on top of the stove and gave off a scorched scent.

"Can't you ever do two things?" she snapped at Ella. "I know you saw the rice cooking over!"

"No, I didn't. I thought tonight was your time to tend to the rice."

"My time. Your time. Whose time? It's burned to a crisp now. Will Ben flip a lid or not. If there's one thing sets him off, it's burned rice and you can be sure he won't flip in your direction. The only name he knows when he's mad is Gertrude. Am I right, or am I right?"

She loved to say, "Am I right or am I right," and added these words on the end of every sentence she spoke as if she thought it added emphasis to her shallow words.

Ella opened her mouth to answer her, but was startled by a rush of fluid from her body that quickly ran down her right leg and she was left standing dumbfounded in her tracks.

Mrs. Simpson noticed the look of terror on her face and stopped frying the smoked meat to ask, "What is it, dear? Sick again?"

Ella could only shake her head negatively. She opened her mouth again, but could not make a sound issue from it. Outside, she heard the long lonesome whistle of the 9200 train and knew that it was right on time. Quarter to six. That's what time my baby started to come, she told herself. It's always be easy to remember. Right on schedule with the old 9200. It was slowing for the depot. That meant someone was getting on or off. Wonder who has been somewhere or who is going somewhere this time of night? What silly things I'm standing here thinking . . .

"Dear, what is it? Your time? It can't be that though. You said in May. This is only . . . what is it, for goodness sake? Why this is only March!"

Gertrude and Faye Ellen stood silhouetted like the imaginary sisters of Cinderella in the light of the kerosene lamp. They wanted to hear all of this conversation. It was too good to miss a morsel of it. They stood suspended in time, too, until the hands ticked on again.

"Are you in pain?"

Only Mrs. Simpson was voluble and this was not unusual for her for she was always voluble.

"No. No pain. But I think my water's broke. My baby must

be going to come early. Ma said that happened sometimes."

She wondered if that were her own voice that she heard. It sounded as if her head were inside a ten quart bucket and she was listing to someone else talking.

If Mrs. Simpson had been highly agitated with Ben Jr. for marrying her or distressed that Ben Jr. had been left in charge of everything or by living in the house with her daughter-in-law, all of these things vanished in the great anticipation of seeing and holding a brand new baby. A baby just newly born. Born of her son! Her own flesh once removed! So new and small and helpless and frightened and she would be right here to hold and comfort it. Why, she would be the first to hold it after the doctor. She had never held anyone's baby first. Not even her own. Her son's baby! This was all that mattered at this moment and she grew in status for the occasion, regardless of her son's low opinion of her capabilities.

"Gertrude. Get Ben immediately. Faye Ellen! Hitch the black horse to the buggy and bring it around to the front. Ben'll have to go for Dr. Kellum. I'll get Ella upstairs to bed. Maybe we ought to put you to bed downstairs though. I don't trust pregnant women walking up stairs."

"I don't want to hitch that old black horse. He jumps at me," Faye Ellen whined, not because she was asked to touch the black horse, but because that it was below her dignity. Ever since Ben had gotten the car, she did not like to be seen in the buggy.

"Hitch the horse. Now, I say!" and the inflections in Mama's voice left no doubt that she meant it for once.

Gertrude left the kitchen on the run and skipped across the back porch that joined the kitchen to the big house and ran down the side steps across the yard and over the boards that covered a deep ditch and through a small pine and holly thicket to the big store.

The store was filled with farmers sitting around the stove, some smoking pipes, some chewing tobacco, some spitting in the over filled tin can that sat side of the heater. Ben was busy weighing out rice from a big barrel that sat behind the counter. It was difficult to keep mice out of the rice barrel and he was carefully inspecting it to see that no mice droppings were in the rice he sold. Papa hadn't cared whether mice had been in it or not. "A little mice turd won't hurt nobody" . . . he'd declare if anyone mentioned it, but Ben Jr. wanted things done right or not at all.

"Ma says you're to come immediately. It's Ella's time. Looks like the baby might come early!"

She had whispered the words to him, but every man in the building had stopped talking, cocked his ear, and had not missed a single word.

Ben dropped the rice and it scattered all over the darkly waxed plank floor.

"Not tonight of all times. My God! Dr. Kellum's just left on the old 9200. Stay with the store, Gert!"

He took the stairs two at the time. Ella had just had time to slip out of her clothes and into a long flannel gown made especially for the occasion. Mama had gone back down stairs to put on hot water and to perk the first up in the stove and fireplaces.

"Don't panic now, Ella, but Dr. Kellum's just left on the train. I'm going to call ahead and tell the station master to tell him to get off at Tar Landing. He can get a horse there. It won't take him over a couple hours at the most for him to get back. Do you think you can wait till then?"

He was so serious about her waiting for the doctor that it tickled her for a moment and she laughed aloud. The laugh brought color back to her face.

"I just don't know whether our boy is going to wait for the doctor or not. You can't tell, Ma says. Maybe you'd better call ahead and go after Ma just in case he don't get here in time."

"You'll be alright, won't you? It won't take me long to get your Ma. She'll want to come anyhow. I mean you won't do anything till I get back, will you?"

"I'm not promising. The quicker the better."

Outside in the hall he met his mother in the semidarkness

and whispered, "Will the baby be alright coming ahead of time like this, Ma? Aren't they supposed to be too little to live or be normal or something?"

One of her pale eyebrows shot up and made a perfect arch over her eye. Was he playing a game with her? Did he really believe the baby was coming early? Did he think her completely innocent in affairs of the heart and actions of the body? Surely anybody with any sense could see that Ella had gone her full time. She had half known it but hadn't let herself speak of it. Well, if he wanted to act like he was fooling her, she'd go along with him now.

"Oh. I imagine the baby will be fine. Often times these first ones come early. The next one will be right on time, though. Get on with you, now!"

And the old woman smiled. She was giving her son an order for a change and he was obeying her for the first time in his life without question.

Faye Ellen had bungled her job of harnessing the horse and she was only too glad to turn the job over to her frantic brother.

"What in the hell did Mama think I wanted the buggy for tonight. Take that damn thing out of the way!"

He pulled the harness rig off the horse and threw his own English saddle over him quickly and buckled the straps. It was impossible to get lost in their community at night as the road made a complete circle and if one stayed on the road there would be no place to go except back to the starting point. However, in spite of this, he was glad the horse could see because he certainly could not and he had not taken time to light a lantern. Damn these muddy ruts! He could have flown over them in a few minutes in his automobile, but the muck and mire made it impossible to use his car during the winter months. He had sent the message ahead for Dr. Kellum, and that at least consoled him. Doc could not do much of a job pulling teeth or curing measles in a hurry, but he had a good reputation among the local folks for getting babies here safely. And very few of his patients had child bed fever. Thank God. Just treat a woman like you would your best horse and everything comes out fine," the doc would say as he sat around the store stove and spit his quid of tobacco halfway across the room and proceeded to put a new chaw in his big mouth.

Ben Jr. knew that he wasn't making sense, but Missouri understood what he was trying to tell. She had seen many a man dumbfounded at just such a time.

"Git on back to her. Jacob'll hitch up and bring me as soon as we can make it there. Git on with you, now!"

He was cold and the horse was hot, but time was a black widow spider now, inviting him to make the wrong move, tempting him to dilly and he wheeled the horse around sharply and left in a muddy gallop through the dark night again.

What in the name of God do they do with all that hot water they heat? Maybe that's a ruse to keep husbands out of the way, he thought.

Meantime his mother had placed bundles of old papers under Ella so that the featherbed would not be ruined, and she had managed to keep the girls downstairs. Their curiosity was killing them and they lurked in the darkness of the hallways hoping to hear anything. The few times that Ella had moaned loud enough for them to hear had brought snickers from both of them. But the miracle of impending birth had changed Mrs. Simpson from a pusillanimous character into a firm dependable midwife. She had drawn a chair up beside the bed and tried to hold Ella's hand.

"You mustn't roll and turn so. You'll kill the baby. Try to lie as still as possible."

"I want my Ma. When is Ben coming?"

"Most any time he should be back, now."

"I want Ma. What if she ain't home?"

"Isn't home? Land sakes. Where would she be tonight but home. She'll be here 'afore you can say Jack Robinson. Try to lie still."

All things had been straight in her mind about the baby until now. It had seemed as if everything was working out as she had planned. Now suddenly she was going to be confronted with an unequivocal lie in the flesh and she suddenly did not know how she was going to explain it to Ben. She had not thought it would matter how he felt, as long as there had been a home for the baby. A home and a name! But it was important. Ben with his ugly nose and his fast balding head had become important to her and she wanted him to believe that the baby was his. He had been so proud of her up till now. What if he suddenly threw her out of the house. Baby and all. A low moan escaped from her dry lips. But the moans were not from the pains that rose and swelled and died suddenly. They were from despair. I mustn't let myself faint. I might get to talking and say something wild. I won't take Dr. Kellum's little white pill. Then I know I won't go to sleep and wake up wild. I must keep awake and I must keep Ben out. Why doesn't Ma come on? It doesn't matter what I say around Ma, but I must get these others out.

What a welcome sight her Ma was in her gray homemade cotton dress and her big white apron, black hair piled high on her head, dark black eyes flashing and sparkling. She had said a thousand prayers that it would be a tiny baby. That would make it easier for all of them. Not even Jacob, her own husband knew the truth. He had suspected the baby would come too early, but he figured that she and Ben had got over anxious and had not been able to wait for the wedding. This kind of affair naturally caused eyebrows to raise in the community, but it was accepted as the inevitable with the young folks in this mad modern world. The war just over. So many men coming home ready to marry. Men who had seen and learned too much. And so it had not worried Jacob very much. The desired land was his and his daughter was safely married to the best catch in miles and people would forget how quickly the months had slipped by since the day of the wedding.

Ben came in right behind Missouri and stood at the foot of the bed, but he had not been prepared for the change in Ella within the hour he had been gone. Youth had faded from her face. Dark pools had come under her eyes, her mouth was a hard straight line, her hair hung bathed in perspiration and was matted to her head. He had thought all of the time he would want to be with her during her labor. None of this old fashioned stuff for him with the man outside the house, but his belly lurched around and his blood left his head and he knew he, too, would be another husband who waited outside. Bending over her and planting a kiss soundly on her forehead, he whispered, "I'll be right outside the door if you want me, honey. I'd better keep an eye out for the doc, anyway. He should be here before too long." She closed her eyes tightly and nodded affirmatively. Better let him make his own reasons than for her to think up one for him, she thought.

Missouri sensed her relief at Ben's leaving the room and also understood her desire to be alone with her for a spell.

"Maybe you'd better be the one to fetch some water, Mrs. Simpson. We'd better have some in here, just in case things go a little quicker. Had Ella herself in two and half hours. Took me ten hours next time. Can't tell bout these things. No sirree." She flung the quilts and sheet back and gently massaged her daughter's stomach. The baby was a hard hunched up lump and did not seem to be moving one way or the other, but she could occasionally feel his little balled up fist moving around.

"It won't be long. Baby's nearly ready to start down the birth canal." Still she hoped Dr. Kellum would get there in time so that Ella would not be torn as badly as she had been.

Ella tried to sit up for a moment and fell back weakly on the pillows. "Oh, Ma. What am I goin' to tell Ben. He'll never believe me. He's read too many books on things like babies and marriages and such like. He knows more'n a woman does about these things."

Missouri gently brushed the blonde curls back from her young daughter's forehead and talked in a monotone so as to soothe and relax her.

"It'll be well. It'll all be well. Won't be long 'afore you can hold him and you'll forget all about these pains till next time. Won't be long 'afore you can bundle up the baby in a quilt and take the buggy and come spend the day with Kate and me and your Pa. Kate's been powerful lonesome since you been married anyhow. And we'll sew and rock the baby. Won't be long."

And on into the night she soothed and caressed her, but still the baby did not come. Dr. Kellum had arrived in a huff and had immediately taken charge of everything as if they all were imbeciles. He did not commend them at all for having done everything they had known how to do and his big moustache quivered up and down as he barked orders around to everyone in hearing distance.

"Baby's staying too high too long. Fix me a big dose of castor oil. We'll purge her good. That'll bring everything soon."

She was too weak from pain to sit up and take the oil, but Missouri held her up in her arms while Mrs. Simpson spooned it into her mouth. Missouri was sure the castor oil at this time would kill her, but within the hour, her contractions became harder and closer together and Dr. Kellum took out his pill bottle and prepared to give her a sedative.

"It's going to come now," she told them through clenched teeth.

"Oh. It'll be a while yet," his baritone voice boomed and they heard him even out in the hall where Gertrude and Faye still huddled on the stairs and Ben still stood just outside the door.

"No. No. No. It's coming now." And a little white haired head literally popped out and a nine pound boy fell into Missouri's hands.

"My God. What a whopper! And a boy, too. Wait'll his old man hears this." He massaged Ella's stomach and gently pushed on it a few times until the afterbirth came and she flowed clear.

"Stick a rag on her. She'll be alright now. And I'll be betting I'll be back here doing the same thing 'afore another year's out, too."

Out in the hallway he knew he had to lie to this young man, but he did not mind lying in the least. What's a lie, more or less, he always said. What's truth for one fellow ain't necessarily truth for another. And he made his own theories to fit the occasion for whatever he had just done.

"You gotta mighty fine boy, Ben. Looks just like his Ma, though. You can go in as soon as the lady folks finish cleaning up, but you'd better not hold the baby till that cough of yourn clears up. Any better since I made you that cough syrup?"

"Can't say that it is. It's worse when the weather is damp, though. First one I've ever had that I couldn't shake off. You say the baby looks like Ella?"

"Just like her for the world. Blond hair and all. He's a boy in a million. Won't be no time 'afore you'll have him in the saddle afront of you just like your Pa used to with you. I'll bet he traveled ten thousand miles with you just like that 'afore you were six years old. Nope, won't be long."

—Chapter 7—

BUT THE DAY NEVER CAME that the little boy with the
head full of sun goddess kissed ringlets sat in the saddle ahead
of Ben and rode over the big, low lying farm. Spring had come
again three times over since the night the little boy had come
into the world and though it had thawed out each time the branch
and the upper mouth of Northeast Creek, it had not thawed the
ice in Ben's heart, and it was obvious to Ella now that time was
never going to heal that wound. In fact, it became more infected
day by day.

He had come into their room that night full of love and
tenderness, all prepared to kiss her pale lips and look upon his
tiny son, full of concern that the little fellow might not live and
already had words of comfort formed in his throat to speak to
her and help prepare her for the inevitability of the difficulties
of raising one so little even if he should survive. Instead, he had
been confronted with the sight of a big husky baby hungrily
pulling at Ella's breast so fiercely that the dark yellow milk was
running from the corner of his mouth down her breast and falling
onto her fresh gown. An invisible fist came out of an imaginary
corner and punched the wind out of his belly in that moment.
And the nasty little memory of how she had suddenly changed
in her feelings for him just months ago reared its ugly head and
glared at him with its green eye. And this time he could not
push the dirty thought aside. It continued to stare at him and its
evidence lay in the arms of his wife and was sucking the very
breast that had given him many exotic moments in caresses and
kisses. He wished through a red veiled mist that he could reach
out and kill the baby. That would rid him of the ugly thing and

he and Ella could pick up the pieces, but as long as that child lived, he could never resume his life with her again. He longed to slap the smile off his own mother's face as she leaned over and crooned to the baby. How idiotic she is! Sure she knows that this is a nine-month baby. Surely it was obvious to the doctor and Mama! Why, they probably think this baby is mine. And they don't even care if it's early or not! They're all in this together. How blind . . . how blind! How blind is a man when he wants to be blind? Did Papa know this, too, and still approve of my marriage. He must have known about it. He must have thought I was still sowing the wild oats he loved to brag about. The oats were sown alright, but I'm not the god damned one who sowed them. If not me, then who? . . . but he had seen blood on her gown their wedding night . . . the light had been dim from the wall lamp, but it certainly had been blood . . . and she had been so frightened of him that it had taken hours of persuasion to get her gown tail up. He had almost given up for the night before she suddenly relented. If not blood, what then?

"He's beautiful, isn't he, Ben?"

Her voice was weak, but it was filled with love and adoration for her newborn one.

Tears of anger and frustration filled his eyes and he whirled on his heel and left the room without a word.

"Well. I never! That's the first time I've ever seen that boy speechless. Him and his mighty words and he couldn't think of a thing to say. You are beautiful though, darling. Grandmother knows you are. You're too beautiful to be a boy. You should have been a little girl. Well, I know I've never seen such a little piggy in my life. Couldn't even wait a few hours to get your first ninny. Grandmother is going to take care of you. Yes sirreeeee."

Mrs. Simpson had found her real place in life at long last.

Ella should have seen the tight line of Ben's lips, but her mind was an empty space. She was thinking with her heart and the heart was not looking for any thunderclouds tonight.

The following day Ben did not go up to their room and his mother made a trip to the store especially to tell him to go and visit with Ella and the baby and she and Gertrude would keep the store.

"Dr. Kellum said for me not to go near the baby till my cough cleared up." He lied as easily as if he had always done so.

"Cough be hanged. If she hasn't caught that hacking thing in the last month, she won't now. Besides, you won't have to breathe right on the baby. Ella's been asking for you all day. Go on with you and your old cough now."

He had not slept a wink all night and his mind was a confused mass of wild distortions and accusations and a love that had gone with the wind. He had not decided on a plan, yet there was one thing he was sure of . . . he did not intend for this damned community to learn that he was not the father of the baby. Knowing that a lot of the tough farmers did not think of him as a real "he man" because he had taught school and had never done real hard labor as they had done, he knew that if they learned he had failed to father this child, they would laugh him right out of the community. No such calamity as this had ever fallen on one of them, he was sure. Even now he would have liked to argue with his mother, but he could not bring himself to do so in front of Gertrude. If only the roads were good and he could fire up his car and ride with the windshield open and top down, sailing along the canal road, past the tall dark pine and the cypress and the gum and the juniper trees, perhaps the wind could have cleared his head and told him the right thing to do and the right words would come to his mind. But this damn mud had closed that avenue to him, too, and his cough really had been much worse today. It did not seem as if his throat were sore, rather that the cough had a deeper origin and he might as well have been drinking sassafras tea as the god damned cough syrup of Dr. Kellum's.

He was sure the doc had boiled roots on the stove and made the darn stuff. One thing was clear in his mind though. He intended to corner that doctor and put it straight on the line to him. He was sure Dr. Kellum knew more about it than he did and he intended to get it out of him the first chance he had. The complexities of the past night and day had given him an intense headache and his nose appeared much redder than usual and his forehead was blanched of color entirely when he finally went into their bedroom.

She looked like a young innocent girl again today, the puffiness having left her face and the rich red color restored to her lips. Raising both arms to him with an humble silent plea for love she asked him, "Oh, Ben. Where have you been? I've asked for you all day. Couldn't Gertrude keep the store for awhile?"

"She's keeping it."

"I meant before now?"

"Evidently not."

"You didn't come in while I was sleeping and take a look at your new son, did you?"

"Don't you dare ever use those words again as long as you live, you whore you."

She knew that she shouldn't ask why because he was waiting for her to say "why?" and that he would never speak another word until she did say "why?" so why prolong the inevitable. Closing her eyes tightly so as not to be able to see his face distorted by anger, she asked him his reasons.

And he was more than glad to explain them to her. He punctuated his words by hammering one balled fist into the open palm of the other hand and ice dripped from every syllable. She had never seen him like this, or anyone like this for that matter, but she had heard of his terrible temper fits all of her life and realized that now she was getting a ringside seat at one.

"You bitch," he seethed between clenched teeth. "You know damn well why. Because that thick haired bastard is not my son. You know it. I know it. Who else knows it? That's what I want to find out. Am I being laughed at all over this damned neighborhood? You and that quack doctor knew about it. Him telling me the baby would come in May. He's stupid, but he's not that god damned stupid. He may be a horse doctor, but he can tell you within a week when a colt's due. You think you've been mighty clever don't you? Well answer me. You could talk plenty before?"

"No, Ben, no. I've never been clever. Kate way always the clever one before I was married, and you've been the smart one since them. You know I've never been clever."

"Don't you get pious with me. You're smart enough to pull a damned fool trick like this and you did a pretty good job of it, too, if I do say so. A pretty damned good job!" and he kicked the white rocker completely over on the floor.

"I'm so sorry, Ben. I did lie to you. It was most common for me to do it, but I didn't know what else to do. He had to have somebody, and I really did think you wanted me enough to forgive me when you found out."

"No, you didn't think that. You thought you'd half starve yourself to death and stay sick on your stomach all the time and that maybe he'd weigh four or five pounds and you'd have it made for life. That's more to your planning, isn't it."

"Please don't holler! You'll make the baby cry."

"Let the bastard cry! It won't be the only thing he'll ever cry over in this world. Answer what I asked you. You did plan to go on lying about it, didn't you?"

"I don't know. I really don't know, Ben. I thought time would work things out. Sometimes when you let things alone, time arranges things for you without a bit a help from you. Maybe that's what I was countin' on more or less."

"More or less, hell. You had it more or less thought out. More, most likely. When I think of how innocent and timid and frightened you acted the first few nights of our marriage it makes me so damned sick. You're a regular Sara Bernhardt."

"Sara who?"

"Never mind Sara who. Who told you all of those things to do? Dr. Kellum? Your Ma? My Mama? Does anyone else know?"

"Just Ma."

"You're lying. That cussed doctor knows, too."

"No. He knew I was expecting the baby, but he thought it was yourn."

Maybe with one more lie she could save his belief in old Dr. Kellum. It would be terrible thing for his faith in everyone to die at one time.

His words and accusations flowed like a scythe in a field of ripe wheat and they cut wide and deep and broad. They were words that both of them were never able to forget, but he could not stop them until the screaming of the baby drowned him out and his mother came rushing into the room.

"What are they doing to Grandmother's little precious? Don't Mama even know when it's time for his good titty. He's starving, Ellie. Out with you now, Ben."

He was a little boy again, having one of his worst temper fits, but Pa was not here now to give him a good smacking and he was willing to listen to his mother, glad for anybody to take the reins for a few terrible moments until his blood pressure could recede, his head stop its terrible pounding, his eyes stop their smarting, and he could again get complete control of himself.

He stood on the back porch and let the cold wind of March bite his face, but for once this was not enough to settle his stomach. The muscles in his stomach continued to tighten and drew him double and he retched until only green bile water poured from his nose and mouth. He was glad to have the sturdy oak post to hang onto. Just as the contents of his bowels were being poured onto the ground with violent force, just so his love for Ella ran from his heart and shriveled and died, a poor pitiful thing of the past, a lovely thing that had bloomed for a short season much like the red rose, had been a joy for them and for others to look upon and then had curled up and withered and died. No amount of watering or fertilizing could bring back the bloom. Maybe in time his heart would feel something but for now, all was dead. He crossed the porch with long steps and went into the kitchen where he pumped up a pan of cold water and cupped it in his hands and dashed it on his face several times. This caused the sickness to disappear, but his body was soon convulsed with coughing spells and he went out into the night and back to the store. There he kept his infernal cough syrup. He had not wanted Ellie and Mama to know just how much he had to rely on it this past winter, but now he did not give a damn who knew he coughed and coughed hard and long, and he reached under the planed counter beside the rice barrel and pulled out a big bottle of the concoction and took two or three deep swallows.

"Looks like being a father is just about too much for you, Ben," Jacob Horne laughingly joked.

He did not know whether Ella had lied or not, whether only she and her mother knew the truth, but the only course for the moment seemed to be to pretend that he too did not suspect a thing out of order. How terrible to be humiliated in front of one's father-in-law, he thought, the one person in the world a man wants to impress, to make him proud that he had married his daughter. And Jacob had been so friendly, so smilingly helpful, so everything, damn it, and all of this time, he might have known. And then again he might just have thought her pregnant and that he, Ben, had got her that way. Perhaps the two fathers had even talked it over and been jubilant together that nature had got out of hand and put through the deal that they both had desired for a long time.

"Sure looks pale, don't he? Right plumb green around the gills, most like Ella's told him that sad news that it'll be a month 'afore he gets anymore. That's most likely what's got him so agitated," Tom Parker added.

Everyone knew that Tom wasn't just right and it seemed as if everything he said was funny to everyone. The five men around the pot belly stove threw back their heads and howled. It was funny because Tom had said it and it was made funnier by the fact that it was most likely true. It was also funny because most of them had been fathers—agitated fathers waiting for their sexual lives to return to normalcy—and at not being the culprit this time added to their hilarity. Tom laughed until the tobacco spittle ran out of the corner of his mouth and down on his homespun gray shirt.

"She'll let you rock the baby when he gits the colic though. That's keep you out of trouble till things right themselves. Wait till he gits the three month's colic. Man, oh man. Will you be entertained then. And he'll bellow right in the middle of your cock. I coulda killed my youngins when they did that and all of them did it, too," old man Parker, the father of the two dumb boys added, as if to pour fat on the already smouldering fire.

This should have been a night of joy, a night of revelry and exotic happiness and I could have found joy in their ribbing. It could have been, but it isn't and I don't know if joy will ever come again. He kept smiling at the men and after a while the smile froze on his face and they decided they had about joked him enough for one night. There would be more nights though. This he did not doubt in the least.

He slept across the hall from Ella that night. Several times he heard the baby cry, but it did not awaken him for he was not asleep again tonight. Something had pinned his eyelids open and it felt as if they would never close again. He knew that she was unable to rise and care for the baby and he hoped with all his hating bitter heart that she, too, was in physical pain. If he could only arrange the thoughts in his mind, he could think who the father of that damned brat probably was, but all was confusion and mercifully a blanket pulled across his mind and he was unable to reason. I'll know soon and when I do . . . but what can I do? Do I even want to know? There is nothing I can do without letting everyone know what a fool I've been. There will have to be another way of hurting her without letting everyone know about me . . . and the baby cried again ... and he heard Ella pattering around. Changing the diaper, he supposed, and then all was quiet. But still he did not sleep.

The next morning he announced to his mother and sisters at the breakfast table that he was going to make a trip to the capitol to learn about the new tobacco seeds that were soon to be put on sale, and to try to learn how to plant it and cure it. Cotton was selling at the lowest price since the war and he had gone in the hole on sixty acres of beautiful cotton last year. He had read that in a few years enough tobacco markets would spring up to make the sale of bright leaf feasible and he wanted to try his hand at the new crop. First it would be necessary to learn as much as possible about it, though, and he wanted to go to the Agriculture School and see what they knew about it.

If his Mama thought it odd that he wanted to go right after their big argument, she did not let on by raising so much as one eyebrow and told him to take his time, that she and the girls would care for the store and for Ella and the wonderful new baby. Didn't he think it favored their own sweet departed father?"

"It favors a baby. That's who it favors. They all look just alike."

He stormed out at her like an agitated adder.

"Well, now. Who put alum on his tongue?" Faye Ellen asked.

"If I know anything, he's had alum on it for the past few days. Don't seem too happy to be a brand new Papa," Gertrude added.

"I hear tell it grates on the nerves, don't you?" His sisters relished taunting him because he had always been the favorite child and now that Papa was not here to command them to shut their mouths, they made a field day of it. Their mother's gentle "now girls, enough of that" went completely unheeded.

"Get a man of your own and find out for yourself, if you're so all fired interested in how and why a man acts like he does."

"Well, I never!" This conversation was getting entirely too modern for Mama.

"I declare, but we have become right vulgar. Just because we are compelled to hear it at the store doesn't mean that we have to reduce ourselves to their level. And by the way, Gertrude, was it really necessary for you to sit with that Eva Belle Morton last Sunday in church? I meant to speak to you about it before now and it just kept slipping my mind."

"What's wrong with her sitting with Eva Belle?" Ben was incensed at their bigotry. "These are your people, Mama, not your slaves or your lessers. Learn to live with them, please, and maybe if these two here will come down off their high horses, they might have more success in getting boyfriends, which is the object of all womankind, isn't it?"

"Well, I think this conversation has gone far enough," Mama snorted and flounced out of the kitchen while both girls turned aside and realized that they had indeed said all that they dared for one time.

❦ ❦ ❦

IN THE MONTHS THAT FOLLOWED, Ben buried himself in his project of learning how to plant and raise and cure the bright leaf tobacco. He had not started in time to plant a crop for this year, but he fully intended to be ready when springtime came round again. He hired men to build two curing barns out of hand hewn logs and had them covered with wooden shingles. A long oven-like tunnel ran the length of the inside of each barn and into this oven they would throw firewood to raise the temperature high enough to cure the leaf of the tobacco. When the barn had been raised, they went down to the clay hole and made buckets of rich red clay and carried it back to the barn. They gathered up buckets of it and chunked the cracks of the barn, wanting it to be as air tight as possible. Most of his neighbors were curious about these strange looking ugly barns with fire furnaces in their bellies and stopped by frequently to see the progress being made on them. Nothing, they declared emphatically would ever replace cotton as their major crop, but they were curious about anything that suggested more money as they too had not been able to pay out of debt with their cotton and hogs.

The nation was at an all time high, prosperity wise. The post war time boom was on and everyone was eating good on the hog except the farmer. Nothing he had to sell brought anything and everything he needed to buy was out of his reach. And still the President of the nation insisted that the farmer must work out his own problems without any aid. The backbone of the nation was poor and very discontented and if the ear of the nation had been tuned in, it could have read the mumblings from Maine to Florida. However, the government was the most corrupt it had been since Grant was in office and the rich got richer while the poor went hungry. Even the taxes on the high incomes had been reduced. Big business and Labor argued, but the government took the side of the Big Man and the aims of the Laborer were crushed.

Finally, the President realized that he had lost the confidence of the American people and decided to make a tour to try to regain some of their confidence in him. His heart was broken. The men around him had failed and deceived him. He had listened to their advice and heeded it and it had been ill advice, given for their own personal gain. The Teapot Dome Oil Scandal had caused the nation to open their eyes and take a good look at the Federal Administration. Surely though, he had given the people what they wanted. They had begged for a return to normalcy from the ravages of war, but he had tried to make the transition too rapidly.

Not a tear was shed for him in the area of Eastern Carolina when they read that he had died on his tour. And it was not with elation that they realized Calvin Coolidge was now their new President. If the trend continued, what they had to sell would continue to drop and they couldn't take many more drops.

Perhaps the time was right to change from cotton to tobacco, Ben told the men in the store. Everything was rapidly changing, the government, the dress of the men and women. Skirts had shot up above the knees. If men had wondered how a woman's leg looked, he need not wonder any longer. But the majority of the neighborhood clung to the old way and they wanted to let Ben try out the new crop first. If he failed, that was it, as far as they were concerned. If he hit it rich, they, too, would try it before long.

In the meantime, he had not relented in his determination not to continue living with Ellie as man and wife. He kept the store open late at night, and had his mother bring his supper over to the store for him. He waited until he was sure Ella would be asleep before he went upstairs. He had moved all of his clothes in the room across the hall, and though he knew that his mother and sisters wondered about the separation he did not offer any information and they did not ask him for any. He was polite enough to Ella at the dinner table on Sundays, but if they were left alone for a few minutes, he ignored her completely.

She did not ask him to look at the baby or to help care for him and if she needed money to buy the baby anything, she sent his mother and told her to get the money from Ben.

"I'm going to spend the night with Ma and Pa. Do you mind if I take the horse and buggy?" she had asked him when the baby was two months old.

"Use it when you want to. Don't bother to ask me anything that stupid."

Words lay like stones in her heart, but they were words which must be torn loose from their soil and spewed up.

"Would you rather I went and didn't come back? I'll stay with Ma and Pa if you prefer it that way."

He had not thought she had the guts. The baby had given her the courage to do or say almost anything. This once timid young woman had become a self assured person asking for anything she or the baby needed. He surmised this, but he was wrong. In her heart, she trembled as fiercely as she had when she had known she must marry quickly, but she had acquired a veneer that helped her to live with two difficult women and a man who hated her and her child.

Did he hope that she would not come back? Did he care if all knew that she had been a whore? No, his heart lied. He could not hate her enough if she went and stayed. He had to keep seeing her in order to keep hating her. Occasionally, her door would be open when he came up at night and he could not keep his eyes from looking in that direction. She would be rocking the baby slowly and gently and the now growing and husky fellow would be nursing her lovely breast and it would fill him with enough hate to keep himself going for days afterwards. He had to hate to go on living, he told himself. He fed on hate and the coughing spells came closer together now and with more convulsive forces.

"Suit yourself. Go if you like. Come back if you like. Why ask me?"

"I ask you because this is your house and I bear your name. Would you rather be free to marry again? Please tell me something, Ben."

"I'll never marry again if you're worrying about that. How could I?" How could I be sure I wasn't being made a fool of. If I was fooled by you, I could be fooled by any woman. No. You aren't keeping me from marrying or from anything for that matter. I don't begrudge you what you eat or wear. Feel free to come back if you want to. Just don't expect anything personal from me. Understand that?"

"I thank you, Ben."

"Don't thank me, damn it all woman. You're not welcome if that's what you're waiting to hear me say. I made a bad bargain and I'll admit it, but I'm not completely backing out of it. Not yet. I'd appreciate it too if you tried to conduct yourself decently while you continue to live at my house."

"Haven't I been conducting myself decently?"

"Have you? Perhaps that lad in your arms was conceived by divine conception. Is that what you wish to tell me now?"

"I was not referring to Woodrow. You know that. I mean since I've been here."

She had indeed conducted herself so properly that she was all that a man could have hoped a wife might be, and even in his anger he could not tell her she was a failure. Failure was certainly present, but whose failure, he asked himself. Was it his fault that he did not love her any longer. Perhaps he had not tried hard enough. Perhaps if the baby were dead? One of these days God will strike me dead for thinking that and maybe everyone will be better off then. He was seized by a coughing fit and he waved his hand to dismiss her.

Later he stood in the back door of the store and watched her set the baby in the floor of the buggy and lead the horse around and maneuver him between the shays and put the belly band under him and put the bridle and harness on him. It would only take a few minutes of his time to run her over to her Pa's in his car. The roads were dry and dusty now, and Gertrude or Faye could stay with the store. But he had not been with her since the birth of the baby and he did not wish to start doing her any favors. If the community thought him a heel, let them think it. Just as long as they did not know the real truth. She is truly beautiful though, he thought, as she wheeled the horse out of the driveway and turned down the road. Her golden curls had grown back long and he knew in his heart how it feels to a man's insides to run his hands through them and kiss her neck underneath them. A strange pain ran down his groin and down the inside of his thigh to his knee.

Thinking about her loveliness brought pain, but he kept thinking about how her waist had narrowed down and she looked like a young girl again except for her heavy bosom, which amply provided for that greedy baby. She had not changed over to the new extreme styles as Gertrude and Faye Ellen had done and he was glad. All those damn bows that women were putting on their dresses. On the neckline, at the waist, around the skirt, anywhere they could find a place, they stuck a bow. But why did he worry whether she wore a short dress or a long one, or a loose one or a tight one. As the buggy disappeared from sight, he turned back to his job of weighing out dried beans, putting them in brown paper bags, and tying them up with a cotton thread. How brown the paper bag looked after having seen the sunlight on her golden hair. How dark the interior of the windowless store. He had never noticed before how dark the flooring was, how long the cobwebs were than hung from the unceiled rafters.

Perhaps she won't come back. Will I be sad or glad? Will that be good or bad? He searched his heart and mind and soul, but his mind was a tangled web of confused thoughts that crisscrossed each other so rapidly that for a moment he felt faint.

—Chapter 8—

"WE'RE GOING TO SING just one more verse, and if nobody comes forward, we're going to close this service with a prayer that none of you sinners will die before we meet in God's house again. Play one more verse, Ella. Just one more verse now, folks, and I'm gonna close for today."

Preacher Cornaby ranted and raved, but no one came forward and he waved his arms in exasperation.

"Must I sing myself to death by myself? If you can't come forward and be saved by Sweet Jesus' Grace, at least open your mouths and sing. Turn the page, Ella. Just one more verse of 'Nearer My God To Thee.' Just one more verse and we'll quit."

The ladies were beginning to fidget. It was already past one o'clock and most of them had to go home and cook their Sunday dinner. A few only had to warm up theirs. The men were mumbling because they were hungry and ready to get out. The babies had long since cried themselves to sleep, but in one pew the four- and five-year-olds were still marking in the hymn books, looking under the benches and staring at the hats on the ladies behind them. Four-year-old Woodrow sat with his Grandmother Simpson while his mother played the worn-out organ, which she had learned to play by ear since her marriage, as Faye Ellen and Gertrude were married and did not attend the church any longer there was no one else to play for them. Ben had given up his lifetime habit of attending and in spite of all the protestations from his mother and Preacher Cornaby, he kept the store open on Sundays. Right on through the services, too. Preacher Cornaby would have liked to have protested more vigorously, but he knew who donated the majority of the money that paid his salary and his protests were more like gentle mumblings.

The congregation liked Ella's playing better than they had the Simpson girls' . . . puts more bounce into it. Don't act like she's dead when she plays . . . they said, bragging on her. The community had fallen in love with her anyway since her husband had turned out to be such a sorry piece of a man. He not only didn't care a darn about her or the baby, but had turned into a puree ole drunkard. It wrung the hearts of the neighbors to see her come into church every Sunday morning and every Sunday night, leading the little boy with the head full of golden curls by his chubby hand. She would deposit him on the front row beside his Grandmother and seat herself on the stool and play her heart out for them . . . every Sunday of her life. The boy was big enough now to know that they all thought him cute and he entertained them more than the preacher with his upside down antics and his childish pranks. Occasionally Ella would glance around while playing and stare hard at him. Then he would wither down on the seat for a minute, but he soon forgot the visual chastisement and jumped up and continued at full speed. And about all the reprimand he ever received from his granny was a soft spoken "Now son. Now really." These words fell like soft drops of rain on a mallard duck's back and rolled off just as lightly, leavin' no signs at all where they had fallen.

Flies flew freely in the upraised windows and flew undisturbed on out the front door and only the frantic fanning of the ladies kept them out of their faces. They were made worse by the fact that it had not rained in two months.

Three other members of the congregation had managed to buy automobiles and they carried every one they could possibly cram into their cars on Sunday mornings. The part of the meeting that most of them enjoyed best was when it would let out and the men would crank their cars. Someone would adjust the spark while the father cranked frantically, and after a while they would fire and sputter and finally run amid the cheers from the young folks. Those who did not have a car or a ride in one still drove their mules and carts and did not seem to mind.

Due to the fact that his mother was getting old, Ben came after them each Sunday, but during the past year, he had taken to coming with whiskey on his breath, and this embarrassed Ella and Mrs. Simpson to such an extent that they told him they could walk home. This had insulted him to the high heavens and he now made a point of driving up drunk, whirling around the yard in a cloud of dust or a whirl of mud, and honking his horn, right on the dot of one o'clock whether the service was over or not.

"What a cross she's had to bear since she married him," Mrs. Kellum told the old doctor, and his moustache jumped up and down as he mumbled, "Yes. Yes. Turned out and showed his true colors, that boy did."

"Colors my eyes. He's as black as the devil. That's what color he is, and I don't care if Mrs. Simpson hears me say so either."

"I don't doubt that you don't, my dear. I don't doubt it at all."

The short ride home beside Ben, his mother and the boy seated in the back seat was the most agonizing time of the week for Ella. She had to put up with the facade their life had taken and the worst part of it was that there seemed to be no end to it in sight. No end ever. She had learned from experience to keep the boy away from him as much as possible, but it was not possible to do so all of the time and the little boy would have liked to sit between them now and jiggle the knobs and pull the levers. However, Woodrow had an understanding with his mother that on days when his daddy was away on buying trips he could sit in the car as long as he wanted to and play driving.

The odor of whiskey was pungent even though he had the top down, and he had drunk enough to be free from most of his inhibitions.

"I'm leaving on that New River Train. I'm leaving on that New River train. Same old train hat brought me here is goina', take me away. How you like that, Ella? How you think Mr. Cornaby would like that. Like me singing to you? Can you play that on your damned old organ?"

She knew better than to try to answer him in this state. If she had said one word, he would have lit upon it like a bird on a lone stick in the ocean and have clawed her frantically to death. And if she let him ride her long enough, his mother would come to her rescue. She had come to love her in the years living with her and accepted her eccentricities as a part of human failings. She overlooked her childishness as a part of old age. The boy had healed any breaches between them, and they clung to each other for each was all that the other had.

"Aren't you going to come in and eat dinner with us today, Ben?" his mother implored when he deposited them at the front end of the walk.

"No. I aren't going to come in and eat dinner with us today Ben," he mimicked. "And I most likely aren't going to come in and eat supper with us tonight, either. How about that, huh? I'm going to take me a little ride in my friend here and if you two ladies would like to continue living in the style you think you live in, you can keep the damn store open. If you want to perish you can sit on your tails and do nothing the rest of the day. Suit thyselves."

And he spun the tires and threw dust all over their Sunday clothes and was gone.

As they put the plates on the table, Mrs. Simpson kept wiping a tear from the corner of her eyes with the back of her hand.

"I'll declare. Ben would turn over in his grave if he could see how his boy has turned out. You just don't know how he hurts me, Ellie. Me, his only living parent and he talks to me worse than I talk to a stray dog at the back door. And you, poor poor child. There isn't another like you in the whole world. God loves you for it and how he can ignore a beautiful child like Woodrow is just beyond me. And his own image, too. The exact image of him when he was that age."

Ella knew that only a grandparent could look at favor that blindly, but she did not interrupt and let her ramble on in her anguish.

"He's going to kill himself in that car. Run into somebody or somebody run into him. There's getting to be so many of those things on the road, it's just not safe to take the horse out anymore and I know it's not safe to ride with him. The world is moving too fast. Too fast. We'd all better listen to the preacher and make sure our souls are right before we lie down at night. That's all I can say. We'd better be sure."

Ella stood at the window that night and felt the soft breeze blow against her face. There was a restlessness in her that could not be denied or fulfilled and she was suspended in the space of her own emotions. I am married, but not married. Single, but not single, she told the wind and the top of the chaney ball tree that stood beneath her window. I am a nobody, and my life counts for nothing. No not nothing. I do at least have the baby. Ben is the one who has no one. I am the one who has ruined his life. Not the devil nor the whiskey nor the free women. I am the one and the only one. She hugged herself and shivered in spite of the dryness and the oppressive heat. But I can't do him any good staying here. And my life is running away quickly. Sometimes she thought of taking some money from the cash register and taking the train right in front of the store and going just as far as the money would carry her. What then? Could she get enough work to feed herself and the boy? Would they know hunger if she did this? She had come close to trying it and had taken the money from the drawer and started to call Woodrow and then had turned back at the last possible moment and put the money back in the register. It was too late at night to go down and play the organ. This usually soothed her restlessness. And there was nothing in the room that she had not read. Ben would not be home before dawn so she felt safe in crossing the hall and entering his room. Taking a match from her apron pocket, she struck it and lit the kerosene lamp that sat on the corner of his desk. She thumbed through three of four of his books. All of them seemed too difficult for her and she was looking for something easy to read, something to take her mind off herself.

"So this is the kind of woman you are? Sneak into men's bedrooms late at night and go through their drawers, huh?"

The sound of Ben's voice startled her so that she screamed a short winded breathless scream. My God! . . . he must have come when we were singing and playing downstairs.

"Cat got your tongue? Don't act timid with me, you bitch. I fell for that line one time, remember that, woman?"

"I only came to get a book, Ben. I didn't realize you had come in."

"That makes it worse. That makes it breaking and entering. Knew I wasn't here and you came in anyway."

Hating to face him, she turned slowly around. His voice told her all she needed to know about his sobriety, but delaying it would not make it easier. She had learned this lesson well during the past five years.

He was naked except for his bottom underwear and he was sprawled across the bed on his back, half propped up with a pillow. She noticed his bottle on the bedside table, but she could not tell whether it was empty or full.

"I'm sorry, Ben. Really. Good night." She hoped it was good night, but without his mother near her, she was suddenly frightened of him.

"I'm sorry, Ben, Good night, old man. Good night. How do you like going to bed every night of your life without a man between the sheets? Huh? How do you like that? Well, let me tell you something, woman. I don't like it and I don't do it. When I need a woman I know right where one is that likes the sight of me. Likes me and likes my money. When I say jump, she jumps in the bed. Now ain't that nice. Such a pity it can't work both ways and be like that for you, too. But I got Mama here to keep an eye on you and I know you aren't getting any right under Mama's nose. Not Mama. So it's tough, huh? And I know plenty of local yokels that would like to oblige you, too. The damned preacher for one and several more squirts I've seen eyeing you all over at the store. That damned ticket master that eats his dinner there for another. It's your innocence that lures them. That's what does it. That sweet innocent beautiful face . . . that fools a man every time."

"I'm not going to listen to you, Ben. You're drunk. Good night."

She spoke as coldly as she was capable and swept past him toward the door.

In an instant he was off the bed and standing between her and the doorway. He braced himself against it, arms outspread against its jambs and suddenly he did not look that drunk. He looked very angry, and though his eyes were bloodshot there was a calmness about him that did not personify a drunk.

"I won't be brushed off when I'm talking, dear woman. Not with an icy good night. Not in my own house. When I'm through you can leave, not one second before."

He wanted to tell her of the woman who lived in the fishing shack beside the river who fulfilled all his sexual needs. He had wanted to taunt and hurt and humiliate her, but he was not succeeding in hurting her. He was disgusting her and that had not been his intentions at all. What kind of a man only disgusted a woman? A beautiful woman!

"Get out of my way, Ben. I'll call your mother in a second if you don't."

"Ah, ha. And I'll just bet you would, too. I'll call Mama. I'll call Mama," he mimicked and the sarcasm in his voice caused chills to run up her arms and legs.

She opened her mouth to speak to him again, but even though he had been a lethargic person a few minutes before he now seemed possessed of more than his usual faculties. He was sharper, more alert, and madder than she had ever seen him and in an instant he reached out and clamped his hand over her mouth. Her eyes widened with fright and anger and she tried to pull his hand off her mouth. She reminded him of a rabbit he had caught once. It was the first one he had ever caught by himself. He had made a small wooden cage and propped it up with a small stick an set it out in the snow and the first thing the next morning he had gone running across the barnyard to see if he had caught anything. He saw at once the stick had fallen and had run his hand in under it, a ball of fur was crouched in the farthermost corner and it had shrunk almost into the ground trying to keep out of his reach, but his boyish hand had been determined and he had dragged the kicking soft animal out, carried it out to the hound's pen, thrown it over the fence. He had enjoyed watching the dogs tear him into several pieces and stood watching the scene until his mother had called him to come in the house immediately to get out of the cold and get some breakfast into his stomach.

Ella was soft like the rabbit had been, soft and lovely to touch, yet he wanted to destroy her, to see her hurt. He had been hurting for years and she had acted as if her life still had real meaning. Her and her damned boy and her organ playing and her fanatic interest in the church and its carryings on. There had been no joy in anything for him. Not in his success with his tobacco crop, or the improvements he had made in the store or even in the love affair that he had been involved in during the past year.

She had been a nothing, a nobody from the wrong sides of the swamp. And he had taken her and raised her above it. And then he had fallen lower than anyone he knew and it was suddenly a compulsion to drag her down to his level. Down. Down. Down. Down. His arm was like a steel band around her waist and he still held his other hand clamped over her mouth as he slowly moved backwards, dragging her toward the desk. He had first intended to turn the wick down in the lamp, but he could not figure out how to do it without letting go of her so he gave up on that idea and forced her over to the other corner of the room and flung her across the bed, awkwardly falling on top of her.

"You're not going to scream," he whispered savagely in her ear.

"You might wake that bastard across the hall and you'd hate for him to walk in here and for me to shut him up in here, too, and for him to see you naked. He's too nice to see anything like that, isn't he?" His voice purred on as he methodically removed her apron, unbuttoned her blouse, tore her middy in three pieces and tossed each piece the length of the room, snapped the buttons off her skirt with his thumb and threw it over the foot of the bed.

There should be something I can say to him that will reach him, but God knows I don't know what it is. Why is my mind so blank? Why can't I think? All she could say was "Please Ben. In the name of the Lord. Please."

"Please, Ben," he mimicked her. "Please. Cheese. Do you think God hears you? Ask him to help you now and see if he does," and he tore her underwear to shreds.

Outside the horse was restless in the stable and made a sudden loud clanking noise, thus catching Ben's attention for a moment. In a flash, she turned and sunk her teeth into the muscle of his arm and drew blood. He laughed hysterically and pushed her back down on the bed.

"So there is some fire there after all, huh?" That's the kind of reaction I used to hope to rouse out of you, but you were the prim one, weren't you?"

And he forced his lips against hers so hard that her lips parted and her teeth cut her own lips. He caressed her body for a few minutes and then ridiculed her. It was not enough to hurt her physically. He wanted to destroy her confidence as well.

"I'll bet old preacher man would like to be doing this now. Many times as he's stood up there and preached and sweated and looked right down your dress. The sigh of that pretty stuff was more than he could stand. You enjoyed teasing him, didn't you? Didn't you?" and he twisted her arm behind her.

She had stopped trying to talk to him. He was a mad man and anything she said only incensed him. Preacher Cornaby had always repulsed her as a man and she could not understand Ben's jealousy of him when she was sure he must know that Leonard was Woodrow's father. Leonard came to the store at least once a week. Ben treated him cordially and had never accused her of being too nice to him. Was she too shallow to fathom this man? Or could anyone ever understand him? His own mother certainly did not. Neither did his community.

After he poured his seed into the depth of her body and all over her thighs, he fell backward on the big goose down pillows and went instantly into a deep sleep. The whiskey and the temper tantrum and the violent exercise of possessing her had completely exhausted him, and for once he was not even able to cough. The kerosene had burned out of the lamp and only the moonlight lit the room now. Ella lay on her side and whimpered much as a small cold puppy who had just been weaned from his mother would have done. The enormity of this night overwhelmed her. While she tried to restore her breathing to normal before getting up from the bed, she contemplated the dangers of continuing living under this roof. Would this happen again if she did? Would she have the courage to take Woodrow away from the grandmother who idolized him and who could afford to give him all the things that her own family could never afford. Would she be able to live again with her own family. Kate had not spoken a civil word to her since her marriage and it was with sadness that she realized now that Kate had really loved Ben. Loved him in the way she had loved Leonard. She always managed to have somewhere to go as soon as Ella arrived home, and it was understood that they could not talk about what lay deepest between them.

"God, please spare me from another pregnancy. I have tried to live by your book the last few years. Now you help me . . . please please God." And she went about the room naked, gathering up her garments, a crushed figure who only an hour ago had been a lovely creature. Her shoulders were now stooped with fatigue and worry. Back in her own room, she poured a basin of water from the night pitcher and bathed herself repeatedly, examining her many bruises and trying to think of what she would tell his mother come morning. She peered at her reflection in the mirror dresser and saw that her lips were swelling and could see the print of every one of Ben's fingers on her neck and breasts. "I made my bed hard," she told herself. "Look good at yourself, Ella. You made your own bed. Tonight you lay in it and it was a very hard bed to lie on, wasn't it? Oh,

Mama. I need you, Mama. I'm not very gown up, and I need you tonight. Please help me, Mama . . ."

❧ ❧ ❧

AUGUST CAME and August is a still hot month in Carolina. The land lies hard and dry and the flies and mosquitoes take turns aggravating every living creature. The once green corn with its fragrant tassel turns a slate brown and withers on the stalk. The milk from the kernels of corn turns hard and the farmer knows that it will soon be ready to pull from the stalk and put into his pack house or corn crib. The cotton has not yet opened its white boll, but turns its leaf a reddish green and waits. The tobacco has been pulled from its stalk, cured in its barns, and removed and packed in dry piles in the barns, waiting now only to be sorted and carried to the market. It is a time of waiting, waiting. A hot time, a dry time. The dog days will soon come, but not this week.

Ella and her childhood friend, Eva Belle, sat grading and sorting the tobacco leaves in the big pack house. The flawless yellow leaves were put in one pile, the spotted leaves in another, the leaves with a red or greenish cast in still another. Then these leaves were bunched together and tied in bundles with the head of each bundle about the size of a quarter. Ella sorted while Eva tied them together. Ben had completely stopped growing cotton and had the land all in corn and tobacco and pasture now. He was doing much better financially than his neighbors, who were still trying to depend on cotton for their main money crop. Crops had changed. So had Ben and Ella. But Eva Belle would eternally be the same chatterbox.

"You're too quiet today, Ellie. A person would think you didn't like living high on the hog? You'll be the only person in church this fall with a new outfit from top to toe. Aren't you the lucky one?"

Ella tried to listen to her enough to give sensible answers, but her own mind was so deeply troubled that it was difficult to follow the line of conversation. She had known for the past three or four days that she definitely was pregnant and the weight of the certainty was overwhelming.

"Ellie, I don't believe you hear a word I say!"

"I'm sorry, Eva. Really. Tell me again. I'm about to go to sleep sitting here so long, I reckon."

"I said you're too quiet. What's ailing you?"

"Nothing more than the usual, I guess."

And Eva well knew what everyone knew was the usual— Ben drinking too much and seeing to much of Lula Tyson, the woman in the fishing shack on the river's edge. Ben was spending too much money, changing cars every fall as soon as the tobacco was sold. The usual with Ben was the unusual with everyone else.

"How about you and Leslie. I thought surely you'd be married long before now?"

"You know we can't. Not with him in college. I don't mind waiting for him, but I'll tell you one thing, girl. I don't intend to wait for no man that can't even take the time to answer my letters. Three letters. That's what he owes me now and I ain't writing him another line till he writes me. I said it and I mean it. He's not the only fish in the big pond and I think I oughta remind him of that more often. Me, I have no way of knowing what he does in his fancy school and a girl's college not two miles from where he is. Don't that take the cake? I wonder if that ain't why I don't hear from him more regular?"

"I declare, Eva. You know I'm not criticizing you. You're such a good friend, but what with him bound and determined to be a doctor and with Dr. Kellum backing him financially, there's no reason he won't make it, and it won't be fitting for you to be saying 'ain't' all the time when you're a doctor's wife and have to live in town and meet all those rich people. You'd better start practicing right now if you want too make him proud of you."

Eva laughed, too, and put down the tobacco for a moment and pantomimed how she should serve tea. "Won't you all be seated, ladies. I must call my maid. Tea will be right out, so will the cucumber sandwiches! How's that?"

"That's much improved, I'd say considerably. Why don't you and he just tie the knot and you go on living at home. You could start your family that way. You're going to be an old maid before he gets out of school."

"I asked Leslie the same thing and you know what he said. Said they couldn't get in medical school if they was married and that Dr. Kellum would quit paying his way if he married before he was through. Don't that put a bee in my bonnet, though?" and she took out her snuff box and twirled a small fuzzy black gum stick around in the snuff and stuck it in the corner of her mouth.

"That's something else that will have to go. That snuff! What does Leslie say about it."

"Oh. I don't let him know. He'd have a fit if he knew it. I just take real pains to brush my teeth and sweeten my breath with a little cloves and he don't know it. He'd have a dying spasm if he did, I'm sure."

Woodrow came bouncing in the doorway, sucking feverishly on a penny sucker, sugar and saliva running out of the corner of his mouth, his hands newly washed by his grandmother, and daring all the world not to love him. He pushed the tobacco leaves out of his mother's lap, put both arms around her neck and kissed her with his sticky lips squarely on the mouth.

"I love you, Mommy. Do you love me?"

"More than anyone else in the world. Now get out of my lap and get to play. Mommy has to work today to help make us some money. Down with you, you little booger."

"I'm not a booger. A booger comes at night. Grandma said so."

"Well. You came at night, too. But you aren't a real booger. Just a little one is all."

Eva dropped her work and watched this play between mother and child. She felt a sharp pain in the lower part of her stomach. This was what she wanted with her own life, someone to take care of her in real style, a baby to tend to, a man that was here.

"You're so lucky, Ellie," the friend said enviously.

"Yes, I'm real lucky," and venom dripped from every word.

"But you are. If you had prayed for years, you couldn't had a prettier baby and he's so smart. He'll be a go getter like Ben."

"I don't know what he'll be. I just hope he'll be happy. Is that too much to hope for, you think?"

"Certainly not. Don't everybody hope that?"

"Not hard enough. If everybody hoped for it, more would have it, don't you think?"

"Well, I don't know. I think most people are happy. Most of the time anyway, don't you?"

"No, I don't. I know there's a lot of unhappy people. The hurting kind of unhappiness, if you know what I mean."

Eva knew that she was referring to the embarrassment and shame that Ben had heaped upon her with his drinking and his boldness with Lula Tyson. He had been seen with her in his car right down on Main Street in town on Saturday night. Several of the local men had been down the river at night time, to set their nets or take them up, and had seen Ben's flashy car parked outside the vertically boarded up shack. And they had asked themselves how a man who had been lucky enough to marry a woman like Ella, who was not only lovely to look at but a good Christian wife and mother besides, could lower himself to such depths. Woodrow was a child more like his mother, unspoiled by what money could buy, loving and affectionate with everyone who came into the store, finding in the local men what he looked for in the man who lived in their house but did not like to be called "Father."

"Mama. Grandmother said I could go to town today with her on the big train. Can I, Mama. Can I?"

"I know Grandmother doesn't want to be bothered with you on her shopping day. Maybe you'd better stay out here with us while she's gone."

If he was loving like Ella, he was not the pusillanimous youngster she had been and he immediately began to wheedle.

"She wants me, Mama. She wants me to hold her bag for

her. Can't I, please?"

"Oh, say yes, Ella," Eva interceded in the boy's behalf. "You know how he loves the train and I know he's safe with her if he is anywhere in this world."

Ella gave his bottom end a playful hard smack and sent him to the house, her words falling happily on his young ears.

"If you eat all of your collards for dinner like a man does, you can go if Grandmother really wants you to," and the delight in his skip and jump made her forget momentarily the living burden that already was bubbling and nauseating her stomach.

Why should I fear Ben, now, she pondered. The worst has already happened. He can only kill me now. Why should I hesitate to try to talk to him about myself. If he's sober tonight, I'll do it. Perhaps it would be better to ask Mother upstairs to read to Woodrow while I go across the hall and talk to him. Then, if I needed her . . . but she remembered how forcibly he held his fingers around her neck and knew that if his temper was roused she would not be able to call for help. But then, if he had been sober, she doubted he would have touched her with a ten foot pole.

He had avoided her completely since that night and did not even eat his meals at the table with them any longer. Instead, they fixed him a plate and Woodrow carried it to him at the store. Some nights he even slept on a cot behind the feed pile. A few times she had gone over and helped him out on Saturdays and Saturday nights and if she needed him to lift anything for her or move anything around, he answered her politely enough. She had caught him staring at her when he thought she wasn't looking, but she could not begin to phantom his thoughts. Was he sorry? Was he glad he had hurt her? Did he even imagine that she was pregnant? If so, would he want her to bear his child? Was the sight of her repulsive to him?

The strain of the past few weeks was beginning to show on her face and dark circles had come and stayed under her eyes, her lips had paled from worry and loss of appetite and the more recent nausea was adding to her complaints. Moreover, even

Preacher Cornaby had commented publicly on her paleness and had told her not to come back to play for the night services last Sunday, and as usual he punctuated his words by beating one fist into the other palm. She had been glad to stay away, for it was almost more than she could do to keep her mind on the playing.

She put Woodrow to bed that night and sat near her door, waiting to hear Ben's footsteps on the stairs, but two hours passed and he did not come. Having made her mind up to talk to him tonight, she felt compelled to do it now while she had the courage. Tomorrow might come and find her with the spine of a jellyfish, but tonight she felt she could tell him anything she wanted to, and she must see him tonight! She checked on the little boy's breathing, a nightly habit with her, then went out of the house and through the small needled thicket. She stood a few feet back in the shadows and deliberated again. A small sliver of light came from under the oak planed doorway and she wondered if he was working on the books or if he was drinking or undressing or in bed and reading. Perhaps it would be better if she just knocked and if he were drinking she would get a can of milk for breakfast coffee and go back to the house and wait until another night.

When he opened the door to her knock, he was holding his pistol, thinking that she was another hobo asking for a place to sleep or a bite to eat. They crawled off the train at the nearby trestle and hid out until dark. Then they would come up to the store for a handout. Nevertheless, she was taken aback by the sight of the raised pistol. He never gave her the satisfaction of asking her what she wanted or even speaking first about anything. The more difficult he made it for her to talk, the more he seemed to relish it. Thank God, he is cold sober for once, she breathed inside. And for once, I'm not begging him for my fare. I won't give him the satisfaction of asking for everything.

"I have to talk to you a few minutes tonight, Ben. Had you rather talk inside the store or out here in the dark?" Even the sound of her words gave her more courage.

He looked at her strangely for a few moments, lowered the pistol and motioned with it for her to come on inside. He closed the door and bolted it behind her. Even this did not frighten her. If he raped her again, perhaps that would destroy the baby, and that was something she would welcome. He sank down on the edge of the cot and had a bad coughing spell, but he did not ask her to sit. She stood erect and looked down on his almost completely bald head. She was not used to seeing him without his cap and she was amazed that so much of his hair had disappeared.

"I'm pregnant, Ben."

"And?"

"And what?"

"And what am I supposed to do about that?"

"I don't know how to answer you, Ben, anymore than I've ever known how to talk to you. You're too smart for me to argue with, and I'm not going to try it. I'm just going to tell you this and go. I'm not going to have this baby. We're not married. We don't share anything. I'm asking you to talk to Dr. Kellum and get him to give you something for me to take. He'll do it for you before he would for anyone else and I know he has something he makes from roots and barks that will bring everything out. I've heard Mama talk about it. I don't want to die and what he has is fairly safe. But if you don't get it, I'll risk something more dangerous. There are other ways and I'll try them all if I have to."

He coughed again and reached under the pillow for a handkerchief. He turned aside and spit in it, but even in the dim lamp light she saw that the spittle was very dark. Dark as blood!

He read the question in her eyes and answered it unflinchingly.

"Yep. You guessed it right. Consumption. And yes. Dr. Kellum knows it and says I'm just as well off here as I'd be in the sanatorium if I'd rest. But who in the hell has to rest up to die. Answer me that?"

"But, Ben? What about the rest of us? Even if you hate me and Woodrow, surely you can't hate your mother?"

"You don't know who I can or can't hate, woman. Don't tell me what I can't do." And when she did not make a reply to his hateful remark, he continued in a more subdued tone.

"No. I don't want any of you to get it. That's the main reason I sleep out here. I'm glad you know it now. You can boil my plate from now on. I should have told you all before, but I don't want your damned pity . . . if you have pity for me . . . maybe you're glad I've got it. You've got every right to be glad. Are you glad?" He felt compelled to ask the last question.

She shook her head negatively and looked beyond him when she spoke. She did not want to like him and if she looked into his face, it might be possible to pity him and pity was dangerously close to like. She was afraid now of liking him. It was easier to live her under their arrangement when she disliked him intensely. Hate had kept both of them living from day to day.

He had suspected that she was pregnant from observing her closely and he had anticipated her coming to talk to him, but he had been wrong in his assumption that she would ask for a divorce. He had never believed that she would have the courage to ask him to help her get rid of the baby, a baby conceived of rape and disgust and uncontrolled rage, even in acute alcoholism, but his life's sand was fast running out and suddenly he did not want to help destroy this minute particle that could live on after his death. He had tried for a year to get Lulu pregnant, but he had come to the conclusion that the bitch was no good. The secret fear had been the doubting of his own manhood, and suddenly he was glad that Ella was pregnant. Big drops of perspiration stood on his forehead, some of them merging into little rivers of water and running down his long nose, falling onto his soiled trouser leg. For one time in his life he was on the short end of the saw horse and it was bewildering.

"I . . . I . . . I don't know what to say, Ella. I don't think that Dr. Kellum would give it to me any more than he would to you. From what I've heard, Dr. Thompkins has been on him about it and has threatened having him put in jail for having used it. I know Dr. Kellum and you know him and we both know he isn't a criminal, but I don't think people in other places would look at him through the same glasses we do. He just does what he wants to and that's that. I don't think in fairness to him, I could ask him."

"You amaze me, Ben Simpson. Fairness is a word I didn't know you knew. I'm not asking you to do the fair thing. Did you do the fair thing to me?"

"I've been sorry about that every minute since it happened. I'm being honest with you now, Ella. But that doesn't undo the thing I did, I know. But I don't want any part in killing a baby."

"Well, let me tell you here and now, Ben, that I intend to do everything in my power to get rid of it. I don't want any part of it. You won't want it. There won't be a living soul who will want it. What kind of life will that be for a new baby?"

His head which had been lowered and covered with his hands came up abruptly. He stood up and came over to where she stood up, his tall sickly thin frame towering over her. He put both of his hands firmly on her arms and spoke between clenched teeth, for he knew now he must beg her. He had hoped to threaten or frighten or scare, but he could now see that these three would be useless with her.

"I do want the baby. If you'll just try to carry it and birth it, I'll do everything else for it as long as I live. I'm not going to ever get another chance to father one, I'm sure of that as I'm standing here now, and I don't want to die leaving no one. There must be someone that I can leave who is a real part of me. There must be."

"Have yourself a bastard by Lula then. But don't beg me to bear you a child. When I have another one, it will be by a man who loves me and whom I love, whether I'm married to him or not and put that down in one of your precious books and mark it well." She shook her arm fiercely and he dropped his hold on her.

"Don't go yet, Ella. Please wait."

She had never heard that tone of voice coming from him, the youth who had everything, the young man who had been the catch of the township, the only educated male in the community, the high and mighty, he who had looked on her as less than nothing for the past four years, now he could say please to her. It caused her to lift her chin a little higher, yet it gave her the compassion to turn and listen to his pleas.

"Everything I have except the house and store is willed to Lula. The house and store is willed to Mama. I had it made up six months ago. I didn't intend to leave you a red cent. Not you or Woodrow. I didn't intend to see you well off and married as soon as I was laid out cold. But if you'll do nothing to harm the baby and will promise me to take care of it as well as you have Woodrow and to raise it as best you can, I'll change the will tomorrow. Everything will be yours. Just take care of Mama and see that she doesn't want for anything. The house. The store. The farms. All will be yours."

"What about your precious Lula?"

"Lula, hell! I've never loved her. She was just necessary to me in the same way vittles are to you. Surely you understand that much about a man. I was leaving everything to her just to hurt you. What do you say?"

"I've got to think about it awhile. Then I'll let you know. Good night, Ben."

He wanted to open his lips and say good night in return, but the knot in his throat had filled it beyond speaking so he dropped his head and locked the door behind her. He was hot and cold simultaneously all night. His teeth chattered as if he had a chill while his forehead burned with fever. One coughing spasm followed another, and the rag which he kept under the pillow was completely red with blood filled mucous he had coughed. He got up three different times and kindled the fire in the heater and boiled the coffee pot and drank some as hot as he could stand it. This seemed to ease the pain in his throat and chest for a while. Laying back on the cot and staring at the cobwebs in the dark loft, he tormented himself for not having been big enough to forgive Ella the moment he first realized he had been tricked. Anyone else could have forgiven her, so sweet and loving she had been and what a wonderful wife she would have continued to make him. Their life could have been filled with little ones by now. Little ones who called him Daddy and who could have filled their bench at church, he on one end and Ella on the other and all their little ones in the middle—every Sunday. Just as Ma and Pa had done. This could never be now and the futility of weeping over it did not seem apparent to him. Can't keep looking back. Must think of someway to make her keep the baby. He longed to reach behind the cot and pull out his quart jar of moonshine, but he did not want his mind fogged tonight. Must keep clear. Must think of someway to convince her. Surely she won't turn down all that property. Is having a baby as terrible as losing all that. Then he remembered the long hours she had labored when Woodrow had been born and he was afraid for a moment that no amount of money could coax her into it again. He thought how soft and white her skin must be. How lovely her body remained. All of the long nights she too had been alone without even a Lula to ease the pains of desire. Funny, he had never really thought much about her sexual needs until now. He had mentally put her and his mother in a class together and had forgotten how young and desirable she was. Forgotten too were all his drunken accusations. Had he been drunk all those times? His mind was an upside down thing. One and two made four tonight and he was not sure of anything. And when the first filter of the dawn slipped under the crack of the back door, he thanked God that the night had finally passed.

—Chapter 9—

A BODY WOULD THINK THAT North Carolina is far south enough to have mild winters, but there is a dampness that meets the cold air which comes from the north and together they do their best to chill bones and chap the flesh. And more often than not, they succeed. It is always just about cold enough to snow, and just about damp enough, but then it pouts and decides to rain and sleet and rain again. The roads turn to mire, the side ditches fill up and freeze, the pump handle freezes standing straight up, the manure in the mule stable is filled with ice, the sow has her pigs and they freeze to death in the pine straw beside her. The branch runs slow and freezes, not hard enough to slide on but almost, enough to tempt the boys out and make them try it and fall in and get a soaking and a whaling. The robins search the already harvested corn fields in search of one scattered remaining grain, the sparrows stay close to the houses in hope of crumbs being flung out the back kitchen door, and the dogs' backs arch with the coldness and their hair takes on a shaggy coat and their bellies are sucked in and ribs protruding. It is a time when a man is glad that there is wood under his shed and plenty of lightwood cut to start fires with in the early hours of the cold mornings. Every corn cob is saved and put in the kindling box in the kitchen behind the stove to help start the fire. The chicken door hangs open during the day, but only an occasional hen ventures outside into the lot. The pickings are too lean to make it worth the effort to peck around. The land lies half frozen, daring man to try to plow it now, knowing that it has bested him again and always will in the end. The sycamore trees are humble though and stand with arms upstretched like naked women, their trunks straight and white and lovely. Every leaf is gone, gone with the time of winter.

And so it was in the winter of their great unhappiness. Ella had decided that it would be better for Woodrow to remain there in the house and grow up with security than to risk being thrown out with nothing. The thought of living alone frightened her more than living under the roof with Ben. There was something about being Mrs. Simpson's daughter-in-law that gave her a warm strong feeling, a feeling that she had never had at home. Kate was the self confident one there. She had talked it over with Ben after a few days of deliberation and uncertainties. During these same days Ben had remained cold sober, perhaps trying to convince her that he could if he wanted to, perhaps wanting to be sober when she did make her decision.

She longed with all her young heart to go home, really go home and talk her heart out with her mother about her problems, but she could feel the animosity in the air the moment she entered the yard. And it all stemmed from Kate's jealousy. She was jealous because Ella had the husband she wanted for herself, jealous that she was not making any progress toward getting one for herself, jealous that her mother was so delighted to see Ella and the boy. If she could not have a husband she did not intend for Ella to become the light of her mother's eyes, neither her nor the boy. Every biscuit filled with grape preserves that her mother handed Woodrow caused a satirical grunt to come from the throat of the jealous sister. Occasionally she would hear her mother and Ella tittering about something they did not want her to hear and she imagined right that it concerned subjects that only married women discussed. She longed to be included in the conversation even if she were single. Every effort that Ella made to remain a part of the family was thwarted from the start by Kate and the pattern of their childhood continued in that Ella often apologized for things she felt were not her fault in order to try to win over the good side of her sister. If her father had favored Kate as a young child, he certainly did not from the day that Ella married Ben and secured his purchase of the cleared land, but he was unreachable as a friend.

So it was that there was no place of comfort or wisdom in which to turn. Again the right answer must come from herself and all the old insecurities came to taunt her. She knew that she was not wise or even smart and the decision was so enormous that it made a tight lump rise in her throat and choke off her air. The palms of her hands would become moist and a terrific pain would shoot through the lower part of her stomach. Woodrow must be looked after. Could she do it if she left Ben? What kind of work could a woman get? Housemaid? Janitor? Scrub woman? Yet the real question was of another nature. Could she ever learn to love the new baby. Would she, its own mother, look upon it with hate and disgust, or would it be a warm little thing that she could nurse and love and in time forget how much shame its father had heaped upon her in the past few years.

Though the day was icy cold, she asked Mrs. Simpson to keep an eye on Woodrow while she went out for a spell.

"Child. In the name of the Lord! You'll catch your death of cold Ben doesn't need you today in the store, does he?"

"I'm not going to the store, Mother Simpson. I just want to get out in the air for a spell. You don't mind watching him, do you?"

"Land sakes. Mind, the dog's tail. I'd mind if he wasn't here to watch. Get on with you. Just wrap up good. I'll never understand you young folks. No respect for the weather. Cold days is time to crochet. No time for walking."

"I won't be long, Mother. Thanks a blue million," she said and she kissed the woman on her forehead.

It was too cold and damp in her favorite woods spot to sit on the log so she leaned against the damp cedar tree and hugged herself for warmth. There was a thin coat of ice over some of the stream, but most of it was free running still. Not an animal moved anywhere. The squirrel was warm in his nest overhead, the rabbit safe in his burrowed home on his warm spot under the log. The moss hung straight down as no breeze moved to swing and sway it today.

"Tell me tree . . . tell me what to do . . . You just have to stand here. The wind will take your cones and scatter your seed to the winds and you won't even know when your babies are born, or even recognize your own children. You won't even cry when they're cut for timber or shingled. Is that why they call you wood . . . because you have no feelings? I wish that the insides of me was all wooden so I wouldn't have such hurtings inside . . . then I wouldn't toss and turn when the night is warm and lovely and dream about what could have been with my life, or lie there wishing some man I can't have was lying on the other side of the bed and all I'd have to do would be reach over and touch him. He would turn immediately and know my needs and fill my heart and satisfy my longing . . . Tell me, tree. You know I can't go back to Mama. There's no turning back and Leonard is lost to me now. If there ever was a chance, there isn't now. Not with another baby coming. Most soon as not, he'll be married afore long. I don't want Woodrow to know hunger and shame from being too poor. I want him to go to school as long as he can or as long as he wants . . . Tell me gentle old cedar ..." And a needle fell from its boughs, hit the water and moved slowly downstream.

"If the next needle falls on the ice and lies there, then I'll stay with Ben. If it hits the water and floats downstream, I'll pack and leave with the boy and do the best I can by him. I'm awaiting tree." And peace came on her while waiting. She had put the terrible burden of making the decision on someone else and that had taken the load off her own shoulders and she waited and when the next needle fell, it looked as if it would hit the water for it fell straight downward toward it until it gently laid the needle on the edge of the ice and it lay there still.

For a moment her heart fluttered. In the very deepest recesses of her heart she had hoped that it would hit the water and that she would be free to go. "But perhaps it's best this way," she told the tree. "I didn't know what was best. Perhaps you do."

The cold was cutting through her heavy wool coat and she turned and walked back through the woods to the house. Standing in front of the fireplace and thawing out her hands and bottom end alternately, she knew that there was no need to delay telling Ben or his mother about the baby now.

Mrs. Simpson sat trying to thread her darning needle by the light of the Alladin lamp, and seemed to be missing the eye of it every time.

"Here. Let me thread it for you, Mother. You've got to see to getting those glasses changed."

"Changed the cat's tail. All Dr. Kellum does is buy these things from the catalog. And I can order me a pair from Sears Roebuck and save myself five dollars. There is an eye to danged blamed thing, isn't there."

Ella had to laugh. Laughter would come more often now that she had decided which way her life would continue.

"Yes. There is an eye. Here. I didn't realize I was so cold. I'm going to have to take better care of myself now that I'm a doing for two again."

"Doing for two? You're joking me, aren't you, Ellie?"

"Nope. Three months already. I thought you'd notice and say something before I told you. There is room in the house for one more baby, isn't there?"

"Room? Huh? What'd you say, Ellie?"

"I said there is room here for one more baby, ain't there?"

"Oh. Yes. Yes. Of course there is."

But Ellie could see that the old lady was perplexed as to how she had gotten pregnant as distant and cold as Ben had been to her. She had been sure in her own mind that he never crossed the hall. She had lain awake night after night just to listen for his footsteps. Not a board had creaked. Not one. Had they been fooling her all along. Was he really not as ill with Ella as he pretended to be . . . but all those stories about him? Her own husband had been an irritable bossy man, but when he slept at night his big arm was outstretched across the bolsters and she lay secure and warm on his arm. Her heart had bled many times for Ellie. Young and vital and warm and tender and missing so much of what was real in life. Perhaps after all, they had merely fooled her. And Ella was not impervious to the trepidations in the old woman's heart and mind.

"Oh, Mother. Don't look so worried. It's going to be a sweet little girl this time. It might even look just like you. And if it is a girl, she's going to have your name. How about that now?"

All of these statements were thought up on the spur of the moment, but she liked the sound of them as they took voice. In the two years following both of Ben's sisters' marriages, neither had become pregnant, and Mrs. Simpson longed for them to have babies and come and visit over the weekend and give her a chance to rock and croon to new born ones. But neither girl seemed the least disturbed about not having produced. In fact, from their conversations, one suspected that they were glad they did not have any babies. Babies would have interfered with their schedules. Faye Ellen's husband was the Honorable Percy Winterville, the town's only lawyer, and if he had been President of the United States, she would not have put on any more airs. Gertrude was satisfactorily, if not happily, married to Ivan Hancock, the local school master at the present, and as his salary was not sufficient to keep her in the style in which she had always been accustomed. She continued to buy the most expensive things and have them charged to her brother, things that Ella and Mrs. Simpson would not have dared to buy for themselves. Although this seemed an audacity to Ella, it was accepted as a normal occurrence by the girl's mother, and she ignored Ben's wild rantings over the bills for twenty dollar shoes and thirty dollar dresses that kept coming in.

Mrs. Simpson seemed to have gained her composure and came over and embraced Ella warmly.

"I'm so happy. It's so pointless to knit and knit shawls and shawls when one should be knitting for a new baby. I'm going to go into town tomorrow and stock up on baby wool and make some sweater sets and maybe a pink blanket with white fringes. Tell me, dear. What did Ben say about the coming of the new baby?"

"Mother, I think he wants this baby more than he has ever wanted anything in his life. Haven't you noticed any changes in him in the last few weeks? No drinking. No shouting and cursing?"

"Yes. Of course I've noticed. I've also noticed his cough is so much worse. Can't you talk him into going to a specialist. Dr. Kellum's medicine is not worth a happy hoot, if I must say so. He looks pale and drawn, too. Haven't you tried to talk to him about it."

"Yes. I've tried, but he won't listen to a word I try to say to him about it. Perhaps if you tried, Mother, it would help. I want to run upstairs now for a few minutes before we have supper. I won't be long."

That night was the first night in over four years that Ben had crossed the narrow hallway and knocked on Ella's door. His mother had told him as soon as he had come in about how delighted she was over the coming of the new baby and his heart had leaped. Was it positive that Ellie had decided then? And decided to try to bear the child? Had she really intended to try to destroy it? Yes. He felt in his heart that she had and he could not have blamed her if she had. But he had prayed, really prayed, for this tiny spark of life that was of his own flesh to continue living and growing. Surely she wouldn't have spoken of it so openly to his mother if she intended now to try to destroy it. His anxiety showed plainly on his pale face as he waited for her to answer his knock. But, she did not call out. Instead she came to the door, opened it wide, read the questions on his face and said softly, "Come in, Ben."

He had forgotten how white and soft this room was—white coverlet, white organdy at the window, white walls, white cushions in the old rocker that had been his own grandfather's, small white bed beside Ella's that Woodrow slept upon. It made his own walnut room seem like a morgue and it certainly was not as if no time had elapsed since last he had stepped into this room. Four years had elapsed and they both felt every minute of it between them. He stood at the window and looked at the frozen ground far below as he talked to her, and she held both hands in front of her tightly to still their trembling. As she looked at him, she realized that he was still above her. Always had been, and even in the face of death still was. He had confidence, money, security, poise and strength that came from inside, and she alone knew the depth of her own weaknesses, although at times she felt that he could look through her and see how she trembled at the world. Only her love for Woodrow gave her the strength to put a strong front. She hoped that she was fooling him now.

For once he did not speak to her in grand eloquent tones, but continued to look out of the window and spoke softly, his voice raspy and gentle.

"Ma said you had spoke to her of the baby, Ella. I presume this means that you have made a decision about the matter at hand."

Still the eternal lord and master, she thought. Still sounds like the school teacher. So far above me, yet.

"Yes. I've decided. Or it was decided for me before I was born. Perhaps that's what decides everything."

"Hog wash. Nothing's decided before we're born. Not even the day we're going to make our entrance and exit. Anyone who believes otherwise is illiterate or downright stupid."

He continued since she remained silent. "Why? I owe my intelligence to the fact that Pa was smart and wise enough to choose a good wife. Breeding. That's what makes smart children."

She wanted to ask him why his sisters were so hair-brained, but decided against it.

"Then may I presume that you have decided positively about the baby?"

"I'll do my part, Ben. What happens in the end though is up to God."

"You and that damned religion. For the sake of Woodrow and the coming baby, Ella, do stand on your own self-reliance. Learn that you can control what happens. Don't sit and be a milk toast all of your life and then no matter what falls on you, say humbly, 'It's the will of God.' It's not God's will that you be ignorant or unlearned or unable to make decisions. Please learn to be strong, Ella. For the sake of the children if not for yourself."

He was looking at her now and she noticed again how thin he had become and pale, except for the two reddish spots on his high cheek bones. Perhaps if she asked him again about going to another doctor?

"I fooled you once about a most important thing, Ben, but I've never tried to fool you about being smart. I know I'm not and I've not tried to act as if I were. I've heard enough times from Kate about how dumb I am to believe it. Perhaps the baby will take after you. I hope so."

Was she trying to rile him deliberately? He tried to hold his tongue and decide. No. There was no sarcasm in her face or in the inflections of her voice. She sincerely hoped the baby would be brilliant. How big her heart and how little his own had always been. How loved she was by everyone and how few people loved him, or even respected him anymore. He was despised by the entire community and he knew it.

"And I hope the baby will take after you too, Ella. You have more good traits to pass on to a baby than I have. Forgive me my remarks. I wish I could say I'm not myself, but I am myself as I have always been and probably will be and that's not complimentary to me, either."

Looking at her he watched her breast rise and fall with each deep breath and he realized what a strain this must be on her. Perhaps she feared him still. How lovely her breast, he thought and he felt an agonizing pain shoot down his stomach from his navel and travel down the inside of his right thigh. Perspiration popped out on his upper lip in spite of the chill in the room. I must not think how smooth her skin and soft and lovely her neck. In spite of hating her fiercely for four years, I know I could love her again, more than before now that she is carrying my child. Yet, I must not dare to think. Or touch. Only the child. I must think of only the child now.

He was untrammeled, yet he could not bring his legs to start walking from the room. There was nothing, not one single word, that remained to be said. Nothing remained but for him to go and yet . . . why did he wait? she was asking herself.

"I'll ring up old Winterville after supper and get him to come out tomorrow and change my will. I want you to see it before it's signed and see if it's to your satisfaction."

"I trust you, Ben. There's no need for me to see it."

"Do you trust me, Ella? He asked as he found his own legs and walked over to her, stopping only inches from her big skirt."

"Why, why . . . yes. Yes, I do."

"I mean do you trust me in your bedroom?"

"I'm not sure. But I'm not afraid of you anymore, Ben. If that's what you mean."

"You stay so young, Ella and so lovely. Like a child still. I'd forgotten how your nose turns up. It could rain in it, I'll bet."

"You'd better go now, Ben."

"I'm glad you let your hair grow back. No woman looks good with bobbed hair. You should never cut it again."

"Please, Ben."

"Please what? Please love me?"

"You know that's not what I mean. Please go now."

"Say that you hate me. Then I'll go."

"Get out of my way, Ben Simpson. I'm going down and help with supper and you can stand here and talk silly all night if you want to."

"Oh. It's silly when a man tells you you're beautiful, is it? I thought most women wanted to hear that."

"I'm not most women and you're not most men, and we're not the most average married couple. So there."

"No, we're not. But I still want you the way any average man wants his wife. Does that embarrass you?"

"I'm not embarrassed!"

"Then why are you so red?"

"You make me so damn mad. That's why I'm red. Now move out of my way!"

It was then that he reached out and took hold of her arm. He felt her flesh tremble to his touch. Her arm is hot, he thought and I'm so cold—cold all of the time lately—and she's so warm and soft.

"You haven't said you hate me. Then I'll go."

"I don't hate you, Ben. I've never hated you, really. But that doesn't mean that you can start where you left off years ago. Get that into your thick, intelligent head. Take your hand off me and move away."

"Haven't you needed me at all, Ella. In four years, haven't you needed a man enough to come across the hall even once?"

"I'm not discussing my needs with you."

"If not with me, then who? Who can you discuss them with? Mother? Your mother? Kate? Some other man?"

"Please, Ben."

"Please, Ben. Please, Ben. Is that all you can say. Don't hide that mind in a shell, Ella. Quit hiding. You can tell me anything you need to."

"Well, in that case, listen Ben. There is nothing I need to tell you. Can't you understand that?"

"No, I don't." And he moved closed to her and caressed her hair with one hand while he held her arm with the other. "I don't understand a woman who could have been as warm and loving and giving as you were and then . . . nothing. I wouldn't have blamed you if all the accusations I made had been true. You and the preacher. I knew they weren't, but I think I secretly hoped they were so that I could justify what I was doing. I wanted to drag you down with me. Still, I can't understand how you did it. Women really are different from men, aren't they?"

She could have told him no. She could have told him of the long cold nights when her body had ached and twitched with desire and there had been no one to kill the fires of longing, the nights she had dreamed that Leonard had come across the fields and told her that now the land was his and he had come to claim his woman and his child, nights she had dreamed he would take them both and hold his arm around her waist and take the child by the hand as they had raced across the field, through the meadow, down the hill, across the branch, up another hill and into the clearing that belonged to him. And in the dream he had filled her needs so that the real daytime had not been as hard to bear. She felt that he was clairvoyant and that nothing was hid from him anyway. So why bare her soul when he probably already knew everything.

He bent and gently kissed the side of her neck. His arm was not holding hers tightly, but she did not pull away. Nor did she respond. He moved his lips gently to the lobe of her ear and kissed it softly. Chill bumps rose on her arm and he caressed her arm until they disappeared. The continuity of his caresses and kisses caused her body to tremble from top to bottom, and he held her tighter as his lips moved the tip of her nose to her unpainted lips. How lovely and full those lips, those unkissed lips, lips that had waited, but not for him. He did not disillusion himself in thinking that she had longed for him as a person, only as a man. And that had to be enough. He reached behind her, slipped the thumb bolt on the door, and picked her unresisting body up and carried her over to the white starched bed. He blew the lamp out with one blow and pulled the covering up over both of them and they warmed the night . . . not with a raging fire, but with a low flame.

Later he lay satiated in bed and watched her try to fit her full bosom back into her corset and admired how tightly she could drawn in her waist. He enjoyed looking at her firm thighs and remembered how hot they had been lying between his own thin legs and how the touch of her breast on his chest had been like molten lead. He looked up from her legs to her face and saw tears streaming down her cheeks.

He sat up quickly and took her hand in his. "Don't cry, please. It won't happen again, if you say so. Please don't cry. It was so lovely. So wonderful. Please say it wasn't bad for you. I can't bear it if it was bad for you." Tears were in his own eyes and he did not care that she saw them.

Leaning over him and holding his head next to her stomach,

she hugged him and caressed the top of his head.

"It was good for me too. The tears are for all the wasted and lost time. That's all."

And she finished dressing and went downstairs to help prepare their evening meal.

—Chapter 10—

FALL WILL COME WHEN IT IS TIME. Summer may come late, almost a part of springtime. Spring also comes later sometimes, but in the Carolina's when the summer is over, fall stands up and marches grandly in. All summer the old corn had weevils in it and the women had to be very careful in sifting it not to let any bugs into the corn bread. Now when the ears hung dry on the stalk, they went out with burlap bags and filled them. They knew that Ben would be too busy to go to the grist mill, but it was only three miles and Ella looked forward to hitching the buggy, taking Woodrow, and driving there herself. Needless to say, Mrs. Simpson thought it dangerous in her condition for she was very pregnant by now, but she had taken some of Ben's advice and learned to depend on her own decisions.

It had been the happiest summer of her life. She thanked God everyday that she had not let her pride stand in the way of forgiving Ben for his past. Then she would never have known how kind and tender her really could be when he so desired. Mrs. Simpson knew too that happiness had come again to their home and she sang like an off key mockingbird. Ben resumed going to church with them and during every sermon, his mother would lean over, look down the pew and smile broadly at him.

All summer she had fanned and smiled and Ben had stayed sober, except for the first time he had carried the tobacco to the market. Dark came and he had not returned. The two women and the little boy were standing on the front porch waiting for a glimpse of the wagon and the lantern that would tell them he was coming. But they heard him by the time they saw him for he was singing, "When they ring the golden bells," and they could tell from his voice that he was loaded. Sure enough, the team was leading itself, the reins laying loosely between his legs, his hat lost somewhere down the road, his shirt unbuttoned all the way, his hairy chest exposed for all the world to see, a most indecent sight. Even his trousers were not completely buttoned and his shoes were untied and his coat wrinkled and dirty.

As was the custom with the farmers selling their crop, they slept on their own piles of tobacco during the night to guard it from shysters and bums. Then to make his day perfect, his piles had sold for one dollar a pound, had graded wrappers, a rare thing for this part of the state, and he was so elated that he went right out and bought a quart of the best whiskey in town. He drove the team awhile, stopped and drank awhile, drove awhile, and drank awhile, and soon the quart was gone. Perhaps he had slept part of the way home. Surely he must have, because it was a good twenty miles from home and he did not remember anything of the last ten miles. It was a good thing that old Bessie and Nell were dependable or else he might have wound up on another road in a deep ditch.

They helped him out of the wagon and into bed and had to wait until the next day to learn how good their tobacco had sold. Ella had left the store for a moment with her daddy in charge and ran back over to the house that morning to see if he was still sleeping, but he was sitting on the edge of the bed rubbing his forehead.

"Who made the damn sun rise today? The light is killing my head."

She pulled the shades down and told him to lie back down, but he insisted on getting up and taking care of the store.

"Why didn't you pour water on me this morning first thing. You've got no business taking care of the store now."

"I don't think even water coulda got you up first thing. You looked too far gone."

A funny look crossed his face and she realized she had said the wrong thing. Instead of rebuking her, however, he pulled her to him and lay his head against her swollen stomach. In a minute the baby kicked him hard and he laughed aloud.

"I know he's a boy, Ellie. A girl just couldn't kick like that, could she?"

"I imagine she could."

"It's a boy. I know it. Oh, Ellie. I wish there were time. Time for lots of babies. I wish I were the father of eight or nine, sons and daughters. I never knew how it could make a man feel to plant his seed inside a woman and wait for it to grow and then suddenly, there is a new human being. It's a miracle. That's what it is."

"Yes. I've always thought it was a miracle too, Ben."

"You don't hate the baby now, do you?"

"You know better than that. I've never hated it. It just frightened me at first. May I say that you're a sight. You'd better clean up before you go out to the store. Guess what. I had a gasoline customer this morning."

"You don't mean it? Where was he from?"

"New Jersey. They were going to Florida to visit their daughter. They bought some of three different kinds of hard candy and ten gallons of gasoline."

"Wonderful. It won't be long before lots of cars will come by and we're right on the main route. We'll sell more gasoline than we do anything else put together within five or ten years."

"I've got to get back. Papa is at the store alone."

She had some more news to tell him, but this was not the right moment, perhaps tonight. She had made an appointment for him with Dr. Bradshaw, a chest specialist from Rose Hill for the following Monday. She did not know if he would go or not, but she intended to try everything to get him there. She did not have too much faith in Dr. Kellum's diagnosis and she wanted to know for sure what was wrong and what they could do about it, if anything. Above all, she had to find out if it were dangerous to others besides themselves.

* * *

DRIVING ALONG THE CANAL route to the grist mill, she and Woodrow sang all the little songs he knew and she tried to teach him a new one, but he was more interested in holding the horse in the middle of the road, watching a blue jay fly across the pines, or watching for turtles sunning on the banks of the canal, and he chatted like a magpie every step of the way. However, he would tell nothing until he knew he had his mother's complete attention, pulling at her sleeve until she answered so there was little time for her to think of her own complexities or happiness.

The air was very warm and still, and it was possible to see tiny particles of dust suspended in midair if one looked closely. The horse was old and beyond hurrying and he swished his cockle burr filled tail contentedly from left to right. The boy chatted on while the woman's mind lay idle, her heart content, however, for the moment.

But rare are the moments of contentment for those immersed deeply in living, and Ella was caught momentarily off guard when she stepped into the mill house and saw that it was empty except for Leonard who was sitting idly in a straw bottom rocker in the far corner. Sunlight filtered through the boarded up window in the back and made his yellow hair take on golden lights. I must not waiver, she told herself. I must persevere, as Ben told me to. I have seen Leonard many times and there is no need to tremble now. The little boy clutched his mother's hand and inquired loudly.

"We want our corn ground. Ain't you grinding today?"

"Aren't you grinding today, dear. You know better," Ella corrected, glad of an opening word.

"Where is Mr. Morton," she continued.

"Over there a piece. Gone after some more bags from the shed. I'm a keeping it till he gits back. Where's your corn?"

She pointed toward the buggy outside the door and he went out and brought in over his shoulder the burlap bag filled with fresh shelled corn. He ran some of the grains between his fingers and commented on the quality of the corn.

"Yes. We've been blessed with good corn every year lately.

How you been, Leonard? I haven't seen you at the store lately?"

"Haven't been there lately."

"But you been alright? Well, I meant?"

"Fitter'n ever."

He started to ask how she had been, but any question about her health might lead her to think he was inquiring about her condition, which was obvious to everyone. No man ever asked a pregnant woman about her health.

"Yes." He went on when she did not converse. "Times is mighty good. Good seasons. Good money and the war's all behind us men now. I'm a thinking mightily about gittin' married soon. Guess Eva Belle done told you that, however?"

"Eva Belle? Why no. I haven't seen her lately? Why should she have told me, though?"

"She's the one."

"The one to tell me you're getting married."

"Yes and yes again. She's the one to tell you and yes, she's the one I'm aiming to marry. Are you addled today, Ella, or something?"

"But I thought Eva Belle was awaiting for . . ." She stopped, embarrassed that perhaps she was letting the cat out of the bag about something that Leonard had no inkling of.

"You mean Leslie Humphrey? Why, he wrote this summer and told her to look for someone else, not to wait for him any longer. His education is going to take years and he didn't want her awaiting, so he told her, but I told her he was just letting her down easy like so as not to hurt her feelings. Most likely he had found him a pretty nurse, interested in the same things he's interested in and they hit it off and he was wanting all strings back here cut free. And she's knowed me all her life, and more important, she understands about Papa. She knows everything is hissen, but that it will be mine one of these days and she don't care if we have to wait for it. You don't look well, Ella. The grinding is not too upsetting for you. Maybe you'd better step outside in the fresh air till it's done."

"No. The grinding is not upsetting me. You know damned

well what is upsetting me. You and Eva? How could you, and right under my nose? You make me so damned mad, Leonard, I could kill you and laugh at your funeral."

"Well, what in the name of God ails you now?"

"But I thought you . . ." she stopped and whirled and ran outside. Woodrow was squatting in the sand outside the door, trying to make a doodle bug come up from his tiny burrow and singing his little chant,

"Doodle bug, doodle bug,
You'd better come up,
Your house is one fire,
You're goin' to be burned up."

He twisted a little stick around and around in the little hole and looked for the tiny bug to come out of the sand. Feeling water dripping on his head, he looked up into his mother's face and saw tears falling.

"What's the matter, Mama? Did a corn bug get in your eye?"

She squatted and rubbed his blonde curls, curls so like the big man's inside the mill. She laughed and said, "Yes. There's a bug in my eye, but I've got him out and I can see very clearly now."

"I'm glad, Mama," and he was satisfied to turn back to his bug work.

In a few minutes, Leonard came out with their meal ground and bagged and stacked it in the back of the buggy for them.

"You ought to learn to drive Ben's car. Think how quickly you could come and go."

"And you ought to learn to tend to your own business. Think how much better off you'd be!"

"I'm sorry, Ella. I didn't mean to upset you in there. I honestly thought it was all over for you. It has been for me for a long time now. For a while I waited and hurt and thought you'd leave Ben as soon as the baby came, but you kept staying on and staying on, and you never had a word to say to me to give me any hope at all, and my last hope died when I heard you was pregnant again. I knowed then you weren't a pining for me at all anymore. And I knowed Eva Belle real well and she was a'ready as I was to talk about marriage. I never thought once you'd care. Honest."

"Honesty, be hanged! You never thought once is right! How'd you think I'd forgot when I look at your image a full two dozen times day. You see that boy playing there. Take a good look at him. How'd you think I'd forgot about you with him a reminding me all the time. Day and night?"

"But Ben . . ."

"Ben did what you wouldn't do. He married me. Does that answer any of your stupid questions?"

Even saying the words she knew that she was not being fair to him, but in her dreams, Leonard had always been awaiting eager to take her back, still loving and waiting for her and it seemed as if her dreams had just been stepped on and ground in the dirt. She turned quickly to call Woodrow and get in the buggy.

"Here. Let me help you up."

"Keep your filthy hands off my arm, you, you beast," and she stepped up too quickly and missed the bottom step and tripped, the front of her stomach striking the iron step board.

"Can I drive, Mama? Can I drive back? Huh? Can I?"

"Are you hurt, Ella," and it was obvious that she was for she was bent over double in agonizing pain that ran from the front of her stomach to the depths of her back.

He stepped forward to try to assist her, but she struck out at him with her outstretched arm and straightened up and climbed into the buddy.

"Can I drive? Can I, Mama?"

"Yes. Take us home, son." And she fell back on the leather black tufted seat and rubbed her stomach with her hands and groaned every foot of the way there.

❧ ❧ ❧

"I KNEW IT! I KNEW IT! She had no business driving that buggy all the way to the mill! We coulda waited for fresh meal till Ben had time to carry it himself. We coulda waited."

Mrs. Simpson was in a great state of perturbation for this baby was not only another grandchild, but the salvation of her only son. Her anxiety was plainly written on her face and she was unable to assist Dr. Kellum in preparing Ella for delivery.

"Shouldn't I call Ben. I can close the store for him."

"No need. These second ones never take as long a gettin' here. Husbands ain't no help anyway. Let him be! Just get downstairs and put on more water."

. . . I had no right. I had no right to let him know anything that was in my heart. Now he can laugh at me the rest of his life and tell Eva, and then they both will lie in bed at night and laugh at me. And in her moments of agony she continued to torment herself and blame herself for her predicament. And to think how badly Ben wants this baby. I've probably killed it. Just like I said I would. He won't believe me when I tell him I didn't mean it . . . and her mental agony was as great as her physical pain.

She reached out and took Dr. Kellum's old brown time worn and age cracked hand and clung to it.

"I oughta die, but please don't let me. I don't want to die. I want to live for Woodrow. And Ben. Please don't let me die, doctor."

Damn these women who always look so pitiful, he thought to himself. Like a heifer having her first one, that's what she looks like and who can stand to see a heifer suffer?

"Oh, a second baby is no trouble. Never lose a Mama with a second one. This one's not going to be a big one like Woodrow, thank heavens. Now you lie still and try to relax, by God," he soothingly talked to her.

His big voice and walrus moustache did not frighten her, for she knew that he loved helping the sick even though he was not a graduate of medical school. She had seen him doctor cows and horses with the same compassion he felt for humans and she felt as safe in his care as if he had been a graduate of Trinity Methodist.

"Did you know that Leonard is going to marry Eva Morton right away?"

"I've heard rumors to that notion. Why?"

"I just learned it. I can't understand why Eva hasn't told me. She's always been my closest friend."

"Maybe there's a reason."

"I know there's a reason. But what is it? That's what I want to know."

"Well, if it'll ease your mind, I'll tell you this much. But if you quote me, I'll just deny I ever said any such thing and that you were out of your head and just thought I said it. Understand?"

She nodded her head affirmatively, bit her bottom lip and hugged the counterpane until the pain eased.

"She's in the same predicament that you were in when you married Ben. Only thing her Papa threatened to put a gun to Leonard's stomach and pull the trigger if a wedding didn't come off and very soon, too. And if I do say so, I'm damned glad. A man like that going around and getting every pretty girl in the community pregnant, be better off married. Maybe she can keep him home nights and we'll all be better off. Now put that in the back of your mind and try to forget where you heard it. Understand, girl?"

"You're right, doctor."

"Right? About Leonard?"

"No. Right about this baby. It isn't going to take long. Not long at all."

He threw back the sheet and counterpane, rubbed her stomach gently, and contemplated for the thousandth time the mystery of birth and death. How young and innocent and lovely they rush into marriage. Glibly. Blindly. Unprepared. Expecting love and roses. And the husbands come like black widows on the prowl. Taking. Taking. Taking. Using their bodies. Leaving them pregnant, and in childbirth alone, a little sweating, a few cigars. That's all he thinks is expected of himself and all he gives. While these give and give and give and are old long before their time. Bodies worn out with giving and childbearing and the man still stays youthful, ready to prance and prowl and howl right through his forties and fifties. True in animals. True in men. Where is that damn woman with the hot water?

The pills he had given Ella had taken effect and though she was awake, she was not in control of her mental faculties and when he told her the child was still born, she thought, "I don't really care. I'll worry about that some other time. I don't think I care at all," and in a few minutes she heard a tiny weak cry and thought, "Why, that's a baby crying. I must have imagined he said it was still born. I know that's a baby crying."

She opened her eyes and saw her mother-in-law bathing the baby and thought, how silly I am today. My baby is alive after all. The baby is alive.

"You gotta girl this time, young woman? How do ya like that?" and he continued to press rhythmically on her stomach until the after birth passed.

"A girl. Is she alright?"

"She a mite tiny. But with plenty of good ninny, she'll be okay, I reckon."

Later she would ask him if she had heard him say the child was dead. Surely she couldn't have imagined it, but then he had said it was alright. Perhaps she was still confused.

Silhouetted in the dimly lit room, Ben sat beside the bed and observed the newborn baby lying beside her mother. Why is it so lethargic? Don't new babies scream? He remembered how Woodrow had been heard all over the house, day and night. How curly her hair is when wet with perspiration. A girl! A pain of disappointment had filled his throat and chest when the doctor had told him, but it had lasted only a few moments. Then he realized he was grateful the baby was alive. How easily it could have died. And Ella too, for that matter.

With an air of indolence, Ella opened her heavy eyes and saw Ben sitting with tired shoulders and clasped hands, a deep furrow running straight up from his nose into his forehead. It was the first time she had seen her baby and she pulled the quilt away from her and looked her over, holding her minute foot in the cradle of her hand. The baby slept soundly in spite of the mother's turning and twisting her, fondling each tiny ear and caressing her fine hair.

"She's so little, she seems like a doll, don't she Ben?"

He nodded but did not rouse from his concentrated study of the newborn one.

"Dr. Kellum said she was going to be fine even if she is little. You don't mind too much that it's a girl, do you, dear?"

Again he nodded.

"Are you feeling worse, dear. You don't look well at all. I almost forgot to tell you. I made you an appointment with Dr. Bradshaw for tomorrow afternoon. I was going to keep the store for you, but I want you to go anyway. Pa will keep the store if you ask him. I doubt Mother will leave the house now that there's a baby in it. Please go."

"I'm afraid to, little mother. I'm afraid he'll say I have to go to a sanatorium. But I will if you'll feel better. I'm not promising anything else though."

The fear of what Dr. Bradshaw might say was not the only fear he felt, but it was the only one he could put in words at the moment.

—Chapter 11—

A MONTH WENT BY and still the baby did not cry aloud or gain any weight. Occasionally she would make a soft whimpering noise and fret, but most of the time she lay very still, the only sign of movement being the opening of her almost transparent eyelids, which opened to reveal pale blue eyes that misted over but did not shed tears. Something about the baby reminded one of an old woman, perhaps the fact that the pupils of her eyes were bottomless and very large. She nursed for only a few minutes before falling asleep with fatigue and Ella would have to shake her gently to wake her, put the nipple back in her mouth, and start her nursing again. Some days she nursed so little that Ella's breasts were aching with milk. She would empty them and give the milk to the cats.

When her mother had come to see the new baby, she had whispered to herself, "Dear God, no!" It soon became apparent to everyone except Ella that something was very wrong with the infant. She continued to nurse and feed it sugar water, croon to it and rock it just as she had with Woodrow, but Ben came less and less often to look at her and he told Ella than until she regained her strength he would sleep across the hall. Sometimes the width of a hall is as wide as the width of the ocean, so hard is it to cross and thus it became with their hall again. Occasionally they exchanged pleasantries at the supper table over their second cup of black coffee, but as soon as the cup was empty, he went back to the store and she up to her bedroom. Often times Ella thought that she detected the odor of whiskey on his breath, but she was too engrossed with the baby to get involved with any other worry. Anyway, why should he go back to drinking? He had said that Dr. Bradshaw said he did not have consumption, but rather a growth on his lungs that might allow him to live for years, and she did not question the validity of Ben's words.

As she started upstairs, Woodrow pulled at the hem of her skirt strongly.

"Mama?"

"Yes, darling?"

"I'm your baby, too."

"I know you are sweetheart," and she stooped and hugged him tightly against her painfully milk filled bosom.

"Can I come up now and sit in your lap, too?"

"Well, I don't know about that. You can come up, but maybe you'd better just stand beside Mama."

This scene was tearing Mrs. Simpson's heart strings and she immediately interceded for the little boy.

"It isn't time to nurse the baby yet, is it dear?"

"Well, I don't rightly know when the time to nurse her is. She eats so little. I thought if she was awake I'd try her again though."

"Let me go up and give her a little sugar water then. You take Woodrow and go to the store for a while. You haven't been out of the house for a moment. I'm going to get Ben to drive you over to your Ma's for the day tomorrow. You need to start getting out again."

Ella started to protest, but Mrs. Simpson simply shooed her out of the kitchen. She stood on the narrow porch that connected the kitchen to the main part of the house and felt as if she were standing at the a gateway of Nowhere. Where now, if not to the baby's room? Where now?

He tugged at her skirts.

"Can I be with you now, Mama?"

"You certainly can be, darling. You're Mama's very first love. Baby sister is so little that Mama has to tend to her very carefully, but she'll be a growing any day now and we'll take the buggy and go visit our other Grandma. That'll be fun again, won't it?"

Tears spilled from her eyes as she realized how much she had pushed him aside during the past month. He had been at her side all of his life and suddenly he was left out of her world and his own castle had collapsed. Together they would have to try and rebuild it, she told herself as she held his hand tightly and decided to walk over to the store with him and sit a spell.

Loud masculine laughter greeted her long before she reached it, and she knew that someone had just told a rank joke, but when she reached the lantern lit doorway she saw instantly that they were having their semiannual spitting contest. She had forgotten all about it. A tin can with a little sand in the bottom was sitting on the top of the stove and the men had to stand behind a line drawn midway the store and chew their tobacco until they had a mouth full of spittle and then try to hit the can. Of course, most of them missed and it ran down the hot sides of the heater, much to the delight of all of the other men. Occasionally one of them would hit it right in the middle. Ben always gave a ten pound bag of flour to those who hit the can. When he saw her and the boy standing in the doorway he came over and laughingly told them, "You'd better stand behind the counter. As bad as some of them are aiming tonight, you might get hit right between the eyes."

"I want to spit, too, Daddy. Let me spit too."

Ben and the crowd of men all laughed together.

"Let him have a chaw, Ben. Let him try it."

"I don't think so. He's too young to get the taste of tobacco yet awhile. He can wait his turn." But his words were not hard words of dripping with sarcasm as they had been in previous years when he had corrected or verbally chastised the boy. And he reached behind the glassed counter and gave the lad a big jaw bone breaker.

Above the heads of the rest of the men, one stood tallest and straightest and most blonde and Ella knew before he turned that she had picked the wrong night to come. She was not quite prepared to see Leonard face to face again, yet she also knew that it was inevitable. They would see each other regularly for

144

the rest of their lives as neither could bring themselves to leave this lowland place of birth.

"Let the bridegroom spit. He needs the bag of flour. Won't be long afore he'll be a needin' a twenty five pounder like the rest of us."

And the rest of the men joined the chorus until Leonard had his turn. His aim was as true as the luck he had with women, and the men slapped him jovially on the back until they almost winded him. One by one the men drifted out and went home, all except Leonard and Ben. Ella wished that he too would leave, but he continued to bake himself in front of the heater as if he were in no hurry to get home to his bride of three weeks. He had moved her right into his home where he was still treated as if he were a boy of eight, and it was only a couple of days before his daddy was commanding Eva as well as his own boy. Woodrow tired of playing behind the rice barrel and went over on the bench and sat beside Leonard.

"Do you have a little boy like me, Mr. Leonard?"

"No. I don't have any children. I just got myself married."

"Do you want a little boy like me? Mama says I near talk her head off."

"You're a real talker that's for sure."

And the question went unanswered for Woodrow but for Ben, standing against the cash register and looking at the two of them sitting there together, a big question was answered beyond any shadow of a doubt. Two thick blond heads, both with huckleberry blue eyes, two Normanic noses, the little one's an exact replica of the big man's, both with short stubby fingers and broad hands. No man on earth could have desired a more perfect child than Woodrow, he thought, healthy, masculine, intelligent, quick witted, good tempered in spite of his grandmother, and yet he was not the father of this boy. He had fathered that tiny mite upstairs. That mite that was doomed to idiocy, and in all probability would never speak a word. That was the seed he had sown. All the grand dreams he had while the baby was growing inside Ella had turned to cinders, and there was no time to rekindle the spark. He had told the truth when he said he did not have consumption, but he had lied in that the doctor had said he had plenty of time. In truth, he had said that he had cancer and that there was no operation that could save him. Only a matter of months, he had said, but he had wanted to live to see his own son born. And he had prayed to never know who Woodrow's father really was. It was possible to even like the boy as long as he didn't know. He realized that perspiration was pouring from his forehead, falling on his nose and dripping as if he had a bad cold. Ella sensed his great perturbation but did not fathom his true feelings or the reasons.

"I think we'd better get to bed now, Woodrow."

"Ohhhhhhhhhhhh, Mama."

"No ohs, now young man. I've got to see to the baby."

"Don't go just yet, Ella," Ben implored with a funny tone of voice.

She was justifiably surprised, for he had never asked her to stay before.

Leonard rose and without a word left, taking his jug of kerosene with an Irish potato stuck on the top for a lid and left.

They turned the lamps out together and walked through the pine thicket through the darkness together, the boy skipping and singing as they walked,

"Teacher, teacher don't whip me.
Whip that nigger behind the tree.
He stole money, I stole honey.
Teacher, teacher don't whip me."

And he chanted it over and over to his delight at the volume he could attain.

Ben took her arm and steered her around a mud puddle left by last night's rain and the touch of his hand on her arm was pleasant again. She hoped that it was pleasing to him, too. Perhaps the baby would show an improvement soon and then . . . but not tonight . . . She must get up there quickly and nurse the tiny thing. It seemed as if a strong whiff of unexpected wind would carry her away so delicate was she.

"Shall I heat up the coffee pot?"

"No. The coals are out by now. I've got some things to do in the shed before I come in, anyway."

"Alright, dear. I've got to hurry in to the baby now."

"Ella?"

She turned on the wood planked step and looked down at him.

"Yes, dear?"

He hesitated. She was so lovely still, all that golden hair piled up, her lovely legs showing in the newer styled dress, her skin glowing with vitality and health, the light shining at her back and playing tricks with her age. She looked like a fifteen-year-old girl except for her over abundant bosom.

"Nothing, I guess," he finally said sadly, and she had no way of knowing the futility of his plans, and turning went inside, hips swaying gracefully much in the same manner in which a snake glides, not with a quick jerk but with a slow gliding motion that taunts a being with its gracefulness.

—Chapter 12—

A YEAR NEVER BEGINS with the first day of January; it begins with the first crocus that pops through the cold ground, the first bud on the bare gray limb of the apple tree, the first hint of green under a world of brown, the first sprig on the willow tree, the cow having her annual calf. These things signify that a new year is at hand. The earth knows her time and waits, regardless of what day or month man marks on a thing called a calendar.

But even though the land felt the breath of spring upon its bare bosom, the days lay as dead leaves upon a slow moving branch in Ella's heart. She had known that morning when she saw old Doc's buggy tied to the tree in the backyard that something was amiss and her heart skipped a beat at the expectation of trouble. Perhaps Papa had a stroke. He had looked so white of late, and Mama was not looking any younger and with her high blood pressure. Surely it was not Mother. If she had taken sick during the night, Ben would have called her first thing. Pulling her faded hand made robe around her plump body she hurried downstairs and into the second sitting room. Doc was bent over the coals on the hearth, blowing on them hard.

"There is plenty of lightwood in the box, Doctor. We don't even try to revive the old coals. What on earth are you doing tending the fire this morning? Ben didn't put that job off on you while he opened the store, did he?"

Silhouetted in the early November morning light, he looked like an old booger, long beard on his strong chin, big moustache, shaggy white hair covering his head and neck, back hunched with work and the years, but knowing that his heart was one that belonged to his people, his looks frightened no one, and they accepted the fact that regardless of how styles of haircuts and years changed, Doc's would remain as it always had been. He shook his head negatively.

"I'll bet you've just borned a baby and think you're going to get some good sausage and grits and hot biscuits afore you get on home. I'm wise to you and your appetite. Has mother come out of her room yet?" Her voice was strangely high pitched, her conversation chatty and pointless.

"Hadn't seen her. Just got here and decided to start the fire before calling you. You're right on one thing, though. Ben Collin's old lady had twins this morning before day. You know old Ben. Lives on the Black Swamp road a piece down from town."

"I don't think so. Are they kin to the Collins here?"

"Same bunch. Just poorer is all. Said he'd send me a ham when he killed hogs. I told him he'd better. Weren't taking no shoulder piece to deliver him two babies. Needn't try to fool me neither."

When the fire flickered, wavered and finally started, he dusted his hands off, rubbed them clean on his trouser legs, and stood up facing her. It was going to be harder than he had imagined to tell her after all. He had carried messages of life and death for forty years and could tell of the going out in the same tone he told of the coming in, but the pitiable beatific look on her face took his courage. It was like a mad man snatching off a rose from an unsuspecting bush and not even taking the time to smell the bloom, just tossing it to the ground and grinding his heel on it over and over. It was like the rain falling on the river and not shedding a drop on the parched fields beside its banks.

"I made another call after I left the Collins, Ella, a most unpleasant one." He paused hoping she would ask where or why, but she waited quietly for the ax to fall.

"Word came to me to go as quick as I could to Lula Tyson's shack, but the last of the twins wanted to take his time and I couldn't get off right away. But I don't think hurrying coulda helped matters anyhow. Oh hell, Ella. By God you do know who Lula Tyson is, don't you?"

He was sure that all the gossip about Lula and Ben had not escaped her.

"Yes, I know her name. Are you trying to tell me something about Ben?" The voice sounded strange and unreal to her, but she was reasonably sure the words had issued from her own lips.

"Yes, I am and I'm doing a mess of it, by God. But then, it's a messy thing to try to tell. Ben's dead, Ella. Burned to death. Seems he and Lula were asleep and she woke up cold evidently and got up and poured some kerosene in the wood heater on the coals and the thing exploded. She broke a window light out and managed to save her life. Ben wasn't so lucky. When she got back with help, not a board was standing. I fixed her face as best I could. Nothing won't ever help her looks. Her face is ruined for life if you can find any consolation in that, which I don't think you are the kind who will, God help, but her days of taking other women's husbands are at an end. Ella? You heard me, didn't you?" for she was standing transfixed, unseeing and unhearing momentarily.

"Here, sit on the davenport. I'm going to fix you a dose of ammonia and I want you to drink it right down. You've got to hold up and try to help support Mrs. Simpson in this hour of trial." Ella let herself be led much as a child might have and obeyed his order to take the medicine. However, she felt no better after having drunk it. The only difference was the awful taste left in her mouth, which soon was dry again.

". . . Oh, God . . . Oh, dear God. Why hadn't she insisted on his coming in the house with her last night. Why had she put the baby first and gone on in? It was obvious even to her that the baby wasn't right someway, and Ben, poor, sad, intelligent Ben, had needed to tell her something. He called her name when she had stood on the step, and then had not told her . . . She thought it strange then that he had work to do in the car shed, but had not pondered on it long, so hurried was she to return to the baby.

Why hadn't she paid more heed to his needs as a man? She realized for the first time that she had given him no encouragement since the birth of their daughter. How many nights had he lain awake across the hall, turning twisting, desiring her, yet not willing to force himself on her again? Why hadn't she comforted him about the baby, instead of pretending that it was going to be alright, and picked up the pieces from there? What had happened in the past week that had driven him back to Lula? That was certainly a part of their lives that she had hoped was dead and buried. She had firmly believed that it was, too. Last week? Yesterday? Last Night? Last night? She had gone to the store, taken Woodrow? Had he antagonized Ben? Leonard had been there. Was it Leonard? But then she was sure that Ben had always known he was the one who had fathered Woodrow. Surely he had known that. Everyone had known that she and Leonard had been sweethearts. Surely he hadn't believed for years that she had let just anyone make love to her? Had it happened last night? What night?

"I want you to listen to me now, Ella. Are you listening?" She nodded as his voice went on and on.

"People are going to talk about this. There is going to be no way to keep it a secret, so don't try it. Talk about it yourself. It'll be better than keeping it locked up inside of you for the rest of your life. And don't try staying in this house to keep from seeing people. They're going to love you more than ever. Understand? Woodrow will never remember it. The one good thing about the very young, they can recall a few nice things, but conveniently forget the horrible ones. People will help you. This is a nice community for that. There will be no need for you to try to move to get away from things. Listen to me, girl!"

The look of blankness had fallen over her face again. She heard the words, but their meaning escaped her entirely. She looked up and saw Woodrow standing in the doorway, his long white gown almost touching the floor, his bare feet on the cold boards, and this part of her everyday duties brought her back to reality for the moment.

"I'll call Mother as soon as I get the boy dressed. Stay with us please. Please don't leave us right now."

"I'm not going any place. Got no place more important to go."

And that settled the matter as far as he was concerned.

Gertrude and Faye Ellen arrived in a couple of hours, and as was their way, they took over the arrangements of everything. Gertrude thought she ought to be the one to sing a solo, but Mrs. Simpson held out that it would be most unfitting for a member of the family to sing at a dear loved one's funeral.

"But who else is there, Mama? Honestly. These country hicks can't carry a tune in a bucket. I know sometimes I'm the only one on key in the entire church. And I do sing myself to death trying to lead them. I know sometimes they're a whole line behind me. You know how hard I try, don't you, Mama?"

"You sing lovely, dear. Yes. Yes. But not tomorrow. Perhaps we should send for Sister Carrie. She could sing for us."

"That holy roller! Honestly, Mama. You just slay me. Honestly. You know she sings the same tune to every hymn. Why, there isn't even any music written in her hymn book. We'd be the laughing stock of the community. Honestly. Don't you think so, Faye Ellen?"

"I certainly don't want her to sing. I know who could do it though."

"Who, dear?" Mrs. Simpson was open to any suggestions at this time.

"Why, Percy, of course, who else."

Ella sat quietly through all of the discussion until Percy had been suggested for the chore. At the thought of that fat, bald headed epitome of a lawyer Calhoon singing at Ben's funeral, she rose and revolted. He might be Faye Ellen's long sought husband, but he was not going to be the soloist at Ben's funeral if she had anything to do about it.

"I agree with Mother. I'm going to send for Sister Carrie. After all, Ben attended her meetings faithfully with his father until we were married. In fact, our first date was at one of the camp meetings. And I do know he liked her better than he did Preacher Cornaby, and he will be in charge of the funeral. She may sing off key, but she did like Ben and that's worth something. What do you say, Mother?"

"Excellent. My dear. Excellent. You send her word, won't you dear?"

After Ella left the room, Gertrude pouted and puffed and blowed and stormed at her mother.

"Well! It's pretty obvious to us whose side you're on. You could have sided with us for once, Mother."

"When I feel that you're right, I'll side with you. Not before, dear. And the day of dear Ben's death is not a proper time for jawing, so why don't you and your sister go in and stay with the guests for a while now. I'm going upstairs and relieve Ella from the baby."

"Honestly, Mother," Gertrude began as she began every sentence of importance to her. "You and that baby. It's perfectly obvious that it's an idiot. Why do you even bother? I do hope Ella will be sensible and never bring it downstairs. What on earth will people say? Bad blood will out, though. That's what I said when he married her and I still say the same thing."

"You haven't had your babies yet, dear. Wait until you do, before criticizing other people's. And as for the baby's mentality, idiot is a word that I absolutely forbid you to use in this house ever again as long as I'm living. Do you understand me?"

The girls had never realized that their mother had this much dander insider her and they were standing speechless looking at their own selves as she left them without another word.

⚜ ⚜ ⚜

THE BABY WAS RESTLESS all night and her puppy like whimper roused Ella instantly. She rose and lit the kerosene lamp again, unbuttoned her gown and put the nipple of her breast in the baby's mouth, for she made no attempt to nuzzle around and find the nipple by herself. Ordinarily the scent of the milk would have stimulated the baby to seek it, but even when she put it directly into her mouth, she pulled weakly.

"Please, sleep tonight, little thing. Please sleep tonight," she crooned to her in a pure soprano voice that irritated her sister-in-laws incessantly.

"Your daddy wanted you so badly," she sang on. "He dreamed you were going to be his little man, but God stepped in and you must have been his plan. We don't know why . . . We probably never will, but we're going to keep you and love you still . . . Sleep little baby, sleep for Mama tonight. Tomorrow may be dark and dreary, but you are warm and safe tonight." The words and the rhyme and the tune came easily to her. She might not have been as bright as Kate in her books, but she thanked God often for the small talents that brightened her own life.

She was standing at the white curtained window when dawn broke, still holding the baby to her breast, unaware that her feet were cold. Her eyes were red and swollen and burning, and she saw the first trickle of neighbors arriving with their picks and shovels and axes.

"Oh, God," she groaned. "The grave diggers. I had forgotten to ask anyone to do that. I wonder who thought to ask them to come," and she noted mentally that a cold drizzle was beginning to fall and she pleaded, "Not today, please, God. No rain, today. Please."

But her prayer went unheeded and the drizzle picked up in intensity and coldness as the day wore on. However, the weather did not deter the community folk from turning out. No one dreamed of ever missing a funeral. It was too good a chance to gossip to dream of missing.

The out of tune organ creaked and groaned out, "Jesus lover of my soul, Let me to thy bosom fly, While the nearer waters roll, While the tempest still is high." And for the sake of the family, Preacher Cornaby ranted about Ben's good points and graciously omitted mentioning his many sins and failings. But Sister Carrie did not disappoint the sensational seekers. When it came her turn to preach, she lit into every sin known to man and beast, and let it be known that she thought Ben had fiddled in every field. "But, I tell you Brethren, a pale horse came riding, came riding. And he picked the one he wanted. And you'd better know, Brothers and Sisters, that the horse was death and I quote from Ecc. Look it up. Look it up! And he ain't going to spare nary a one of us. It might be your turn this very night. Git your barns in order, and in conclusion I've been asked to sing. Listen well to my words. Listen well. You might never have another chance to darken the doors of this church."

And she sang six lugubrious verses while the congregation twitched and turned. This had been a little bit more fire and damnation than they had expected to hear.

Mrs. Simpson had been overcome and had not been able to attend the services. For this, at least, Ella was thankful. She knew that Faye and Gertrude were throwing meaningful looks at her, but she was well hidden behind her black veil and pretended not to notice. Perhaps after all in a few minutes I'll wake up and say, "Thank Goodness. It was just a bad dream and I certainly am glad it isn't true." I would be just like a lot of dreams she'd had before and awakened from with a wonderful sense of relief. Her mind was temporarily untrammeled and she heard nothing the preacher said. Mercifully grief had made her numb.

❧ ❧ ❧

WHAT WAS IT Doctor Kellum had told her? . . . People are going to be helpful to you from now on? Not quite, but something like that. People are going to like you even better. That was what it was and he couldn't have been more wrong. The very women who had been her best friends at church now looked on her with suspicion, and the men who had been helpful to Ben before now hesitated to offer their services for fear of catching hell from their wives when they got home. Even Eva, whom she loved better than her own sister, held her husband's arm a little tighter when around Ella. She continued to run the store, but the men did not sit around the heater for hours at the time as they had done when Ben was alive.

Even Faye Ellen and Gertrude did not come out on Sunday afternoons as they had always done since their marriages. They had been distraught to the point of hysterics when they learned that Ben had left everything to Ella, who soon made it plain to them that she would not longer be responsible for the debts they incurred in Ben's name.

"Honestly, Mother, aren't you even willing to try to break that damn will? It can't be much of a will when it doesn't leave you anything."

"I'll be amply provided for, my dear. I'm not worried."

"But what about me and Faye. Don't we get a thing? I knew that Ben meant the most to Papa, but not a thing for us? That's not fair, Mama!"

"My dear, the land was Ben's. So was the store, and he left it to his own wife and dear children. That should be plain enough for anyone to see and understand. And I have no fears whatsoever, but what Ella will provide for me well. Now, let's talk about babies. When are you going to surprise me with a dear little grandchild?"

"Don't knit any booties anticipating it. Babies are so revolting and cheap. Runny noses and messed up bottoms all the time and think how ugly I'd look. All paunched out in front. Percy gets all fired up about it every now and then, but I know how to handle him. I just cut him off completely and then after four or five days, he'll talk turkey my way."

"I'm certainly surprised at you, dear. How do you think you came into the world. By me simply wishing for you to come and when you're old like me, there won't be anyone to come and see you or even love you. You'll wish you had some little ones to call you grandmother. Why, Woodrow is the light of my life."

"You aren't telling us anything we don't already know, Mama," and venom dripped from each word.

"Well, dear. You have to live with your own decisions, but I do hope and pray that Gertrude and Ivan will be more sensible and have a nice family. Everybody ought to fill a pew at church if they're able, your Pa always said. You will try, won't you Gertrude?" Mrs. Simpson was most distressed to learn her daughter's view points on child bearing.

"Not if I can help it." She was a parrot of her sister. "And even if I had planned to before, one look at that, that . . . that baby upstairs would have changed my mind for good. It might just possibly come from our side of the family. Are there any others like it on our side that you know of, Mama?"

"Well. I don't guess you do remember your Papa talking about it, but he had a sister that lived to be fifteen and she never spoke or walked. I do pray to God in Heaven that Ben's poor little one will not be that bad off. Poor Ella if it is. However, when you come right down to it, I don't know a family tree anywhere that doesn't have something like that in it. You just can't use that as a reason, dear. If God intends for you to have normal babies, you'll have them. You'll just have to depend on His judgment, that's all."

"Well for right now, Mama, I'm going to depend on my own judgment and that's all there is to it. How did you happen to learn about Mrs. Wilson?

"The conductor told Ella about her and she's so wonderful with the baby. I don't know how we managed before we had her. And what with Ella at the store all the time. Maybe it's a blessing in disguise that her milk went dry. If it hadn't she'd have insisted nursing it even if she had to run back and forth from the store to the house."

"Well. I do hope that's all the conductor's been telling her." Faye Ellen couldn't resist this underhanded jibe because even Percy commented on Ella's loveliness occasionally when he dared.

"What on earth do you mean by that? There's not many men nicer than old Mr. Barnes."

"Why, I mean Ella, of course. She's still very young. And

men seem to find her quite nice to look at, though heaven knows
she's certainly on the fat side to my notion. I don't intend to let
marriage get me looking like that. And what with brother dead,
it won't be any time before she'll be sporting again. I do hope
she'll let brother get cold in the ground before she cuts loose."

"If you had a few babies to occupy your time, you wouldn't
have time for such foolish idle gossip, mean gossip at that. Ella's
a dear sweet child. Ben couldn'ta done better if he'da scoured
the world. And so smart! Why she runs that store just like Ben
did. Everybody says so. I do hate for her to have to pump gas,
but then there isn't too many calls for that. How does Percy like
his new Ford?"

"He likes it fine. Personally I think it's sorta cheap. I tried
to talk him into getting a Lincoln like Ben's, but he said a Lincoln
wasn't practical and the Ford was so economical. Still, I guess
it's better than a buggy if it comes down to that."

"I'm sorta glad I lived my life before these autos took over.
There's no need for getting everywhere faster. It doesn't give a
body time to think what you're going to say when you get there.
And the horse isn't a friend anymore. He's just a horse. I don't
know that I like that part of it. If Ella was to take my advice, I'd
have her sell Ben's in a flash. It's not doing anybody any good
sitting there. She can't drive and I know I certainly can't."

It was a grubby handed, dirt smeared little boy who came
into the siting room and pleaded his case.

"Grandma? Can I please have one of your good rolled out
cookies? Not the fat puffy ones. A big flat one. Please?"

Mrs. Simpson welcomed the pleasant intrusion, which put
an end to the most unpleasant conversation with her proud
daughters. She had always had a lot of pride, but she had not let
it separate her from the masses or the problems of everyday
living. Perhaps there was no one to blame for the girls now but
herself. It was times like these that she needed Ben's strong
willed person to lean upon.

❧ ❧ ❧

THERE HAD BEEN MORE than a ring of truth in Faye Ellen's words about the way in which men now looked at Ella. They had thought her lovely before. Lovely and safely married to the most prominent man in the community. Now they thought her lovely and unmarried, and new thoughts entered their minds when they looked at her. They hoped when she handed them their change that she would lean over a little father so that they could get a good peep down the neck of her dress, or that she would brush by them closely so that her hips would touch them in the little aisle between the feed and the flour and meal, or even that her hand would lay in theirs just a moment longer than in their neighbors'.

And she was not oblivious to their attentions. She was not a hypocritical person in that she pretended to go on grieving openly for Ben. There had been good days and bad days with him, but Ben was gone now. She did not even blame him for the shame he had brought upon her in the way of his death. For that incident, she wholly accepted the fact that she had driven him to it. Perhaps she did not comprehend the exact way in which she had accomplished it, but nonetheless, she accepted the fact that it had to have been her fault. And perhaps the time would come when someone could love her and accept her two children. Unless they could accept the second one as willingly as they did the first, they need not nourish hope of winning her. The hard work at the store helped her to exhaust herself physically, which was necessary for sleep for her. She had leased the land to her father on halves and it was a relief to her mind to know that it would be well tended. If the winter had been her hardest one, one wonderful thing had come out of it. Kate had found an ardent suitor. Ella did not realized that Kate had not accepted dates as long as Ben had lived, but immediately after his death had accepted a date from Bernard World, the hog feed salesman. She had been going to church and prayer meetings with him regularly since. This alone was a miracle.

Ella prayed that Kate would bite her tongue often enough that he would not get discouraged and it seemed now that her prayers were being answered. And in Kate's own new found happiness she was kind to Ella and her children for the first time and did not seem to resent their coming home as she had before meeting Bernard.

As for Bernard, he was neither handsome nor ugly, rather an in between kind of man, one that a person couldn't describe two hours after having met him. Perhaps the word slick clung to him best. And he did own his Model T six passenger Ford and he wore white shirts with real cloth collars. That should have impressed most anyone.

Kate had forbidden her parents to let him know that she slopped the hogs or milked the cow, because when he came courting she pretended to be enormously frightened of all animals, living or dead. When they walked out to look at Pa's hogs, she climbed on the edge of the pen and squealed with mock terror when the male hog walked over near her. Bernard took her by the waist and lifted her down beside him while he patted her arm to quiet her fears. When a woman is not pretty, there must be other ways in which to capture a man. And oddly they seem to be as effective as beauty. Mrs. Horne watched this scene hopefully from the open kitchen window and said a silent prayer that a marriage would come of this relationship. No woman needs to be an old maid. Man plus woman, that's what life is all about. It don't take an educated fool to explain that to a body. And man plus woman means babies and that's the turn of nature for sure. At least Kate was being wise enough not to let on how smart she really was. That alone would have frightened most any man.

The following Sunday was a dinner-on-the-ground service and every member of the congregation was present at such affairs. The preacher closed his fire and brimstone service a little quicker than usual and the women hurried out of the church and began bringing their boxes of food out of their cars and carts, such as their lot in life permitted them to possess. They proceeded to spread their very best table cloths over a wire table and set out the most delectable vittles in the land. Irish potato salad and candied yams, coconut cake, baked hams, fried chicken and bowls of rice were set the length and breadth of a fifty foot table and the men stood impatiently by and watched the proceedings, their mouths watering and their minds full of hope that the preacher would not pray a long winded blessing. It was an unspoken rule that Ella and Mrs. Simpson had the places at the head of the table. After all, Mr. Simpson had been the head of the church for almost thirty years. The poorer the family, the further down the table was the father's place. It was near the end that Leonard and Eva spread their faded cloth, and Eva set her vittles on a cotton spread. They were not particularly troubled by other members coming and sampling their vittles. The cruelty of the poor to the poorer exceeds that by far of the rich to the poor.

At the conclusion of his shorter than expected blessing, Preacher Cornaby took off his spectacles and wiped them with his white monogrammed handkerchief and cleared his throat.

"Fellow Members, I have an announcement to make that gives me great great pleasure. I have been asked to announce that Miss Kate Horne and Mr. Bernard World will be married next Sunday here in our own little house of God, and they wish to cordially invite every one of you to be here. I know we won't want to miss this happy occasion. You may eat now."

The announcement came with such shock to most of the congregation that their appetites were momentarily stunned. They had known that she was receiving a beau, but it had been such a short time. In the minds of many the question arose: Is it a matter of a shotgun affair. Can it be real love already? But here was not the place for the questions and there was so much delicious food just awaiting to be eaten.

—Chapter 13—

THE OLD LINCOLN CONVERTIBLE was now nine years old, and the cloth top had rotted away completely so that Ella usually did not take the car out on a cloudy day. Just in case an unexpected shower caught her out unaware, she carried an old piece of canvas in the back seat. Now it looked as if she and Woodrow were going to have to pull off the road, stop, and get under the canvas any minute now.

She had decided that the opinion of the people in the community was not high of her anyway so why pamper their nasty tongues by letting the car rot away while she paid a train fare every week to and from town to buy supplies for the store. She had run into a few ditches, killed a few chickens, lamed two dogs, and killed one cat learning to steer it. She had even run right through the back end of the car shelter and on out into the clover on her first try, but she did not intend to let this mechanical monster lick her. If she could drive a horse, she could steer a car. And even Mother frequently said now that she was a much safer driver than Ben had ever been.

They turned off on the Pumpkin Center Road, trying to beat the approaching rain by taking a short cut. They crossed Deep Bottom Branch and turned the corner in a whirl of dust, but the cloud was traveling faster than they were, and she pulled up under a big oak beside Haw Creek and crawled under the canvas on the back seat. Lightning flashed and thunder rolled around the sky for a short while. Big drops of rain pelted them as hard as if it had been mixed with hail, but it was soon over and the ground was steaming and drying off. Ella and Woodrow emerged from the soaked canvas looking like a couple of moles coming out for the first time that day. They shook themselves like a couple of hounds in front of a good hot fire.

"I'll be might surprised if this thing starts now. I'll bet it's wet as water clear through."

"Let me turn the crank, Mama, please."

"Maybe I'd better do it. You might let it fly back and break your arm. I don't know how I'd manage if you had a broken arm, son. You're Mama's most faithful helper."

And indeed the eight-year-old boy could almost do the work of a man. If the neighborhood thought it funny that he did not have a build like either Ella or Ben, she did not know or care any longer, for it was obvious to her that he would always be the spitting image of his father. Already his shoulders squared away and his hips trimmed down like a young man's should, and his legs were thick in the calves and thighs, not thin as Ben's had been. He could put the rope around his neck and plow a furrow as straight as his Grandfather Horne and even though he could not handle the plow well at the end of the row turning around, that too would come with another year. Ella and Mother stood at the end of the garden row often and bragged about what a good plower he was while Ella turned the mule around for him.

His very existence had added years to Mrs. Simpson's life. He was the extra reason she needed for living. Neither of her daughters had produced her a grandchild as of yet and with the exception of Sybil Ray, now three and as helpless as the day she had come into the world, Woodrow seemed to be the only one she would ever have.

But turning the crank did not start the car, and she leaned on the side of it exhausted and tried to catch her breath.

"It's had too much gas. I can smell it everywhere. Maybe if we raised the hood and let the sun dry it out . . ."

"I sure do hope night don't come and ketch us here, don't you, Ma?"

"Catch honey. Not ketch. Your father spoke properly."

"Aw, Ma. Who's listenin'?"

"I am. That's who. And I think you'd better say catch before you ketch something you aren't expecting."

"Shucks, Mama. You know I hate school. I'm going to be a farmer like Grandpa. And you don't need schoolin' for that. He says so, too."

"Well, never you mind what Grandpa says about schooling. He's a mighty poor one to ask advice about it. Ask Grandmother Simpson and see what she says. The way to make money in this day and time is to get a good education. It'll be someday where you won't even be able to get a job if you don't have a high school diploma."

They heard the motor of a Model T Ford a long time before they saw it, and it was indeed a welcome sight for it was obvious by now that they were not going to be able to start it by themselves. As much as Ella had grown to despise Bernard World, even he was a welcome sight to see now.

He putted to a stop beside them and they were a forlorn sight to behold. Ella's hair was wet and curled tight to her head like a sheep's when wet. Puddles of water stood upon the worn out seat. The rusty hood was thrown back from the front end of the car.

"Now this is the kind of position I have been looking forward to finding you in. One in which you will have to ask me a favor and then I will say, 'But you never do me any favors,' and you will say, 'I will do you a favor if you want me to,' and I will say 'Eureka! At last. A woman of good taste,' and this will begin the most rewarding experience of your life."

"Please, Bernard. Drive on if you must be vulgar even in front of Woodrow. If you'd care to help us, we'd be obliged to pay you, though."

"Take pay? From a lovely sister-in-law. Indeed not. What do you take me for?"

"That I shan't answer as I need you to help me start this damn car today. Will you or won't you help me?"

"My dear lady, to help you has been my fondest desire since first I laid eyes upon your lovely face, but you resist me. Of course, I'll help."

"Careful. Careful. How can such language issue from such fair lips? It grieves me to see them slip between such perfect teeth." And he leaned over her a full foot and a half and looked down upon her.

"We were rained out, I guess," she stammered. "Then it flooded. If I could turn the crank harder or quicker, I think it would have caught."

"Elementary, my dear. Strictly elementary. What I've said from the beginning is that you need a man. And I've offered my services on numerous occasions, but you rebuff me. Your sister finds my loving quite to her taste and sisters usually have similar taste, don't they? That's why you perplex me, dear. Truthfully I don't repulse you. It must be that stuffy mother-in-law that causes you to behave in the Victorian manner. This is the freest era ever and the gayest. Don't you want to stay up with the times? Live modern?"

"You're going to push me just one step too far, Bernard, and I'm going to tell Kate everything about you. If you love her like you say, don't you care that she'd pick up and leave and never live with you again?"

"Leave? Kate? With her face, she knows that she is lucky to have found one husband and, furthermore, she would not believe you and then she would hate you and you wouldn't be any better off than before."

The truth of his words defeated her in that avenue and she steered his attention again to the automobile.

"I must get back to Sybil as soon as possible. You know she won't eat a bite for Mother. Will you please help us or shall we start walking?"

And as blandly as if he had never insulted her womanhood, he bowed and took an iron crank, leaned over her, set the spark, rolled up his white sleeves, flexed his muscles, and proceeded to the front end of the car, prancing as if he were about to enter a boxing ring. He gave the crank a magnificent turn and stood back to gloat over the fact that the car chugged, sputtered, and started.

"As I said, my dear, a man would cure all of your troubles. And you know my address. Good day, dear Ella." He bowed again and was gone as fast as his Model T would take him, leaving them standing open mouthed beside their own faded outdated contraption.

And as Ella drove the last mile home, tears of frustration poured down her cheeks, cutting rivers on her now mature face, tears for the time when the car was new and exciting and the thing of the day, the only car anywhere that had brake lights and a spare tire in the rear, tears for the time when the mere fact that Ben had been her husband had restrained men from making advances on her, tears for the empty pillow beside her every night of her life, and many many tears for the growing girl upstairs who would never walk or talk, but stared at them with eyes of love.

"Don't cry, Mama. Please. I'm your man, ain't I?"

"Yes, darling. You're the best man anybody could ask for."

"Uncle Bernard ain't very nice, is he?"

"He's not nice at all, but let's keep it a secret and not hurt Aunt Kate by telling her that. What say?"

"Alright, Mama. When I'm bigger, I'm going to punch him right in the nose for you."

"That will be wonderful, son. I'll look forward to it."

The boy had not understood the shallowness or the depth of the words he had overheard, but it was with an innate instinct that he felt the animosity aroused in his mother by the mere presence of Uncle Bernard, and he too bristled whenever he came around and he did not hesitate to turn down his offer of jelly beans.

* * *

"WHAT AM I EVER going to do about you, baby?" Ella asked as she leaned over the crib and put the bottle of milk in the mouth of the child who now was a long as the length of the crib.

Dr. Kellum had begged her the month before his death to

please not spend any more money trying to find help for her.

"Those doctors are going to take all of your money and your baby is going to stay the same, child. Just try to learn to live with her and, if you can't do that, put her away in the State Hospital. But for God's sake, quit throwing your money in the ditch!"

Still she had not heeded his advice and had taken her to Duke hospital in Durham. They had observed her for weeks and it had cost her over a thousand dollars, and then the eldest of the doctors who had cared for her told her sadly, "Take her home, Mrs. Simpson. And love her if you can. That's the only thing anyone can do for her."

"By why? Why my baby?"

"If I knew that, I'd tour the world telling every doctor in hearing and then we'd all know. Some are normal. Some are not. But you forget that hogwash about sins of the fathers visited on the children. I don't know a lot of answers, but I know that if there's a God in Heaven, he is not sitting up there making deformed babies just to punish the parents. And you try and believe it, too. Hear?"

She was glad now that she had asked Mother's permission to spend as much as it might cost to take the child there. Now that she had traveled every avenue possible to help her, she had resigned herself to the inevitable: Sybil Ray would never walk or talk or learn. She would have to be waited on as long as she lived, and the doctors had predicted fifteen years life expectancy for her. It was a yoke on her neck and when she stopped to think about it, every inch of her body trembled; therefore, she tried to keep so busy that there was not time for thinking.

Although she did not regret spending the money, it made her uneasy that she had to put a mortgage on the farm and store in order to buy supplies until the fall. This was the first time that there had ever been a mortgage on the place and she prayed that the tobacco crop would be a good one and that the creditors would be prompt about paying their bills come fall. Still, Mother had confidence that they could pay off, and if she could have faith, what was causing the tiny flutter in the core of her stomach whenever she thought of that paper with her name on the dotted line? And Pa had persuaded her to buy on credit from Bernard rather than running the loan from the bank. Surely nothing could go wrong with that between now and the fall!

Saturday night came, and one by one the local folk thinned out until there was no one left sitting on the warehouse bench with red letters which stated boldly, "Sell Your Tobacco With Us for the Best Prices in the South," all except Leonard. Since he had become a father three times over, he had grown a sandy colored moustache, which added several years to his general appearance. And although his father continued to boss him around like a six-year-old and begrudge every mouthful his children ate, he continued to live under the same roof with him and accept anything that his father was might to give him, which was mighty little. And nothing dampened Eva's effervescent personality. She bubbled right on as if they were not the poorest family around.

"The years shore are kind to you, Ella. You don't change a bit."

"I do so, too. And you change too. You don't look at all like the boy I knew one time." And her words were natural, neither warm nor cold, but the kind of words one speaks to a stranger so as not to be unkind but yet so as not to encourage him either.

"You know I don't speak well with words, Ella. Ben could do that, but I'm not very slick with them. What I wanted to say is you're still pretty. And I guess I was afraid to say it like that."

"Well. I thank you kindly, Leonard. True or not!"

"Why haven't you been to see Eva? You can drive and you two used to be friends. Don't many people come and Eva is pretty tied down with the babies."

"And I'm not tied down, I suppose?"

"I didn't mean that. But you are free on Sundays. The store is closed and all and Eva's job is a seven day a weeker."

"My job is never over, either, Leonard. Aren't you forgetting Sybil. That's a seven day a week job, too."

"Well, take her out, too. People are going to see her sooner or later. Everybody knows how she is and nobody is blaming you for that. Ain't nobody who don't know Ben cut up. Most everybody has seen her already and Eva would be so glad to see you again. You and her could chew the rag and sew and talk."

Ella wanted to explain to him the dim witted fact that one did not socialize with one's ex-lover's wife. Oh. Damn. That was all too complicated for her mind and she did not feel any kinship or friendship with Eva; nor had she since the moment Leonard had told her of their forthcoming marriage. She watched the flies buzzing around the cheese box and took the homemade swatter and killed some of them, shooing the others out of sight. The mosquitoes were coming in the door also, and biting her on the legs in spite of the smoke rags she had in buckets outside the doors. She wished that he would leave so that she could close up and get to bed—to bed if not to sleep.

But he packed his pipe after having knocked the burned out tobacco against the summer cold heater and lit it again and puffed and talked and puffed. Ellie had her back turned to him as she pretended to straighten the cans on the shelves. That's why she did not see him when he stood and reached up and turned out the gas lantern, immediately putting them in complete darkness.

"Well, I do declare. To be sure the gas isn't out. Maybe I can find my flashlight."

"Don't look too hard for it, Ellie," and he was standing right behind her, both of his strong long arms reaching out and pulling her backwards until she was pressed against his body. "Who needs light anyhow?"

"Take your damn cotton picking hands off of me, Leonard. This instant!"

And he held her in such a vice grip that she knew words might help her, but her strength could not.

"Why? When you know you need me. You've needed me for a long long time, but you just won't let yourself go. I'm not a boy now, Ellie. I wouldn't make love to you like an ox this time. You'd enjoy it this time as much as I would and who would ever know."

"I'd know, that's who. Please let me go, Leonard. You've just been sitting there telling me how much Eva meant to you. What ails you tonight?"

"I do love Eva. What's that got to do with us? I've always loved you. You know that."

"I don't know any such thing. Let me go. Besides, you told me at the grist mill that you had forgotten all about me."

"You didn't take that serious, I hope. I wanted to say something that day to hurt you like you done to me. You were so proud acting that day. In your fancy buggy, and your silk dress, acting all above your raising, the high and mighty Mrs. Ben Simpson. I knew I had to marry Eva or get a seat full of buckshot from her Pa and I thought to strike out at you. But Eva's one of a kind. She's good and gentle and loving, but it's still not like the eating inside of me for you. That's the same as it's always been. And I know it's the same for you, too. Or you'd have said yes to some of these other fellows who's been a trying to make love to you these past few years."

"And how, may I ask, do you know so all fired much? Perhaps I have been turning out the light other nights and letting men stand here and make love to me in this very spot."

"You might have. But you haven't. I've been a watching you like a hawk and that painful look ain't been eased nary time. That little hungry look around the eyes that a woman has when no man loves her. You know what I mean, don't you, Ellie?"

"No. No. I don't," she lied as he turned her slowly around facing him and bent until his lips found hers. The salt on them told him what her words had not, that she was bewildered and frustrated and still in love with him. He kissed her gently until her body ceased trembling and her lips sought his eagerly every second that he took them from hers. Perhaps it was wrong for them to lie on the very cot that Ben had slept on in the back of the store. Perhaps a lot of things were wrong, the conception of Woodrow, her marriage to Ben, the way Sybil had been conceived, the way Ben had died, the way she managed the business. Her life was full of wrong things, but Leonard's loving was the one thing that seemed right. Indeed, he had learned the art of loving and if anyone should have come to the door and knocked they would not have heard the knock or call, so deep was their absorption in each other. The things she whispered in his ears were things she had never told Ben, the things Ben had longed for her to say, things that surprised even her. He might go home, but he would not love Eva tonight. No man had that much strength!

✄ ✄ ✄

"NEVER THE MUDHOLE, only the sky," that's what Pa had always said about her, and it was true. And it is not the simple minded alone who dare to dream, for there are those whose names are synonymous with greatness who spent their lives in dreams, and out of these very dreams came their greatness. There are those who live next door to poverty and look above it and below it, but never quite squarely at it, never notice the ache in a small girl's eyes when all but her are clad in new finery and the sadness on a boy's face when he is the only boy who does not own a bicycle or who has to work on Saturdays and Sundays. There are those who clasp their hands in sheer ecstasy over the bloom of an African violet and who would not cross the road to save a sick sister, those who know the correct name for every cloud formation and spend hours watching the birth and death of the sunset, and who would not walk down the road yonder with a friend. Beyond. Beyond it all. Out of it. And who are we not to say they are the lucky ones?

The next morning she threw both bare arms above her head and smiled like the cat who had just licked the cream off the top of the milk, her mind a blank page of happiness. She would not look or listen to the words if they took form. She would not indeed let them take form. Instead she would crush each memory of last night, but she would delight in its after affects. It had brought a calmness to her life that she had needed desperately, a void had been filled that neither Woodrow nor Mother could begin to fill. All the ugly thoughts that wanted to rear their nasty heads would be crushed. I'm not going to let myself think about Eva. She's had him all of the time and I'm not going to think of Ma and Pa. They had each other. Or Kate, she had Bernard, perish the thought. Or Mother. Dear God, how mother would be hurt if she ever found out. But I'm not going to think of that. I'll just be more careful, that's all. And I'll probably pay the piper. I always do, but today I'm going to be wonderfully deliciously happy.

You can come right into my room today, mockingbird, and she hopped out of bed with the bounce of the very young, put a record on the Victrola ,and dressed while humming to the accompaniment of "The Death of Floyd Collins." The sadness in the song always seemed fitting with her own troubled life and she had shed many tears while listening to it, but she played it for another reason today. Sybil would try to turn her head and smile when ever she heard the music, and today she wanted even Sybil to be happy.

And pay the piper she did, but in a very different way than she had expected. Even knowing that the rest of the nation was in the same boat with her did not ease her pain. With the foreclosing of the banks, the last bit of her savings had been wiped out and Bernard had given notice that unless she could raise the cash in the near future to pay off her note he was going to foreclose, too, taking almost everything she owned, the house that had been Ben's birthplace, the store that had amply provided for them for years, and the big farm that surrounded it. The only possession that had not been listed on the mortgage paper was an old piece of run down land with an unoccupied tenant house on it that lay down the railroad a couple of miles, and if Bernard had known that she had owned it, there was no doubt that it too would have been included on the mortgage paper.

"What in the name of Heavens can we do, Mother? You know well that I can never raise that much money?"

"There'll be a way opened for us, dear, I just know that God won't let us down."

"Well, I hope he does something quick. Bernard isn't going to wait on God or anyone else for that matter."

"Don't let him get you to talking like that, child. God hears every word." The gray haired lady of the truest southern tradition whispered just in case He was near.

"Oh, Mother. I don't have your faith. When things are going right, it's easy to love God, but when everything is as wrong as it is now, I can't help but wonder if He couldn't have helped me if He had seen fit to. And I don't really care if He hears me say it. What else could go wrong that hasn't already? Ben gone. Sybil like she is . . ." She could never bring herself to say that awful word deformed. "The house, the store, the farm, everything about to go down the drain. You must hate me something terrible, Mother."

The old lady seemed to be in a trance, but she roused to come over and put her arms around Ella's shoulders and state vehemently, "Don't you ever believe it for one minute. You're the nicest thing that ever happened to a Mother. You've brought me more joy than the very ones I birthed. They were raised in my nest, but they flew and don't come back except to fill their purses. I've never said it before. I hoped you wouldn't say it either, even though I knew it hurt you. But I'm saying it now. You're everything to me, you and Woodrow, and Sybil, too. Dear, she's a part of us, too. And you wait. There'll be a way. I'll go in tomorrow on the train and sell my diamonds. The bottom may be out of everything else, but I know a man who will still pay a handsome price for my engagement ring. Ben bought it in New York. There's not another one in this part of the State like it. If it brings just a part of what it cost, it'll pay the mortgage. You're giving up too quickly."

Ella wanted to say that no one in town had the money to buy the rare solitaire, but she did not have the courage to stomp the old woman's faith into the floor.

She was standing in the dusty doorway of the store when

Mrs. Simpson alighted from the train and she could tell by the tremble of the woman's hands and the grayness of her face, that she had been unable to sell the ring. That night as they dried the last of the knives and forks, she tried to console her.

"Don't be so put out, Mother. I didn't have too much faith in your selling it so I'm not too outdone. Really."

"Well, I'm outdone. All these years I've thought it was a valuable thing. I've flaunted it in every woman's face I've ever met. I've sat in church for years under the right window just so the sun would hit it on the hour of twelve and make it send rays of light all over the church. And all this time, it's not more'n a piece of old glass. I could have sold a window pane for as much as I could have got for it. Not worth anything. Here." And she snatched it from her wrinkled finger. "I never intend to wear it again. I want it to be yours anyway, Ellie. When times settle down and people act normal again, maybe it'll be worth something then."

"You're just upset, Mother. You couldn't bear to be parted from this ring for one night, let alone for the rest of your life and it rightfully should go to your girls."

"Both of them? Ever see two sisters wear one ring? That'd be something to see, wouldn't it? And it rightfully should go to whom I choose. That's who it should go to, I say. Here. Put it on and not another word. Who knows what we'll be reduced to before long."

"I know, and if we don't raise the money, there will be no other place for us to live except in the tenant house. Perhaps you'd rather live with the girls, Mother, if it comes to that."

"If you move down there, I'll move there too. You aren't putting me off somewhere I can't see my grandchildren every day. Why do you suppose neither of my girls have had a baby yet? To be sure there isn't something wrong with both of them."

"Oh. There's plenty of time. They'll have babies yet."

"After four years? Isn't that giving them plenty of time? I've given up on both of them. Some marriage with no babies."

"Well, don't Mother." But she was glad the old woman had

got off the subject of the mortgage and the ring and onto her favorite subject. Babies.

❧ ❧ ❧

THE FIRST THING that the girls noticed upon arriving after their mother's unexpected death was that her ring was on Ella's finger.

"I always said you had the brass of Job, but to take Mother's ring off her finger before she even got cold, that tops anything I could have imagined. Honestly, Ella, you don't think we're going to let you keep it."

Ella opened her mouth to explain why she was wearing the ring, but before she uttered one syllable, Gertrude chimed in, "Well you may be wearing it today, but that doesn't mean that it will be yours, I can tell you that. I always said Mama's ring was going to be mine and I intend to have it."

"Just because you did say that, Gertrude, doesn't give you any right to it. Not just because you said you wanted it. I'm the oldest and as such I'm entitled to Mama's jewelry. Mama always said I was more dependable than you anyway."

Faye Ellen's bottom lip protruded and she pouted for a minute before reaching into her purse and getting a handkerchief which she used to dab the tears that flowed intermittently between her demands and her grievances.

Fools . . . fools . . . fools . . . thought Ella. What fools. What value the ring when here lies their mother.? Flesh is flesh. She lies here like no more than a piece of old clay . . . cold clay . . . and the words made cold chills run down her arms and legs. She hugged herself to stop trembling and wondered, am I grieving for Mother or am I frightened that the death leaves no one in front of me to die next? When I was little I always thought, there's lots of time before God will want me. First he'll take Grandmother, then Ma, then me. Lots of time, but not that Grandmother has been gone a long time, and here lies Mother, there's no other generation ahead of me now. God will take me next or do we always grieve for ourselves at funerals. We make believe we are heartbroken over a loved one's death when, in reality, we are terror stricken that there but for the grace of God lie us . . . and the moss sways cold in the winter time . . . and the earth is damp and frozen, and the linden trees leaves are all fallen and dead. "Oh . . . Mother . . . I did love you, but I don't want to be dead yet. I've just begun to live. All of this that has passed before has been nothing. Leonard will never be mine, but I will never be without him. That's better, far better than nothing. Perhaps it's better you never lived to know, Mother. I loved you, but I can live without you. I don't know if I could learn to live again without Leonard.

"Mama, when do you think God is going to take Grandma to Heaven?"

"It won't be long, I'm sure."

"If I wait up, will I see Him come for her?"

"No. I'm sure He won't come tonight. Off to bed with you."

"I'm scared. Do I have to go now?"

Looking almost squarely into his eyes now, she realized that he was still a very small boy at heart in spite of his overgrown size, and had the instinct to know that what he needed more than anything in the world was to sleep with Mama. Oh, what sleeping beside Mama can do for us, even as we grow up and have long since been weaned. No other bed in the world has that same odor. No wonder the wild can find their own mothers in the forest. Woodrow lay between the very white sheets that smelled of homemade soap and rose perfume, and knew that before long, she would come and he could curl up beside her and put his arm around her stomach, and she would press his hand gently and say, "Are you Mama's man?" And he would answer, "You know I am." And they would both go to sleep contentedly.

During the funeral services, the organ grunted and groaned its usual dirges, and Preacher Cornaby ranted for a full hour, and of all times, a funny bubble moved around in Ella's tummy. I do hope I don't have colic today, not here and now. She put her hand to the spot and rubbed it and the bubble disintegrated and died away only to be born again a few minutes later. I'm going to be sick, she thought, all this sitting up at night and Mother dead and the mortgage. I'm going to be mighty sick were her last waking thoughts before she crumpled to the floor. The woman next to her moved aside to let her fall rather than try to catch her and let her down easily.

"No one sent for me, but I took it on myself to come and see if there wasn't something I could do? The good looking doctor told her that night. The poor Humphrey boy had finally made it through medical school and had come home to try to fill Dr. Kellum's shoes, but the community was slow to open its arms and purses to him. Perhaps if he grew a moustache, Ella thought. At least he'd be like Doc in one way then, for he was a real made medicine man, not a self-learned one like old Doc with his coffee grounds and molasses for the measles, ash tea for a spring tonic, sassafras tea for what ailed you in general.

"I'm obliged to you for coming out, but there was really no need. I'm not really ailing, just tired. You can be seated though." She raised a still weak hand and motioned him to the white rocker. Instead of seating himself, however, he walked over to Sybil's bed and stared at her. He had heard the neighbors' accounts of how terribly deformed this child was and he was amazed at their distortions of the truth. He felt that he had never looked upon a lovelier face in a child. Black ringlets circled her head and her complexion was the color of a pink sky right before a hail storm. Blue eyes looked at him uncomprehending and the compassion and the futility he felt in his heart were overwhelming. They didn't teach me enough, he told himself. They don't know enough to teach me. Why don't they know? With such an animal one would merely knock it in the head, but man has not come to the place yet where it can eliminate the deformed, the mentally ill. And from such intelligent parents? What was the reason? The answer?

In answer to his unasked questions, Ella volunteered the information he wanted.

"I've tried everything. Been everywhere. Spent more than I could afford to. They all said the same. There's no where else to go with her. And aside from that, I'm broke and hopelessly in debt."

"I know."

"You do?"

"Of course. Bernard has told everywhere that he intends to dispossess you and move in himself. We all hoped that it was a part of his endless bragging. Don't you have anything you can sell and meet the debt."

"There's nothing except the Neck Piece, and no one would buy that."

Ben's Daddy had jokingly named the small piece of land that because it was so poor that even watermelons grew knotty upon it.

"I wish we could help, Ella. But there's not five hundred dollars in this entire community. I just can't advise you. You'll have to listen to your own heart."

"Listen to my heart. My heart tells me many things tonight, and none of them are good to hear. But it does not tell me what to do about the mortgage." And she turned on her side and wretched until she was so weak that he had to support her head to keep her from rolling off the bed. After he had put cold cloths on her forehead he told her, "You have enough trouble to be emotionally upset, but you vomit like a pregnant woman. But that couldn't be."

He waited for her to confirm that the impossibility of that diagnosis, but her silence told him that it could be true. Lovely, lovely Ella. Pregnant without a husband. The women of the community would crucify her. This was the kind of thing they loved to get a hold on, and they hung on like a kid on a bull's tails, never knowing when to turn loose. How small her nose was, and turned up so that it reminded him of a little puppy's.

"You'll have to make your mind up that you aren't going to pay any attention to what people say. The baby is the only thing that is important. Think about him."

"Is that what they teach you in your fine medical school in Richmond?"

"That! Yes, and many more things."

"Did they teach you how to write letters to your sweetheart and tell her to marry someone else."

"Eva told you that, huh? But, then I know she always told everything there was to tell. And added some more just for good measure."

"She didn't make it up about loving you, that was real. And she'd have gone on waiting, if you'da let her!"

"There's a lot you don't know. People thought Doctor Kellum paid my way through medical college. Nothing could be more wrong. He stood my bond at the bank so that I could borrow the money to go. It'll take years for me to pay it back. The bank won't take a bag of taters or a blueberry pie for repayment. Even the best smoked ham in the county won't do. Just cold cash. You got any idea how I could support a wife?"

"She'da helped you. Wasn't that worth anything?"

"I didn't want her helping me. When I can support a wife, I'll get one. In the meantime, take it easier, and come into town to see me in about two months."

"Don't look for me. I won't have money for any doctor, the ways things are."

"Did I say anything about damn money. I said come to the office. Can I make it plainer than that?"

And she knew then that a lot of Dr. Kellum's blunt ways had rubbed off on his protege. She wished that he had lived to see him back here fighting disease and ignorance and poverty and petty women.

—Chapter 14—

THE DAY DAWNED BLANK and chillingly cold, not a glimmer of sunlight anywhere. The thick gray cloud threatened sleet or snow or a combination of both, and the ground lay frozen so that if precipitation fell, it would stick and harden. She lay in bed longer than was her habit and hugged herself under the thick covers that she and Mother had made. This was the last night I will ever sleep under this roof or in this room or on this bed. All that was Ben's and mine will be gone today when I leave—all except Sybil. She is all I have left of Ben. All the warmth and security that had been mine will be gone, too, and those who looked up to me because I was somebody will look down on me now because I will soon be a nobody—nobody with nothing, that's me. Not one piece of this lovely furniture will be mine any longer, nor will my beloved organ. Oh, what will I do when I can't play my hymns at night? I hadn't even thought about that, so many things not thought of. That comfort will be gone. Everything gone! Oh, God. My Babies. How will I feed them? Woodrow not even nine and Sybil, poor, poor Sybil. Maybe it's a good thing you don't know what today holds for us. You'll be just as happy anywhere we go, won't you baby?

"Oh, God" she moaned, and even while moaning knew that she must rise and pack what few things Bernard and Kate were allowing her to take with her. Not even Ben's precious books. She put her fist to her mouth and bit it and sobbed. Oh, I wanted Ben's books so badly. I wanted them for Woodrow. He'd have wanted me to have them. I know he would have. Not even one. Not even *Les Miserables*. She had loved that one well and read and reread it during the past ten years. I hope you fare well in this room, sister, she thought with bitterness. I hope you sleep well here tonight. On my bed, on my sheets, in my room. I pray to God you will be barren as long as you live. You're too mean to have a baby. You and Bernard both. Oh, God! Forgive me. I am the wicked one. And I do need your help. I need you terribly today. Where are you, God, when I need you?

If time could turn back and I could live over the minute in which I signed that damned note, how different, how different . . . but damn it, no turning back . . . I'll bet that's probably what Custer was saying in those history making twenty minutes. Time isn't going to turn back for me, and there is no way to go 'cepting ahead and I won't get there laying here in bed.

"At least it's not a cold house you'll be a going to, child," her Papa told her as she tied the ropes around her suitcases. "I got up mightily early and went down and made you a good roaring fire. I don't want to hear of you going cold now. As long as I can cut wood, you won't neither."

Poor Papa. All this had been harder on him and Mama than on her. One of their daughters was being put in the road by the other, and it left them straddling the fence. Mama felt that Kate could make Bernard let her keep the property and pay off the note as she could, but Papa felt it was Kate's bounden duty to go along with her husband's notions, not that he approved of what Bernard was doing. He just didn't hold Kate responsible.

"Oh, I can cut wood, Granddaddy. You oughta see me swing the ax!"

Woodrow felt that it was a sad day for his mother, but in his boyish misunderstanding, something new lay ahead, and something new meant adventure, and he was all for anything different.

"You're going to cut a foot off if you're not kerful, youngin'."

"Well. That about does it, Papa. There isn't much to take."

"I been wanting to tell you. I'm powerful sorry I ill advised you 'bout borrowing the money. Hope you don't hold any hard notions."

She knew he must be feeling deeply about the matter to

have offered this much of an apology. It was the first apology she had ever heard come from him and it left her powerless to speak. She patted his arm and swallowed a hard lump in her throat.

"Is the cart ready?"

"All ready and waiting at the back door. I'll carry Sybil and come back after the bags. You can go on down if you like."

"No. Let's go together. I can still carry Sybil easily." She wrapped a quilt around the five-year-old child and picked her up as easily as she would have an infant. She planted a kiss on the smiling lips of the child and whispered, "You are the lucky one here today, dear heart."

⁑ ⁑ ⁑

IT WAS BITTER COLD in the cart and the wheels jogged over the frozen ground, bouncing her around on the floor of the cart. Woodrow sat on a board beside his grandfather, while she hugged the small child to her bosom. I shouldn't look back, but I'm going to look just as long as I can see. I want it to remind me of what a fool I've been. I want it to hurt so much that I'll remember it as long as I draw breath, and let it help me to hate Kate with every one of them. Kate and that damned son of a bitch husband of hers. She wondered how Kate would feel if she were to tell her of Bernard's last proposition regarding the debt. Only two nights ago he had come into the kitchen without knocking, that ass of the man, daring to act as if it were already his house and home. He had chatted pleasantly for a few minutes. Then he had hemmed her up beside the stove, pinning her against the wall with both of his long arms, breathing his cologned liquor breath down on her face.

"There is a way, sweet and lovely lady, to pay off the debt so pleasantly. And you could go on living here forever. You and yours. All this and heaven too. It might take a few young years to pay it off. It might take only months. I couldn't say. But you'd be no worse off for the wear. Besides, it's just what the doctor ordered."

"Take your damn hands off me."

"I'm not touching you, my dear."

"Well. Get out of my way, then. I'll call . . ."

"That's right. There's no one to call, is there? Why do you play the virgin saint with me. I've been hearing rumors that you're not the virtuous organ playing woman you lead us to believe. If one man can, so can others, I always say."

"I don't give a happy damn what you always say."

"Tut. Tut. Tut. How such language ever passes such lovely lips, I can't figure out."

"Well, if you'd slopped as many hogs on cold mornings and nights, and run after spring fevered mules all across the field trying to put a bridle on her as many times as I have, you'd learn words to fit the occasion."

He leaned closer to her until his chest was pressing against her bosom and her back was burning the boards behind her.

"Can you say you don't like the feel of a man?"

"Can you say you like the feel of this woman?" And she raised her knee with a sharp jerk and caught him right between his legs. His arms dropped from their braced position against the wall like two broken matchsticks, and he doubled over in pain. He sucked in air like a hog just stabbed for the kill and when he could talk, he whispered, "You bitch. You be out of here by Friday and don't take one thing with you either. If you do, I'm coming after it with a warrant. You'd better believe I mean it, too."

"I believe you, Bernard. Every word of it. You better believe me, too. The next time you come after me, I'm going to kill you. No jury on earth would convict a woman for killing a son of a bitch like you. I've been sorry for myself with no husband, but I'm ever sorrier for Kate tied to a horny jackass like you."

Woodrow came in the doorway with an arm full of stove wood, and he felt the tensions in the air in his child's perceptiveness. As soon as Bernard had left, he threw the wood in the box and went over and put his arms around Ella's waist and buried his head against her.

"Uncle Bernard is a mean, mean man, ain't he, Mama?"

"Yes, he is."

"I'm going to kill him for you one day."

"Hush. Don't say that."

"I am, too, Mama. I lie awake nights thinking of what ways I could do it that would hurt him the most, like he hurts you."

"He isn't going to hurt us much longer. We're going to be free of him very soon. And one thing is certain, he won't come to visit us in our new house. I can stop him and I will."

And as the cart jogged over the frozen mud ruts, she knew that one of the things she was going to have to learn to do was use a shotgun. The old house stood near a water tank, and hobos frequently hopped off and slept under it at night. When she and her mother had gone to scrub down the place, there was evidence that they had even slept in the house. She was grateful that Ben had bought a good iron cooking stove for the house when the last family had lived there, and even though the top had several coats of rust, once scrubbed down, it looked serviceable, which was all that counted at the present. Mama had cried and pleaded with her to bring the children and come home, but there were more reasons than she could tell why she could not do this. Her pride would never let her be a yoke around Papa's neck and most important, Leonard would not be able to come and see her if she moved back home. Papa would never stand for that for one moment. Already the baby inside her had begun to make bubbling motions, but she told herself that no one had noticed it so far, not with full dresses and starched aprons. And if they had? Well, they had. That was all.

She watched the house disappear from view as they turned a curve in the road, and whispered, when I see you again, someone else will be living in you. Good-bye, Ben. The cornstalks were covered with ice in the fields. The cows stood dumb like, not having the good sense to get under a shelter, the peach trees stood like naked women, their arms upstretched over their heads, their trunks straight and firm, the pigs in the pastures they passed rooted around trying to turn the hard earth with their noses, looking for one last peanut from last fall, or one new sprig of grass, one anything to fill their lean bellies. Dogs barked at them as they passed different houses and they were a sight to bark at. A women huddled down for warmth, holding a big child in her arms, an old man huddled on the board and a chattering bundled up boy beside him, battered suitcases in the back of the wagon. Curtains moved aside slyly as they passed by and she knew but did not raise her eyes to confirm that every woman was looking at her descent and privately enjoying it. I'll be giving them more to talk about before long, she told herself and a smile born of despair, futility, and sadness merged into a satanic grin.

In spite of the fire burning brightly in the fireplace she had to hug herself continuously to stop trembling. Am I really cold, or am I just angry? She did not know and bent to turn the sweet potatoes she had laying in the coals. She could feel the cold air coming through the cracks between the boards on the floor. I'll kill us all, I reckon; we'll all die from pneumonia and then I won't have to worry about what I'm going to feed us on from now on. And the unborn one will never have a chance to know the mess I've made of things.

She said a prayer of thanks for her Mama who had sent over her oldest pots and pans and cracked dishes and discarded linens. I don't visit Mama enough. I'm going to do better about that, she thought as she put the frying pan across two logs and dropped in some smoked sausages. Woodrow was fascinated by this type of cooking and was underfoot every minute. Even the hot grease popping out of the black pan did not dampen his enthusiasm and they ate their first meal in their new home squatted before the open fire. Tomorrow would be time enough to start battling that old cooking stove.

It was not much after eight o'clock when she heard a soft tapping on the front door. My God. A tramp? A blasted hobo? Our first night here, too. And she tiptoed over to the window and pulled aside the flour sack curtains Ma had put up. To her immense relief, she saw Leonard standing there with a peck bucket in his hand. She was hysterical with laughter when she lifted the wooden latch and faced him.

"Well, now that you've scared me to death, welcome to the end of the track."

"Can I come in?"

"What a dumb question, Leonard. Of course."

"I been thinking 'bout you all day, but I didn't see no way I could come without raising too much talk. I brought you some vittles. I didn't know whether you had any here or not."

She took the bucket from him and set it down near the fireplace.

"I just brought ourselves and a few clothes. Ma sent over a little food. I reckon I'm depending on the Good Lord from now on to provide for me and the babies. No use depending on myself, seems like."

"Woodrow tuckered out?"

"Yes. He went right to sleep after supper. Thank God he isn't unhappy over our moving. I couldn't stand it if he had acted up. How's Eva Belle?"

"Middling good. You know she's pregnant again?"

"You told me. You think you're some man with two women carrying your babies at the same time, don't you? They put men on the road for less."

He leaned against the fireplace, spread his legs apart, pulled her between them, and held her close to his body. After a time the coldness left her and the warmth of his body flowed over her. She raised her lips and eagerly found his lips.

"I knew you'd come," she whispered as tears flowed freely for the first time today.

"How?"

"I just knew was how. I been a waiting for you in my heart every minute."

"I told Eva I was going possum hunting. I got my gun and lantern outside."

"Has she heard yet that I'm pregnant?"

"It was told at a quilting this week, but Eva blessed every one of the women there out for their nasty tongues. Said she wasn't staying and sewing on a quilt with women who loved to dirty the name of her good friend. She asked me if I'd seen you lately at the store and I told her yes, but that I didn't see any sign of any baby on the way. She said she knew it couldn't be so, and she hadn't mentioned it since."

"Well, the blame is going to have to be put on someone, that's for sure and some may point you out. What you going to tell her then?"

"I'll just say it's a damn lie is all. Can't nobody prove it."

"No. It can't be rightly proved. But people have got two eyes in their heads and they may even begin to notice how Woodrow is in the spitting image of you when another turns up just like you."

"You don't know. It might look just like you. With a nose that it could rain in," and he hugged her closer and kissed the end of her nose.

"One nice thing about living, Leonard. No matter how bad the day, it only has twenty four hours and then we have another chance. That's obliging of God, wouldn't you say?"

"Don't nothing dampen your spirit with Him? After all this?"

"Of course not. He's just testing me now, to see how strong my faith is. All these things are my trials. I know he's watching after me same as ever."

"I'll be God damned, Ella. You take a cake."

She pressed her tiny finger to his lips to silence them and pulled his head down again. All tiredness left her and she could feel her heart beating against his chest.

She turned the kerosene lamp very low and spread a quilt on the floor in front of the fire, and he loved her in the way we hope our children will never know we are capable of loving, the kind of love that is never told about in the lessons on bird and bees, for he loved her gently and strongly, the perfect merger of two opposites that every woman craves, and he fulfilled her own needs before his. He left her feeling clean and warm and happy.

She stood at the window and watched him go down the path with his lantern and gun and knew that life was going to be hard in this home, but life was going to be good, too.

—Chapter 15—

"WE TOOK IT UPON OURSELVES, you understand, Ella, to come and talk with you. We know it's God's will, cause we all prayed about it and felt a positive answer to our prayers, didn't we girls?"

All three meddling women agreed they had indeed prayed over the matter.

"And we know that you wouldn't want to be a source of embarrassment to your church any longer. And my lands, there ain't anybody that hadn't got eyes to see with that ain't talking about it. Now you understand we ain't going to ask you not to come anymore. That's entirely up to you whether or not you see fittin' to continue with the ones that tries to live God's will, but we don't feel it proper that you should play the organ anymore."

The woman, delighted at the sound of her own words, stopped for breath and moral support from the other woman.

And it came.

"Tell her the rest, Isabel. You know . . ."

"Oh. And we decided, only after prayer you understand, that it'd be better when you do come, if'n you do, that you sit as near to the back as possible. There's no need to flaunt before the young folk your condition . . ."

So far, Ella had held her peace and let them wander through their speeches. They called themselves a delegation from the church, but Ella knew how much delegation was involved in them. They had more than likely had a quilting party and dragged her over the coals and hemmed and hawed about the paternity of her baby, and had then conceived the brilliant idea of confronting her in the name of the church. She knew that all they had said was only leading up to the main reason for their coming. And she was not wrong in her assumption.

"And not meaning you, Ella. You understand, dear, but we want to help you. And the way things is, we just ain't able to take food off our own tables and bring it to you. Not even enough taters in the banks to see us through till springtime, but we don't intend that you go hungry. And if you'll just tell us who this scoundrel is that inflicted this condition upon you, we aim to take him to the law and see that he provides for you like he should, the rascal. We don't put the blame on you, Ella. We know you was took advantage of, and we'll help make it right. And everybody is not as broad minded as we are, are they girls?"

"Oh. Nooooo," they chorused in unison.

"So it all remains that all you have to do it tell us who he is and we'll handle it for you. We know you have your hands full here and can't leave poor Sybil for any time at all." And her breath stopped with a big question hanging in the air between them like Dracula's sword.

Please don't let me be a coward in front of them today, God. Please help me just for now, just for this moment. I don't want them to know they're hurting me. Please. I don't want any tears to show, at least not now.

"I'm sorry I've been a source of embarrassment, as you say, to our church. I guess I thought we were all going there for forgiveness, but it seems that I'm the only one that's been going for that. The rest of you don't need it for anything, evidently. I distinctly remember that your baby was a seven monther, Bessie. An eight pound seven monther at that!"

"Why, why, why, how dare you, you hussy. Jimmy was a premature little fellow. You know how pitiful he looked at first, don't you, Isabel?"

And though Isabel blushed she agreed that he had looked pitiful. They had to hold together now that they had waded into deep water, lest they all drown.

"I don't see anyone else staying home because they're pregnant. Is it the fact that I don't have any husband that is embarrassing, or should I say, delighting you ladies?"

"Ella! I told you we didn't come to judge, but to help."

"Excuse me. I don't seem to be able to tell the difference. Yes, I'll admit to you one thing. This wonderful baby that I'm expecting was conceived in sin, but don't the Bible say we all are? Yes, man, a man you're dying to know, was involved too. And I wasn't taken advantage of either. I want to be sure and put that in. I was just as much to blame as he was, and we didn't do a damn thing that night that all of you don't do when you crawl between the sheets. If'n you're not too tired, that is. Or too contrary."

"Let me tell you one thing. These is a heap of difference between what we consider our bounding duty, and what musta' took place that black night for you. We suffer through it for the sakes of our men, don't we girls?"

And the girls agreed they suffered through it.

"Well, all I can say is that I'm mighty sorry for the lot of you. I know mighty well that my name isn't on a wedding certificate right now, but I don't feel wicked in my heart and I'm letting that be my guide just like it's always had to be. If God had intended for it to be terrible, he wouldn'ta made two kinds of everything. Man and woman. That's everything. That's what we're born for and when we die we leave sons and daughters for the same purpose, if we're lucky."

"Well," The leader reported haughtily, "you need a heap more praying than we ever suspected. You not only are in a bad way, you ain't the least repentant. You better pray that you live through your coming ordeal. God just might take your soul for your sinning ways. But I don't feel no harshness in my heart for you, and I'm willing to forget and forgive what's been said here today, and I know the rest are, too. We must not let our tempers get away from us. But we can't help you a step till you go first and help yourself now, Ella."

"By that you mean, who is the father of my baby?"

"Of course."

"Are you prepared in case I might name one of your husbands

as the wicked soul?"

"Our husbands?"

"Why not? You called me a hussy, and I understand a hussy takes one and all, come what may, so tonight when you go to bed, ask your own old man where he's been when he stepped out lately. He might not be able to account for every single night, and then you can wonder if he's the one. Now get out of my house. It's not much, but it's mine and you came to see and you've seen, so get."

She could hear the starch in their best aprons rustling as they swept by her with their eyes straight ahead and their chins up in the air, but not a tear slipped from her eyes until she slammed the windowless door behind them and leaned against it and sobbed. She bit in her fist to keep from making a noise because Sybil was sensitive to crying more so than to any other noise . She went and fell across the bed and buried her sobs in the ragged quilt. At least Woodrow was at Ma's today and for that, at least, she was glad.

Why, oh why, had she said so much? She had not intended to say so much, but they had just kept egging her on and insisted that she name Leonard, and now they would tell everywhere that she said she laid down with any and every man, and each person would add more to it. Poor Mama! She had never meant to hurt Mama so much and she regretted that most of all.

And only a few weeks later their visit was followed by that of another malicious woman, this one her former sister-in-law. It was obvious that Faye Ellen had deliberately put her very best finery in order to widen the social position and Ella's fallen one. She wore a blue silk sailor dress with a big red bow hung at her hip and sharp pointed black leather shoes, and she twirled a black leather purse nervously around her fingers.

"I'd never a believed it, Ella. I had to come and see for myself. Percy said what for, as it didn't affect us any and wasn't going to cost us anything, but still I had to see."

"Knowing you, that's understandable, Faye Ellen."

"Well. It's not like you hadn't ever been one of the family.

I'da thought you'd respect my brother's memory enough not to put such a mark on the Simpson name."

"You seem to be forgetting the night your brother died, he was in another woman's bed and I had just born his child."

"Well, men will be men, you know that."

"That depends on whether you're talking about a brother or your own husband. If it had been Percy, could you still casually say, men will be men?"

"Why that's different, and you know it. Besides Percy would never stoop so low. Why he's the superintendent of the Sunday School in town now."

"Superintendents and preachers, too, for that matter, put on their pants just like the rest, and you'd better remember it, too."

"I wanted you to stop calling yourself, Ella Simpson, but Percy said it was still your lawful name, so I'll forget about that, but I do want you to promise me that when the bastard is born, you certainly won't call it by my brother's name. After all, sister and I have positions to uphold. Ivan is getting a bigger school next year, and with jobs scarce like they are, I think he's doing wonderfully. Just wonderfully."

"Well. What would you suggest I call my baby? Little Black Sambo, perhaps? Or Nicodeamus? Why, it's not the baby having Ben's name that bothers you, it's the fact that I'm lucky to be having the baby and you don't have one. That's more like it, isn't it?"

"I want you to know that Percy and I don't have time for babies. There'll be plenty of time later on."

"Well, I do have time. And plenty of love besides, and if Mother had lived, she would have loved this baby just as much as Woodrow and Sybil."

"I don't doubt it at all. But then you fooled her so completely, with your sweetness act and kindness all the time. You near turned her against her own flesh and blood and she would have forgiven you anything, even this, I imagine. I'm certainly glad she didn't live to see this shame brought on our name."

"Well, you can just tell people we aren't related, that we're the old Simpsons down the railroad way, and that you're a different set entirely. That won't be a lie exactly and it'll save face for you."

"I see you're wearing Mother's ring every day still."

"Yes. I don't think a diamond will wear out, do you?"

"You could at least save it for Sundays. You must feel real smart having both Percy and Ivan on your side about the ring."

"No, Not real smart. Just happy that they'd believed what I told. After all, Mother did give it to me, and it could not be divided two ways between you girls, maybe that's why Ivan and Percy took my side."

"I want you to think over what I said about using Ben's name, now Ella. And if you get to needing money too badly, I'll buy Mother's ring anytime from you. Just don't mention it to Gertrude."

She drove away in her Ford and Ella noticed that a few jonquils had burst through the ground, some that had been planted by someone else and had lived unattended. I just wish I were as happy and as brave about the baby coming as I tell people. Me and my big mouth. What in the name of God I'll ever do with it, I'll never know.

They had survived the winter with an old rifle that Pa had given Woodrow, who had killed birds of all kinds. They had eaten them fried for breakfast, warmed over for dinner, and stewed with rice and dumplings for supper. And the rice box was never empty. Leonard saw to that. I'm going to get a pig from Pa, a good gilt. Then we'll be having more pigs and more pigs, and we can eat good again. Maybe I can even sell one along. I'm going right over and ask him about it. No, I can't. Who would stay with Sybil? Maybe Pa'll be by in a day or two and I'll ask him.

🌫 🌫 🌫

AND IN THE NEXT TWO YEARS she added to the pigs one mule, who was very old and slow but still strong enough to pull the bottom plows and still capable of telling gee from haw, though she liked to act as if she did not know the difference; one milk cow, quite young and frolicky and capable of jumping the best fence Ella had, but she provided all the milk and butter they could use, besides having a calf every year which they could sell; and thirteen dominickle hens that alternately laid and set; and one very beautiful baby girl. These wrought noticeable changes in this woman who belonged to the land. Wrinkles came around the corners of her eyes, and her hands looked much like those of the men who still gathered at the store around the heater in the wintertime and sat on the tobacco benches in the front of it in the summer.

There are those who think North Carolina is all mountains and cool breezes, but those who truly know the state know that there is no place east of the Mississippi where the temperature rises higher than it does on the coast, and those not working in the field seek any form of shade they can find, come summer. Working the fields in the sun took a terrible toll on her once beautiful features. All of the beautiful dresses that she and Mother had made and bought were faded and worn and she had not been able to buy a single new one, but dresses were not a pressing problem. Clothes for Woodrow to wear to school and food for the children's mouths were the things that were important and she did not let pride stand in her way of obtaining them either.

When word came that all those who needed Federal Relief could come to town and sign up, she was one of the first ones there, and the boxes of dried prunes, raisins, field peas, and grapefruit were a God send straight from Heaven to her and others like her. They did not talk much to each other in the line. What could they had said? I have gone hungry. Have you? I am ashamed to take relief, but I have no other choice. How's things been with you? It was obvious how things had been to all of them or else they would not have been there. When things picked up a little and she could manage she planned to build herself a tobacco barn and raise a little tobacco, but it was not bringing a cent a pound now, and one could not raise it that cheap.

The years had also taken her father in death, and Bernard lost no time in informing everyone that he was going to be generous and let Mrs. Horne still live in the old house as long as she still lived, but that everything would go to Kate as she was the youngest child, and though Ella doubted the validity of his reasoning, she didn't have the money to force the issue in court and thought that the less involvement that she had with him, the better off she would be.

While helping her Mother make the cakes for the forthcoming quilting, Kate took the opportunity to spell her views on Ella's children.

"You'd let them tear the house down if they wanted to, Mama. Don't you every care that she lets them footloose the minute she steps inside this door?"

"Oh. They don't do bad. They're just children is all. Wait till you have some and I'll bet you they do just like Ellie's do."

"Well, God spare me from having any if they are going to act like barbarians like hers do. That Priscilla is a demon."

"How can you say that, Kate? She's your own niece, and she's a lovely child. She's just at the age that they're into everything is all. You'll learn."

"I don't want to learn."

"Oh, you don't mean that. One of these day you and Bernard will have one and . . ."

"You don't know what you're talking about, Mama. Bernard is as sterile as a castrated pig."

"Kate! Such language. How do you know that?"

"I asked Dr. Morton and he told me the truth of the whole matter. He's had syphilis and it left him completely sterile. Doc said it would have been dangerous for us to have any if he hadn't been left like that. The kids could have it, too."

"Oh, my! How terrible for you! I'm so sorry, dear."

"Well, don't be. We don't have any and we don't want any, so let's forget it."

But her mother read her deep hurt and saw then why her own sister's children antagonized her every moment. They were living reminders of her own failures, and she had never been able to face failure of any sort.

"Mama, who does Priscilla favor to you?"

"Why, she's the very image of Ellie when she was at that age."

"Oh. You'd say that anyway, Mama. I mean really? Who do you know around here that has that thick blond hair and big blue eyes?"

"Well, that fits a lot of people hereabouts."

"You know darn well who I mean, Mama. She's the spitting image of Leonard."

Her mother stopped beating the cake batter, held the spoon suspended in midair, batter dripping back into the crock bowl, and looked at her daughter for a moment, dumbfounded.

"You don't mean Leonard Johnson? That nice man?"

Kate nodded affirmatively and let it sink in her mother's head for a few moments before adding more fuel to the fire.

"But he's so helpful to Ella. She tells me regularly how he cuts her some wood and carries off the cow when she's in heat and the sows. And just the other day he carried her a mess of turnips."

"I'll just bet that's not all he carries over there either. Carries her something in his pants more likely."

"I won't hear another word of that kind of talk, Kate., about your own sister. You should have your mouth washed out with lye soap."

"Mama, wake up for God's sake. How do you think she got pregnant with Priscilla? Immaculate conception?"

"Immaculate what?"

"Like Mary did with Jesus. By God, I mean."

"God is going to punish you for talking about him like this, Kate. You do carry on so and it worries me."

"Well, doesn't she ever talk to you about it. About who Priscilla's daddy is, I mean?"

"No, she hasn't. And I haven't asked her and I don't intend to. If she wanted me to know, she'd tell me."

"Well, I know I'd ask if I were her mother. Me, I'm only her sister and Bernard doesn't like me to have anymore association with her than necessary."

"I should think that you'd want to be associated with her. Her with all her needs and troubles and you with so much. You could take her a box of food from the store anytime and Bernard would never miss it."

"And give it to her?"

"Of course, give it to her. You can't take everything with you when you die, Kate. Ellie's children are your flesh kin and they need all the help they can get. I bought Woodrow's books this year myself out of my egg money and you should hear him read. That boy's going to go places in this world. He's got a brain, he has."

Ugly red jealousy filled Kate's throat as she realized how much of her mother's love went to these children. If she could, she would have grabbed hold of all her mother's love, put it into a burlap bag, carried it home and hid it under her bed. Mama had no right to love anyone but her. Those snotty-nosed children didn't need any love.

"Well, I don't intend to steal from Bernard from behind his back, at least to feed her. I'm embarrassed enough to let people know that she gets food from the relief. Honestly, Mama. How did she sink so low?"

"Well, one way is that your husband stepped on her back and crushed her. That's why she's so low and you're so high. Take care you don't fall off the ladder yourself."

"You love her more than you do me. If you didn't, you couldn't say that to me." She flung the old accusations wildly.

"I love you both just the same." But Mrs. Horne knew that her voice did not carry conviction and she did not know how to make it sound true when in the bottom of her heart, down under all other emotions and hid from even herself and her own conscious, there lay the truth and the truth was that she did have a special feeling for Ella that she did not have for Kate. Yes, she loved them both, but not the same. And she was glad when Eva

Belle arrived early for the quilting and put an end to the unpleasant conversation.

Ella often wondered whether people talked and laughed less when she was around, or was she only persecuting herself in thinking this way. But, then again, why shouldn't she feel guilty when she was sitting only a width of a quilt away from a women whose husband lay in her bed nearly as often as he lay in his wife's? I don't feel hard toward you, Eva, for having him. It's his own fault, dammit, that he didn't have the guts to marry me in the beginning, and I guess if the truth were known, I'll never quite forgive him for that. What a mess we've made out of all our lives, all of us.

"Ouch, darn it." She knew that she'd better quit daydreaming or else the needle would go clear through her finger with the next mistake she made. It was a beautiful quilt top, one made in the Martha Washington design, and she knew that her mother had filled many lonely hours putting the tiny pieces together by hand.

Eva sat back from the others after a time, unbuttoned her dress top and took a breast that would fill a ten quart pail. She put the crying baby against it. He gurgled and half choked and half cried before settling down to contented nursing. The women stared, for it was a sight that warmed the hearts of all of them and made them a little sad that they were not the lucky one at the moment. Poverty! Lack of food! No money! Nothing to sell! The nation crying for jobs. These were all nothings when a mother looked upon a baby nursing. It made her forget all hardships and caused a pain of yearning and longing to prick the area around the midsection. It was unexplainable and it was also undeniable. Only Kate looked upon the sight with an insidious air. The young child intermittently nursed and played and the conversation soon turned full stream to babies.

"I do know, you'd hardly weaned little Thomas before he got here, had you, Eva Belle?"

"Why, I hadn't. But I soon dried up and he can eat a tater as quick as a grown man. He gets aplenty."

"Well, I just asked, because Ella still nurses Priscilla and she's over two, isn't she, Ella?" Kate's voice had an ominous sound to the two women in the room who had known her longest and best, and they wondered what she was about to drop on them.

"Yes, but I really have got to quit it. My milk's much too thin and watery and she don't eat like she should."

"She is a lot smaller than Thomas, but other than the size, they could pass for twins."

"Twins?" three of the women chorused together.

"Why I don't think they look alike at all, do you Mama?" Ella's voice pleaded for support.

"No indeed. Thomas's little face is too round and fat and Priscilla's is thin and white."

"Yes, but a little weight would change that. They both have the same blue watery eyes and thick blond hair. If I were Eva Belle, I'd keep my eye on you."

The laughs that followed were thin and shallow. Kate's iniquitousness remarks had found their way into the minds of all the women there. She had answered the questions that had plagued them for the last three years. Who? For Eva Belle they awakened new suspicions that she had never dreamed of and made her recall how Ella had loved Leonard fiercely when they had been young friends together. They had never doubted then but that Ella would marry him and she would marry her own Leslie. But when? Not when he went coon hunting for he always or usually always brought home a possum or a coon. Or when he went looking for the sow? Oh. These doubts were too silly to mention to him, but just the same, maybe she'd better keep her eyes open. Or should she keep them closed more tightly, her with four babies and a husband who was kind and hard working and loving enough for any woman.

For the remainder of the quilting party, she talked too quickly and too loudly in an effort to hide the perturbation in her heart, and she was immensely relieved when the last stitch had been sewed in place and they all gathered their babies and bundles and went their separate ways. Walking home with a baby straddling her hip, half pulling and half dragging another, and two small ones running ahead part of the way and behind part of the way, she was filled with anxieties: some of the cares of everyday life such as the guinea nest she should have searched for this afternoon, and the four o'clock seed she had planned to plant around the back door, and the supper that had not been started, but the worry that lay like a stone around a drowning puppy's neck was the seed of suspicion that had been planted that day.

Ella, too, lay awake that night and turned over in her mind the conversations of the afternoon. She knew that every woman there except her mother had been glad to believe Kate's gossip. I don't give a damn about them knowing about Leonard, but I really didn't want to hurt Eva. But am I being honest with myself? Am I just afraid that if she knows, she will make it impossible for him to come?

The oil burned low in the kerosene lamp and though she had long ridded the room of cobwebs and dirt, it still looked bare and ugly and unpainted and shadows danced around the corners of the room as if they were puppets pulled by strings. Some innate reflex caused her to look up at the manhole in the ceiling and a long black snake was swinging down over the foot of the bed. A scream came from somewhere, not from her surely, but from the depths of the unseen, or the bottomless pits of fear, but not from her, or else she would have recognized the sound of her own voice.

"What is it, what's the matter, Mama?" the half man child asked anxiously from the doorway.

But she could only point to the snake, her voice had left her completely. She had the presence of mind to snatch Priscilla up from the backside of the bed and hug her close and safely while Woodrow ran back to the kitchen and got his rifle, which he kept loaded with rat shot all of the time, and he was as proud as a man killing a buck when he fired and the long snake jerked convulsively and dropped on the foot of the bed, a long black slick thing dripping with blood.

"Throw him out, throw him out, son. Get him off the bed."

He poked the barrel of the gun under the still wriggling snake and carried him out into the yard.

Ella sank into the rocker where she hugged the baby and rocked and sobbed. Still the young child slept on through the frightening ordeal.

"I'm alone . . . I'm always alone when I need a man . . . and I need a man all the time—daytime to make me feel safe, nighttime to make me feel warm and loved. But I'm alone . . . all the time. Dammit, I hate being alone. I need someone. I need Leonard, but that can't be . . . too much water under the bridge . . . too much time gone by, and too many things in the way now."

The smell of the new turned earth filled her nostrils and the odor of burnt broom sage filled the room with the door ajar and she knew that all things were pregnant now. The cows, the sows, the hens on their nests, the dog in the yard, but not her, and a longing beyond all sense and human comprehension filled her to be pregnant also. The fact that she was unmarried, penniless, and had three children already were facts of truth, the longing was a fact of the heart and completely unexplainable even to herself. She hugged the baby again and knew that the child was really too large to go on nursing at her breast, but perhaps this would be the last baby ever, be the last one to draw milk from her breast, and she did not want to say good-bye to that part of a woman's life. Not yet. Not quite yet.

Long after Woodrow had gone back to bed and asleep she continued to rock and try to sort her incoherent thoughts. So deeply absorbed was she in her own self that she was not really sure she heard someone at the door until he repeated again "May I come in for a minute, Ellie?"

And she looked up to see Dr. Humphrey standing in the open doorway, bag in hand and a tired smile on his masculinely handsome face.

"I saw your light and door open and hoped someone would

still be awake. I had a flat down the road about a mile back and my darned pump wasn't in the rumble seat. I'd like to get my hands on the rascal who took that thing out of there. Mrs. Barnes had a big boy tonight. Eight and a half pounds if he's an ounce. "

As he continued to talk, Ella realized she was sitting in her nightgown and she pulled the baby up in front of her, but the man did not appear to notice her apparel.

"I really need to get back to town tonight. I'm halfway expecting one of my patients there to have her baby tonight or early tomorrow. Can I borrow your mule? I don't think my feet will hold out for four miles. They barked every step of the way here. I could send her back early by my nigger boy."

"Oh. Certainly. She's in the barn lot. Can you still put the bridle on one after all this time?"

"Are you kidding? I can still plow a row as straight as any man."

"I'll bet. I'll bet you wouldn't last half a row. Your city hands would have blisters as big as a silver dollar."

"Well! I know how much of a man I am in your sight now. I'll prove it to you the next time I'm out this way and you're plowing anything. Do all the people out here feel I'm a city doctor? Tell me honestly?"

"Well they did for quite a while, but I think you're winning them over. It'll take time, but I think a mustache would help too, but I wouldn't come down to that even to make them like me. They'll all have cars as soon as things are better. Things will get better, won't they, Leslie?"

"Bound to. Country can't stand many more years like these past ones. Roosevelt is bound to bring us out of it. The banks are open again. That's certainly a good sign. Are you making ends meet?"

"Well, we have enough to eat—if that makes ends meet— but never any money. If I can sell a hog now or then, we owe it for food, and I have to buy clothes occasionally for the children. Me, it doesn't matter, but I don't intend for them to wear rags. I certainly lost everything, didn't I? And you have it made for life. You were the wisest one of all of us. But I did want to go to school. You'll never know how badly I wanted to. But Pa wouldn't hear of it and look at me now."

"I'm looking, Ella, and you're still very nice to look at." She knew that he was looking at her gown.

"The mule is out back. We'll need her tomorrow, but you're welcome to ride her."

"That was certainly a quick dismissal. I'm not through talking."

"I'm sorry, Leslie, but you caught me undressed for company. I'd rather you left now."

"You women really kill me. Don't you think I've seen every inch of you when I delivered Priscilla? And you weren't embarrassed. But now you're embarrassed and you're covered from head to toe."

"Get the hell out of here and hush, Leslie. And bring my mule back early."

"To hell with the damn mule. I'm talking about you now. I haven't had a chance to tell you all you told me when I gave you the sniff of ether. You told me many interesting things. Wanta hear them?"

"I certainly do not. And you'd better not go all over the place telling them, anyway."

"They might not be bad. I didn't say they were bad. I said they were interesting. And you just leaped to the conclusion that they were bad."

"Well, were they?"

"Depends on what a person thinks is bad."

"You started this conversation. Now finish it. Either shut up or get out."

"You told me to get out. I was much too young. You kept saying that. You're too young to be here. I was flattered, you know."

"Is that all?"

"No. That is just a sampling. You told me about you know who."

"No. I don't know who."

"About Leonard. And about how clever you two were in fooling everyone."

"Damn your hide. You can't borrow my mule. Or anything else. You're the blabber mouth that's told it all over creation. No wonder Kate knew it today. You're some doctor. You're a louse!"

"Anything else?"

"Yes, everything else, but I can't think of enough names to call you right now."

"Well, while you're thinking I'll tell you something else. I haven't told a damn soul about it but you here tonight. If Kate knew it, Bernard must have told her. Men talk at the store, you know, and you can't hide something like that forever. So quit blaming me for what you're doing."

"What I'm doing," she gasped and stood up with the baby still in her arms. "What am I doing that you're not doing? What am I doing that all other men and women that you know are not doing? Maybe I do a little differently from most people, but I don't do anything new or original."

"Let me put her to bed for you," and against her protest he took the child from her and gently lay her between the covers.

"I always say that when bedtime comes, the rich don't have a thing over the poor. All one can do is bathe, put on something clean smelling to sleep in, crawl in to a clean bed and go to sleep. And when they're sleeping, they're not a darn bit better off than the poorest one of us."

"Oh, stop your fancy wording. You know what you just accused me of and now you're trying to get off the subject."

"That's exactly right. Let's do change it. And it was all my fault it was brought up. Will you forgive me this once and let me borrow your mule tonight?"

"No, dammit. I wouldn't let you ride my mule if you had to walk all the way to Jerusalem. And get out of my house and stay out."

And it was with relish she slammed the door as hard as

possible behind him. She leaned against it, her hand still on the knob, and tried to slow her breathing and still her heart, but she could not recall when she had been so agitated at anyone. Not even Kate could rouse her to such anger. Or was it anger? Of course it was anger! She went over to the four paned window, pulled back the curtain and saw him, bag in his weary hand, trudging down the railroad track. Perhaps he did have a patient expecting. And perhaps she would deliver before he could walk back to town. Surely her anger was not worth having some poor woman have her baby without a doctor. But he had been downright nasty to her. And hateful! And he thought he was the pure stuff since he had come back. So almighty good and right. Did he have to be right about everything? Just because he was educated, couldn't he ever be wrong like the rest of them? But he would send the mule back early. And he had let Jim come and plow for them last year before Woodrow had been large enough to plow a straight furrow. Oh, dammit, I can't even win in anger, and she jerked the door open and hollered loudly, "You can ride the mule, but just make sure you don't keep her."

"God almighty, Ella. Make your mind up. Can I or can't I?"

"I said you could, didn't I?"

"Thanks a blue million. I'll get her back early tomorrow."

And when he rode around the corner on the old plug's back, he said to the closed door and the woman behind it, "What you need is a good husband."

She jerked the door back to tell him to put the mule back in the lot, but he kicked her sides and took off on her jogging back. She could hear him laughing loudly for a good quarter of a mile.

"You'll pay me for using her I'm going to charge you," she hollered, but he continued to laugh in the darkness of the night and the dust of the path.

When the first light of day came into her solitary window, she still had not slept a wink, but had lain trembling in anger and frustration the rest of the night. What had happened to the shell she usually kept her head and heart in? Why had she let him arouse such anger and frustration in her over such a small thing? But then, was it such a big thing to be classed as a whore? But wasn't it true? All night these questions revolved in her mind and tormented her and she welcomed the morning sun. Maybe it could bake some sense in her as she hoed the cockle burrs and the Jerusalem weeds out of her corn field. The child that never cried looked up at her from her homemade crib and grinned a pitiful smile that revealed rotten teeth and gurgled like an infant newly born instead of a seven-year-old. Ella changed her diaper and bent to kiss the black curls that were so much like Ben's hair.

"I'm not much wiser that you, little one, and I'd be better off if I couldn't speak a word either. So there, Mama'll feed you in two jerks of a cat's tail, so be good."

While the grits and side meat were cooking, she looked out and saw Jim riding her mule. She smiled a sheepish smile. How transparent I was to Leslie! I let him look through me and hurt me because what he said was true. If he comes again, I'm going to laugh with him and act as if I don't care what he says. He's no more than anyone else around here.

"Miss Ella, where you wants I should put da mule?"

"You can put her in the lot and give her water, please, Jim. And then wash up and eat some breakfast with us. It'll be ready in a jerk."

"I can shore use some. Mr. Leslie was in a pure notion about gittin' this creature back as soon as possible. He said it was a matter of life or death, and I said, is Miss Ella sick and he said, no, she ain't sick, but she's powerful agitated, and I couldn't tell whether it was so or a right and out story he was telling."

"It was a right and out story. I'm not in the least agitated. The doctor must be delirious from over work. Tell him so when you get back."

"Yas, mammmm!"

Although he did not eat at the table with them, he ate exactly the same fare as they did. He took the plate she handed and went and sat on the doorstep where he enjoyed every mouth full of it. Woodrow gulped down his food quickly so that he could watch Jim whittle before he had to go back. He could make a wonderful whistle out of a reed, one that would play eight different notes, and he had the prettiest pocketknife that Woodrow had ever seen. It's handle looked like real glass with tiny flecks of colored marbles scattered around in it, and it had two whole blades, one long and one short. It must have cost a lot of money and Jim did not miss any chance to show it off. The morning sunlight streamed down on the dark boy with the whittling knife and the white boy with the golden hair and the woman in the doorway with the small girl pulling her dress tail and crying, "Mama."

March filled the house with sand blowing under the windows and doors, and April brought forth the first seeds sprouting in the garden. May brought the most pressing money problem that had confronted her in a long time. Woodrow was going to graduate from elementary school and all of the boys were supposed to wear a navy blue suits, white shirts, and ties. He not only did not have a navy blue suit, he did not have a suit at all, and the only white shirt he had was one Ella had made out of a bleached flour sack. Woodrow had vowed he did not intend to go to his own commencement if he did not have a suit and shirt like the other boys. And where in the blessed name of God was she supposed to find five dollars? On the railroad track just as likely as in her own purse. If only Bernard had let her have Ben's clothes, she could have worked something over and made it do. Perhaps they hung there still. Perhaps Kate . . . ?

It had been preposterous to even imagine that Kate would give her anything. Her sister had stood on the steps of the front porch with her arms folded over her flat ugly bosom and had not even asked Ella to come into the house.

"Why, we threw all those old things out of Ben's and burned them. Bernard didn't want them in the house. Gertrude and Faye Ellen wanted their mother's clothes and I couldn't wear any of them so I let them have them. And I do hope, you won't go running to Mama and borrow the last cent off her. If she has any, she needs it I'm sure."

Yes, I'm sure that she does, too, Ella thought, because you and Bernard see to it that you get every cent off Daddy's place that's made there.

"I really have got to have five dollars, Kate. I know you have it, and I could pay it back."

"With what?"

"Why, with my hog money this fall."

"They might all die with summer cholera."

"Yes, they might. But then, we might too."

"I'm sorry, Ella. Really, that boy has no business in school. You need him full time at home, and if you're might to put mule reins around your neck and plow in the sun just so he can sit in the school room, it doesn't make any difference what you need. Use your brain."

"I am using it. I wanted to go to school and you know how Pa was. If Woodrow'll just go, I intend to give him every chance to do it."

"In that case, I don't see how to help you if you won't help yourself."

"Is 'no' your final answer, sister?"

"How touching, Ella, calling me Sister after all these years, and just when you want something."

"I'll get it some way. You can be sure of that!" She turned to go down the steps.

"I am sure of that, Ella. I'm very sure of that!"

And the sarcasm in her words left little doubt in Ella's mind what her sister was implying.

❧ ❧ ❧

"I TELL YOU, MAMA, she hates me. She hates me something terrible."

"Oh, I'm sure she doesn't. You're her blood kin!" Mrs. Horne tried to soothe Ella's troubled mind with a few lines.

"Blood kin! That's the worst kind. They're always the

vultures. People that ain't your blood kin wouldn't dare to pull the things on you that your relatives do. Look at Kate and Bernard. If anybody but them had held my note, they would a waited for me to raise the money. Anybody but them!"

"You mustn't hold Kate responsible for what Bernard does. He's a hard man to please and Kate must really try hard to please."

"Mama, you just don't know the half of it. He's so ugly and nasty. And he doesn't give a damn about Kate, or about anyone else except himself. She didn't say she didn't have it. She said she wouldn't lend it to me."

"Well, I'm going to talk to her. I'd certainly let you have it. And Pa was buried in his only suit. What are we going to do?"

"Don't you start worrying about it, Mama. The money is going to come from somewhere, and I'm certainly not going to mortgage my land this time to get it either. There'll never be another mortgage on anything I own."

Out of desperation and despair came one last hope—the doctor whom she had shouted at and cursed at and hollered at the last time she had met him. The collards were bubbling away in the pot, and the sides of the iron pot were red hot, too hot to put the bread in just yet, but just right for the sweet potatoes baking inside.

"Stand side of the road and when you see him coming, wave him down, son. He won't be up that way long, 'spect."

And the tall barefooted boy in the bib overalls and with the big knuckles stood on the railroad track that ran parallel to the dusty road. He watched the sun change from yellow to orange to bright red, and then suddenly fall behind the scraggly dark pines. The twilight was a time of haste usually. Hurry to feed the mule. Hurry to feed the chickens. Hurry to get wood in for breakfast. Hurry to keep from starving. So he welcomed the chance to stand and wait in the twilight of the old day. Old blue clouds, you aren't really white, are you? You're just any color God makes you be. That's what you are. And he wiggled his toes and caught up a piece of charcoal between them. He raised his foot up and took it in his hand. Why bend? What's a foot for anyhow? Don't go, sun. Tomorrow will be another day like today and I don't want it to be like it today. All those hateful boys at school with their damn new suits and shirts. All those silly girls talking about the white dresses they're a going to be wearing. And Miss Hargett wanted to know right in front of everybody if I had got a new suit yet. "Well try, son. You must say your piece, you know. We're counting on you as our valedictorian."

Valedictorian, hell. Don't count on me, Miss Hargett, cause there's no money and there ain't going to be none, and I'm going to say ain't as long as I live regardless what the book says, or you either. So there . . . And his young boy's thoughts filled every moment till he saw a whiff and a whirl of dust and a car coming and knew that the doctor was in his usual hurry.

"Ma wants you to stop by for just a short spell."

"Who's the sick one? Not your Ma, I hope?"

"No sick one today. Just for talking."

"Well, I'll be." He switched the engine off, left the car at the side of the road, and crossed the narrow foot path that led over the tracks and into the barren yard.

"I take it you're a wanting pay for using the mule. I thought you were kidding or I'da sent the money by Jim."

"No. No money for the mule. You know better'n than that. Hurry to your feeding, son. The hogs' slop is in the bucket out back."

She opened the Kerr jar of homecanned tomatoes, poured them into the iron skillet, sprinkled them with salt and pepper, and set them back on the stove to heat. Nothing was any more filling than collards and good cooked tomatoes and potatoes. She had been right when she planned on the land feeding them, and the land had kept its promise, most of the time.

He noticed that her face and neck still had a youthful line and she had kept her waist trim unlike most mothers of three children. He would love to see her in beautiful clothes again. Lovely clothes make a woman take hope and keep trying to stay beautiful. He had not forgotten how lovely she had looked when she had clerked in Ben's store and how desirable she had been to all the men sitting around. He had been no different from the others who had hoped that she would lean over the counter and give them a chance to look down the neck of her dress for a quick exciting glance of her ample bosom.

"But it is about money, Leslie. I need five dollars in the worst kind of way. I just got to have it is all. I've already tried 'bout everybody I know. Can you let me have the loan of it for a while? I'd get it back to you as soon as I possible could."

His heart formed the words, "Of course, I can let you have it," but when he opened his mouth to speak, his mind spoke words that he did not even recognize as his own.

"I can let you have it, but it'll cost you in a very nice way."

So startled was she that the big metal spoon fell from her hand and clanged on the boards of the floor. It unnoticed by either of them. Priscilla played happily between their legs, singing her childish songs and humming, unaware of the tension in the air above her curly head.

"Why, you're no different from any other man. I thought you were somebody! You're just like Bernard. I can get it from him at the same price. You're, you're . . ."

"That's right. I'm no different from any other man. Just a man is all any of us are when you get right down to it. And what's so different between Leonard and myself? He's come to see you just like he's worked all day in the fields, and I can bet you're not in the least insulted when he crawls in bed with you. And knowing his Papa, I bet he can't give you a dime. Well? Can he?"

"You know he can't and I never asked him to, either," she lied and he could tell from the way that her eyelids veiled her eyes that she was caught in her own untruth. For it had been only last night when they had lain on the cool clean grass and she had asked him to get her five dollars.

"I could get you five thousand just as easy, you know that."

"I don't know that. Your Pa has plenty of it salted down. What kind of man are you to let him take every penny that's there and give you nothing? You know where he keeps it, go to it and take some when he's not looking. You do all the work anyway. It wouldn't be stealing. It's yours."

"You're just upset, Ella. You're asking me to steal from Papa and I could never do that. Why Eva never asked me to take from Papa." His words were filled with sadness that she would even ask him to take some of the money.

"Well, I'm not Eva. And she has you, and all that there will be yours and hers, someday, if you're lucky enough to outlive the old cuss, but I can't wait for him to die to get what I need. If you don't love me enough to bring me one five dollars, don't cross this railroad again, cause if you do, I'm not going to let you in the house, and I mean now or ever."

For a few minutes he tried to soften her and change her determination, but she would not even let him put his hands on her again or bend to kiss her. "A sow will bite the flesh out of the boar if he threatens her pigs. A bear will kill her mate if he comes in the den. A chicken will attack a grown man if he upsets her setting eggs, and I'm no different. This is my boy that I'm fighting for now. And no man is worth loving if he can't help me when I need it most."

He could not see the features of her face, but he knew well enough that her mouth was in a tight line and that there would be no reasoning with her tonight, so he fastened his clothes together and left her trembling with anger, dead desires, and frustration.

"I do love you, Leonard," she told the grass and the fireflies above her, "but you'd better know I mean what I say this time."

And now in her own kitchen stood a man, a man in his early thirties, tall and good looking and very educated, so unlike Leonard in every way, a man any woman would be proud to own, proud to stand and wait in the night for him to return, and he was offering her, not his name, but his loving, and she did not know herself well enough to know whether or not she was insulted that he thought her available for money or flattered that a man still desired her. Why this would be a way to make Leonard open his eyes and see I'm no puddle jumper. Maybe it would put a spine in his backbone. And I could close my mind and eyes and make believe it never happened, like I used to with Ben sometimes.

She was about to open her mouth and tell him she would, and if she had, the course of her life the next twenty years would have been very different, but he had taken her moments of indecision to mean a firm no, and at that precise moment he took out of his wallet, handed her a five dollar bill, and said, "The money is yours, Ella. Try to forgive me for what I said. I don't know what got into me tonight. I'm not usually like that, really. And don't worry about paying it back. Take your time."

He turned on his heel and went quickly out into the darkness where he stood beside his car, lit his pipe, and smoked it for a few moments before leaving. Looking at his own house, he trembled at his own folly.

"My God. My God. I nearly threw away everything tonight. My reputation would have been mud. No one out here would ever have called me again. Everything would have been gone. And he pulled deeply on his pipe and blew the smoke from his nostrils, trying to clean his own mouth from the words that had issued out from it. Our deeds are unintelligible to ourselves even. What in the name of Jesus came over me? I am not a lecherous man like Bernard. That's what she said I was like. And he lies down with white and black, young and old. Is that what I really looked like to her? Why do I throw Leonard in her face every time I see her. I know she's loved him all her life. Always loved him. And I know Eva knows that, even if the knowledge is hid deep within her heart. And the only line between immorality and morality is love. I know there is enough love there to justify their actions, but I let it irk me that he has her and Eva too. Face yourself, Leslie. Look at the truth even when it hurts. Drag it out into the open. And once you view it, you'll look at it objectively and put it aside. I am a jealous man. That is the cold truth. I am a jealous man. He's never done a damned thing to win any woman and now he has two. And I don't think it's right. That's what makes me so damned mad. And I have no one, no one but Jim and me every night at the table, and lots of women having babies and men with pneumonia, and children with measles and whooping cough. That's what I have, and by God, it's not enough any longer."

He started the car and was embarrassed at how loud the engine sounded. He would have rather crept away like a camel in the night, but here he was chugging away like a big baboon in his motor car and he told himself on the ride home that now he had admitted that his life was no longer complete, he was strong enough to change his destiny.

—Chapter 16—

. . . THE COLOR OF THE DAY is blue . . . it all depends on you . . . and the day had never been as bright and beautiful as it was this beautiful early July morning. It had rained a whopper the night before, all of the dust had been settled and the leaves were green and fresh, and the clover that grew richer around the edges of the fence was dark as a hunter's green when only yesterday it was a parched and dusty patch. The sand bedded cow paths were beaten hard again as the earth had tried to absorb every drop that had fallen. For the first time in weeks the corn had not wilted in the morning, and the cows just ahead of her walked briskly, swinging their cocklebur tails as if eager to get to the pine meadow knowing that there might be water in the stream bed today. The wet earth felt good between her toes and beneath her feet, for it told her heart that the corn now would have a full grain on the ear, and she would not have to carry every bucketful of water that the hogs and cows drank. Now the ditches would run for a few days. She noted that the persimmons had formed good on the trees along the woods and knew that if she could beat the possums to them this fall, she could make them some good persimmon beer this winter. Oh sky, I could hug you all day! I want to live and live and live. I don't want to be old. I want to be young like this cow carrying this calf. Stand still, time! Stand still and wait for me today.

A full year had passed since Woodrow's commencement and she had not backed down in her determination not to continue her relationship with Leonard. For a few weeks he had been very insistent, but she had told him flatly to stop coming or else she was going to go and tell Eva Belle the whole truth. The absurdity of this caused him to laugh. A few days after his next visit, he walked onto his yard in the afternoon to sharpen a hoe and found Eva and Ella sitting on his front porch, chatting in dead earnest. The sight of them together, plus the thought of Ella's latest threat, caused the blood to drain quickly from his head. For a moment, he was afraid that he was going to faint. He nodded to both of them, and went over to the well where he pulled up a half gallon of milk that hung by a long rope and lay in the bottom of the well in the cool clear water. Turning the jar to his head, he drank long and hoped that he was appearing nonchalant enough to the women watching him.

"Better git out of the sun some, honey," Eva called to him. "You're apt to have a sun stroke one of these days at the rate you work," she added sweetly.

"He's most too hard headed to have a sun stroke, if I remember well." Ella's words were said jokingly, but he knew the meaning she was trying to convey to him.

"Don't know anybody who says you remember well," and he hoped his words would cut her off.

"Why, Leonard! You ain't even polite today. And it's the first time Ellie's visited me in a coon's age. She's being courted, she says, hot and heavy. Ain't that the thing, though. It makes me feel so old and married, Ellie."

He was glad that he was not facing them at the moment so that they did not see his mouth fall open in surprise. In the name of God, had she told her and his wife taken it as a joke? Surely she hadn't told her and stayed on to talk sociably. Eva looked happy enough, yet the words, "courted hot and heavy" . . .

"And by my old beau, of all things. I can't git over it. I'd thought all this time he was doomed to be a bachelor. Can't even tease you anymore about him, can I, honey?" Eva rocked back and forth in the enjoyment of the good news.

He came over and sat down on the edge of the gum planked porch and was glad that they did not have anyway of knowing how weak his knees were at that moment.

"You don't mean the doctor, Ella? Well, this is certainly

news! You can't be pulling our leg, could you now, Ella?" he hoped he sounded objective enough yet still neighborly in his inquiry.

"Why should I joke about a thing like being courted. He came last night, and he brought Woodrow a record for the Victrola, a new song called 'Maple on the Hill.' It's the prettiest thing. It's so sad like. It made tears come in my eyes and keep falling for the longest time. I declared to Leslie, I could have listened to it for the longest time. And he brought me a bag of white flour. Said he'd planned to bring candy, but he figured we needed flour worse, and that certainly hit the nail on the head. We've been eating corn meal for weeks now. And you should see the way Woodrow and Priscilla have took to him. He's told the boy so much about what to choose in high school. He's so encouraging to him about going to the town school and I just know he's going to keep on a going. He asked me to go riding, but you know I don't have anything fitting to wear off. Course, like he said, it'd be night, and we'd just ride around and I'd not have to get out, but that's not much of a date, I said, and I put it off. And last week when he came he brought us two ears of popping corn and we put it in the skillet on the stove and I never seen the children have so much fun. I declare, I didn't know I could still laugh like I still did . . ."

He could not bear to listen to more and her words kept pouring out about the doctor's visits, so he took his hoe, which he had leaned against the well, and left abruptly for the fields. He stopped under the barn shelter, leaned against the cart and hung his head on the cold steel of the wagon wheel rim. It cooled his fevered forehead. So many things were running around in his mind, that it had him addled. She had come for a purpose alright, but it had not been the purpose she had threatened. She had found someone who could fill his place, and fill it better than he would ever be able to. He looked across the wide acres of cotton and corn and peanuts and knew that surely all this would be his someday, but had it been enough just waiting for it? It had cost him the woman he had first loved, cost him his son, and now was taking her again. He had imagined that she was as satisfied with the arrangement as he was. What had he done wrong? Surely not one five dollars that he could not raise? Surely his loving had been worth more than a five dollar bill. Was that all she had loved him? His stomach turned over at the fact that it was all over, for he knew that the doctor not only had money to offer, but he had his freedom and he might even be willing to marry her. If he did, all was lost. From down the field road a piece, he could hear Pa yelling, "What in the hell is taking you so long? Git on down here." And he said to the still air and the ducks and guineas about him, "Go to Hell." But he turned away from the cooling shade and the cart wheel and went quickly down the path.

She had not lied to taunt him. It was a fact that Leslie was a regular visitor to her house, and quite a different one from Leonard. He did not try to touch her in any way, but he let it be known that he was paying court. He'd lean back in a straight bottomed cane chair, prop his feet against the heater, and smoke his pipe. A stranger would have sworn on first sight that he was master of the house. He had woven an incantation on her children that moved her to see, if he did not bring to her the same thing of satisfaction that Leonard did, he brought a quiet, still happiness to the faded boarded house that she would never have thought possible.

Some nights, she'd cook a big potato pudding and a mess of fresh corn and fry some fresh perch that Woodrow had caught that afternoon in the swamp, and they'd wait supper for the sight or sound of his car, and it would not appear at all. Then they would know that it was not possible for him to come that night, and they would sit and stare at each other with nothing to do. When they tried to think of how they had spent their bedtime hours before they had known him so well, their minds were empty. Even the old Victrola sounded squeaky and worn out when they were alone. Moreover, he looked on Sybil with compassion and was not repulsed by her abnormalities as were most people who saw her. He well remembered Dr. Kellum telling that he had suspected even from the first that she was too limp and inactive for a newborn. He liked how lovely Ella had looked when Doc put the baby in the curve of her arm and watched her hair fall over it. It made him proud that he had been called to deliver Priscilla, though even under sedation Ella had strongly protested against the doctor's youth. He smiled remembering it and puffed his pipe. He longed to put her in pretty things, especially clothes. He had seen a white organdy dress trimmed in wide powdery blue braid that he had gazed at for a long time. It would have been beautiful on her, even with her tanned complexion, but would it offend her? Would she think he noticed how ragged her own dresses were? The smile faded from his lips when he recalled his encounter with Bernard on the street corner a few nights past.

"I . . . I . . . I been a wanting to have a little talk with you, Doc," Bernard stammered out, and it was obvious even to the dogs that he was very drunk.

"Well?"

"I hear tell you been a courtin' my sister-in-law. I just . . . I just want it made plain that I'm not taking any tampering with her affections. I mean to look out after her. Yes, sirree. I'm going to see that she's taken care of."

"You've already taken care of her? Taken is the word. You've taken everything you could possibly get away from her. Now you take this. If you go around her while I'm courting her, I'll personally knock those shiny teeth of yours out of your mouth into the street, and then I'll enjoy seeing you bleed while I stomp your fat belly in. Is that clear?"

He had not even known that he was capable of such anger and even at that moment thought, how little we know ourselves.

"I . . . I . . . I git the message, Doc. I didn't mean any harm. Just joking. Just joking." He staggered past Leslie on down the dark street and out of sight. The doctor's hands were trembling so that he clenched them together and gritted his teeth. Would he have really struck the man? Yes. He believed he would have and thought of his professional reputation later. Soon, soon he would ask her. It was not courage he was lacking, but the time had not been right just yet.

❧ ❧ ❧

SHE SAT IN HER SMALL corn crib and shucked corn, tossing the ears into the homemade wicker basket. The sun light filtered through the crack of the barn. It illuminated the dust and made it appear to be rays of golden flecks. Something about the corn husks made the diamond on her finger sparkle and she smiled as she thought. How silly you look on my finger, my ugly work worn fingers. And how Gertrude and Faye Ellen want you. I won out in something at any rate. She leaned forward and peeped through a crack to see if Priscilla was still playing safely in front of the house, but she did not see any sign of her. Where on earth . . . ? I told her to stay right there. She stepped out quickly and started calling at the top of her voice. Woodrow had gone to Mama's to borrow a cup of sugar. She planned to make a batch of rolled out cookies. Leslie might come, and he loved sweet things.

"Priscilla! Where are you? You'd better answer me right this minute!"

Not hearing any answer or seeing any sign of her, she walked a few yards down the road. As soon as she had turned the bend she saw what was fascinating the child. She was squatting beside the Mulberry Branch and apparently talking to herself, but as Ella approached she saw that Old Tom, the half-witted boy who had frightened her many times, had fallen into the branch and was sitting on the bottom like a crawdad.

"What on earth! Get out of there, Tom, before you're drowned!"

"Howdy, Ella. Two things I'm looking for and I ain't coming out till I find them. My bottle fell in and I ain't getting out without it. And I'm hunting a guinea nest. It's around here somewhere. Ma is going to make some sweet bread if I find the eggs."

In spite of the scare the child had given her, and aside from the fact that she did not really know how safe Tom was to be around, she had to laugh.

"You quit that laughing," he stormed out at her. "You know where that guinea nest is, don't ya! And you just want the eggs for yourself. I aim to have 'em. Quit laughing, I say!"

"Well, Tom. You don't have any guinea hens that lay over this way. If there are any nests around here, they're mine."

"'Tain't so. Finders keepers. And I aim to find them."

"Even so, I don't think you'll find them sitting there. Come on, honey?"

Knowing it might be dangerous to argue with him, she thought the best thing was to take Priscilla and get in the house until he left.

"Oh, you don't mind having me drowning, do you?" he called after her. "Just ole drunk Tom. Don't care if I live or die. Hain't got no sense. You think I don't know nothing, don't you?" He proceeded to get up and crawl out of the run of the branch. She turned in time to see him crawling up the bank and thought, why he looks just like a gorilla. And he's so drunk. I do wish I hadn't sent Woodrow. She tugged harder at the child's hand, hurried inside the house, and bolted the door with its wooden latch. I'm being silly. It's broad open daylight and surely he's not crazy to try to come on the house. But then . . . He knows that there's no one here but me and that no one can hear me holler. I'll bet a car wouldn't go by for nothing now, and she pulled the curtain to one side and peeped out. Sure enough he was coming into the yard staggering and falling and getting up again, but steadily coming forward towards the house.

Oh Lord! I don't know if there's even a gun shell in the house or not. She hurried and found one under the underwear in the top drawer of the dresser and put it in one side of the double barrel shot gun, but when she pulled the curtain and looked out, she did not see him anywhere. She went from window to window peering out, heart thumping wildly and breath coming short and raspy.

"Don't make a sound, darling. It's nothing but old Tom and we don't want him to hear us today. We're making out like we're not home. Don't make a peep now."

The child snickered and thought it was all good fun. Even the gun did not disturb her illusion of joviality. For what seemed an eternity, Ella waited and peeped, but did not see him again. Assuming that he had slipped off and into the woods, she opened the door to look around and was startled out of her wits. He had tried to crawl under the house and had got stuck about half way. His big hips and legs were sticking out from under the house. Oh, Lord. I do wish Woodrow was here with me. We'd all be together at least, even if we aren't safe. That was perfect logic to her. Why doesn't he come on? As if in answer to her prayers, she saw his big yellow nondescript dog turn the corner and the boy was close behind. He was running excitedly, swinging a brown, twisted, much used paper bag in his hand.

She opened the door to warn him, but he hollered, "You'll never believe it, Ma, but old Tom was drunk and he came to Grandma's and he wanted her to give him guineas eggs, and she told him we didn't have any, and he said she'd better git some and he weren't fooling Dixie, and she told him there wasn't an egg of any kind on the place, and he went right on in the kitchen and broke some of her dishes . . ."

Ella was frantically motioning for him to hush and pointing to the part of the drunk that was exposed, but the boy was not upset at the sight. He threw back his full grown head and laughed.

"Do your job again, Jack. Sic 'em. Sic 'em, boy."

And the much loved nondescript dog grabbed at Tom's pants leg and pulled so fiercely that the cloth tore away. He proceeded to bite at the flesh until the drunk began to back out. Saliva was running out of the corners of Tom's mouth and he tried to hit at the barking and biting dog.

"Put your God damned dog on me, will you? You won't be forgetting this. And I was just about to find my guinea nest, too. It's all your fault," and he shook his fist in Ella's face. "All your fault, you bitch."

"Take him out of the yard Jack. Take him!" The dog who was used to bringing the cow or cornering a hog, jumped at him until he went in the direction leading from the house.

Ella sank down on the porch step and breathed a heavy sigh. "Well, I never. And on such an ordinary day, too. Did he scare you to death, son?"

"Grandma said she was surely glad I was there or else she didn't know what she'd a done. Gosh, Mama. I didn't know you were a needing me too."

"I always need you son, but I'm glad you were with Ma. Priscilla and I had the gun loaded. We were safe, at least, even if we were scared to death."

"The gun! That thing wouldn't have fired, Mama. It's been where it kicks out the shells for a long time, now. You know I told you that."

"Good Lord! You certainly did! But I forgot all about it. Well, maybe when the shell popped out, I coulda hit him on the head with the gun."

Mother and son laughed together, and the little girl laughed because the others were laughing. That night when they sat on the porch and ate some of the still warm rolled out cookies and drank milk, they had much to tell the doctor, and they told it as if it were the most hilarious thing that had happened in a coon's age.

"I do know, Leslie. You shoulda seen him. He looked like a big baboon, and he was so mad with us, he coulda busted us right open.

"You were right to load the gun. A man of his mentality is unpredictable. I wish I had been here."

"Old Jack tore into him, didn't he, Mama? That got him on the move."

"It sure did. I knew we'd been feeding that critter for something special just like this. He did us proud, too."

"Most likely, he won't remember a word of it when he wakes up, so don't be upset by his threats. You don't know how long he'll be drunk on the other hand. I'm going to carry back that gun with me tonight and the first thing in the morning put that thing in the shop. You're too close to the water tank for comfort anyhow. Do you know, these taste just like the ones Mama used to cook on Saturdays. And rainy days! We called them rainy day cakes.

"I'm glad." She rocked in contentment and hugged the big girl who sat in her lap, tired now from chasing fireflies and trying to find the chirping locusts.

Long after the children were asleep they continued to sit on the front porch, Doc glad that his presence made her feel warm and safe inside.

Now, he told himself. Now is the time to try and ask her. Now while the children are asleep and she is fairly happy. Suppose old Tom had managed to break into the house today. God knows what he would have stopped at. And her here alone. The more frantic his thoughts, the harder he puffed on his pipe.

Even Ella became aware of how rapidly he was smoking.

"I do know, Les. You're puffing like the afternoon locy. What's got into you?"

Never again would there be an opening like this one.

"Ella, would being my wife be worse than being out here alone all the time?" The words literally poured out of him.

"Why, I don't worry about being alone. I have the children with me all the time."

"You know what I mean."

"I don't know whether I do or not. Are you asking me to marry you?"

"Yes, dammit. Something like that. I've never asked a woman before. It's not an easy thing to say, is it?"

"I wouldn't know. I've never asked a woman either."

They laughed and then the words came easily for him at last.

"I've been wanting to ask you for months. I know you know my feelings by now. And I'd be good to the children."

"I don't doubt that for a moment, Leslie. But you're just starting out. I am an old woman."

"Don't say that. You're not a day older than I am."

"Not in days, maybe. But in living. I've had my family, and I've had more troubles than you can even imagine. Troubles make a woman old. They just can't chuck them off like a man can."

"You're still beautiful to me. I need you for my wife, Ella."

Her hesitation told him that her answer would be negative, and in a way, it was.

"I just can't tell you now. I'd be such a weight around your neck. And there'd be Sybil. You'd be ashamed of us before long and then it'd be too late. And I'd get used to having something for a while, and have to lose it again. It's not bad on the bottom. It's the falling down that hurts. Once you're there, though, really it's not too bad. I've seen a lot of things down here that I didn't know human beings were capable of doing and saying. Everybody ought to have to hit bottom one time, don't you think?"

"Ellie, I'm not following you. None of that mess makes sense. Will you or won't you?"

"I, I just don't know. If you feel might to wait, I'll be obliged to think about it."

From the corner of her eyes, she saw him nervously twisting the stem of his pipe around and around, recalling how easily he had been embarrassed when a young boy dating Eva. Perhaps he was still as shy as he was then. But he seemed to be so much at ease with her. She stood up and walked into the yard, knowing he would follow her. The moon was in its second quarter, but it gave enough light that she could see that pain in his eyes as he stood beside her under the China Tree.

Turning to him, she blurted out what she had been needing to tell him all night.

"Oh, dammit, Leslie. You don't know me. If you did, you wouldn't want me at all. Go and look for a nice young girl seventeen or eighteen. Not one that is second handed like me. You just don't know all about me. If you did, you'd run and run fast. I just don't feel the need to tell you as long as we were just friends. Friends don't need to tell everything, but a husband and wife ought not to have any secrets. And if I told you about myself we wouldn't ever be husband and wife. Please. I'd rather never be your wife than have to tell you everything. You'd want to put your foot on me then. I couldn't bear that."

He reached out and for an instant she thought he was going to strike her, but instead he very gently put his forefinger to her lips and caressed them.

"You need never tell me another word. I know all I need to know, that you're warm and loving and a wonderful mother, the kind of mother we doctors prescribe for every baby, and that you enjoy bringing happiness to other people. I know you'd be loyal to a man. That's all I need ever to know. We could set fire to this old house. We'd pack the children and say good-bye to it. I don't even have to stay in this old town. We can go to some other place just as well."

"No. No. You're like all the rest of us. This is our place on earth. There is no other place for you either. And all the people have come to need you. I'm a very wicked woman . . ."

"Hush. I won't listen. You're trying to make me hate you. I'm not going to let you tear yourself to pieces like this."

"You don't have to marry me to make love to me, Leslie. I know you've needed me, and loved me. And I know the need's been a growing. But when I love a body, there doesn't have to be a marriage license to make it right. All you have to do is lead the way to a nice soft spot in the broomsage and I'm like Woodrow's old dog. That's me."

He grabbed her shoulders and shook her with such force that her hair came unpinned and fell all over her face and neck.

"Stop it. Shut up, I said. I don't want you to destroy yourself to make me leave. I'll go without that. And if I don't hear from you to the contrary, I won't be back. Not tomorrow. Not any time."

"You're so dumb for a doctor sometimes. I'm not trying to make you hate me. I'm trying to beg you to love me. Love me, you dunce head. How plain does a woman have to spell it out for you? No man at all. I've been faithful to you in my heart for over a year now. Isn't that enough? I might not be good enough to marry you, but I could love you like no other woman could. And who would be the wiser? I don't give a damn for your precious reputation! Put that in your pipe and puff it for a while. Even if I got pregnant, people would blame Leonard. They always blame Leonard. You'd have nothing to worry about."

He backed away from her until he was leaning against a tree, but she came on and on, egging him with her words, and finally pressing her body against his, letting one of her legs slip between his thighs and gently caressing him, standing on tiptoes to find his lips, teasing them with the tip of her tongue, until he groaned in ecstasy and forgot all that he was supposed to remember. He picked her up bodily, his hips still pressing hers. With her, he stumbled across the yard and into the broomsage patch that bordered the south of the yard where they sank down into a deep grassy bed. On and on the night owl screeched, and the locusts cut his shrill screech, and the June Bug, his call, and a rooster mistakenly crowing for day, and fireflies flashing their lights. On. Off. On. Off.

It was a night of love for all kinds of creatures, but none enjoyed it so much as the man who had given himself to medicine first, and sought a woman last. His experience in whore houses had not prepared him for the response of a woman who cared and who could give freely. He had been right, too, in his assumption that she would be so lovely in newer clothes, and before he had carried her back into the house and eased her down in the bed, he had loved every inch of her body and still he wanted to kiss her. I'll be back tomorrow. I'm not going to take no for an answer. We'll talk about it some more tomorrow!" She was not been able to argue with him about it anymore tonight.

Driving home, his knees shook like rubber bands stretched too wide too much, and he chastised himself for all the lectures he had given women on getting pregnant too often. All the information he had given them. Why? He had asked them in desperation. Why didn't they ever use it? They had smiled shyly and knowingly, for he was only a bachelor doctor in their eyes, and this irritated him to no end. Now the wicked truth reared its head. All knowledge is useless at such time. All hopes, all plans, all dreams . . . these are all nothing . . . and time stands still, and the moment is suspended, and all the minutes are as if they had never ticked by. That's the answer. That's the answer I couldn't find, because I hadn't made love to a woman I loved with all my heart. I've been a narrow minded fool. No wonder they loved Dr. Kellum. He had loved women, and he had understood women, and he did not scold. He merely accepted human frailties as the natural thing. And if one had a baby while two still crawled, he accepted this too as products of loving in a home.

He stopped the car beside Reedy Cane Creek and watched the water run darkly beneath the bridge. Run on, water. I've got all the time in the world now. He felt like a silly boy, just out of school for the summer, like one who wanted to reach up and pull the sky down and hug it tightly. All the many frustrations he had yesterday could not be recalled, no matter how hard he tried. That's why they can sit for hours around that damned heater in the store, listless and happy. It's not laziness like I accused them of at all. I've been blind. Blind . . . And he tried to pack the tobacco in the bowl of his pipe, but his hand still trembled so that he gave it up for the moment and put it back into his pocket.

—Chapter 17—

October 1934

And though she continued to put off her answer to his proposal, he began to court her more openly now, bringing her fine dresses and store bought shoes, and she accepted them, and wore them to church with him by her side, holding her head as high as any one else in the building. And why not? she asked herself. I am as good as they are. I don't do a thing they don't do, except maybe I do it better. Maybe I get a little pleasure from life and they begrudge me that. If a tiny mite of conscious pricked her, she shoved it back to the farthest corner of her mind, and closed the door to that compartment and threw away the key. Now. Today. That became everything for her.

We all want to live and go on living. Yet we none want to ever grow old. We can't picture ourselves bent with age, and gray and wrinkled, but rather picture ourselves as perpetual youth. Oh, our friends may die, but we will go on living, and with that consoling thought, we face each new day with confidence.

It seemed so wonderful to have a car to ride in again, and her mother would come and stay with Sybil while they put Woodrow and Priscilla on the back seat and took a picnic basket to the river for the day. Sister Carrie had long since moved her tent and people came there now to swim and eat basket lunches, but the trees still echoed with her fiery sermons and Ella had only to close her eyes to still hear her loud voice shouting, "He'll come. He'll come in a whiff and a whirl, and he'll get you. Every last one of you here. Not one., not one will escape him. He rides a pale horse, and his name is Death . . ." She still shuddered even as she had as a child. She wondered if Sister Carrie was still preaching her messages for the sinful. But that didn't include her, surely. The day was too blue—the sky, the river, the powder puffed upside down clouds.

While Woodrow caught crabs with a net, Priscilla waded at the river's edge, and she and Leslie sat on a quilt and watched them, both full of food, full of love, and content for the moment. He reached over and rubbed the inside of her thigh.

"Stop that. The children'll see you."

"They will not. They're not looking."

"Well, they might look. And then it'd be too late for you to move your hand."

"Say you don't really want me to move it."

Even as the touch of his strong hand made cold bumps rise up on her leg, she lied, "I do so want you to move it."

"I don't believe you for a minute, but I'll do it anyway. You know you're like Dr. Jeckell and Mr. Hyde."

"Who're they? Friends of yours at college."

He could not resist throwing back his head and howling.

"You're so cute, Ellie. I'll swear you are a prize among women."

"I'm not cute, either. I'm a middle aged woman with a near grown boy. Now who are the men?"

"They're friends of mine."

"You're lying. I can tell by the way your eyes are dancing." She gave his hair a good strong jerk.

"Ouch. You want me to be bald before my time? Alright, I'm pulling your leg, honey. They are men in a story, a very famous story. They were both one man, but he changed so completely during the night that he was two completely different people. You know what I mean?"

"I think so. But I don't see how I'm like that!"

"You don't?" Incredulity filled his words. "Why, you're the perfect picture of a mother during the daylight, and at night, you just blossom out like a flower, all waiting for a honey bee to come."

"I think you're being plain nasty, and I'm not going to listen to another word you say," and to prove she meant it she put her fingers in both ears.

He pulled her down on his chest and moved her hands.

"You are going to listen, too. I didn't mean I wanted you different. Just as long as I'm the bee you wait for, that's what counts with me."

She bent and kissed his lips very gently until he pulled her tighter to him, and bruised her lips.

"How about marrying me before you ruin my good name?"

"I told you I'd . . ."

"I know what you told me, and you've had three months to think about it. Seems like you could have given it a lot of thought during that time."

"I have, and to the best of my thinking, Leslie, I don't think I could be rightly happy living in town. You know how foolish I am about the land, and my chickens, and I know I'd be all shut in down there. Why I couldn't even hang my underclothes on the line without the whole town seeing what size bloomers I wore. And I . . ."

He sat bolt right and put his hand over her mouth.

"Not another word. Do you mean to tell me that you would turn down marrying me, regardless how you feel in your heart, just to live out in that miserable house."

"It's not so miserable. I thought you had nice times with us there.,"

"Oh, for the love of God, Ellie. You know what I mean. I want nice things for you. Can't you get that into your silly head."

"You're pressing me now. Aren't you happy like things are."

"You know I am. But any day the thing could blow up in our faces. We can fool the public with our dating as long as you don't turn up pregnant. That's something that won't wait, Ella. It tells its own secret in its own good time. And I need you for my wife. Loving you is wonderful, but I want you in my own bed, so I can reach out and touch you the first thing when I wake up in the mornings, and see you the minute I open my eyes. I want to sleep curled up beside you even when I'm saturated with loving you. There's lots of things that could be so much better."

"Leslie?"

"Yes?"

"I wish I could tell it so that you'd understand me. You don't know what it was like the day I moved out of the big house. How I felt when I looked back and knew that all that had to be behind me, or the things I told myself that day. One of them was that I never intended to be talked out of what little land was left me, or to sign my name on a mortgage. It's like I just can't say good-bye to it. It was the only salvation for me and my babies. Can you understand me?"

"I don't really know, but I know myself and myself is willing to live anywhere as long as it's with you. I can have a phone put in and it won't take too long to build a new house out there."

"You can't do that. All of your paying patients are the ones in town. You'd be as poor as I am before a month was out."

"Oh, some of the ones in town would call me. I'm sure they would."

"I won't hear anymore of it. I don't want you to be as poor as Dr. Kellum. You've just spent too many years getting ready to help people. Maybe we'd better forget it and try to be satisfied like things are for now."

"I'm not going to forget it, and I'm not going to let you have any peace of mind till you say yes." He reached over and pulled her against him again. Even under the thick needled pines and amidst the cooling breeze from the wide blue river, she felt like a hot coal laying beside him. He wished the children were miles away, and that they were in some deeply secluded spot. The time to love is when the heart and body tells one to, not when the time is right for everything and everybody. Instead, he took his harmonica from his hip pocket and played her "Oh, sail tonight my pretty red wings, pretty red wings, sail tonight . . ."

❧ ❧ ❧

HOW SWIFTLY THE WEATHER had changed from one day to the next. Only yesterday had been long and golden and hazy blue, and today the sky was gray and overcast, layers of dark blue clouds laying on the horizons telling her that cold weather was just around the corner. The wind whipped at her legs as she bent over the washboard and rubbed the pieces up, down, up down, and occasionally stood and rubbed some homemade lard soap on them. Then she tossed them into a second tub beside her on the porch, which was filled with clear rinse water. The now empty gourds whipped around in the wind, high on their pole, the birds all hatched and gone, the young having learned to fly and feed for themselves, the old ones seeking a winter home. The noise was an empty shallow sound as the wind whipped into the tiny openings in their sides that had been cut for a doorway to the improvised bird house. The feathers on the chickens stood out ruffled from their body as they came and drank from the waterer made from an old automobile tire cut in half, some drinking water, some drinking in the intermittent specks of sunlight. Down the field a piece, the cow bellowed because the calf couldn't come to her and her bag was full of milk. For a city dweller, it would have been a time of sheer loneliness, but to one with an ear tuned to the country, it was a day pregnant with noises. That's why she didn't hear the footsteps behind her until she saw a ragged overall pants leg standing beside her own.

It had been over a year since Leonard had come to her house, and she had told herself during all this time, that all was dead between them, and had told herself so convincingly that she had made herself believe it, but the sight of his leg standing beside her did something to her that she did not think the sight of him could ever do again. She felt her stomach tighten up against the washboard and she backed away and wiped her soapy reddened hands on her apron.

"I told you not to be coming around anymore."

"Hain't been."

"You're here now, ain't you."

"Looks like it, don't it?"

"Damn you, Leonard. Watcha wanting?"

"You want I should tell you now."

"Tell it or don't tell it. Suit yourself. But stay away from me."

"I could love you so damn good, Ella." There was a combination of eagerness and sadness in his voice that she could not separate.

"And I could love you better than anyone else has ever loved you. But I won't! Because I know now, I have to live with myself, and you can't be a part of that anymore. I'm just sorry. But that's all there is to it," she said.

"That won't ever be all there is to it. Not as long as you live, or I live. You'll know I'm just across the swamp, and that will keep reminding you of how good it's been. And you'll come. I can wait meantime. You want me to bring you anything from the store?"

"I want you to go to hell and stay there. Get out of my yard, you, you, buzzard!"

His eyes and lips were smiling when he picked up his kerosene jug with an Irish potato stuck on the top for its lid and turned and left. She knew that he was recalling her anger and her loving. Sometimes they had been synonymous. But he was wrong. She would never cross that path again and wait for him under the thick swamp cypress, or on the meadowed field, or on the edge under the pines. He had his chance and didn't want it, and never again would she offer herself to him. Watching him walking down the railroad track she noticed how stooped he had become and she reckoned it was from letting the plowline hang around his neck while he worked. He's so much older, so much is gone, and she leaned over the tub of clear water and examined her own reflection. "Face was still smooth, but God, look at those lines on my neck, and it's all saggy. And that hair! Still curly but all uncombed and coming unpinned. And skin as brown as a Cherokee. I'm the only brown skinned woman in church, I guess, but then I'm the only one who plows in the fields or works uncovered without a big bonnet or long sleeves and gloves. What does Leslie see in me? I should count myself lucky and say yes this very day." She leaned over and steadied herself holding onto the pump bench and vomited until it seemed as if her guts would come next. "It's because I'm all upset. He had no business coming here on a Monday morning and saying that to me. He had no business coming here any morning. Damn him. Damn his smart mouth and his smiling lips. Oh, damn him!"

She was glad that Woodrow was in school and didn't hear or see Leonard. The boy hated him with such violence that she wondered if she had covered her deeds as well as she thought. It was a weak woman who turned back to the tub and tried to continue the washing, she was not prepared for the sudden lurch her stomach gave against the board. She straightened up and put her hand to the spot. "Why, that felt like, but it couldn't be . . . But what else could it have been? Surely it wouldn't have moved, yet . . . her period had never been regular and she could never tell a thing by that. But surely she would have known it before now, but then . . . would she? Oh, my God, if that's so, Leslie will hate me, and I'll be alone, alone with another baby and no husband. Oh, I couldn't bear that." She was unconscious of the fact that she was wringing her hands and talking aloud to herself until the small girl interrupted her.

"What the matter, Mama?"

"Oh, oh, oh, nothing, honey. Run and play and don't bother Mama right now . . ."

"But, Mama . . ."

"Run on, please honey."

The following Sunday when preacher Cornaby had said the last amen after having showered them with fire and brimstone for an hour and a half, he begged the congregation's attention to the fact that the entire congregation was invited to attend a wedding the next Sunday, the wedding of their own beloved doctor and one of their faithful members, Mrs. Ella Simpson. Everyone was cordially invited, and every head in the church

turned and gasped and stared at them on ...ck seat, for
though they had all known he was paying co...ot one had
thought that he would ever marry her.

"Not her, of all people," the women said.

"And why not?" said the husbands.

"You would defend the hussy! Just like a man."

"I'm not defending her. I just said why not."

"I should say why not! Just such attitudes as that is ...hy
she's like she is. She knows all you men stand behind her. A...d
if one won't, the other will . . . Oh."

"I don't think Ella's like that at all. She seems to be mighty
kind, and you gotta admit she took ahold of that scrub farm, and
had pulled them a living out of that land. Not many women
coulda done it."

"Not many women coulda turned men her way like she's
done, I'd say ain't enough for her. And she picks the cream, she
does. First Ben. And now Dr. Humphreys. He'll find out!"

"Find out what?"

"Why, what a hussy she is, that's what. You mark my word.

"I always, do, dear."

She had first thought it best not to tell Leslie until after their
marriage about the baby, but she had fooled one man and the
man had hated her with a passion that knew no bounds for
years. However, that baby had not been his . . . surely that had
made the difference. A man wouldn't hate his own child,
reputation or no reputation, would he? She had decided that she
would try the straight line this time by telling him.

"Is it possible, doctor, to be four or five month's pregnant
and not have known it."

"It's been known for a woman to be nine month's pregnant
and not know it. Thought she had a tumor. Why?"

"I think I'm the woman in the first case."

"I know."

"You what?" Incredulity filled her voice.

"I know. I've known for sometime. I thought women knew
these things first. I thought you'd never mention it."

"I kn... ...is doesn't sound right, but I just suspected it today."

"Ell... ...or the love of God!"

"I ... ...n it. I didn't know it. I'd move away where people would know if I could afford it, but I can't. I'm really sorry, Lesli...

...ell, I'm not. Not if this means you're going to marry m..."

"You're not just feeling sorry for me, are you?"

"The only person I've felt sorry for is myself. I'd been doubting my own manhood."

"You men and your manhood! That's all you ever think about?"

"Aren't you glad we're like that?"

"I certainly am not!"

"I know better and I'm glad."

His kiss told her all the things she longed to know—that he was good, and tender, and kind, and strong . . . and he loved her, and wonder of wonders, he wanted to marry her, family and all.

—Chapter 18—

THE BABY CAME in its own due time, as all normal babies have a way of seemingly doing, and though every female tongue in the community wagged, every male was as delighted that the doctor was a good man as well as a good doctor. As old Dr. Kellum had been both, they looked for the same trait in his protege. For one, the people did not wonder who the father of this young one was, for the little eight pound newborn looked exactly like the doctor and completed the link in the chain in his maturity. He now held the newborn more tenderly, doctored the pregnant with more care, hurried to sick children more quickly, and became less detached to all his patients. And as spring to summer changed, he would sit in the porch swing, holding her tenderly and talking to her as if she understood every word.

"That's a martin in the gourd, honey. He's fussing because his wife won't let him out the door. He couldn't find a worm this time for the baby and she won't let him inside until he brings food. How about that old wife . . . That's Mama's pigs grunting. They're fighting over the last grain of corn. What we ever going to do with Mama and her pigs? Take them all to town?"

But he knew that he would never take them all to town. Here was the land, and the land was theirs and the land was real. His patients had not minded calling him on the phone during the night, and he still spent the day at the office in town, but there was so much to be done here, so much that must be done to the house and the yard, and always there was the woman waiting for him. That made the day, the year, and the life worth living. All the days that had passed before he had known her had merged into nothings and each day since stood apart warm and happy and golden and individually wonderful. Not often given to eloquent words, he said over and over to himself, "Oh thou art everything, Ellie. My life. My everything." The sudden gust of wind made him shiver and hold the baby closer and he knew that before long, a summer shower would break and the big warm drops would drop on the tin roof, each like a dancer holding its own pit, pat, pit, and the air would then be cold and the earth new all over, and while the rain fell, he would love the woman, and he, too would be reborn. How lovely she had become again since he had forbidden her to work in the fields. He had brought Jim with him, as he refused to leave, even at the threat of having all his pay severed, so he had relented. At first he had slept in the corn crib with a pile of old quilts, but he and Woodrow worked together and made him a one room house between theirs and the barn. He had an old cot, and a lantern, and that and his harmonica and guitar were all that were necessary for his happiness. That plus being near the doctor.

Every day brought new things to Woodrow's life. He had put aside his apprehensions and hates and feelings of guilt, and taken joy in learning to play the harmonica and to sing all the songs that Jim knew. Music had always been a part of his life. Even though they had only a few records, they had been played over and over on the Victrola, and he had inherited Ella's love for music. It was not long before he could take up Jim's guitar and play songs that he had made up, songs with a very good rhythm that astounded even Ella and Leslie.

"It's all right to play those things for fun, but you mustn't let them make you forget about studying. You won't amount to a hill of beans without an education . . ." And Ella would turn to Leslie and ask him silently to back up her argument.

He understood her plea and jumped into the void. "There's so many wonderful things to learn about and you won't be able to do all of them if you don't keep up at school. Music is for funning. That's all. When school starts back in the fall, there won't be time for these playing sessions every night. Maybe on weekends."

And Woodrow would take their arguments and turn them into a song right before their eyes and play along.

"Oh, the doctor man, says, the music's just for fun. But I say long before man was begun, music filled the air, the land, and the sea, and I know that music's the making of me. And Mama she say, you gotta study hard, to pay for your taters and beans and lard. But I know that man will pay to see my homemade music, my harp, and me."

And he could go for verse after verse until his mother would break down in laughter and Leslie would smile at this boy, full grown in size, if not in years.

"I do know, I don't think you could hear it thunder, Leslie."

"Sorry, honey. You been calling me?"

"All the commotion and you ask if I am calling you. There's something in the hen house just raising cain. Woodrow and Jim went a running with the rifle. Please, go on down there before they shoot one another."

"Why?"

"Why? I said, they'll shoot one another."

"You're getting yourself anxious over nothing. Both boys could shoot the eye out of a possum at a hundred yards. And that's a hell of a lot better than I can do. Let them be men, Ellie, especially our boy."

"He's always been a man. Had to be. I want him to be a boy some, and let you be the man. He wasn't wearing long pants before he'd tell me, I'll be your man, Mama. I'm going to take care of you."

"I'm whipped. I'm always whipped in an argument with you. Here, take the baby. Night time anyway, and I'll take a look. Feel better?"

"Get on with you and your wise old owl ways. I'll take care of you later on."

And he knew that she would.

The possum was a white short haired beady eyed creature and he had already killed three of the laying hens. The rest of the flock was squawking madly and the rooster was trying frantically to attack the animal. Jim had a long stick trying to beat him out of the roost so that he could kill him without killing one of the chickens, but the animal lay down and acted as if he were dead until Jim tried to pick him up by the tail. Then he hissed through his sharp teeth and tried to bite the colored boy's hand, whereupon he dropped him like a hot potato.

Leslie stood and observed the boys for a moment before they were aware of his presence. Yes, I do love these two. And very much. But how much more I love that little bit of humanity that was conceived in the damp broomsage last summer. That's what the Bible meant when it said, "out of man's loins." These were just words once. Now they explained his deepest feelings. His seed had been planted in the belly of the woman he loved. How lucky could one man be? He had thought when he graduated from medical school that nothing could ever be more. Only less, from that day on. How dumb the young—and unmarried. And how all fired wise they feel. Even now I'm just beginning to learn.

"Give up trying to shoot him, boys. Just club him to death. You might get a serious bite."

"Oh. He's a wise creature, Mister Leslie. First he dead. Then he ain't. Then he am. I do wish he'd make up his feeble mind."

"He's a hopper, Dad. His belly is full of Ma's best hens. Wait'll she takes a look in the morning. She'll bristle like a hog."

After they had killed him, they took his hairless pink tail and threw him outside the house till morning when Jim would bury him.

"That's a sorta mean thing we did to him, don't you think, Dad?"

These were the kinds of questions a boy needed to ask a man all his life and had never had the opportunity, and right from the first, Leslie had asked him to think of him as his real daddy and feel free to ask him anything.

"Perhaps more so to a city fellow, I guess, than to a farmer. You can't live out here without the rule of survival of the fittest."

"What's that?"

"Well, in a way, it means killing those things not fit to live, such as the possum, for instance. There is no good that he does at all, but he kills many helpful farm creatures, so we eliminate as many of them as possible. And still they are prolific enough to keep their race going strongly so there's no danger of getting rid of them all, if that's worrying you."

"No, I wasn't thinking about that. I guess I mean, he was trying so hard to fool us into thinking he was already dead. Then he could have slipped off and back to his family."

"Maybe he's a bachelor."

"Nope. Mama one. I looked."

"Well. I wouldn't worry. She'd have been back tomorrow night after more hens and the night after that. We did a good thing."

Leslie had thought that his explanation had settled things in the boy's mind, but later that night when Ella and he sat on the porch and swung, the rain falling gently now, he swung the door open to Jim's house and in the lantern light, he saw Jim mouthing his harp, and Woodrow playing his guitar. He and Ella stood swinging to listen, and they heard him singing of the poor old mama possum who had wanted a chicken supper for her babies, and had died trying to get the best for her family. "And still the small ones lie and wait for the mammy who lies cold and will not come again . . ."

"Well, I'll be damned," was all Leslie could think of to say and he took Ella's hand and led her into the house.

She was lovely in the lamplight, and it was a nightly ritual for him to watch her undress. Something about her slip coming slowly up over her head thrilled him just as it always had. Occasionally she fooled him by taking it down from the top and letting it drop to the floor in a crumpled heap. It was wonderful to wear silk again. The years in between had led her to a point to where she wore no slip at all. What a funny thing my life is, she thought over and over again. From rags to riches to rags to riches again. Perhaps not riches in the sense of the really rich, but rich enough to her and her kind of people. Rich in the sense they did not want for food or clothing anymore, and the fact that they owned an automobile and could buy gas for it all the time. But I'll be on my guard this time. If all this leaves me. I'll never let it hurt me again. I'll never let myself be in such a fix again as when I moved away from that big house where my sister sleeps in my bed, the bed that should be my children's bed right this moment. I'll watch. Even silently, I'll watch, and try not be hurt again.

They had not done much to repair the house, but he had a telephone put in from the beginning because it was necessary for his patients in town to reach him, too. She had not been sitting nude in his lap many minutes before it rang with its clanging solo, and he deposited her on the bed with a bounce.

"I'll lay money on the table that's Mrs. Morgan and she's about to have her baby. I'd forgotten her time was about up. Want to make a bet?"

"No. If I bet, that'd make it come true, and I hope it's not tonight."

"You shoulda bet me. I was right. Her water broke an hour ago," he told her after answering the phone.

"Did anyone ever tell you you're a teaser?" she asked as she put her clothes back on.

"No, and I'll whip your pretty tail if you tell me that now."

"Well, you are!"

Whereupon he smacked her hard on her bottom and she screeched.

"I'm sorry, honey. Really sorry. Women do have babies, you know."

"Yes. I know it quite well. Better than you think. I'm pregnant myself!"

"You're kidding?"

"No. I'm not kidding. Don't you think it possible."

"Yes. I know it's possible. But the baby is so young . . ."

Ella had to laugh. "I wonder how many husbands have ever said that. And didn't you tell me with all your doctor knowledge that I wouldn't get pregnant nursing."

"Well, that's what the book says."

"Throw your old book away then. Are you mad?"

"Mad? No. Startled for the moment, but very glad. You're so pretty pregnant. Warm and round and rosy." He pulled her to him and kissed her neck.

"I want to live a long long time so I can spend all of it making love to you. Did you know that, girl?"

"Uh, huh. But get on or Mrs. Morgan will have had the baby."

"Call Woodrow in as soon as I leave. I don't want you in the house alone."

"Oh, silly, if anything happened, they could hear me call."

"They might, and they might not. Do like I say, please, Ellie."

"Yes, lord and master!" She leaned over and brushed his lips with hers.

"Stop your fooling. And do it."

After her husband had left her, she went to the back doorway to call Woodrow in, but she stood for a moment and listened to the music coming from the doorway of the cabin like structure. The guitar was soft and the harp was sad and the song was of the Indian princess who had died and left her lover alone. On and on they sang. "Oh, sail tonight, my pretty red wings, My pretty red wing, sail tonight." She did not have the heart to make him stop and come to bed just yet. Of course, they were nearby. How pretty the music was, but don't get too involved, son. Music is a playing thing, a thing for pastimes, and work is for working and making a living. Too much playing will get in the way of learning to work, and you must do better than Leonard has done with his life. Be a doctor, or a lawyer. We can afford college for you now. All things are possible when you go to school. These things filled her heart and mind as she lay in bed and breathed the clean air through the open unscreened window.

The sharp snapping of a twig under the pear tree made her heart lurch, then her mind told her that it was only a dog. But would a dog have been so heavy footed as to break a branch? Maybe just to be on the safe side, she'd better look. Oh, I'm just being a silly goose, she thought. But her apprehensions had foundation when she peered from the window and saw a dark human figure bent over under the tree picking pears off the ground and filling his pockets and cap. Who on earth? As a cloud moved away from the moon, there was enough light for her to see that it was a raggedly dressed man. Of course, a tramp stealing pears. Should she call the boys or let him steal in peace and go his way? Jim might come with the rifle and shoot. There might be even a man dead—and over pears. Leslie would want her to call them, she was sure . . . still. It was only a few pears, and if he came closer to the house, there would still be time to call out. Try as she did, she could not make the thick lump go down in her throat and she did not take her eyes off the man until he raised up, looked all around, and crept down the back path and down the track toward the railroad water tank. There he would divide the pears with his less bold friends who were waiting for him to come and bring anything edible. She did not doubt that they had a fire lit on which they anticipated roasting a fat hen, but the light coming from Jim's cabin had probably discouraged him from approaching the chicken house just behind. She hugged herself tightly to stop her body's trembling and went into the kitchen where she lit the lamp again and put on a pot of coffee to boil. It may be late when he comes, but I'm going to wait. I'm going to wait for the man of this house to come . . .

She went into the adjoining room, looked down upon the retarded girl child and whispered as she pushed back the jet black curls that hung on her forehead, now damp with perspiration. "Sleep well, poor baby, poor, poor, baby . . . always my baby. The rest grow quickly and forget me, but you're always my baby, and the child turned her head and smiled in her sleep."

How often in the past year Leslie had tried to talk to her

about Sybil, but she had closed her mind to every one of his arguments and continued to love the child with all her heart.

"I'm not asking you not to love her, Ellie. Just please don't let yourself go overboard with it. You know you can't keep her like with the others. She can't live a normal life. They seldom live to be ten years old."

She put her fingers in her ears like a small child trying to avoid hearing his parents scolding her. Gently he came and took her hands down and held her.

"Just try to think of her as a small wounded friend who needs your care. Like the birds you mend who soon fly away. You hate to see them leave, but you know they must."

"I don't want to listen. Please stop, it, Leslie. She's really no worse, is she, really?"

"No. Not really. No worse and no better. But she'll never be better and she certainly will get worse. I'm not trying to hurt you, honey. I'm trying to help you from being too deeply hurt later on. She doesn't know whether you talk to her or not. Why spend all that time cooing to her?"

"She does so know it. Don't you see her smile and her eyes light up when anyone talks to her?"

"No, honestly I don't, honey. But perhaps you do."

When she heard the car come into the yard, she tried hurriedly to arrange her thoughts. Should she tell him about the hobo? Or should she just say she had been restless and unable to sleep. The complexities of truth and untruths did not bother her. They never had. What fitted the moment best was what was right. If it hurt anyone by telling the truth, she told the lie, and did not ever have fringes of conscious about it, but in his embrace this time, she trembled so that he did not believe her feeble tale of restlessness.

"Why in the hell didn't you call Woodrow? A few shots over his damn head would have scared him and his friends off for good. They just know they can come and go free here is why they come so often." He scolded her after she had relented and told him.

"But they don't really steal. They take. Because they're hungry, they take food. That isn't really stealing."

"Well, it is sure as hell in my book."

"Perhaps. But I don't draw the line quite as sharply as you do."

He had to laugh in spite of his fears for her safety, for he knew there would be no reasoning with her. If it was right for her animals, then it was right for people. The kindest way was the only way regardless of the risk. She thought nothing of stepping into the pen with a sharp tusked boar and rubbing his back while he ate. "But he loves me," she would protest to her husband. "Why should he want to bite me?" The thought of what those ugly teeth could do to a human's leg made a cold hard pain come in the bottom of his stomach, but he could not deny that the hog loved her. Yet when she loaned him for boar service to the neighbors, they had to crate him up and nail the door to haul him home. Foam would be running out of the corners of his mouth and out the hog box before they left the yard. "Poor fellow. He doesn't know why they do him like this."

"Oh, he'll get over it as soon as he finds out what's waiting for him when he gets there."

"Get on with you. You're just jealous because he plays the field."

"Nope. There is no greener clover than I find here. Not if I looked the world over." He bent and kissed her between her breasts."

When they finally lay inside each others arms that night, the strains of "The Maple On the Hill" were coming from Jim's house, and Woodrow's strong soft voice filled their room.

⁜ ⁜ ⁜

TIME BRINGS IRREVOCABLE CHANGES to everyone's life, but for Ella, the changes were for the better, and her happiness made time stand still for her. Once again, she was the envy of the women at church. Her skin was softer, rosier, more youthful.

Her bonnet was wider and had more flowers, her gloves of pure lace, her dress of pure eyelet embroidery. There were only two women at church who did not once again admire and envy her.

Time had not been at all kind to Kate. Her face had always been long and bony. Age had made it appear to be skeletal in appearance and the sharp line of her mouth made it even worse. Bernard had drunk himself to death, and the store had folded like a long overplayed accordion. She had been able to hang onto the land and keep it and rent it, but the tobacco and cotton were so cheap as to hardly pay for the fertilizer it took to raise it. The paint had peeled from the once stately house and the boards of the front porch had rotted and sagged. She had hoped to remarry, but there had been no gentleman callers. The very fact that Ella had made two good marriages had infuriated her. Her perturbation upon seeing Ella each Sunday was obvious to the whole congregation, and the fact that Ella and her family filled up a whole bench made her own life obviously empty. It only showed people how barren her life had been. Just behind her sat Eva Belle and her five young ones in their homemade clothes. "Ha," Kate would tell herself. I'm certainly glad I don't have that motley crew hanging onto my coat tail day and night, and with a husband that won't even come to church with me. But alone in her bed and the big house at night, her heart spoke louder than her mind and she wished that there was someone, anyone who could share the days and nights with her. Her lacquered front fell away and she saw herself getting old and ugly and years of loneliness ahead of her. She had not been the kind of sister with whom Ella would want to share her good fortune now. Kate could never stoop to ask them to visit her. They might think that she was without friends or even needed them. So it was that she sang louder than anyone else in church. Even if it was off key, it was louder.

The second woman who resented Ella's good fortune was the woman who sat on the back pew with the five small ones. Ella's lifelong friend had come to face the truth and live with it. Her husband had been unfaithful. Even so, he was the father of that tall handsome boy on the end of the most prominent pew. This she knew with a dead certainty and had at last accepted it. She had tried to talk to Leonard about it, but he had laughed at her and told her, "You're so silly, Eva. Get on with the dishes." He dismissed her similarly every time she tried to talk about it, and his abrupt dismissal of the subject told her it was so and that it could not be aired between them and hung out to dry like their hand rubbed washing. It would have to stay in the bottom of the dirty clothes basket for their lifetime. And surely, too, it could not happen again, not with Ella safely, and she hoped happily, married. But how on earth did she stay so young looking? She had matured more fully in body since her first marriage, but old age had not claimed her. Why didn't she get old like the rest of them? Just look at me and Kate. One thing is certain, she'll never put her foot under my table again. Not if I have to bust the whole damned thing open right in front of her and Leonard, too.

And though the Cornaby preached his heart out, there were few there that paid heed to what he said, so absorbed were they in their own thoughts. They were always startled that the time had passed quickly and it was time again to sing the invitation hymn, Number 100, "Softy and Tenderly." And as if to compensate for their idle minds, they sang as if they were really traveling the road to glory that minute. Flies flew in and out the unscreened windows at random, lit on the top of hot and hairy hands alike, perched at will on hat and babies, and were fanned away by Jones's Funeral Parlor fans.

"God is not going to be so lenient. He's going to burn down your barns one night. You needn't wait, I tell you brother, thinking you will get right with God tomorrow or next Sunday. You might not live till another sun rises. I tell you, sisters, the time is now! You don't want your tiny children living with parents of sin. And the only way is to repent. Repent, I tell you now. Now."

And as they shook his hand as they filed out, some of them told him, "I tell you, Preacher, you really told it to them today. You hit it right on the head." But not a one thought he could be the preacher's man target. And so with life.

Time also claimed the lives of two of the people dearest to Ella's heart, but she accepted each death in a way that Leslie did not think possible. It had been near Christmas time when she noticed Sybil was not drinking as much milk as she usually did, and she had Leslie check her thoroughly, but he could not find anything out of the ordinary. Looking down on her for a moment, Ella's chest suddenly constricted and she felt faint. What's wrong with me? Sybil didn't even have a fever; nonetheless, Ella had a foreboding sensation that she was looking down on her baby for the last time. My baby. My baby. Always my baby. And so pitiful now with her baby teeth gone and no permanent ones coming in after them. You really are a baby. The child filled a full sized cot, but still could only wave an arm occasionally and open and close her eyes. Any movement of her head was entirely reflex. I'm just being silly again, she thought and she bent and kissed her. She was glad that her children accepted Sybil as a part of their lives. Since Woodrow had learned to play the guitar he would play for hours beside her cot. If Sybil flashed a fleeting smile, it was all the reward he craved. Then Ella would go over and put both plump arms around Woodrow's neck and kiss him. "You're such a good boy," she would tell him.

"You said you found me in a stump hole, remember? And that a buzzard had laid the egg and the sun hatched it, and you felt sorry for the ugly buzzard baby, and went out and brought it in your apron, and that buzzard baby was me."

She shook with laughter, "It's been years since I told you that. I'd never have though you'd remember it. That's an old tale."

I remember lots of things you don't think I do. I can still remember Daddy."

"Daddy?" the word started her momentarily.

"Sure. In the big house, and the store. He didn't like me very much, did he?"

"Why Woodrow. Of course, he loved you. Why on earth do you say that?"

"I never went with him like I do with Dad now. I was always with you or Grandma there."

"Well, mostly, but your Daddy was a very busy man. And a very smart man with books. I hope you'll continue with your books, too."

"You're trying to get me off the subject, ain't you, Ma?"

"Aren't you, Ma? Please don't say ain't all the time, son."

"Well, aren't you, then by gun?"

"Yes. And no. I'm not trying to get off the subject of Ben, but yes, I'd really rather talk about us now. I hope you won't be hurt, dear, but I was never happy with your father like I am now."

"Neither was I!"

"I don't think you really should say that, son. You can't remember too well."

"I remember, all right. And I know I wasn't happy with him like now."

She had given up on the conversation. Lying in bed that night, she tossed and turned so that even Leslie could sense that she was not sleeping. She told him her fears about Sybil.

"They're not silly at all. That doesn't mean they will come true, but the sensations of the mind are beyond all of our understanding. The spiritual is what we call God, dear, and, of course, we don't understand that."

Nevertheless, she was not comforted, and she went again and felt of the child. But again she was not feverish, and was breathing evenly. Looking down on her again, she did not feel the presence of death as she had earlier. She heaved a sigh, went to bed and was soon sleeping soundly.

Even though they had remodeled the house and bought new furniture, they still heated with a wood heater, and Jim would come in mornings before they were awake and start a fire with lightwood splinters and seasoned pine wood. By the time they arose, the sitting room was warm as toast, and the fire was burning in the kitchen stove so that there was little to be done except fry the meat and cook the rice and biscuits. They kept Sybil's cot in the corner of the living room because long after the fire died out, the coals would give off heat, and she was the only one in the household who could not cover herself. Though Jim called for the doctor first, his tone made Ella hit the floor in a second and run into the living room still in her gown.

"Don't look, Miss Ella. Let the doctor look about her." But she did not have to wait for Leslie to tell her that the child was dead. The fact that she had turned on her side and that her tongue was protruding and bloody told her that Sybil had had a fit and in a convulsive moment had been able to turn. For a few moments her sobs filled the house, but then the sorrow on Priscilla's and Woodrow's faces and the compassion in Leslie's, made her think, I am thinking of myself. Why cry now? God's angels are these children. Preacher Cornaby said so himself. She went over and hugged Priscilla tightly.

"Please, don't cry baby. God is going to give us another baby very soon. Not one to take sister's place, because she was her own herself and one person can't take another's place, but one so that we won't be lonely for her. Maybe it'll be a little fat boy. Daddy would be proud of that, wouldn't he?" The child nodded affirmatively with tears streaming down her face.

"But Mama? Now there won't be any Christmas at our house. Just a funeral is all."

What do people do who don't have children at moments like these, she thought, and she hugged her tightly again.

"Of course there will be Christmas in this house, just like always, and you're going to help Mama make the cakes and cookies, same as always. Only today we mustn't celebrate. Today is Sybil's day. Understand, honey?"

Looking up she saw more love in a man's eyes than she had ever hoped to live long enough to see. His worry about her had disappeared and he knew that everything would right itself again in its own time.

"Do let me bear this man a son, God. Please . . ."

They spent the day after Sybil's funeral hunting holly with berries and mistle toe. Leslie cautioned them to be careful with the ax, and to take care not to get chilled. Ice lined the banks of the branches and wet leaves lay atop the stream like a cold brown blanket. Birds were scarce now and even the rabbits did not show themselves. For once, Jim and Woodrow did not sing. Yesterday was still too much with them, but they talked incessantly and helped Priscilla over the logs and through the briars. Ella would have loved to have tramped the woods with them, but she was too heavy with the child she was carrying and there was Miranda Lee still unable to walk good, so she sat by the heater and rocked her and closed her burning eyes and hummed. Leslie had had the cot taken down and put in the barn but she still had to glance over to the corner every few minutes, and it still shocked her to look there and not see it. I mustn't let them all see it. I must only cry inside. I must keep saying, it's for the best, and then I'll believe it soon. She swallowed hard and closed her eyes again.

There never was a baby born who had a father who loved it more, she thought as she bent and kissed the hair of the one in her lap, and the child's big luminous eyes looked up at her questioningly.

Momentarily startled by a hard rap at the door, she recovered quickly and called out, "Come right in," but she did not expect to see Leonard standing in the doorway. How old he looks, and so unkept! His gray beard unshaven and his bib overalls patched in many places. What did I ever see in him? Leslie would kill him if he caught him here. She held the baby tighter to her breast and tried to act as if this were not a man she had known and loved intimately for years. Surely he could understand that things do come to an end. That all was a yesterday and today was an entirely different world.

"I come to say we're sorry 'bout Sybil."

"You said that yesterday."

"So I did. But I come to say it when your husband ain't home."

"Well, he will be home promptly, so say it and leave."

"You lie the same as ever Ellie. Eyes dancing like an Indian's, and red spots in your cheeks. He won't be home till dark.

Everybody knows that. I watch a lot a days from my field. Don't you ever see me?"

"No, I never look."

"I see lots of things—you and him hugging, same as you hugged me, and you and him walking in the woods. I coulda touched you lots of time and you never knew I was there."

"You've got a lot of nerve. That's called spying."

"I don't care what it's called. That's the only way I could see you. I waited lots of time for you in the meadow thinking you'd come." There was a sadness in his voice that she would not let herself hear.

"I told you how it was going to be. No more coming—not now, not ever. Can't you get that through your big dumb head."

"It may not be filled with learning, but it's filled with loving the same as your old man's. The rich and poor put their britches on the same way or hadn't you noticed?"

"I don't know about how the rich do. We certainly are a far cry from being rich. If you'd pay for the last two babies at your house, it might help." She was instantly sorry that he had said that. Leslie would find it unforgivable to have asked for money owed him, and it was out of her hands. She had meant to be cruel, but not that cruel.

"I ain't forgot the debt. We don't have the money. You should know how that is. We'll get it though, come fall, if the taters sell good this year."

"We aren't suffering. I didn't mean to say that anyhow. Please forget it."

"No, you were right to mention it, but that's neither here nor there. I come to say if you don't meet me this week, I'm going to tell the Doc everything about us—about Priscilla, and Woodrow, and all the times. I'm not fooling this time, Ellie. I been a wanting you too long to hold my peace anymore."

"What good do you think that would do? Leslie would take the gun to you in a second. And aside from that, I told him everything about us afore we was married. He said nothing mattered that had already passed."

Glibly she lied on and on. Truth to her was a thing for the occasion. As a child it had been necessary to lie in order to compete with Kate and stay out of trouble with her father.

"Well, I'll be damned," was all he could think to say. He looked like a small boy at a birthday party who had not received a single gift and who realized that the hour was too late now for any guest to come. His cheeks suddenly seemed to have shrunk, and the lines deepened in his face.

"You're not foolin' me for a minute, Ellie. I know one man is still not enough for you."

"Get out of this house. Get out before I call Jim to make you get. And if you so much as try to talk to Woodrow, I'll find a way to kill you myself. You'd better believe I mean it to." The baby whimpered in her lap, and the nearby dog's hair bristled on his back.

"I don't want to hurt the boy. I'll never want that, Ellie. I'm so sorry I was such a coward when you needed me and loved me so damned much."

"You could say you're sorry for the rest of your life, and that would not be enough to change things. I'm very happy now. I wish you were, too, Leonard, and you could be if you'd let yourself. There's only one chance to plant a garden, one chance to tend your fields, one time to harvest, and one time when love is young and new and real, and we missed that time, and it's over, over and dead as a doorknob. So forget it!"

"I'll never forget . . ."

But she had clamped both hands over her ears and he knew that she did not intend to listen to another word he had to say. He was visibly more stooped when he left.

How cruel the land is to the ones who love it, she mused. It drains youth away quickly, dries one's skin, bends one's back, breaks one's bones, and yet we are as chained to it as if we were behind bars. All these years when we were going to really make money on it, and we have barely paid our fertilizer bills. Tobacco still selling cheap, corn that a body couldn't give away, potatoes that could only be banked in dirt mounds for eating during the winter and early spring. No market for their hogs, or cows, all beef being shipped in from the west, and still we cling to it.

"What's he want, Ma?" Woodrow asked angrily as he put the holly down on the back porch.

"Came to say he was sorry about your sister."

She was glad that Leonard had aged so that the two no longer resembled each other in appearance.

Moreover, when summer came again and they were happily engaged in the harvest of their green tobacco and their frolicking around the barns, Sybil was a pleasant memory, a part of her life that she could recall and not be unhappy about. When the last of the green leaf was put in the barn to cure, they killed a passel of chickens, stewed them in the big iron wash pot, and invited all the people who had helped in the harvest. Young and old came, and it was a saying that the one who ate the neck piece would be the next to marry. The aroma of the curing tobacco was pungent and rich smelling, and the music had a quality that was not often found around a barn. It could make the rowdiest child calm down and listen, make courting couples reach for each other's hands, and older lovers wish for the bedtime to come. It could make one hear the sound of the waves, or the clump of horses, or the approach of death, or the depths of sorrow, or make one's foot tap incessantly to a happy tune.

"He's got a way with music, Ella. I know you're a heap proud of him."

"Yes, yes, we are," she'd answer quietly as if trying to make her heart be quiet also.

"There'll be heaps of people wanting him to play for dances."

"Not yet. He's too young."

"Have you heard yet about Cleep Humphries?"

"Why, no. What's he done?"

"Got drunk as a hoot owl last night and broke into Bessie's kitchen and broke her dishes all up, and when Ed went to put his boot on this morning, he thought it was a might damp, and so help me Jesus, Cleep had peed it half full. Bessie talked like he done him some cussin' . . ."

"Sounds like him. Did you get your pencils in the mail?"

"Yeah, and the kids near fought over them."

This time of year brought advertising pencils from tobacco warehouses soliciting dry tobacco and the coming of the pencils was a much looked for advent. The music and the dust and the night and the tobacco were one with the land and the people. And what else was there anywhere on earth?

Part II

—Chapter 19—

A LONG, FOUR-DOOR, shining black 1930 Ford pulled into the yard and dragged its brakes, scaring guinea hens every which way and sending the old yellow dog yelping under the house and the bantam rooster high and safe into the top of the chaney ball tree. Its horn was loud enough to have waked the dead, but its owner meant for everyone to come out and admire it. Ella was standing at the pump bench in the side yard washing collard greens and scraping the rust off a piece of side meat out of the pickled barrel. I'm too dirty to go out, she thought. I'll slip around in the back and let Priscilla go to the door. More'n likely a traveling sales man anyhow, and she looked down and saw that she was barefooted. But the horn continued to blow with a sharp persistence, and it did not look as if Priscilla was anywhere to be seen. Oh, to hell with how she looked. It wouldn't take her but a minute to send them on their slick tongued way. She wiped her wet hands on the bottom of her worn apron and walked heavily around to the car. Her once blonde hair, now heavily streaked with gray, hung damp on her forehead and the back of her neck. He looked like . . . but then every young blond headed man looked like him . . . but he grinned like him. And there grinning beside him was, praise Jesus, none other than Jim.

"How you like me now, Ma?" Woodrow was grinning broadly, both hands on the wheel, his chest thrown back and his hair in a greased pompadour.

"Get out of the contraption, son, and let me hug you. You coulda wrote me. You coulda wrote me just one line. I looked every day for a letter."

"I didn't want to write till I had some good news to tell and we been real busy. But I've come to tell you 'bout it now."

She was lost in the big man's strong embrace, she of the small frame and he built like the man who had sired him, but she hugged him as tightly as she was able.

"Three years and not a line. I thought you was dead, son. Where you been?"

"I'll tell you all about it tonight. Where's Priss and Miranda? I'll bet they won't even know me. I've brought something pretty for everybody."

He stopped talking for a moment and looked around. How different things looked than he had remembered them. The white paint had peeled from the house. The porch had sagged again, the fence on the side of the yard had rusted down. And how old Ma had become. She who looked like a young girl just three years ago now looks like a plump middle aged woman. Even the atmosphere around the place smelled differently. The shine off everything had gone . . . or does every traveler think that because he has seen so many shining new things. I'm just imagining this. Home, where are you? Please be the same again for me, home!

"How 'bout this suit, Ma? Ever seen anything quite like it? And she had to admit that she hadn't. Its lapel ran the full length of the coat, except for one low slung button, and his collar was buttoned high and he wore no tie at all. From his waist hung a long gold chain and some gold looking fan dangles were dangling from it. Yes, it was different alright. She had never seen anything like it.

"Wait'll you see Jim's. Come on out, Jimmy Boy. Let her take a gander at you, too."

She did not find that Jim had changed in his physical appearance as Woodrow had for he had been a full grown man when they had run off together. And it had been easy, so easy. All they had to do was to lie in wait at the water trestle a few hundred yards down the track and hop on the freight when it took on water, and then they were many miles from home before it stopped again. They had repeated that all over the country.

Oh, cursed train that took my boy from me. Damn you. Damn you, but Jim had changed in his dress and manner. He had gold put on his front teeth and he was wearing one of the most expensive suits that she had even seen. With it he wore a white shirt and a tiny black string for a tie. Only his appetite had remained unchanged.

"We been hoping to make it for supper. All the last hundred miles, Woodie wouldn't even stop for water. Said he intended, the good Lord willing, to put his feet under his Ma's table this night. Got any good collards and back bone cooked?"

Convulsive sobs wracked her body and she pulled her apron up and covered her face deep in the heart of it. Down in the hollow a hoot owl screech and a locust sang his mating song and she was deaf to the sounds she loved. Even the air so pregnant with the aromas of blooming flowers and tall green corn did not penetrate her nostrils. Between sobs she managed to cry, "You coulda wrote me one line . . . I thought you was dead, son, I thought you was dead, all those days and nights just thinking of nothing else . . ."

"Oh, Ma. Don't take on rightly so. I knew you was well taken care of what with Doc and all, and I didn't want to come back till I could come and say I'd done what I set out to do. This car is ours, Ma. These clothes are paid for. And we got a suitcase more that's full just like them. And a guitar that makes the sweetest music this side of heaven. You have to plug it in to play it. How 'bout that? I gotta lot of new things to show you."

Just like he had seen the Doc do often, he took her face in both hands and lifted it and kissed her on her forehead.

"No more crying. You'll know from now on where I'll be for the rest of my life, I hope. You're going to be able to turn the radio on and hear me every Saturday night, maybe during the week days, too, on records. What time you looking for Doc home tonight. I gotta tell him a lot of things, too."

She continued to shake her head negatively, but he could not understand what she was trying to tell him.

"He's not coming in time for supper?" he asked her.

"No . . ."

"Not coming tonight?"

"No . . ."

"Well, what then, Ma?"

"Not coming at all. He's never coming again."

"Oh, you don't mean you and him could have ever fell out, not you and Doc . . ."

"Doc's dead, son, killed right here in front of the house. He was driving in and a waving and I was a waving to signal that the train was coming and he just kept waving back at me and never looked till it was too late for him to get out of the car. Right here it was. Me and the girls, we been alone two years now. Me and the girls and the son Doc wanted worse than anything. You've got a new brother to see. Friends have been kind. That's all that's kept us together. Everybody owed but not many paid their bills. That's the way it's been."

"My God, Ma. Oh, my God. How terrible for you all. I'da come in a minute and be hanged with my music if I'd a dreamed things weren't right for you and the kids. But this music thing, it was something I had in me and just had to get out. I felt like Doc understood that more'n you did."

"No more talk. No more talk. Get unpacked and I'll get the collards on. Time to talk after supper."

By this time the girls had come from the field and though Priss threw herself on her brother and hugged him as a leech would a victim, Miranda did not know him and hid behind her Ma's dress tail and eyed him with big blue wondrous eyes. Most of all she eyed the big shiny car and the tall well dressed negro.

Priscilla thought there had never been finer suitcases anywhere in the world than the ones they took out of the trunk of the car and she could not wait for them to open the guitar cases. Jim hung back and took it all in, the hugging, the crying, the joyful yet tearful reunion, the depths of loneliness a body can sink to when he has no family of his own. It was to be his real song, the theme that people would associate with him for years to come. It was a song born of the soul.

It would be preposterous to think that they could tell each other all that had happened in the missing years, and they did not try. They sat and enjoyed each other's presence for a while on the porch after supper. The swing had the same sharp squeak that he remembered, the top link in its chain grating against the rusty hook that held it to the ceiling. Jim sat on the front door steps and looked beyond, beyond to the flat land, beyond to the railroad tracks, to the tall short leaf pines sprinkled with an occasional cypress or gum tree, beyond to the dark blue skyline where clouds lay like upside down mountains on the horizon, to the half filled moon that was in no hurry, and he knew that his place should not be here, not at this moment. But where else?

"How 'bout me taking the car and going into town and see if I can stir up something?"

"What brought that on?" Woodrow asked quickly. "You've traveled enough miles for today."

"Oh, there's some folks down town I might look up."

"There's not a damn soul there that you still know or who knows you and you know it. You're thinking you're going to eat and run, but you're not getting off that easy. Get your music down, boy. Let's show Ma what we play."

Ella had not been moved like this since the Doc's accident. The music was sad and alive. It made her see trees and soft shady spots. It made her guts tremble, and it had also been perfected since she had last heard it. Why it sounds better than what she heard daily on the radio, much better. And my boy is helping make it. But is it right to get paid for having fun? Work had always been a thing of misery to her and she could not comprehend having a good time and making a living at it. The two could never be synonymous in her way of thinking.

She and the girls clapped as hard as they could when the men paused between songs.

"And now, ladies and gents. Pardon me, just ladies in the house tonight I see. You are going to see the only men in the country who can play two instruments at one time," and he bowed and turned, then took out a wire like contraption and fitted it around his neck. In this he placed his harmonica while Jim did likewise. This enabled them to play the harmonica and the guitar at the same time. And this time it was happy music, foot tapping music. After they had played several songs, they looked at each other and began to play right on cue for her, "Red Wings." Tonight however, it was not the Indian maid who had died and left her lover alone. This song was too real, too close to her heart, and in spite of all her intentions she felt hot tears streaming down her face, falling in cooled drops on her bosom. She wiped them away with the back of her rough hand, but they were quickly replaced by more. The men were unaware of how their music was affecting her and one could actually hear a flutter of sadness in the air from the soft music. Putting her apron to her eyes for a moment, she stumbled past them down the steps and crossed the yard. I'm a big fool. I'm such a fool, but she did not want them to see her carry on like this.

She walked slowly down the well beaten path to the pasture, sat down on the dew wet clover and buried her head in her lap. There the sobs tore her body. Only the night wind and milk cow were there to hear. Later she was so weak that she stretched out full length on her back and looked up at the sky. There are still stars there . . . I'm surprised. She had not looked up since Doc died. Everything had weighted her down to the ground, she of the airy feet and the flighty ways, she with the heart filled with music and love, all happiness had left her for a long time, what with Woodrow gone and never a word and another small boy baby lying in his crib asleep now just awaiting and depending on her. I'm not able to raise another one to leave me like that—so much love poured on them and then they're gone in a moment and they don't bother to even look back. All the nights of getting up to see if they're warm under the covers or feeling their forehead. These are nothings to children, and only having some of their own will ever teach them the fullness of the heart, or the anxieties of parenthood.

She felt much older than her thirty-three years. She felt sixty years old. Early marriage and having children and hard work in the fields and sorrow had aged her beyond her years, but tonight she did not care. She had wanted to be beautiful for Leslie. His loving had made her so beyond man's imagination, and his presence made people afraid to look down on her for her past mistakes. They did not dare because they did not know what hour they might have to call on him in a matter of life and death. It had been different than when she lost the big house. That had been a disillusionment. It had made her bitter with everyone for a while. But losing the Doc had been a heart break that all the years that God might make could never heal again. She hugged herself and remembered how strong his arms had felt around her, how eagerly she had waited up for him to come in nights, how warm the night with his love when the light had been turned off, how safe the hours lying inside his arms and curled beside his body, how wonderful to awake first and look over at his handsome face. She always had to touch his face softly with her hands. Then she knew that all was real, and he'd awake like a growly bear at first, but she'd tickle him under his arms and he'd grumble, "Now stop that, damn it. I'm not in the mood for your fool messing this morning." She'd mimic him and say in her own voice, "Now stop that, damn it. I'm not in the mood for your messing," and it would wind up with him slapping her tail, which was inevitable when she was in bed with him anyway. He'd smile and say, "It even spanks good," and she'd kiss him and say, "Good morning, Daddy of four." He'd bite her neck and whisper, "And perhaps the Daddy of more to come."

How lovely. How foolish to anyone else. And gone. Gone. All gone. The warmth. The loving. The kindness. The playing. The fullness, the security and the dreams. Gone just as much as the locomotive that went by each night at nine o'clock. How many times they had sat in the porch swing and looked at the people inside the train as it went by, trying to imagine where they were all going.

"I've never been on a trip," she'd say.

"Where you want to go?"

"I can't think of any place right now. But I will." But in her heart she knew that even then she lied. There was no placed she wanted to go. Here was everything. She could read about the world, but here was everything for her.

She had closed her mind to the day of the accident and she was not going to open it for anyone, not even Woodrow. He could ask someone else and he would, she felt sure, but she was not going to recount those hours for any soul. Even the days following it had become blanks in her mind and she intended to keep them that way. Preacher Cornaby had tried to console her.

"You mustn't carry on so, Ella. Think of the children. They've lost their father. They are suffering now, too."

"They'll have their lives. Theirs will come. My life is dead. Dead."

And she had been inconsolable. If only Ma had lived to be with me. That would have helped, and she thought, but her mother had preceded Sybil in death by a month. She had vague recollections of Kate standing near her, looking truly sorry for her, but all she could think of was, What does she want? Every woman in the community had called on her several times afterwards except one. And it was months before it came to her that Eva had not come at all. Eva? Friend of childhood. I'm so sorry, Eva. I don't blame you for not coming. You never could lie to me, so open and frank about everything. And you couldn't say like everyone else how sorry you were. Even now, I don't guess you are sorry for me. Sorry I don't have a husband maybe, but not sorry for me as a woman. You're safe from me, this time, friend. Never agin'. Never.

Out of it all, she came to thank God for one thing—that Doc had lived to see his boy. The baby had been four weeks old at the time, and his daddy had already planned his college education. It was going to be the best. Times were going to be more prosperous. Things were picking up already, people would begin to really pay for having a baby or getting shots instead of a few dollars now and then and a mess of meat and a bushel of potatoes. And they could build their dream home. It was all right around the corner for them, and now they would never turn the corner at all. She doubted that she would be able to give the boy a high school education. Perhaps! At least the local country schools had been consolidated and school buses now came and carried the rural children back and forth to town each day. What will they think of next? she asked herself. Riding to school, no less. It seemed only yesterday that she and Kate had taken their tin dinner pails and set off through the woods for school, terrified that they might run into old Tom, hoping it wouldn't rain before night and the swamp swell and run over their foot log so that they couldn't cross without wading . . . only yesterday. There is no such thing. It is as if it had never been at all. And certainly there is no tomorrow. Just as there had been no tomorrows for Leslie or Sybil or Ma. Only today. That's all that counts. I'm not going to let my heart be happy that he's home. It's only a jumping off place with him. Here today. Gone again. It may be years before I hear again. I can't let my heart be done like that. I'll just smile and cook for him and iron his clothes while he's here, but I won't let my heart have any part of it. Out of the depths of her soul came a wee voice that cried out, "Coward. Coward." And strangely it did not sound like her own voice. It sounded like Ben's. It had been Ben who had taken so much of the timidity out of her and made her a more adult responsible person! "Be somebody. Have an opinion, even if it's a wrong opinion!" he had told her often. "Be something." "I'm not listening to you, Ben Simpson. You've been dead for years. You brought me misery and embarrassed me so many times in front of everyone I knew . . ."

"But I gave you something, too," the voice whispered. And she had to listen for she knew the voice was right. He had given her confidence in herself, the confidence that Kate had destroyed all the years of their childhood—always being the smartest, the quickest, the most alert. She had only been the prettiest, and that had not been enough to win Pa's approval. Funny now how it still hurt that he had never bragged on her. "I wanted to please you, Pa. I really tried. You know I'm the one who found the sow for you when she went into the swamp to have the pigs. You said I just went to dwaddle along the day, but really I looked for her. Kate just made everything I did look terrible to you. I wanted to please. Really I did." Like the time she had drawn a tub of water for Ma to wash with when water was low in the well and Kate had tipped it over when she wasn't looking and let it all run out. Pa had whaled her good and said she should have put the tub more on the porch and not so near to the edge. That night in bed Kate had confessed, but Ella knew better than try to tell Pa. He'd say she made it up and spank her for lying. She had turned over and cried into the night, same as tonight here on the clover.

She had not been aware that the white tops of the clover had been hurting her back, and when she sat up at last, her dress was soaking and her back ached all over from the hard clods beneath and the clover tops pressing into it. She listened for a moment, but the music had stopped, and she felt ashamed to have to face them. Perhaps they had gone to bed. Maybe I can slip in the back door, but there was no need to have worried. The car was not even in the yard, and the girls had gone to bed. Priscilla, however, was not asleep.

"I been worried 'bout you, Ma. Woodrow said for me not to, though."

"Well, he was quite right. I just been sitting and thinking and a person can't think with other people 'round him. Where they gone?"

"Said they were going into town to get a beer! Did you know Woodrow drinks beer, Mama?"

The word electrified her. "I should have thought of it, but I hadn't. He's grown and out in the world, and I imagined he had girlfriends, but drinking just hadn't crossed my mind, not Woodrow." And visions of Ben drunk and staggering in leaped into her mind. But he's not Ben's seed. Surely that won't affect him. He told me once he remembered a lot I didn't think he did about living there. Maybe the drinking was one of them. She was sure of one thing, however, wherever they were drinking, they were not doing so together. The aura of the South's past hung heavily of them still, and though her family accepted Jim freely, it was the only one that did. She did not doubt Woodrow's word that he was accepted up North, but she knew how tightly the rope was drawn between the two races in her own state. However, she had not reckoned on the influence their music would have on people. They merely walked in together, sat down and played, drank their beer, played again, and soon the beer hall was filled to capacity. Men begged them to play favorites, and there was nothing they'd rather do than oblige.

He's so young, she told herself that night. Too young to be finding his mark in life. This will be a passing thing and then he'll settle down and get a job. He's just too young to know what he's doing. Maybe he might come back and want to farm with me and the girls. But would I really want that? It's been too hard. But traveling all the time? How can a man put down roots like that. He can't even have a family. She was still awake when she heard the car come into the yard and heard them laughing together as they came into the house. Only the young can laugh like that, she thought. The young and the dumb!

During the rest of the year and the year to come, she and the girls would hurry through their chores on Saturday so that they could get to the radio on Saturday night to be sure and not miss Woodrow's program. It came from Nashville, and it made the muscles in her neck constrict so that breathing was difficult when the announcer said every time, "It is with pleasure that we bring to you that new singing and playing sensation, Woodie Simpson and his guitar picking partner, Jim Nabo. Take it away boys."

At first they had a fifteen minute spot, but within a month, their popularity had grown so that they had sponsors for a thirty minute program. During that time, he always dedicated one to "My mother who's down on the farm in Eastern N.C., and I know she's listening tonight"; but he did not sing "Red Wings" for her again. The boy and the woman had been close enough during their years together that he understood her as well as a child is able to understand a parent. Occasionally his show would be broadcast from another town, sometimes as far North as Cincinnati or Columbus, Ohio. The continuity of his letters and packages soon warmed Ella's heart toward him again, and she began to feel that he would not forget them this time. He sent them recordings of the songs he and Jim sang, and they managed to buy a new record player, the old RCA Victrola having squeaked its last squeak several years ago. During the weekdays they'd play the records, and then on Saturdays it was as if he were alive in the room with them.

His last letter was always pinned to her dress so that she could take it out and read it at any time of the day or night.

". . . I know it's useless to ask you to sell the farm, or even rent it, as I know you well enough to know you intend to hop around on those clods as long as you live. However, enough money is enclosed to make part payment on a tractor for you and the girls and give the old mule a rest at last. I don't mean for you to spend this on anything else except a tractor as I am looking to see one there when I arrive in a few weeks."

Why, there weren't many men around who had a tractor! What wouldn't they say about her? But could they really find anything new that they hadn't already said to say? But to ride and plow? It seemed almost sinful to think about it.

—Chapter 20—

THEY HAD HARVESTED two crops with the second hand tractor before he came home again and though she could understand that there were towns large enough to pay him for appearances and that he had recording contracts he could not break, she could not understand what he had been doing on holidays until he finally arrived with a new car and a pregnant wife. The time of winter was on the barren land, and the ground lay frozen and uneven, last fall's tobacco and corn stalks standing crazily upward still, and the rows still in ridges waiting for the spring plow to cut them down. Only the pine and cedar trees were green at this time of year, all the rest were naked and shimmered with ice on their leaves and branches. The school bus got stuck in muddy ruts more days than it arrived without mishap, and the cows did not wander far from their shelter. The mule was glad even to see a good mess of dry shucks, so scarce was the feed. The bridle hung unused on the nail in front of the stable door and gathered dust. It was a time of waiting, the grass seed just waiting in the soil for the first warm day to spring up and choke to death anything they tried to plant, and the trees waiting to bud nine days after the last hard freeze. But no spring could thaw Ella's heart toward the girl that Woodrow brought home as his wife.

She was a rare dark beauty, having come up from New Orleans to sing on his program in Nashville, and soon she had been a regular on his show. "Sweet Bird" they called her on the air. ". . . and now the Sweet Bird is going to sing for us. Her hair was long and blue black and hung in one long curl down her back, tiny curls falling on her forehead, her skin darker than olive but not as dark as tan, and she was a full head taller than Ella with her long slim legs and fancy shoes.

"It's been most nice meeting you, Mrs. Humphries, but we'll just run into town and eat supper. We don't plan to put you out any."

"Put Ma out! She'd be put out if we went into town and ate. We're eating here tonight. Got any potato pudding, Ma?"

Before she had a chance to answer, she saw the girl's face cloud over like thunder about to break and her bottom lip pucker up in a big pout. She flounced over to the sofa, folded her arms and sat down with a thump. Trying to change the subject as quickly as possible she hurriedly began, "Where is Jim? You shoulda brought him."

Unknowingly she had dropped another bombshell. It's not difficult to say the wrong thing between loved ones when a great deal of time has passed between each visit.

"We've split now, Ma. I think he's in New York City."

"Split? But I still hear you sing together on the radio."

"Oh. That's just some records that we made some time ago. He learned to play a new instrument. One you've never seen, Ma. It's called a xylophone, and there's nobody ever took to one like he has. Plumb gone wild over it, and took to a new kind of music, too. It's called popular. Not for me. I like my old country and hillbilly kind. It tells the true tale."

"Popular? But your music is popular with everybody, isn't it?"

"Yessssss," he said and laughed. "Ma, you're a birdy. It's popular, but it's not what's called popular music."

"Oh, you know what he means, Mama," interpreted Priscilla. "Like Bing Crosby sings. You've heard him, Ma. He's neat."

"That stuff. That's not from doodle. Sounds like they just talk."

And he embraced her the way he used to when he was growing up, hard and long and kissed the top of her head.

What is this a stopover for, she asked silently. Beware, heart.

This is just an in between for him. But I'm being ugly and mean. Perhaps he's come just to come this time.

An old pick up truck rattled by, its body filled to the brim with dry corn going to the market to be sold to get a little spending money in the poorest time of year. Across the field, the cow bellowed to her calf shut up in the stable so that he couldn't suck all of the milk. It's the same. Things are the same here, but everything else in the world is changing swiftly. The war that had been fought to end all wars had in reality never ended. In that sense it had been a failure, for the nations were clawing at each other's throats again. Many of the neighbors' boys had been drafted. Drafted! But surely he would have written about it.

For two days he did not mention to her why he had come or when he would leave, but when Mildred took the girls into town to buy them some new dresses and underclothes as a Christmas gift from Woodrow and herself, he found that he could again talk to his mother easily.

"I've brought you something to stay this time, Ma. Hope you won't mind too much."

"How can I say without knowing."

"Well, rightly, you can't. I've got my call. Got to be at Fort Bragg by Saturday week. And what with Mildred pregnant, I didn't want to leave her out there. She told you she was brought up in an orphanage. I want her to be with you when the baby comes. This war mess may take a long time. Some say it'll be over in a year, but I don't rightly know. You'll like her. She's just like a little girl. Pouts and gets mad and then she's over it in a minute. Jim said she . . . no never mind, forget it . . ."

She looked at him and waited. What had Jim said about Mildred? Jim with his black probing eyes that saw beyond what most of us see. But her lips did not form the words. Better let them lie unsaid for now.

"And the baby? When will it be?"

"About three more months. Couldn't you tell, you wise old bird?"

"Well, I thought she was mighty big, but you said you just got married a couple of months ago."

"That's right. These things happen frequently with the first one." And he lit a cigarette as if he had been saying, it will freeze tonight.

"Well, Woodrow?" exasperation sounded clearly in her voice. "No one down here knows when you got married. Don't be going around telling everyone two months ago. What people don't know don't hurt them."

"I was expecting you, of all people, to be broad-minded about it, Ma."

Her heart skipped two beats and lurched around in her chest before regulating itself to a more rapid beat.

"Why me, of all people?"

"Don't play act with me, Ma. I know all about myself. You don't think the boys in school would have missed telling me all about it years ago, do you? I was called a bastard more times than there are pines in the woods."

A deep red came over her face and neck and she turned to the window so that he could not see the hot tears form in her eyes. So he had known all along. All those long hard years he'd known. You fool, Ella. Fool. Fool.

"I hated you for a while, Ma, but it was hard hating you, when I knew how you loved me and the girls. Then I just hated him. It was easy hating him. He's so ugly and unclean looking. I could still kill him. And didn't you think I could add when Miranda was born four months after you married Doc? I figured what was right for Doc to do was right for me. Fact is, the only reason we married at all was so that she could get my allotment check, and this baby would have a name. We were happy like it was before."

My God. My God, what a image I am in his sight. No wonder he went and stayed. I'm just a whore to him, a whore who loved him and gave him birth and fed him. He doesn't see me at all like I see myself.

Here I've seen myself for years like any other mother in the world, just loving the kids and working for them, and caring for them, and all the time, my first born has felt hate and repulsion for me. Why he doesn't even like the sound of me. All the miles and days that had separated them seemed wider suddenly.

"Please, Woodrow, please, believe me. I can't tell you how bad I wanted to marry your Daddy, but he wouldn't marry me. I begged him, I threatened everything. I said everything, but he wouldn't marry me. Can you understand that much? I was in love with him. I had always loved him, as far back as I could remember, there had been no one but him. Pa was set on me marrying Ben. There seemed to be no other way. I thought if I was pregnant, Leonard would marry me and I'd have him and be happy for the rest of my life. It was a big mistake. It's taken all these years for me to be able to say it aloud, but I'm telling you, it was a mistake. You just can't make a man love you enough to marry you if he doesn't want to. It's got to come from inside of him."

"But he's so damned bad looking, Ma. How could you have loved anything that looks like him."

"Look in the mirror, son. Look good! And tell me do you think Mildred thinks what you see there is ugly. Well, that's how he looked. So straight and tall then, and blonde curly hair, and dancing devilish eyes. He was young and full of life. I was young. We were crazy, that's all. We were too young to have any sense at all. But years don't let a body stay right on looking the same, especially here. Of course he looks old. He's worked hard every day of his life and got nothing to show for it. No more, no, not as much as I have. And to think I once wanted you to stay here and help me tend the land. Keep going, son. As soon as this is over, just keep going. If people are crazy enough or got enough money to pay to hear music, keep making it. After a while they might change and not pay anymore."

He knew that she was talking too fast and frantically to make much sense and he felt that she was still embarrassed over his confession.

"Mama, I'm not judging you. You can look at me. I'm the

same boy who rode on the board in the front of the wagon with Grandpa the day we left the big house. I've never forgotten that day. It was so cold, I couldn't wiggle my toes in my shoes, and Grandpa slipped me a piece of chewing tobacco and said, 'Chew, son, it'll warm your insides.' And when I swallowed some of the juice, I forgot all about being cold. But I didn't dare let you know what I'd done. It's your life, though, Ma. That's all I'm saying. You don't have to tell me anything."

"I'm telling you so that you'll know there was a good reason. There was a good reason for everything I did."

"There's a reason for what I do, too. I enjoy it. That's reason enough, isn't it?"

"No. No. It ain't! You've got to set your sights on something."

"Don't preach, Ma. I don't care to hear it . . ."

Not from you . . . that was what he was saying. Not from you, I don't care to hear it. And if he knew, Priscilla probably also knew. But they were close, closer even than she and Woodrow had been. Surely she didn't hate her. It seemed right at the time, and the reason had been good. She had loved Leonard, but circumstances had killed that love deader than a chicken snake with its head cut off by a sharp hoe, and the love for Doc had been all new and shiny and clean, an entirely different thing. Why, this is the way my neighbors have looked at me all these years—like a whore—and they have merely tolerated me the past few years out of pity.

The baby boy wandered into the room, and pulled the hem of her dress.

"Eat, Mama. Eat."

Looking down a the small boy, she did not know if she had the courage to face the years to come. He, too, will grow up and learn to not like me. He'll hear, like they heard, and he won't like what he's heard. Yet, he says he loves me. Why has he come back? For me to take care of Mildred. Another child, really. Love did not bring him back. This is his changing place. And she took the small chubby hand and went into the kitchen to fix him a biscuit with syrup in it to make do till supper time.

From inside the room, she could hear the man playing and singing.

"From the great Atlantic Ocean to the wide Pacific shore
From the Queen of lowing mountains to the south land
   by the shore, she's mighty tall and handsome,
She's quite well known by all,
     She's the combination of the Wabash Cannon Ball . . ."

She was to hear the record of him singing this song many times before the war would end and he was free to record songs again.

That night as she lay awake and listened to the bed springs squeaking from their room, she was excited in a way she did not ever expect to be again, and she cursed herself silently for having let them have the room next to hers. That part of me must lie silent, lie silent. That part must die. I'll make it be dead, if I have to kill myself.

—Chapter 21—

THE ENTIRE LIFETIME of a woman is haunted by many fears—fear that she will be an ugly old hag and never attract men, fear that she will attract men and will be possessed and hurt physically, fear that she will not be possessed and will have to live a long life of emptiness, fear that she will be pregnant or that she won't, that she will die in childbirth, fear that her children will grow up and leave and never look back or that they won't leave and she won't be able to care for them, fear that there will be no grandchildren to love her in her infirmity, and finally fear of old age.

Deep in the chasms as her heart, she had known that he had come merely to leave her again, and that this time he was leaving to go to a war in which many fine sons would die. She had loved him so deeply from the very first that perhaps God would mark him for death to punish her. Be still, silly heart . . . it may be over soon . . . and he might just be in any Army band and might not even get to the fightin' and shootin'. Shallow words, she thought, and could not swallow her own saliva.

"I don't want you to get up in the morning, Ma. Just sleep and I'll be gone early. That way'll be best," he told her while his strong thin arm encircled her plump waist.

But the aroma of country smoked ham frying, grits bubbling, and biscuits browning in the old oven filled his nostrils before he could turn over. This won't be easy, was his first conscious thought, and I have hurt her more than I ever meant to. Still, she knows I love her. I'm sure she knows that. And sure as hell, I'm no white rose. Still, maybe I shouldn't have mentioned it, and he cringed, recalling the pain he had seen on her face that day.

We're strangers, all strangers. Born to her, but a stranger to her still. Just a strange as if we'd met in the bus station. Love don't do a damn thing to make a body understand.

She was the only one to see him off, and she hugged the post of the front porch hard and long after the black shiny car had made a swing in the bare yard and gone. The tears fell hot and swift so that her apron was limp and damp.

But the racking sobs never came. Those had already been, and the body is capable of just so much sorrow at one time. Thank God, she whispered, thank God there's a limit to grieving, and she turned and went out to her chickens, filling the old tire trough with fresh water from the pump, filling the pan for the setting hens in the tobacco stick coop, throwing out a few shucked but unshelled ears of corn, noting that she would have to spray today for the mites which were swarming all over the roosts. She scratched her arm thinking about the pesty things and recalled that she needed to buy some creosote dip to make the spray. The blood suckers would soon make the hens anemic and they would stop laying. Thank God for a bad task. A body needs a bad task to get the mind off a bad thing, and she scratched her arm again and bent so as not to strike her head on the low door.

Three months later, she pressed her nose hard against the cold glass of the nursery window at the hospital and gazed with fixed maternal love at the small bundle that was Woodrow's and Mildred's. He's so dark . . . so very dark . . . maybe too dark to get by down here. His head was covered with thick black hair like Mildred's and one of his fists fought the air and waved wildly, before he let it fall back on his side. It's a long road, sonny. You might not make it. I don't know if I even hope that you will. God knows what is in for you at the bend of the road. It would be wonderful to take you home and nurse you, and what a pity that Mildred with all that good milk going to waste, has insisted on giving you a bottle. Didn't want you to slow her down, she said. Poor young ignorant one. Thinking a cow could give better milk than a Mama. All the love you're going to miss when he never nuzzles your breasts and you know for sure you

are the most important thing in the world. Thinking about it
made her own breasts come alive with sensation and tingle with
warmth and love. We'll take you home, little fellow. Dark or
light, you're ours and we're going to take you home.

She was so absorbed in her own thoughts that she was
unaware of the line behind her waiting to view the babies.

At home the baby appeared even darker than he had at first
and she rubbed his soft head and thought, how coarse his hair!
How like Jim. Like Jim, my God! What any ugly thought. Ella,
you know better. But then . . . they had been closer than brothers
and they had split up. It was a friendship built on poverty and its
appurtenances, and then at last, on success. But then perhaps it
had been just as Woodrow had said. Perhaps Jim had just wanted
to go his own way. She had been hearing his recordings lately
on the radio. He had even formed a small band to play in the
background. Personally she did not call it music, but a lot of
folks seemed to like it. Especially the youngins. As for herself,
she loved "Maple On the Hill," "Sunshine," and "Wabash
Cannonball." But to each his own. She hugged the little dark
head to her full breast and sang to him the kind of songs she
loved.

Within three weeks, Mildred was dressing herself up every
night and leaving in the car, not to return until early morning.
She dropped word around that she had been dead long enough
and, now that the baby was here, she was going to live again.
Priscilla told Ella that Mildred had confided that she was dancing
and drinking beer with servicemen in the local beer halls every
night. This can't be right . . . it just can't be . . . maybe I'm
getting old. But who am I—my own son said that—who am I to
cast stones. Who am I? I wonder. Just a collard eating, baby
loving, middle aged woman.

The wind blew mournfully the night that the baby had the
high fever, and it seemed as if the train whistle had never been
sadder. On and on and on. Surely she won't go tonight and
leave the little mite, Ella thought. However, Mildred ended her
dressing session by dabbing on too much cheap perfume

and putting on four-inch heels. She is really beautiful and I know the men can't keep their eyes and hands off her. I was like that once. They said I was so beautiful . . .

"Have you taken his temperature, Mildred?"

"Nope." She tossed her long black hair around like a Kentucky mare showing off her beautiful mane in the mountain breezes. "Don't know how. He's alright, ain't he?"

"I don't think so. Maybe you'd better bathe him off in cool water."

"Really, Ella. I don't have the time. I'm late now."

"Late! Late for what?"

"Ah, ha. You'd like to know, wouldn't you? Well, that's for me to know and for you to find out. If you can."

"I'm not interested in finding out. All I know is that this baby is sick—and very sick."

"Well, in that case tend to him. Call the doctor if you think it is necessary."

Keep your mouth closed, Ella. You are only a mother-in-law now, but in spite of her hearts admonitions, her mouth opened and the words just fell out.

"Do you think Woodrow knows how you do all of the time?"

"Yes, I know he knows me, and he knows that whenever I can, I have a good time."

"I doubt that very much." She still carried today's letter in her apron pocket saying that they were shipping out for an unknown destination.

"Why do you think I came to this crummy place in the beginning? Woodrow said that you would take care of me and the baby, that's why. And right now, I don't need any taking care of. By you, that is. But little Woodie? So good night, Mother, dear." With hand on her beautifully shaped hips, she went out into the night.

Well, it takes all kinds. But if he searched the world over, he couldn't have found one more to my disliking. She went in to bathe the new baby and try to comfort him. By midnight, his fever was dangerously high, his deep blue eyes glazed with the abnormal body heat. Gently, she wrapped him in a faded quilt, awakened Priscilla and told her to look out for the younger children and to tell Mildred, in case she should come back, that she had gone to the hospital with the baby.

The morning light slipped soundlessly into the hospital waiting corridor and fell upon a weary woman who had not closed her eyes all night. The doctor had been with the child all of the time, and this alone was enough to make her heart hurt. Surely with so many new drugs, surely they should be able to do something. He had been sick but such a short time. "Doctor, please, please do something!"

"Are you the baby's mother?"

Unable to make words, she shook her head.

"Grandmother?"

Again she answered with a nod.

"I'm sorry. There was nothing we could do. Nothing anyone could do but God. First case of meningitis I've seen this year. It's most always fatal to babies this young. Are you all right?"

Alright! Her mind cried out. Am I alright! A baby is dead. I called him my grandson. I've loved him and rocked him and sung to him for three whole months. His father has never seen him. His mother is God alone knows where. Am I alright? I guess I'm alright as a body under the circumstances can be. I'll make do . . . that's how Mama always answered anyone's inquiry about her health. For years it had slipped her mind. Under the circumstances, I'll make do. Under the circumstances I'm nigh about dead. Poor Mama . . . Well, Doctor, under the circumstances, I'm all right.

Numbly, she went out into the brilliant morning light.

She did not take an "I told you so" attitude with Mildred. That would have been wasted on the arrogantly lovely girl, but as soon as the funeral was over, she did not break any bones about telling her that her free ride was over. Free bed and board and maid service discontinued, she told her, as of now.

"You'll be better off somewhere else. Far enough that I can't see and hear about the things you do. Be sure and go that far. You're not one of these people. We're just plain folks. Folks that love the land, and in our way, the Lord.

"What are you going to tell Woodie?"

For once, for once something seemed to have penetrated the girl's shallow shell. She might not be in love with Woodrow, but he was just too good to lose.

"I'm not going to tell him anything. That's up to you. What man would take his mother's word over that of his wife's? Make up your own tale and tell it well. He'll believe you, but be out of my house afore night falls agin."

The train's whistle was shrill that night. It's always a lonesome sound she told herself. It takes people to where they want to be going and others to where they don't want to be going. Roll on, steel wheels. Take her just as far as you can, and don't bring her back. She's not one of us and never will be.

Standing on the front porch cooling she tried to bring to mind a picture of her when she had been nineteen, married to Ben, young and beautiful, admired and desired by every man that came into the store. Yes, she too had been guilty of leaning a little to far over the counter, deliberately letting them peep down the neck of her dress, delighting in their glances of admiration, but secure in the fact that she was safely married. Ben had said that, a delightful teaser. I mustn't judge her, "I just mustn't judge. You're no one to throw stones, he had said. God would never grant enough years, not even if he granted a thousand and one, for her to live down all her past mistakes. The neighborhood was not all that forgiving. They simply didn't want to forget. It gave them something to laugh about, tease about, toss around in the air like a new ball when the things got dull at home.

❧ ❧ ❧

AND WHEN ONE YEAR LATER, Priscilla came into her room right after a good supper of turnip greens, new Irish potatoes, and fried side meat and stood nervously beside her, she was not surprised to hear her say nervously, "Ma, I'm pregnant."

"I'm not surprised. Do you know who the father of the baby is?"

"No. Not for real sure like. It's between two, though."

"Well, between two isn't good enough. You can't marry two."

"I'm sorry, Ma."

"Well being sorry don't help matters none, but don't look like that. The world won't come to an end. Are you in love with either of them?"

"I don't think so. I felt sorry for them. They are going overseas now. They may even die."

What a good line men have these days, but then they always have a good line . . . and it takes two. One thing was for certain she knew that Priss would love and tend for the baby. It would be different than it was with Mildred. Thank God, for that much at least.

After Priscilla had dressed and left with the tall Marine with dancing eyes, she went in and bathed and dressed in a cool flowered print. Looking over the articles on Priscilla's dresser, she put some of everything on it on herself. Peering closely in the mirror, she thought, "Why, I'm not beyond repair after all. I could still be good looking if I half tried. And why not? The world is not waiting for the sunrise. It's waiting for the sun to go down, so that the love can begin, like it's always been since time began, and always will be . . ."

And checking to see that her young ones were sound asleep and feeling each forehead as has always been her way, she went out across the unpainted cypress planked porch, down the clay path, across the pasture and down the meadow road. "Oh sky, I could hug you so tight. I'm so damn glad to be alive. So damn glad that I could shout to the high heavens. Oh, I love you, sky!"

And she sat down on the wooded damp road to wait. He always comes this way coming home from the store, and he had said that she would come again. Even if it took years, she'd come again.

And she smiled thinking how good it would be to be warm with love again.

The End.